A glamorous Eastern social
she found peril and paradis
in the arms of the
magnificent outlaw
who captured her
defiant heart.

THE FIRES OF PARADISE

"I want you," he said.

"No," she replied, not meaning it.

"I want you," he repeated, moving closer. She gasped, her eyes flying to his. "Hold me," he said harshly. "Hard."

She stood motionless, her heart slamming, and, as if the devil were instructing her, her fingers curled around him.

"Yes, princess," he said, and she felt his warm breath on her cheek, his mouth brushing her face. She gasped, reaching for his shoulders. Crazy desire trailed in the wake of his lips. She no longer knew herself. His face was pressed into her neck, his wet, hard body covering hers, his powerful arms crushing her in his embrace. And he was rocking his hips against her softness, and Lucy thought she might die, trapped between heaven and hell . . .

Other Avon Books by
Brenda Joyce

FIRESTORM
INNOCENT FIRE
VIOLET FIRE

THE FIRES OF PARADISE

BRENDA JOYCE

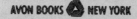

AVON BOOKS ◆ NEW YORK

THE FIRES OF PARADISE is an original publication of Avon Books. This work has never before appeared in book form. This work is a novel. Any similarity to actual persons or events is purely coincidental.

AVON BOOKS
A division of
The Hearst Corporation
1350 Avenue of the Americas
New York, New York 10019

Copyright © 1992 by Brenda Joyce Senior
Cover illustration by Victor Gadino
Inside cover author photograph by Roy Volkmann
Published by arrangement with the author
Library of Congress Catalog Card Number: 91-93025
ISBN: 0-380-76535-7

First Avon Books Printing: April 1992

AVON TRADEMARK REG. U.S. PAT. OFF. AND IN OTHER COUNTRIES, MARCA REGISTRADA, HECHO EN U.S.A.

Printed in the U.S.A.

RA 10 9 8 7 6 5 4 3 2 1

PROLOGUE

New York City, 1890

She was so bored.

She sighed, staring at her reflection. Her husband, Roger Claxton II, would be home in several hours. Tonight there was that charity affair at the Bragg home. She hoped it would not be an utter bore—like the last one. Should she dress and go out, maybe do some shopping at the Lord & Taylor store? She could still return before Roger, if she wanted to. Although why should she bother? He probably wouldn't even notice if she wasn't home, for he'd head straight to the study and the damn telephone. Marianne stared at herself, with utter stillness.

She was undeniably beautiful. Blond and slender, she had that elegance of bearing which comes from generations of upper-class breeding. She studied herself in the mirror of her dressing table, not critically, but with satisfaction. At thirty-eight, she still stopped men in their tracks. She placed her small, perfectly manicured, heavily ringed hands on her waist, pushing open the thin silk and lace peignoir. A wickedly black lace corset revealed all of her charms: breasts not too large nor too small, a tiny waist, slender hips. She smiled. Maybe she should get dressed—she could make it back just before Roger if she hurried. But she would not go shopping.

"Expecting me?" drawled a rough, masculine voice.

Marianne knew that voice. She was white before he'd finished the sentence, white before she even raised her eyes to meet his in the mirror. She stifled a scream.

He laughed.

Marianne could not drop her gaze from his. Her heart was pounding so madly, she became even more frightened. She was aware that she was clutching the edge of her dressing table. She could not move.

His smile was dangerous.

This could not be the same man she had last seen almost a year ago. But it was.

She was terrified.

How had he gotten here? What was he doing here!

"What?" he mocked. "No welcome?" His voice dropped to a satin purr. "Come here, Marianne."

As if a marionette, she slowly rose and turned to face him. Oh, God—would he kill her? She was so sorry for what she had done!

He was grinning, leaning negligently against the door to her boudoir—which he hadn't even bothered to close despite all the servants in the town house. He was a deep red bronze, as dark as she had ever seen him, as if he'd spent the entire summer bareheaded in the blazing sun. His hair was jet black and shaggy now. Never had his Indian heritage been more apparent. Unable to help herself, she dropped her gaze. His shoulders, always broad, were even broader, his shirt carelessly tucked into tight, faded denims that hugged compact hips. The threads were white over his fly. Something swept her, hot chills. He was so hardened now. Yet there was still that inescapable sexual magnetism.

He had probably come to kill her.

And remembering the past, she licked her lips and said, "What do you want?"

He laughed, low. "What do you think?" His gaze swept her with contempt, lingering where it shouldn't. "I want to fuck."

Desire crashed over her. She knew him, knew how he felt, how strong he was . . .

He reached her in three strides, grabbing her and hurting her as he hauled her up against him. "Still hot for it?"

She whimpered in both pain and need as he thrust his

hard erection against the bone of her pelvis, hurting her purposefully. "Please, Shoz . . ."

His powerful thigh lifted abruptly, jamming between hers and lifting her up and back onto her dressing table. Perfumes and powders and crystals went crashing to the floor. Her head hit the mirror, but she was barely aware of it. He was rearing over her, reaching for his fly. She watched, mesmerized. His hand stilled midway down the buttons. "Say it."

"Shoz."

"Say it," he demanded, hatred in his voice.

"I'm sorry," she gasped, spreading her thighs wide, straining for him. She darted a glance up at his startling gray eyes. "I never meant to hurt you."

He laughed. "Liar." He yanked open his fly, and his member thrust out. "Once a liar, always a liar," he said, and he penetrated her.

She cried out in pleasure and pain. Her head knocked against the mirror, a porcelain bowl dug into her shoulder. He was merciless, pumping against her, holding her knees, keeping them wide apart. "Come."

It was a command. He didn't have to say it. She was already convulsing, sobbing with the ecstasy, keening his name. "Shoz, Shoz, Shoz . . ."

He pulled out and grabbed her hair, destroying her careful coiffure. He had one denim-clad knee on the table, jerking her down as she continued climaxing, and then he was thrusting past her lips. She gasped. He went deeper, emptying himself.

She sat up, swallowing, watching him cautiously. His large hands deftly closed his pants and then his pale eyes met hers. There was no sign of spent passion on his features. His smile was cruel. "Aren't you going to ask me about the last year of my life—Marianne?"

She felt the piercing of terror, and pulled her peignoir closed tightly. Logic and confusion warred. He shouldn't be here. *He couldn't be here.* Only a year had passed; how had he gotten out? "I never meant—"

"No? You meant it, all right."

"No."

"You had all of two days to tell the truth." He laughed harshly. *"Two days.* Justice was a bit swift in my case, wouldn't you say? But you didn't, did you?"

She didn't dare respond, because he was right.

"Ask me."

She couldn't breathe. He stood aggressively, legs spread, and she knew the power that rocked his muscular body. *"Ask me."*

Tears came to her eyes. "Was . . . was it very bad?"

"It was hell."

Their gazes locked. His lips curled up at the corners. *"Prison was hell."*

PART ONE

DESIRE IN PARADISE

PARADISE, TEXAS

Paradise, Texas, 1897

Her name wasn't Trouble, but it could have been.

She had gotten into more trouble between the ages of two and twenty than all five of her younger brothers combined. And each and every one of them was a born hellraiser.

As her mother said frequently, it wasn't that she *always* looked for trouble, sometimes it looked for her. At two she spent most of her waking efforts determined to discover the meaning of her universe by investigating (and often breaking) everything she touched. At three she decided to see if the family pet, a miniature terrier, could fly. (It miraculously landed in a bush, unhurt, from the second-story window). That Christmas she stayed up all night, hidden behind the couch in the living room, to see if Santa Claus would really come down the chimney. At four she decided to go visit Grandma and Grandpa—in West Texas. She was very serious when she asked the cabbie to take her "to the train." Fortunately, he took her home instead.

At four she was also in her first riot. Her mother was an active suffragette, and during one rally, her fervent speech was interrupted by tomatoes hurled from the audience. The little girl was attending in the first row, atop her father's shoulders. Pandemonium broke out in the auditorium. She was not to be outdone. As her father raced to her mother to hustle her out the exit and to safety, she grabbed a gentleman's bowler hat from his head and threw it at another

7

gentleman, shouting her own war cries. She loved every moment.

Her earliest near-disaster was when she was six and she tried to ride her father's favorite hunter—alone. She got the seventeen-hand beast across Fifth Avenue and into Central Park, before being chased down by her furious parent.

Her name was Lucy Bragg. Her grandparents said she was an exact replica of her own father, Rathe, who had raised more hell as a boy than all of *his* siblings combined. Her mother begged her to just stop and think before acting. Lucy always promised she would. But . . . usually she didn't.

Now she was twenty and had just finished her third year at Radcliffe College. Going to Boston had been a triumph of major proportions. Her father had insisted she stay in New York, close to home. He had even wanted her to live at home (the better to keep an eye on her). Lucy wouldn't hear of it. She had fought that idea tooth and nail, promising to be on her best behavior, and in the end her sensible mother ruled the day, and her father reluctantly gave in.

The past year had been quiet, to her parents' immense relief. Too quiet, Rathe had said, as if expecting a crisis at any moment. Her freshman year hadn't been quiet at all. She had almost gotten expelled. By mistake, of course. She should have never been caught returning to her dormitory after curfew—and if the hansom's horse hadn't gone lame, she wouldn't have been, either.

Lucy had come home from her sophomore year feeling a bit smug. Not only had her grades been excellent, she'd only garnered a half dozen demerits, as well as an equal number of marriage proposals. She figured that one canceled the other, and she was right. When her father exploded about the demerits, she demurely countered with the marriage proposals. That stopped him in his tracks, effectively shifting his attention from one topic to another. He relaxed when Lucy assured him that she wasn't really interested in any of her beaux.

This past year she seemed to have settled down. Although she'd received twice as many marriage proposals as she had the year before, she had had one steady beau for the last semester and hadn't received a single demerit. Little did anyone know that Lucy was now an expert in the art of avoiding detection for her escapades and had perfected a few questionable techniques to insure that she would never be caught out after curfew again—techniques that would have done any amateur cat burglar proud.

Every summer her family left New York City. Her parents had a summer home in Newport, and the family spent one month there. For a college woman, Newport was wonderful. Half of New York society spent their holiday there, including many of her friends, and it was an endless round-robin of picnics, outings on the yacht, and evening soirees.

Each summer her family spent the other month with Lucy's grandparents on their ranch in southwest Texas. Ever since she was a child, the highlight of the year for Lucy was going to Texas, which was even better than the summer home in Connecticut. Last summer, business had brought her grandparents, Derek and Miranda, to New York, so they had all shared their holiday at her parents' summer home in Newport. They hadn't gone to Texas, and Lucy had missed Paradise terribly.

Paradise was a small, idyllic town, aptly named by her Aunt Jane and Uncle Nick some years ago. It had been spawned by the D&M, her grandparents' ranch, which had grown so big over the years that the little cluster of homes and stores on its outskirts had finally hatched into a full-fledged town. It boasted a bank, a railhead, a post office, plenty of shops, several eateries, and the most modern of hotels, which even had an elevator. The storefronts were freshly painted each spring, and the boardwalks swept clean of dust every morning. Lucy knew practically everyone in town by name, if not by sight. And they certainly all knew her.

This summer was going to be special. It was her grandfather's eightieth birthday, and her grandmother was holding a party which was fated to be talked about from coast to coast. More than a thousand of Derek's friends and peers were coming from all over the country, and from as far away as London and Paris. Derek Bragg was held in the utmost esteem, and all these powerful men and their wives

were coming to pay tribute to him and his lifetime's achieve-
ments. There would be senators, congressmen, and political
bosses present, the Texas governor, the San Antonio mayor,
and the New York City police commissioner, Theodore
Roosevelt, who was a good friend of her father's. There
would be Vanderbilts and Rockefellers, Goulds and Astors,
and even the Republican nominee for president, William
McKinley.

The entire affair was to be a surprise. Lucy's grandfather
was oblivious to the plans going on behind his very back.
Had he known, he would have heartily protested such a
fuss.

Lucy's family intended to arrive several weeks before the
grand event, in early July, as they always did. Just before
they were to leave, however, a problem in Lucy's father's
vast, multimillion-dollar empire occurred, taking him to
Cuba. Lucy had overheard her parents talking and knew
that there was some rioting down there, although her father
had assured her mother that his trip would not be dangerous.
Lucy had been to Maravilla, the vast sugar plantation near
Havana that Rathe owned. It was a tropical paradise, quiet
and beautiful, the undulating valley of sugar cane surrounded by thick, lush jungles and blue mountains with
cascading waterfalls. It had been so peaceful and quiet the
one time she had been there that she was sure the distur-
bances were greatly exaggerated and would be over in no
time.

Concurrently, her mother decided she had to be in Washington to attend a fund-raiser for the young Democrat, William Jennings Bryan. (She did not support her husband's
choice, McKinley, much to his annoyance.) This meant that
their vacation would be delayed two or three weeks, and
Lucy was terribly disappointed—until she had a wonderful
idea. Why shouldn't she and her best friend, Joanna, who
was also coming on their holiday, go ahead with a chaperone, so as not to lose part of their holiday? Lucy had
inherited a bit of her father's opportunistic instincts, and
she seized the moment. Why not? Traveling alone across
the country would be fun, even if they were chaperoned. It
would be an adventure. Lucy had never traveled farther than

the Berkshires without her parents, and Joanna agreed, as she always did with Lucy, that it would be exciting. The girls were clamoring to go, and Rathe and Grace succumbed.

Her father departed for Cuba via one of his brother-in-law, Brett's, freight steamers, and Grace left for the rally in Washington. And at the last moment the kindly Mrs. Tilly Seymour came down with a terrible case of hay fever, which she claimed she hadn't had in ten years or more. She could not possibly travel in such a state, and was terribly sorry that the girls would have to wait for the return of Lucy's parents and travel with the entire family. It seemed as if their vacation would be delayed no matter what.

But Lucy had a blazing inspiration. She and her best friend would go to Paradise ahead of the family, *alone*, for their holiday!

Mrs. Seymour certainly wouldn't know, and when her parents returned and found her gone, it would be a fait accompli. Lucy would feign innocence, widening her big blue eyes at her father and exclaiming, "But, Daddy, if I'd known you didn't want me to go, I would have gone to Newport with the boys!"

Her mother was a bit tougher. Lucy couldn't pull the wool over her eyes. But her mother would forget about her escapade soon enough. If some political or social or economic crisis did not arise, Lucy could always count on one of her brothers to do something to divert her mother's attention from her.

The trip to Texas had been ridiculously easy to accomplish, and now she and Joanna were standing in the dusty yard of a carriage dealer in the blazing heat of San Antonio at noon. Her friend was whispering nervously in her ear. "Lucy, are you sure you know what you're doing?"

Lucy grinned. She ignored the little warning bell going off inside her head. After all, they had made it this far without a single mishap. An elaborate Parisian hat bedecked with ribbons and flowers shaded her face, and she tossed her head. "Absolutely."

"Lucy . . ."

Lucy grabbed Joanna's arm and propelled her aside. She was tall for a woman, and built like her mother, long-legged and willowy yet full-breasted. It was a figure that turned men's heads, and even now, as she bent over to whisper in Joanna's ear, the dealer was staring at her—as were three salesmen through the large display window from inside the red brick store. "Look, we missed the local to Paradise—think of it! Our parents will kill us if we stay the night here, unchaperoned." Joanna started to waver, not mentioning the obvious fact that they had just traveled across half of America unchaperoned. "Besides," Lucy added, "we'll have more fun once we get to Paradise."

Joanna looked at Lucy.

Lucy smiled. "Didn't we say we wanted an adventure?"

Joanna nodded, looking none too reassured.

Lucy turned to the plump little man standing before her in plaid trousers and a white linen jacket, with an oversized bow tie and a straw boater hat. "I'll take it," she announced, then added, "How much?"

All three pairs of eyes turned to regard the gleaming black Duryea standing in the dealer's front yard. It was outstanding amongst the carriages and coaches for sale—the only automobile present. The dealer's voice was eager. "One thousand five hundred dollars, but for you, little lady, one thousand even."

"That's fine," Lucy said enthusiastically. She had always wanted to own an automobile! And she never quibbled over prices. Besides, a thousand dollars for a brand-new motorcar sounded right to her. Hadn't the salesman explained that it had an electric ignition as well as a one-cylinder gasoline-driven engine? And it had four wheels, not three, like some of the new automobiles.

"You're crazy!" Joanna cried, but she was regarding the shiny automobile with awe.

Lucy was flushed with excitement. She imagined herself and Joanna driving into Paradise in the splendid black roadster. Two young women in the beautiful new car . . . What a stir they would create! What a sensation! Lucy liked doing things with aplomb.

She turned to the salesman. "I will give you five hundred cash. I have an unlimited line of credit at Paradise Bank. They will wire you the rest, I assure you."

The salesman blinked. "Look, ma'am, I can't do that, I don't know who you are!"

"My name is Lucy Bragg." The man's eyes widened. Bragg was *the name* in these parts, and Lucy didn't have to continue, but she did. "My daddy is the industrialist Rathe Bragg, and he owns the bank. My grandpa is Derek Bragg, and he owns the D&M, the D&M Railroad, and probably the rest of Paradise and half of West Texas, too. I assure you, you will not be cheated."

Sometime later, after all arrangements had been completed and the dealer had given them a few brief instructions and traveling directions, he left Lucy and Joanna standing with the road car in the dusty yard in the blazing sun.

It was so hot. Lucy pulled an immaculate white linen handkerchief from her reticule and dabbed at her face, wishing she could swish it between her breasts. Paradise was at least a two-day ride—or drive—from San Antonio, Lucy thought. She hadn't mentioned that fact to Joanna. As she and Joanna circled the car, Joanna asked, "Now what?"

"We get in and go."

"Lucy, I didn't want to bring this up, but you don't know how to drive this thing."

"Pooh! Of course I do, it's easy; any idiot can see that! Come on, get in!"

With no small amount of pandemonium, they hauled their luggage and filled up the roadster's tiny backseat. Both girls were huffing and sweating. Lucy wanted to remove her hat, but didn't dare, for it would ruin her fashionable appearance, and her skin was ivory white—the bane of a redhead's existence. They climbed in, tucking their skirts around them. Unfortunately, or fortunately, nothing happened.

"Lucy," Joanna began hesitantly. Lucy understood.

"Great balls of fire!" she cried, using a favorite new expression that she had picked up from her Harvard beau, Leon. She climbed out, dragging her sumptuous skirts with her. She was dying to remove her perfectly fitted, velvet-lapeled jacket. It was so hot and wet.

She grabbed the crank. "I'll turn it, and when it catches, pump the gas pedal, just a little bit."

Panting, Lucy worked the crank until the auto started up.

"Told you this was easy!" Lucy cried, straightening her back with a wince. She clambered back into the Duryea. She'd watched many of her beaux drive. It had always looked like such fun. She stomped on the gas. The car shot forward and slammed into the wooden corner post of the dealer's brick store.

"Oh, damn!"

"Lucy!"

They were simultaneous wails. Lucy stumbled out, thoroughly flushed now. "Are you all right?" she cried, barely able to believe they'd gotten off to such a start. Joanna assured her she was, although she was quite white, and shaking. Lucy inspected the car. The dealer and the three salesmen also came running out, the dealer screaming incoherently because they'd somehow cracked the big display window. Lucy ignored him, worriedly regarding the automobile's front fender. Miraculously, there were only a few scratches—and one perfectly round, melon-sized dent. "Why didn't you turn!" Joanna cried.

"I didn't have time," Lucy explained, rubbing one of the scratches as if she might erase it.

Joanna consoled her. "You can always buy another motorcar."

Lucy gave her a look. "I just spent my entire allowance—and then some."

Lucy gave the dealer another hundred dollars, along with a bright smile, and they were on their way. Joanna said nothing, even though she knew Lucy had overpaid the dealer for the damage they'd done to his window.

They drove down the road at ten miles an hour. It was wonderful, despite the heat and the humidity; they actually caught a small, hot breeze. Lucy sighed, relieved to be finally on the road. She would never admit it, but she was a bit shaken from the accident. However, she was sure the rest of their trip would pass without incident.

Lucy decided to forgo her original intention of driving down Main Street. Traffic was often heavy in the city, a few roadsters, many horses, riders and carriages, and many business conveyances, wagons, buses, and the like. Sometimes there were even cattle, a hangover from days gone by. She had learned her limitations, and would stick to the relatively quiet open roads leaving town. An hour later, they had left the last residential homes behind them. It was blazing hot.

"The train was cooler," Joanna said quietly.

Lucy didn't answer. The train had been cooler.

The car was bouncing over each rut and hole in the road, and they hadn't seen another rider or carriage in ages. Lucy's backside was already sore, her back stiff and aching. Why was the road so quiet? The hills around them were dry and yellow from the summer sun. Stunted trees dotted the landscape. Not a cloud marred the sky. Above them, buzzards circled, and Lucy didn't want to know what they were scavenging. So it wasn't exactly like a picnic in Oyster Bay, she thought, but it was still an adventure.

"I wonder if these roads are always so quiet," Joanna remarked uneasily.

"Of course they are," Lucy said cheerfully, hiding her own unease. "Joanna, what time did we leave San Antonio?"

"At two," she said, automatically looking at her eighteen-carat pocket watch. "It's almost four-thirty."

It didn't seem like they had been driving for two and a half hours. It seemed like they had been driving for ten hours. Lucy was starting to have doubts, which she refused to entertain. "See how the time just races by! Before you know it, we'll be in Paradise!"

Joanna just looked at her.

Lucy could see that they were approaching a man on foot. Instantly worry arose. A man on foot this far from the city? They were in the middle of nowhere! It became evident that he was carrying a saddle, but she did not relax. Because of the depression, there were too many tramps around these days, even armies of violent unemployed drifters. It was only last year that "Coxey's army" had marched on Washington. Caution and determination won the moment. In order to give the man a wide berth, Lucy steered the car carefully to the other side of the road, and landed hard in a pothole. The car bounced rigidly and Joanna groaned. Lucy darted a glance at the man. He wore faded, form-fitting Levis, boots, a bashed Stetson, and an unbuttoned shirt, hanging open. He had been looking over his shoulder; now he stopped to watch them approach. Lucy told herself she was ridiculous for suddenly feeling afraid. She wished the Duryea would go faster.

"Lucy," Joanna whispered, staring at the stranger. "He wants a ride."

Lucy saw, with a sinking sensation, that he was thumbing for a lift. "I will not stop."

"Don't! He looks dangerous!"

Lucy hushed Joanna as they were drawing alongside, because she didn't want him to overhear. Of course, inwardly she agreed with Joanna and even condemned him as a thief, or worse. However, sensing Joanna's real and rising fear, she whispered, "Don't be silly, he just needs a bath. He's probably a cowboy from one of the ranches around here." She caught a glimpse of tightly clad thighs and hips and a bronze, slick torso, and then they were past.

Lucy let out a breath. There was something menacing even in the man's stance.

Fifteen minutes later, Joanna cried out, "Lucy! Watch out!"

Lucy had been admiring a roadrunner darting into the shade of some brush. She jerked her eyes to the road just as the automobile crashed hard into a huge hole, jamming both girls up against the dashboard. A few yards later, a slapping, irregular noise signaled that this time they had done some damage to the auto. Lucy could feel that something was dragging on the ground. She stopped the car and slumped at the wheel. "Oh, damn," she whispered.

It was so hot and they had been driving forever and there was not a house in sight and how could she have been so stupid to think up this whole scheme? "Please just stop and think before you act, Lucy," she could hear her mother saying.

Lucy took a deep breath, managed a smile for Joanna's benefit, and climbed out of the cab. She looked at the car and noticed that it was sagging on the right in front. Something was surely wrong, but what? And even if she could find out what, how was she going to fix it? She circled the car. The other side seemed fine, upright, except for the scratches and the dent. She came back to the driver's side and saw again how the chassis sagged over the big spoked wheel. "Something's broken," she said, trying not to sound despondent.

"Lucy, what are we going to do?"

"I don't know."

Lucy stared at the car for a few minutes, thinking. She immediately ruled out walking. They were two young women, unchaperoned and unprotected, dressed in their eastern finery. Impossible! Even if they escaped mishap, should they somehow arrive at the D&M safely, her father would kill her once he found out. *And* never trust her again. It was one thing to travel by rail or auto, another to travel alone on foot. And besides, what about all their luggage? How could they leave behind all their clothing for their holiday? By the time Grandpa Derek sent someone to fetch their things, undoubtedly they would be stolen.

"Damn," Lucy said fervently.

She would have to fix the car herself.

Determined, Lucy began taking the pins out from her hat. She was horrified when she saw that dead bugs had accumulated on it, and went crimson thinking of how she had looked to the cowboy they had just passed. She threw it aside.

Her head gleamed like golden fire in the sunlight. Her chignon had become loosened, and tendrils were spilling around her face. It was a face that captivated and mesmerized men everywhere.

She was more than beautiful. Her face was classic—oval shaped with high cheekbones. Her eyes were big and sapphire blue. Her lashes were a dark gold, like her brows, startling against the pale ivory of her skin. Her complexion was flawless. Her nose was small and straight except for a slight tilt at its tip. Her mouth was lush and full and coral—too lush, too full, for it drove men crazy.

Lucy dropped to her knees and peered under the car's carriage. It was dark and she couldn't see anything. On her hands she crawled forward, straining to see. Joanna started giggling.

Angrily Lucy raised her head and slammed it into the car. "Ow!"

"You looked so funny, with your fanny in the air like that! If Leon could see you now!"

Lucy sat on her haunches in the dirt, mad, her head throbbing. Then her gaze widened and she stared.

He stared back.

Her breath caught. She hadn't heard him approaching, and he stood so close, she could see, for the first time, his face beneath the battered cowboy hat. It was roughly chiseled, stark, completely masculine. His skin was dark bronze, and his eyes were so light that they seemed silver. The contrast was stunning. She was ensnared in the hot light of his eyes for a long moment.

The corner of his lip curled up unpleasantly. Lucy didn't move. She couldn't. Joanna was stock-still, too. But he never looked at her. His gaze released Lucy's eyes and slid down her face to her mouth. There it paused, and Lucy's heart began slamming wildly in her chest.

His gaze slid lower lazily. No man had ever looked at her the way he was looking at her. He eyed her full breasts, straining against the confines of her traveling suit, the jacket opened now. It slipped quickly down her to her dainty pearl-buttoned shoes, then back up. He hefted his saddle up to his shoulder and started walking on.

He was leaving them.

Lucy was so stunned, she blinked.

"Maybe he can help us," Joanna whispered urgently.

Lucy was staring at his masculine swagger. That very thought was also occurring to her. "Or maybe he'll kill us," she whispered back. "Or—worse."

She suddenly realized that he might have heard her, and she flushed. But if he did, he never broke stride. Rapidly she weighed her choices. He was a tramp, or worse, there was no doubt about that. Still, he hadn't hurt them . . .

She leapt up. "Wait! Mister, wait!"

2

He didn't stop, or even slow down. He just kept walking away as if he hadn't even heard her.

Lucy was shocked. No man had ever ignored her before. Amazed, then with a rush of determination, she lifted her skirts and stumbled after him. "Wait! Mister! *Sir!*"

That stopped him. He turned, thrusting out one hard hip and resting his saddle upon it. He waited.

Lucy paused when she was still a good distance from him. There was no expression on his face. Nothing. And the way his hips were cocked, so arrogantly . . . Frowning, Lucy came forward so she would not have to shout, but remained far enough away to dodge him if need be. "Excuse me." She tried out a brilliant smile, but there was no response.

"Do you think you might be able to help us?"

He stared.

When he did not respond, she grew uncomfortable and began to have serious doubts about approaching this rough-looking drifter for help. The way he was branding her with his gaze made her shift uneasily. There was no one around for miles, except for Joanna, and Lucy could not help but be aware of the two of them face-to-face and alone, in the overwhelming space of the Texas desert, which stretched as far as the eye could see. It made the situation disturbingly intimate.

They needed his help. Lucy took a breath and smiled charmingly. It never failed with the opposite sex. "Our roadster has broken down, as you can see. We can't leave it, because of all of our luggage. I haven't the faintest idea

what to do!'' She gave him an appealing, helpless look.
''Do you know anything about autos—sir?''

''Not a thing.''

She hadn't expected that short, flat response. In truth,
she hadn't really crossed paths with his sort before and
therefore didn't know what to expect. The social circles in
which she traveled were very exclusive. As a little girl, she
had attended some rallies for workers, and had even gotten
caught up in a strike, but she could barely remember those
events. Despite the man's station in life, whatever it might
be, Lucy had anticipated a certain amount of chivalry from
him. She stepped back in surprise.

His eyes blazed briefly in what looked like anger, and
then they went flat. When he eyed the roadster, Lucy rushed
on. ''Would you examine the motorcar? Please?''

For one long moment, Lucy thought he was actually going
to refuse. He looked at her, his mouth curling slightly.
Lucy's heart was slamming thunderously. He unnerved her.
It was a new experience, one she did not particularly like.

Wordlessly he moved past her, so closely, his body
brushed hers. Lucy didn't jump out of his way in time to
avoid the contact. She ran after him, following him to the
auto. He laid his saddle carefully down, then squatted, regarding the carriage.

''Can you fix it?''

''Yes.''

Lucy and Joanna exchanged bright, relieved looks. Then
he rose to his full height, lifting up his saddle. ''But I
won't.''

Lucy gaped at him. He appeared madder than hell. ''In
about an hour you'll reach a ranch,'' he said. ''I imagine
the walk will do you good.''

He began striding away. Lucy stared incredulously at
Joanna. He would leave them now?

''Go after him!'' Joanna cried. ''Quick!''

''Damn,'' Lucy exclaimed, torn. He was very rude;
worse, she was sure he was dangerous. He did not look like
the typical unemployed worker, oh no. And he was certainly
not like any man she had ever met before. In addition to
the obvious difference of background, no man had ever

turned a deaf ear to her appeals before. But they were desperate. Her mind made up, she was about to run after him.

Suddenly he stopped in his tracks, cursing audibly, throwing his saddle on the ground. Lucy jumped involuntarily as he came striding back to her, his open shirt swinging around his narrow hips. His stomach above the tarnished silver belt buckle was flat and looked as hard as a rock. A sheen of perspiration covered his skin. Realizing where she was looking, Lucy blushed and met his smoking gaze.

He came to an abrupt halt. "Don't tempt me."

"What?"

"I must be out of my mind."

"You'll help us?"

"Like I said, I'm out of my damn mind."

"Thank you!"

"Don't thank me, I don't have a kind bone in my body. *Comprende?*"

Lucy didn't understand. Not really. She stared at him. Why was he so angry? Why did he seem to dislike her so? He didn't even know her.

"Turn those baby blues elsewhere, princess," he said. "I'm not doing this for nothing. I'm not doing this for you. I'm doing it for me."

She stiffened. "Of course, how silly of me. How much do you want?"

He laughed as he took off his shirt. "I don't want your money." His gaze slid over her.

Lucy's head went higher; inside, she shook. His look was scathing . . . and something else. Something unfamiliar and scalding. She decided she disliked him. He was terribly rude, the lowest sort of riffraff. She didn't want his help, but she needed it. "I don't understand. If you don't want money . . . ?"

He threw his shirt on the auto's hood. He whipped around. "If you'd lowered your little nose a ways back and given me a ride, I'd have fixed your axle right away."

She stared at his gleaming, thickly sculpted chest, his powerful rippling arms. Her body temperature, already high, went higher. She had never seen a man half-naked before. She knew she should not stare. Now she was being rude.

He stood very still. A silence had suddenly descended. He broke it. "Take your time. Take your fill."

Aghast, Lucy realized what she had been doing, and worse, what he had caught her doing, and she looked away, her face flaming. "We'll give you a ride." The words came out breathless and low.

He turned away.

Lucy covered her pounding heart with her palm.

Lucy and Joanna stood side by side while he jacked up the Duryea. Lucy used the respite to regain control of her emotions. Logic intruded, and with it, a few tiny warning bells went off. Now they were going to have to give him a ride. If anyone ever found out that they had given a stranger a ride . . . It would be bad enough if he were a gentleman, but he wasn't, and this was much, much worse. If he could fix the car. Lucy almost hoped that he would fail. Then he would continue on his way—and she and Joanna would be stranded. They could not win. She supposed that giving him a ride was better than being stuck in the middle of the desert with a broken car. She just had to make sure that no one ever found out.

He had elevated the auto with stones, and now he laid a hand on the nose and pushed. The auto swayed precariously.

"What are you doing?" Lucy cried.

The look he shot her made Lucy sorry she'd asked. "You're going to knock it down," she managed.

"Better it falls now," he said, "or would you rather it crash down on me?"

He dropped to the ground and shimmied under the auto. She understood and she wanted to protest. He might be a tramp, and a nasty one at that, but she didn't want him crushed beneath her car.

Joanna nudged Lucy for the fifteenth time. Her blue eyes were wide in her pale face. She mouthed a silent question: What are we going to do?

Lucy knew Joanna was also just as worried about being stranded out here, in the middle of nowhere, as she was about their "savior." Now it was past five, and in a few hours it would be dark. Even if he fixed the car, then what? Before, when they'd left San Antonio, she had just assumed they'd find a hotel to spend the night in. But now she wasn't sure they were anywhere near a hotel. It appeared that the road to Paradise wasn't the same as the rail route, because didn't she remember passing a few quaint little towns after San Antonio in the years past? Or, come to think of it, were all those white picket fences *before* San Antonio?

If he fixed the roadster and they didn't find a hotel—then what? She would have been horrified with the possibilities, so she decided not to think about it and to deal with that problem later.

He pulled himself out from beneath the auto and rose to his full height. This time Lucy carefully kept her gaze on his left shoulder. "Is it fixed?"

He eyed her averted profile. "For now."

Lucy's gaze was drawn to him, met his, was riveted there. "What was wrong?"

"The axle is broken. It should hold until you can have it fixed properly. Where are you headed?"

The Duryea was repaired. Lucy hesitated, her mind filled with the new crisis facing her—giving this hard, rough stranger a ride.

"We're going to Paradise," Joanna ventured shyly from the background.

He was staring at Lucy so intently that she flushed, sure he could read her thoughts. She couldn't meet his gaze.

"Planning on welching?"

He spoke so softly, Lucy wasn't sure she heard him correctly. "What?"

"You heard."

The anger in his tone made her glance quickly at him. "Of course not. I promised you a ride, didn't I?" She attempted a bright smile.

"Don't look so damn happy about it."

Her bosom rose. How did she dare go anywhere with this man? She exchanged glances with Joanna. But she wasn't a liar, she always kept her word. She took her friend's elbow. "Let's go."

"Lucy?"

"It's all right."

"Dammit, just get in the car!" he said from behind them.

Joanna obeyed with alacrity. Lucy dug in her heels. "Your manners are questionable!"

"Lucy!" Joanna cried in fright.

"Really?"

Lucy regretted her outburst, and turned to get in the roadster. He stopped her by actually grabbing her shoulder. She was stunned.

"My manners may leave a lot to be desired, but so does your attitude—princess."

It was intended as a slur—it felt like a slur. "Why are you insulting me?"

"Did I insult you? No one ever call you 'princess' before? Fancy that! Betcha this is the first time a man didn't swoon and become cow-eyed over you, too."

Angrily Lucy wrenched free. "Your manners do belong in the slums!"

"You might say that, *princess*."

"I regret promising you a ride!"

"I'm sure you do." He pulled on his shirt. "Now, get in the car."

Lucy considered refusing.

"You can get in under your own steam," he said flatly, "or I can put you in."

He meant it. She got in.

"Paradise." He suddenly grinned, with real humor. "Paradise." He chuckled. "You girls really going to Paradise?"

Lucy was too angry to respond, but Joanna said, "We're going to the D&M."

Lucy jabbed her hard in the ribs with her elbow. Joanna gasped, and Lucy bit her lip. But she was looking at the stranger, who was staring at them. At her.

"Fancy that," he drawled. "You two belong to that spread?"

Joanna didn't dare speak, and Lucy cried quickly, "No!"

He sort of smiled. He had stopped when Joanna had mentioned her grandfather's ranch, and Lucy felt the knot of fear increasing. What if he made the connection between her and Derek Bragg and kidnapped her for ransom? He cranked up the car, and the engine roared immediately to life. He jumped into the cab, jamming his big body down.

He smiled at Lucy, baring his white, even teeth. "Just for your information," he said, "Paradise is that way." And he pointed back the way they had come.

"What?" Lucy cried. "Paradise is north of San Antonio, not south!"

"That's right," he said. "That way." And he pointed back down the road again.

"Oh, Lucy! We spent the entire afternoon driving the wrong way!"

Lucy was red with embarrassment. How had she made such a mistake? The auto was idling and he reached for the tiller. His hand brushed her thigh. Lucy tried to shift away from him, but there was nowhere to go in the cramped front seat.

They drove away. Mutinously she stared at the endless road ahead. Her anger cooled rapidly. She darted a glance at him, but his expression was inscrutable. He was watching the road, carefully steering. His elbow brushed her arm. She became aware of the length of his thigh from hip to knee pressing against hers.

All thoughts of their awful predicament temporarily fled. His leg was hard, warm, and big, straining the worn, near-white denim of his Levis. There was a hole on his knee, and soon there would be another rent on his thigh. The fabric was pulled so tightly over his groin, it looked like it might rip asunder at any moment. Quickly Lucy averted her gaze. She tried to remove her body from all contact with his.

"Stop wriggling," he growled.

She went very still. God, how had she ever gotten into this mess?

Lucy's heart was slamming too fast and too hard. She didn't like sitting there next to him, squashed in together like fish bait in a can, much less giving him a ride in the middle of nowhere. With no one else around. No one to help them—if they needed it. How had she ever been so stupid as to promise him a ride? He had practically forced them into the car. What if he did something to them, something terrible? What if he realized who she was, and kidnapped her? What if he was worse than a tramp? What if he was a down-and-out criminal?

He looked like an outlaw.

Lucy had a gun. She had a small, pearl-handled derringer in her purse, and she was a dead shot. Her grandfather had made sure of that. But she was not reassured. On the contrary, to even be thinking about the gun now, to even consider that she might need it to defend herself, fueled her fears. It pointed up just how bad the situation might actually be.

She and Joanna must escape—tonight.

She sat, rigid and breathless, scheming. He appeared just as rigid, his mouth pressed in a hard line, his gaze glued to the road with utter concentration. There was no conversation for the next hour. Then the auto suddenly ran out of power and coasted to a halt. He cursed graphically, but both girls were too upset to blush. He got out and began to turn the crank. It started, but when he stepped on the accelerator, there was nothing. The auto rolled an inch or so and then the engine died.

"What is it?" Lucy asked, alarmed.

"Damned if I know."

Suddenly he gave Lucy a look and went behind the front seat and peered at the fuel tank. "Damn!"

"What is it?"

"We're out of gasoline."

"But . . ." Lucy started. Slowly she went crimson.

"You fill this monster up in San Antone?"

Miserably, she shook her head.

He laughed mirthlessly. Then he reached into the car and withdrew his saddle, hoisting it on his shoulder. He eyed the girls.

Lucy scrambled out of the car. "Are you going to get fuel?" she demanded.

"No, I'm not, princess."

"Somehow I didn't think so."

"You're learning. Leave your stuff. Let's go."

Lucy and Joanna exchanged glances. Joanna needed no

encouragement; she nearly leapt from the car. Lucy grabbed the stranger's sleeve to halt him. "How far are we from San Antonio?" Suddenly she was overjoyed and thoroughly relieved—they had been backtracking, so they had to be close to town. Town—where they could get rid of this stranger, find a bed and bath, *and* take the spur to Paradise tomorrow.

He smiled. "We're not."

"What do you mean? Of course we are! We've been driving for an hour back the way we came!"

"Don't have much sense of direction, do you?"

Lucy had enough. She intended to put him in his place, once and for all. "I was born and raised in New York City— on *Fifth Avenue*." Her tone was superior.

"Guess that explains just about *everything*," he said with contempt.

Somehow, she had lost that round. They stared at each other. Lucy would not give him the satisfaction of seeing her drop her gaze first. As the standoff lengthened, the amusement she saw sparking in his gray eyes riled her. "Where are we?"

"About eighty miles dead west of San Antone," he drawled. "To make up for lost time, I took a turnoff a ways back. We've been heading straight north, princess, and if you'd been paying attention, you'd know it."

Lucy backed up a step. Stuck. They were truly stuck, out in the middle of nowhere with this dangerous-looking stranger—and it was almost dark. They both looked up at the dusky sky.

"Let's go," he said. "We've got another hour of light left." Then he smiled. "And whatever it is you're planning, I would think twice about it if I were you."

3

She was near tears.

Generally he despised sniveling females, but surprisingly, he felt sorry for her. He hadn't known he could still feel compassion for another human being; he had thought any empathy had been beaten out of him long ago, in prison. He supposed it was because she was so plain, and just an innocent victim of the other one's schemes. He had already sized up the girls' relationship. The plain one was the supporting act, the other one was the leader.

The other one. Shoz stopped and turned to let the two girls catch up. The other one, the princess, was not crying, oh no. Her mouth was set in an expression like a mule's, telling him she wouldn't give an inch. This, too, was a surprise; he would have assumed she was all fluff.

"When are we stopping?" Lucy demanded. She was supporting Joanna. The smaller girl did not have her strength. "Joanna is exhausted."

"But you aren't?"

"Not at all."

"Sheathe your claws, princess; we'll stop for the night here." He turned away with a hidden smile. It was a downright lie. Her face was red with exertion. And she was glaring at him as if he'd just told her they'd go another few miles, while her friend, the pale, mousy one, was gazing at him with wide teary-eyes.

Shoz began gathering wood for a fire while the two girls sank down in exhaustion. He watched the redhead strip off her expensive suede shoes without a thought for modesty; in fact, he paused to admire her stockinged ankles and the hint of calf she was showing him. On purpose? He was sure of it. She was a practiced flirt, used to gaining male attention whenever she wanted it. If she thought she could manipulate him, she had another thing coming. And if she wanted to play with fire, it was okay with him. Someone should warn her that he hadn't had a woman in two weeks, not since he'd left Carmen in Death Valley.

"Lucy," Joanna protested, tugging at her sleeve.

Lucy followed her friend's glance to Shoz and saw his interested gaze. A flush rose to her cheeks while a tingle ran down her spine. She hastily let her skirts fall and cover her nearly bare legs.

"What are you doing?" Joanna scolded.

Lucy looked at her. "My feet hurt. I don't care."

"Do you think we'll be safe tonight?"

There was tension in Joanna's voice, and Lucy followed Joanna's gaze to look at the stranger as he dumped a pile of wood and brush. He squatted. His faded jeans stretched taut over his powerful legs, and Lucy realized there was a constriction in her chest.

Joanna did not know their plans to escape, because there was no way Lucy could tell her without risking being overheard by the stranger. Lucy knew Joanna would willingly follow her when the time came. It was just a matter of finding the right moment. Having made the decision to escape earlier, Lucy did not question it now.

But she debated Joanna's question. If they were to remain here, she wasn't sure if they would be safe or not. She was filled with doubts. He confused her. She sensed he didn't like her. He was so different from any man she had ever met before that he was impossible to fathom. And his gaze was unnerving. Predatory. Lucy wasn't exactly frightened, but she wasn't exactly calm, either.

It was almost dark, and they were going to escape as soon as possible. But how?

Shoz stood, his pale gaze sweeping over her. Lucy rose, too, as if on a puppet's string. He had a way of making her feel naked. It raised goose bumps on her skin, and she didn't like it.

"Can you cook?"

Lucy blinked.

He repeated the question.

"We have servants who cook."

He picked up his saddlebags and shoved them at her chest. "Not anymore you don't."

She was genuinely amazed. Lucy opened the bags to find coffee, dried beans, and a few tins of meat. "What am I supposed to do with this?"

"You want to eat?" He squatted and lit the fire. "Make the food first. After it's done and we've eaten, you can wash the pot out in the stream that runs behind those trees. Then make the coffee."

Stiffly Lucy threw the saddlebags down. "I am not your maid," she said, insulted. She turned her back on him. "Come on, Joanna, let's go refresh ourselves." She picked up her reticule.

Shoz crossed his arms and watched her friend get up tiredly, nevertheless obeying her. He called after them, "Don't go too far. There's wolves, mountain lions, and snakes around here."

That froze Lucy, but only for a second. She took Joanna's arm, and said, loudly enough, "Ignore him. He's only trying to scare us."

"Are you sure?" Joanna quavered. "Lucy, what if—"

"Trust me," Lucy replied with more confidence than she felt.

Shoz poked the fire. He made no attempt to cook. If the spoiled princess didn't do it, she would go hungry—he'd already made up his mind on that score. Fair was fair—and he'd been too damn fair. He'd made the fire, and he certainly wasn't going to wait on her and give in to her uppity airs. Never. He wasn't her servant, even if she thought so.

He felt it, again, the rising pressure in his loins. He avoided ladies like the plague and his arousal made him angry. She was probably a looker when she was cleaned up, not that he cared. Her body would make any man crazy, and after two weeks of forced celibacy (he hated whores), she was making him crazy.

He looked at the sky. There was a full moon and a skyful of stars, making it a gloriously bright night. Until the sun had set, he had been heading in the right direction, and now he checked his position against the North Star. He might be off by a few miles, but the meeting wasn't until mid-morning tomorrow. Automatically Shoz's palm went to the waistband of his jeans, touching the thick wad taped there. He had been a fool to become involved with the girls. What was he going to do with them tomorrow? Was he becoming softhearted? That would be dangerous. Then he heard a scream.

He kept a knife strapped to his ankle inside his boot, and it was in his hand even before he was running toward the stream. He already knew it was her friend who had screamed, and he recognized the sound as surprise and fear and pain. He burst through the three trees to see Joanna on the ground, moaning, holding her ankle. Lucy knelt beside her with concern. They had crossed the stream and were on the other side. "Damn," he said, wading through the ankle-high water. He could not miss his meeting tomorrow, he absolutely could not. There was too much at stake.

"Let me see," he said, sheathing his knife and squatting. He gently took Joanna's foot in his hands.

"It's not broken, is it?" Lucy cried.

Joanna kept moaning, rocking back and forth.

"She slip on the rocks in the creek?"

"Yes."

Shoz took off her shoe. She yelped and began to cry. Shoz wished she had just a little of the debutante's backbone. Fortunately, her ankle wasn't broken, but it was twisted. "It's sprained," he announced with a sinking feeling. He knew he should just leave these two and go on about his business, but how could he? Damn! How could he leave them alone in the middle of this barren country—inhabited only by snakes and wolves? Especially now that one of them was hurt. He *was* becoming softhearted.

"We need ice," Lucy stated.

"Sorry, princess, but the icebox is broken and the butler has the day off."

Lucy stood abruptly. "Stop making fun of me."

"You bring it on yourself," he said shortly, and gave his attention to Joanna. She was regarding him steadily out of big, pretty blue eyes, her best feature. He gave her an encouraging smile; she smiled back. "I'll splint this up and it'll feel better immediately."

"Thank you," Joanna said softly.

"What in hell were you two doing, anyway?" Shoz asked, staring at Lucy.

"What do you mean?" Her eyes were wide and innocent, like an angel's.

"Why'd you cross the stream?"

She opened her mouth, but no sound came out. Two pink spots appeared on her cheeks.

"Talking a walk?" he drawled. He didn't wait for her answer. "Stay with her."

Lucy eyed him as he left, and dropped down beside Joanna, taking her hand. "Don't worry," she said, but she herself was distraught. They had tried to escape, but had failed miserably. How could they escape now? The answer was obvious; they couldn't. And she couldn't escape by herself and leave Joanna alone with that monster. She would never abandon her friend like that!

"His hands were gentle," Joanna whispered.

Lucy gaped at her.

"I don't think he's going to hurt us, Lucy," Joanna said hesitantly.

Lucy stared at Joanna, who rarely offered an opinion unless it was asked for. Then she squeezed her friend's hand. "I'm sure you're right," she said, to ease her fears. "Don't worry, I won't leave you."

Shoz returned with material for the splint, and Lucy jumped guiltily. He looked at her sharply as he knelt down. Lucy got the impression that he had overheard them—and knew what they had tried to do. Her heartbeat accelerated, but he didn't comment. Instead, he worked surely and fast, as if he'd tended sprained ankles dozens of times. Watching him, Lucy began to relax. If he was going to hurt them, would he be so helpful now?

She didn't think so.

Had she overreacted to their situation? Lucy bit her lip. Knowing herself, she could honestly admit it was a slight possibility. After all, other than being rude, had he done anything terrible to them? He'd only asked for a ride, and he had fixed the Duryea.

Joanna seemed impervious to pain. Noting this and the way Joanna was gazing at the outlaw's dark head abruptly drew Lucy to the present. Lucy felt her hackles rise, one by one. He wasn't really handsome, although he did have a profile that could have been carved by a master. She grudgingly admitted that he was attractive, in an unusual way, in a rough, dangerous way. She watched his hands. They did, indeed, look gentle.

"Is that better?" he asked.

Lucy scowled at his back. Joanna nodded, whispering a thank you. The outlaw lifted Joanna into his arms without even asking her permission. Joanna clung to him as he carried her back to their campfire. Lucy's anger grew, and she didn't question why.

"Feel better?" she mocked. "Oh, thank you!" She stomped after them.

Joanna was settled comfortably in the outlaw's bedroll and he was stoking the fire when Lucy returned. That sight annoyed her, too. He rocked back onto his heels, squinting at her. Hands on her hips, Lucy stared back. He reached into a saddlebag and tossed a can at her. She just managed to catch it. He dumped the pan out, along with a small can opener. "Start cooking," he said.

"Why me?" Lucy asked mutinously.

"Your friend is hurt."

"Why not you?"

"You're the woman."

Lucy had never opened a can in her life. She wasn't about to start now. His attitude was irritating. She threw the can at him. "I refuse to cater to you," she retorted. "For your information, women are equal to men—in every way. So you can cook yourself."

"Women are equal to men, huh?" He laughed. "In every way? Really?"

He was making fun of her and she did not understand the innuendos, but was certain they were there. "In every way. But I don't expect a backwoods person like yourself to be familiar with liberal thinking."

"Oh, I'm real liberal," he said, still laughing. "If you come on over here, I'll show you just how liberal I am—and we can test out your theories of equality."

"You would make fun of something you don't understand."

He stood up, his smile vanishing. It had been a startling smile, very white and dimpled. "If you're so damn equal, princess, why didn't you get down on your knees in the dirt to fix that fancy heap of metal?"

She flushed.

"You don't believe in equality, honey, you believe in aristocracy."

"That's not true! My mother is a leading suffragette, Grace Br—"

He waited.

Lucy didn't dare reveal her family name, just in case he was as immoral as he looked. Just in case he wasn't averse to kidnapping. Unable to speak, she glared.

"To hell with equality, start cooking. If you want to eat, that is."

"I happen to be full."

"On what? Caviar blintzes?"

"We dined sumptuously in San Antonio this afternoon," she lied. "I couldn't possibly eat another thing."

"Fine," he said, and he opened the can.

Lucy couldn't believe she had won so easily. Agitated from the exchange, she sat down next to Joanna, who had fallen asleep. She watched him cook the beans and the meat. Her stomach began to growl and she flushed, hoping he hadn't heard. What he was making did not look appetizing, but it smelled wonderful, and the truth was, they'd only had a continental-style breakfast that morning. She swallowed. She regretted her lie and wished she could take it back. Never would she let him see that she was famished. She should have fought harder with him over the issue of cooking instead of pretending to be full. Or confessed the truth—that she hadn't the faintest idea how to cook.

He never looked her way, stirring the pot with concentration. Once a wolf howled, and he cocked his head to the side, listening. Lucy decided she would pretend nonchalance when he ate. He took the meal off the fire and began to eat right from the pan.

At first, she was shocked by his manners. Then, when she realized that he really had no intention of offering her any food, she cried out. He turned sharply. His look was questioning.

Lucy stood, trembling. "I'm going to wash my face before bed." She hurried away.

It was a small brook, really just a muddy trickle, not far from the circle of firelight, but hidden from sight by a cluster of scrubby trees. She scooped up water and splashed it on her face, thinking about how awful he was—and how stupid she was. He had not one ounce of gentlemanly blood in his veins. To eat in front of her without sharing, even if she had said she was full!

She found, dismayed, that the water was gritty and full of dirt, and she sank onto her buttocks in the loamy bank. Her feet throbbed, her entire body felt like it had been run over by a dray, she was starving, she was filthy, and she realized she felt like crying.

She settled for a sniffle or two, and started to feel better. This would pass, she told herself, carefully wiping her eyes. Soon she would be at Grandpa Derek's and this would be one big joke; she and Joanna would laugh countless times remembering this adventure. Wouldn't they?

And then she heard a noise.

An animal, grunting. Or a man.

4

What was she doing?

Restlessly Shoz's gaze swept the circle of firelight, passing indifferently over a sleeping Joanna. He tried to penetrate the darkness beyond, where he knew the muddy little stream trickled past the three scrub oaks. He could not pierce the engulfing night. Before, he had heard her splashing water, then he had heard her sniffling. Now he listened intently and heard nothing but a lonely night owl.

What was she doing?

It seemed that she had been gone for a long time, but he knew no more than ten or fifteen minutes had passed. Why was he impatient, when patience was a skill of survival he had learned so long ago? His mind was even playing tricks on him, cruel ones, vivid ones. He imagined her unbuttoning her blouse and baring her big white breasts, to bathe. He stood and began pacing, tugging at the crotch of his Levis. He was not used to this kind of predicament.

He was spoiled when it came to women. Women found him irresistible—all of them. There had never been one he hadn't been able to get, not that he could remember. But this one . . . She was a rich girl, a spoiled girl, a brat, and he did not like her. He liked very few women other than his mother and sister, and Lucy was not one of them. He knew her type intimately; she was another Marianne. He had given up *ladies* a long time ago.

Of course, he thought with a smile, she wanted him. She despised him and had condemned him as a lowlife tramp, but she wanted him. He could have her if he lifted his little finger. He'd seen how she looked at him, and knew damn well she'd gotten a thrill in showing off her pretty little ankles. He wanted to laugh. Ankles! As if that could arouse someone like him. Didn't she know her perspiration-drenched jacket and blouse were more provocative than a bare foot?

So—what was stopping him?

He knew damn well it wasn't decency—he didn't have any left.

Still, in a way, just the tiniest way, she reminded him of his half-sister, Christina. They didn't look alike, not at all. Christina was dark blond and beautiful, a real heart-stopper. She was a little bit spoiled, a little bit arrogant, but *her* heart was all gold. Unlike the princess's. Maybe it was because of Christina. Maybe it was also because she was so young.

After all, he hated virgins.

He had a few doubts on that score, however. He wouldn't be at all surprised if the high-society deb wasn't a spoiled bird as well.

He stubbed the ground with the toe of his worn boot. What in hell was she doing? Had she fallen asleep? Been eaten by a mountain lion? Tried to escape again?

That thought jerked him out of his reverie, and with a low curse, he plunged into the darkness after her. He moved soundlessly. It was not a conscious attempt to maintain silence. He was three-quarters Apache, had been raised steeped in both his Indian heritage and western civilization, and the past five years had forced wariness upon him. It had become a way of life.

He paused when he saw her, deliberately stepping back behind one of the oaks. She was bathed in moonlight. She wasn't doing anything, just sitting there with her knees tucked up under her dusty skirts, her smudged chin in her palms, and he could make out her forlorn expression. She looked like a ragamuffin—and he almost softened.

But he didn't. He wanted her too much. She had a siren's sensual body, and he was nearly oblivious to her dirty face and orphaned look. Two weeks without a woman was his problem, not the little princess's. What was her name? Lucy. Lucy. He rolled it over on his tongue silently. It didn't help

ease the flow of his racing blood; if anything, it worsened
his situation.

He wanted her, and if his thoughts hadn't been so damn
sentimental a few moments ago, if she didn't look so damn
young right now, he would seduce her. She would be willing. He was experienced enough to recognize this. He
grunted at the thought of what she would feel like.

She whirled, on her feet, and saw him. Her immediate
surprise faded. She stared. The way she was looking at him
made him become very still.

He edged his shoulder against the tree. Her riveted gaze
made him forget all his saintly intentions; he was destined
for hell anyway. "Look at me," he commanded softly.

They were strangers, but the night was magical, the moment deeply intimate, and he compelled obedience. Lucy
obeyed. She stood very still, almost afraid to move, the
thick, hot night wrapped around them like wet, crushed
velvet. Everything seemed to have stopped, frozen in time:
the air, the crickets, the owl, her heart. In the moonlight
she could make out the glistening sheen of his damp body
where his shirt hung open, and his strained expression. His
jeans were stretched taut. She should lift her gaze, drag it
anywhere but there, and finally she did. He smiled slightly.
There was no mistaking the raw look in his eyes—although
Lucy had never seen such a look before.

The air was very sticky, and a wet heat seemed to have
risen all over her skin. There was a shortness to her breathing, making it difficult to fill her lungs, and Lucy became
aware of the strange tension, throbbing between them, mesmerizing her. She knew she should leave, go back to the
campfire and Joanna, but she did not want to leave.

"Come here, Lucy," he said.

Lucy knew she must leave, now. Or it would be too late.
Her instincts were ripe, bursting. She did not move.

Shoz smiled. The smile was lazy and sensual, but he felt
tense and determined. His chest rose and fell, hard. He
stalked her. She backed up a step.

"Don't be afraid," he said softly. "I won't hurt you."

Lucy stopped. He was so close, and his eyes commanded
that she wait for him. There was fire there, like the fire

running in her own veins. She looked at his mouth, sensually sculpted, parted slightly, and she felt an insane desire to kiss him. To kiss *him*. Taste him. She could already taste him, damp and salty . . . He gripped her hand, forcing it down between them.

"I want you," he said.

"No," she tried, not meaning it.

"I want you. Are you a virgin?"

She shook her head no, a protest that was automatic—having nothing to do with his question.

"Good. I hate virgins."

He pressed her hand against his erection.

She gasped, her eyes flying to his. What she saw in his eyes, silver in the moonlight, stilled her initial shock. She felt him pulsating beneath her palm, felt the burning heat. "Hold me," he said harshly. "Hard."

Lucy stood motionless, her heart slamming, and as if the Devil were instructing her, her fingers curled around him.

"Yes, princess," he said, and he slipped an arm around her and guided them both to their knees. Lucy felt his warm breath on her cheek, his mouth brushing there. She gasped, reaching for his shoulders. Crazy desire trailed in the wake of his lips. Lucy no longer knew herself. His face was pressed into her neck, his wet, hard body covered hers, his powerful arms crushing her in his embrace. And he was rocking his hips against her softness, and Lucy thought she might die, trapped between heaven and hell.

"Please," Lucy moaned, her nails digging into his shoulders. A second later he was crying out and arching against her belly.

"Damn," he said, into her neck. "That wasn't too good for you, was it, princess?"

Lucy whimpered, unable to make a coherent sound.

Then his hand was in her chignon. She gasped as he anchored her by a hank of hair while flipping up her skirts. His other hand slid up along her silk-clad thigh.

When he slipped his fingers beneath her drawers, Lucy fell back, spreading her legs wantonly. "God, you're ready, aren't you, princess?" he said with a shaky laugh. "Come on, baby, come now."

It was an order that made no sense. It didn't matter. He was stroking between her thighs rhythmically, expertly, and Lucy could not bear it.

He locked his arms around her hips and buried his face between her legs. Lucy was shocked. She felt his tongue. Any desire to protest ceased instantly, as he stroked and laved her intimately, mercilessly. She began climbing peaks, racing from one to the next, higher and higher . . . Her world shattered. She fell.

Drifting downward, Lucy became aware of many things gradually. The night air was a pleasant and balmy caress upon her naked legs. A rock was digging into her shoulder, hurting her. And he was propped up on one elbow, staring at her.

What had she done?

Very cautiously, Lucy looked back at him, her eyes wide. He smiled, a smug, satisfied look that seemed especially male; it instantly infuriated her. She sat up abruptly, hastily pulling her skirts down over her naked body; he caught her palm. When he didn't release it, she lifted her gaze to his face.

This time he wasn't smiling.

"I . . ." she began breathlessly, and stopped. Her heart had picked up its beat beneath the intensity of his stare. What had they done? Actual realization and total recall struck her. My God!

He silenced her abruptly with a hard kiss. Lucy forgot everything. His mouth was demanding, hungry. It became greedy. So did hers. She could not get enough of him. Soon his tongue delved into her mouth, stroking insistently, soon hers was mating with his. Lucy had kissed many men. But never like this.

His hands were on her breasts, seeking, searching, intent. Without her having been aware of it, he had undone the dozens of tiny buttons and insinuated his palm beneath the many layers of her underclothes. She felt him cupping her with growing urgency. He touched her nipple, teasing it into erectness.

Pushing corset, bust bodice, and chemise down, he took the distended tip into his mouth and began to suck gently.

Lucy arched wildly into his rock-hard body. She wrapped her thighs around his waist, undulating against him and the fullness grinding against her. They strained at each other like fierce mating animals, panting and heaving. Lucy's teeth found the tender skin of his throat.

He reached between them to free himself and then he was thrusting deep inside her.

The pain was brief and instantly forgotten. Lucy clung to him as he thrust once, twice, again. Heaven and hell. Hard and fast. Fire, fire and . . . ice. He was on his feet. Lucy lay stunned and bereft and open at his feet. A knife glinted in his hand. "Who is it?" he demanded.

Lucy sat up, reflexively covering herself, shocked.

Shoz, poised to fight, relaxed, and sheathed his knife.

Confused, her senses returning, her pulse racing, Lucy tried to comprehend what was happening. And then she saw Joanna.

5

Derek Bragg squinted down the railroad tracks and into the early morning sun. On the platform beside him, his diminutive wife tugged his sleeve. "Do you see anything?" Miranda asked.

"It's going to be a scorcher today," Derek said in reply, something of a shout. His hearing wasn't what it used to be, and he tended to shout. Although, for some reason, he always understood every word his wife said to him. "Don't see a thing. Train's late."

"It will come," Miranda said calmly. Yet her eyes, and her dress, belied her calm. She couldn't stand still, a tiny figure dwarfed by her leonine husband, who was, in her view, still the finest specimen of man around. Now her purple eyes danced excitedly, making her seem sixteen, not seventy-one—to her husband at least. She was wearing her Sunday best, a fine day gown of sprigged yellow linen with leg-o'-mutton sleeves and a bell-shaped skirt.

Suddenly Derek put his arm around her, squeezing. "Can barely wait," he roared.

"Oh, it will be so good to see Lucy again," Miranda agreed, beaming.

Derek grinned. "I'm glad Lucy came on ahead of Rathe and Grace. Although I'm real surprised Rathe let her travel this far alone."

"She's not alone, she's with Joanna and a chaperone."

Derek snorted. "Some old biddy's gonna keep Lucy in line? Hah!"

"Derek! You've never met Mrs. Seymour! Did I tell you Lucy's beau will be coming to visit in two weeks, too?" Among many, many others, Miranda thought wickedly, barely able to wait for the surprise she was planning for her husband.

Derek's eyes narrowed. "She's got a serious beau?"

"Yes, but you can relax, it's Leon Claxton, and that should please even Rathe!"

"How serious is serious?" He removed his Stetson to wipe his forehead, and frowned. "He related to Roger Claxton, the New York senator?"

"Yes, Leon is his son, and he hasn't proposed, if that's what you want to know."

Derek smiled wolfishly. "Yeah, well, if he's at all like his old man, then he's not for her."

"Why not! You like Roger—and he and Rathe are good friends."

"He and Rathe are close associates, with many of the same interests. That's not quite the same thing as good friends. If Leon's like his old man, he won't make a good husband: ambition will be his first and only interest."

Miranda frowned, absorbing what he had said. "I hear something." They both listened, and in the distance, there was the faint sound of a train's whistle.

"I don't hear anything. Now I remember. We met Leon once, briefly, when we were in New York last summer. He had just returned from Spain, where he had his first post as assistant consul in Madrid. Roger has big plans for Leon. I think he was just awarded the post as assistant to the police commissioner, Teddy Roosevelt. Do you know why Leon left Spain?''

Miranda shook her head.

"He was married—and his wife died over there in childbirth."

"I didn't know that."

Derek's mouth set. "He may have the right bloodlines, but he's not for Lucy."

"Here it is: look, Derek!" Miranda interrupted.

The big black locomotive came roaring into the station. Derek grabbed Miranda's arm. "Stop getting so excited, you'll have a heart attack!" he shouted over the roar of the train. He was flushed with excitement, too.

"There is nothing wrong with my heart, and you know it," she returned more calmly. But she was clutching her hands. The train had stopped, and two blue-suited conductors with their red-trimmed caps leapt off, and then the passengers began disembarking while a few people boarded. But there was no sign of Lucy.

"Derek." Miranda gripped his elbow in alarm.

Derek patted her reassuringly and strode over to one of the conductors. Although sometimes his right knee acted up and was a bit stiff, today his strides were long and agile. "Sir!"

The conductor handed a woman passenger up and turned to face Derek, whom he immediately recognized. "Mr. Bragg!" His smile was genuinely pleasant, not at all obsequious—even though Derek owned this spur that the train was on. After a lengthy exchange, Derek told Miranda to wait while he climbed aboard. Five minutes later, he appeared, grim-faced, and re-joined her on the platform. "She's not on the train, and the conductor said he hasn't seen a girl fitting her description. He's been working the line from New Orleans."

"What do you think happened?" Miranda was too upset to think that Derek had probably referred to Lucy as he always did, as "my little redheaded granddaughter."

"Lucy was on that train," Derek said. "She sent us a telegram the day she left."

"Oh my Lord," Miranda said.

"I'm going to wire New York. Just in case she and her friend didn't leave."

"Lucy would never be that irresponsible!"

"And then I'm hiring the Pinkertons," Derek roared.

"And Rathe and Grace?"

"Rathe's in Havana at the villa or at Maravilla. Grace is in Washington, but I don't know where the hell she's staying. If I have to, I can find out. But right now, I don't want to worry either one of them—not yet."

She was barely awake, and just for an instant she thought she was at home in her sumptuously canopied four-poster bed. When her elbow made contact with a stone and a lot of dirt, reality came rushing back to jar her. She recalled Joanna's hard, accusing glare, and remembered instantly what she and the stranger had done.

She smiled.

No one had ever told her that being with a man was the height of ecstasy. No one had even hinted it could be so wonderful. His image assailed her forcefully. Dark, powerful, his broad chest wet and slick, his thighs braced hard in the tight jeans. He wasn't really handsome, his face was too rough and masculine, but he was utterly compelling. Delicious feelings were washing over her just thinking about him.

Now she knew why some of her mother's suffragette friends espoused free love. They insisted that women were equal to men—in every way. Her mother believed in equality, too.

But not in free love.

Lucy sobered. She was wrapped in his bedroll, the stranger's, and she had shared it last night with Joanna. Oh, God! She didn't even know his name! And Joanna had seen them!

Lucy closed her eyes. She had done many harebrained, wild things in her life, but never something like this. If her parents ever found out, she was finished. In fact, if anyone ever found out, she would be ruined, forever. She would

never make a good marriage and she'd have to marry someone old and fat or become a spinster. This was a very grim
thought indeed.

She didn't even like him, really. He was the lowest sort,
or at least, his manners were. She could never bring him
home, even if he wore decent clothes. He was too rude and
mean. Too dangerous. Lucy shuddered. What had she done?

And until last night, she hadn't thought that he liked her.
Of course, she had been wrong. Hadn't she?

Unsure, Lucy sat up. Then she dismissed her uncertainty.
Of course he liked her; why shouldn't he? Everyone liked
her—she was very popular. And she was pretty—almost
everyone she knew told her how beautiful she was.

But—how should she act with him now?

How did a woman act with a man she barely knew but
had been so intimate with? Lucy smiled. Now she was being
silly: she knew what to do—she was a woman used to men's
company and their adoration. She would treat him the way
she treated all her other beaux.

"He is not here," Joanna said.

Lucy shifted around to find Joanna gazing at her from a
perch on a boulder. Joanna knew. No one else knew, and
God forbid they should. How much had she really seen?
Last night she hadn't been able to talk at all to Joanna, who
had been very distraught. "Good morning," she tried cheerfully.

"He's not here," Joanna repeated, clearly distressed.

Lucy did not want to talk about him. "He's probably just
gone off to do whatever it is that men do in the morning,"
she said, getting up. She started to fuss with her hair, hastily
braided last night when Shoz had propelled her back to camp
after Joanna had discovered them. She had to find out exactly what Joanna had seen.

"He left way before the sun came up, hours ago. He's
gone." Joanna was dismayed and on the verge of tears.

Lucy's hands stilled. He had made love to her last night;
he couldn't have left her. She smoothed down her hopelessly
soiled and wrinkled skirt. "No, I don't believe it."

"He's left us out here, alone. Because of you."

"Of course he didn't leave because of me!"

"He had his way with you and left!"

"No, he didn't! Joanna," Lucy said slowly, "I tried to tell you last night, it wasn't what you think you saw."

Joanna looked at her.

Lucy smiled. "Really, it wasn't. We didn't do anything. Oh, a few kisses, but no different from Leon Claxton."

"I saw you," Joanna cried. "I saw *everything*!"

Lucy stared back as color rose high on her cheeks. Abruptly she sat back down, stunned. "It really wasn't what you think." Had Joanna seen everything? Certain memories that Lucy had been carefully editing began to surface. Knife-like panic stabbed her. She grew calmer only by recalling that she and Joanna had been best friends since they were eight, living on the same block, and Joanna had never ratted on her despite her many other escapades. It was awful that she had been a witness to Lucy's shameful behavior, but Lucy knew she could trust her to remain silent. Now Lucy could face the other disturbing issue. "He's really left?"

"Yes."

Lucy stood. "He's really left?" Her heart was slamming against her chest. "He didn't leave," she said. "He couldn't!"

"He abandoned us! He is gone, Lucy, *gone*."

Lucy felt like exploding. He had made love to her, used her, and left her? She paced wildly to the fire. "Damn him!" She picked up a burnt piece of wood and hurled it, as far as she could. And then she saw his saddle. "He's coming back! He left his saddle! No cowboy would leave his saddle!" Lucy cried. She turned to her friend. "You are wrong—he didn't leave us, Joanna!"

It was blazing hot.

The sun beat down mercilessly upon the parched plain. Trees that looked stunted dotted the landscape. The grass was a harsh yellow. And nestled amongst a cluster of surprisingly lush green cottonwoods that grew by a small creek, was a weathered, doorless shack.

In the shade of the sagging, overhanging roof, Shoz conducted his business. First, they shook hands. Two swarthy men had brought the goods. The old one was fat and grizzled; the lean young one had a red cast to his skin. Spencer rifles filled the scabbards on their saddles, and six- shooters hung from their hips. The young one had a knife sheathed in his belt, and Fat Jack, Shoz knew, had a blade hidden in his boot—as did Shoz.

"I want to see the goods," Shoz said, stepping out into the blinding sun. His shirt clung to his back, soaked. He had trotted Apache-style most of the ten miles he'd traveled that morning, and he'd arrived way before his "friends." Just to make sure it wasn't a trap.

"Be my guest," Fat Jack said, spitting out a wad of tobacco. The young one said nothing. He couldn't; his tongue had been cut out long ago.

Shoz strolled to the two burros sleeping in the sun. Both were packing mounds of canvas-covered gear. Shoz flipped up a tarp, unlashed a bundle, and gently set it on the ground. There he opened the burlap feed bag and nudged out twelve standard U.S. Army carbines.

He smiled, replaced them in the feed bag, relashed it closed, and then fastened it to the burro. Both burros packed five bags each, and he checked every one to make sure they contained rifles and not anything else—he'd never been cheated yet.

"Satisfied?" queried Fat Jack from beneath the sagging roof.

Shoz strolled over. "Yeah. I'll take the mules, too."

"Sorta figured that," Fat Jack said. "Bein' as there ain't no pack animals around—no mount either. Rattler?"

"Dog hole," Shoz said shortly. It had only happened yesterday, yet whenever he thought about putting his magnificent chestnut to sleep, it killed him. He'd had no choice, for the stallion had broken his foreleg.

Shoz lifted his shirt and tore the tape from his abdomen, without a wince. He unrolled the thick wad of bills. He counted out five thousand dollars in twenties, then added one bill more for the mules. The deal had been negotiated in Laredo weeks ago.

After the men had left, Shoz led the mules away. Their progress was slow, but he didn't care. He was sure Fat Jack and the mute wouldn't try to kill him and steal back the already stolen guns, only because they'd arranged to do business again in a few months time. Also, Fat Jack knew him. Knew he didn't kill so easily.

So his thoughts drifted to the girl.

What a piece of baggage.

Hadn't he sensed it? Known it? Known she'd be hot? Being with her had been an explosion, and he could explode now, just remembering. Then he recalled Joanna, and he laughed.

Poor Joanna had been shocked and rigidly disapproving and maybe jealous. He had been amused. Lucy had been just as shocked as her friend at having been caught in the act. He wouldn't have minded continuing, but Lucy had run after Joanna, trying to explain that they hadn't done anything. Joanna refused to listen.

How long would it take to get to the Bragg ranch? Now that they had the mules, they could make it by tomorrow noon. Too bad. He wouldn't mind having the Princess warm his bed for a while. But it wasn't to be. Still, there was always tonight.

He started to whistle.

Five miles from the hut at Geoffard's Hanging Tree, he stopped and unpacked the mules. The spade was where he'd left it, buried very shallowly ten paces north of the hanging tree. Shoz started to dig.

An hour later, he'd buried all the rifles, and an hour after that, he rode back into the camp.

They were waiting for him. One with a smile of relief. The other one furious.

6

"Where have you been!"

She didn't exactly mean to shout. But she had begun to think that Joanna was right, that he had deserted them, deserted her, as the sun rose and rose with no sign of his return. And with the soaring heat, her temper rose as well. No gentleman would leave them alone all day like this, virtually abandoning them, without even a note as to his intentions. Without even a personal note, for her. But then, he wasn't a gentleman, was he? He wasn't from her circle of friends, he wasn't anything at all like the men she knew back home. He was a tramp, and she shouldn't be forgetting it. The hotter it got and the longer she waited, the more Lucy remembered his rudeness and insolence. "Where have you been!"

"None of your business."

She recoiled.

Joanna sat complacently, watching them. Shoz nudged the ashes of last night's fire with his boot. "No food, no fire? What have you girls been doing all day?"

Lucy froze at the implied criticism. She was already regretting her outburst—this wasn't how you greeted someone you'd been intimate with even if that someone had abandoned you for an entire sweltering day. It wasn't the first time her temper had gotten the better of her, and she resolved, not for the first time, to make amends. Yet she couldn't help thinking that he didn't act as if he really liked her, which could not be possible, not after what they'd done.

"We thought you weren't coming back," Joanna said. "Isn't that right, Lucy?"

It was still unbelievably hot. The sun was just starting to

set, but it would be a couple of hours before it cooled down. Lucy turned slowly to face her friend, knowing it was the heat and their desperate circumstances that made her want to murder her. "Not exactly," she said, giving Joanna a look. She gave Shoz a strained smile. "I had no doubts that you would return."

"Really?" He was smiling, as if he knew she was a liar. He was also carelessly eyeing her with lazy sexual interest. Lucy had long since thrown off her jacket, which was ruined. She had rolled up her sleeves and had removed her shoes and stockings. She knew she didn't look the least bit attractive, and that, combined with his disgraceful lewdness, made her turn away and struggle to maintain her composure and her resolve. He was supposed to like her, care about her. She was supposed to be pleasant and flirtatious. All reasonable behavior seemed to be a scant instant from slipping from her grasp. Irrevocably.

She didn't dare ask him where he had been all day, so she watched him reach for one of the saddlebags, her hopes suddenly soaring. Maybe he was going to cook for all of them tonight! She and Joanna hadn't eaten all day, because neither one of them had the slightest idea of how to prepare the rations he'd left. Lucy had tried her hand at coffee, and it had been a gritty disaster. Not to mention the fact that she'd burned her thumb lighting the fire and gotten three splinters gathering wood.

He removed some hobbles from the saddlebag and inspected the pan with the burned, muddy coffee. "You can stand a knife in this," he said with disgust.

Now was the time to be humble, and Lucy knew it. "I've never made coffee before," she admitted.

"Don't widen those eyes at me," he scowled. "You can damn well learn, princess. I am not *your* servant."

Why was he so testy? "I didn't imply any such thing."

He turned away and walked to the stream. Lucy watched him, confused and agitated. This was not going well, not at all. Why was he being so nasty to her? Was it possible that *he* regretted last night? The thought was horrifying!

One of the burros brayed. Her attention diverted, Lucy saw both mules, drinking from the stream.

"Donkeys," she breathed.

Shoz had reached the animals and was hobbling them. Lucy ran after him. "You left us to get donkeys?"

He leaned his shoulder against one furry flank. He looked at her.

Lucy hesitated. This explained why he had left them. He hadn't abandoned them, and he could have; he'd gone to find them transportation, so he wasn't as bad as he seemed. This was more like what she was used to. She smiled tentatively and laid a hand on his arm.

It was the way she remembered it, all silken steel, and she felt a thrill just touching him.

"Now what do you want?" he said bluntly.

She dropped her hand. "Nothing, I . . . I don't even know your name." She blushed, because under the circumstances, she should be embarrassed that they had not even introduced themselves.

"Shoz."

"Shoz? What kind of name is that?"

"An Apache one."

Lucy blinked, and was about to tell him that there was a drop of Apache blood in her veins, too, but he continued in a hard voice, "I was named after my uncle. Shozkay. A real, live full-blooded Indian. At least, he was alive before U.S. soldiers hung him. Aren't you going to faint, princess?" He sneered. "Gasp or scream?"

Lucy stepped back at the cold anger in his tone. He abruptly turned away. "Wait!" she cried, reaching for his arm.

"Now what?"

She withdrew her hand hastily. "I came to say thank you."

"For what? Last night?"

Her eyes widened at the unspeakable reference. She glanced over her shoulder. "Don't you ever speak of that again!"

"She didn't hear. Besides, she saw us."

Lucy wanted to hit him. He was so obviously enjoying her distress. "She won't say anything!"

He shrugged. "I don't care one way or the other."

She had the terrible feeling that he meant it. "You don't mean that," she whispered.

His gaze narrowed and he cursed. "Don't look at me like that. Like I hurt your feelings. This isn't New York, and I'm not one of your love-struck swains."

A long moment passed. He had just made himself very clear. "Believe me, you did not hurt my feelings. You could not."

"Bravo," he murmured.

Her eyes flashed. "I only wanted to thank you for taking the trouble of finding us the mules."

He laughed. "Honey, I don't do anything for nothing, much less if it's trouble."

"What are you saying?"

He stared at her. "I guess you're used to being waited on hand and foot. But I've never waited on anybody in my life. I hate to disillusion you, but I did not spend the whole goddamn day looking for mules for your little backside."

"Why are you so insufferable? Why are you trying to push me away? Why didn't you just accept my thanks!" She was hurt, very hurt, and furious with him, and with herself for even bothering to be pleasant.

"I'm not trying to push you away," he said, and he grabbed her hips before she could blink and pulled her up against him. "Meet me tonight."

Lucy struggled, hurt and enraged, and when he released her, she stepped back, panting. Her chest rose and fell, hard, and to her immense frustration, he openly ogled her. "You are the worst scum imaginable! I've tried to be nice, tried to be charitable, but it's impossible! I thought we felt something for each other, but I was wrong—so very wrong!"

His face, usually expressionless, was dark with strained anger. "Oh, we felt something for each other, all right, and it's called lust with a capital L. You can try and put another fancy name on it, but it won't change the fact—or the act."

"Damn you!"

"No—damn you—and your goddamn charity. I don't want it!"

Lucy was shaking. He stalked away. She swallowed

hard and turned away, only to come face-to-face with Joanna.

Lucy could not sleep. She lay beside Joanna, determined not to cry. Never had she been so abused, and she was thoroughly shaken from all that had passed. She wanted nothing more than to weep in her mother's embrace.

She knew he was stretched out with his head on his saddle, just across the dying fire.

She despised him. Last night had been a mistake, and it would never happen again. Ever. No man could treat her the way he had and get away with it.

Still, she thought she could hear his every breath, his every movement. It was annoying. Her body was coiled tight.

Later, when Joanna was breathing deeply, she heard him get up and stroll away. Lucy wished she could sleep instead of thinking about him, and the humiliation. Instead of listening to him. She didn't care what he did, what he was doing. She swallowed. Her mouth was dry. Arrogant bastard. At least he couldn't sleep, either.

Five minutes might have passed, or fifty. Lucy had no idea. But she heard him returning, and every inch of her went stiff. He came to her as she had known he would.

Which was why she had her reticule within easy reach.

"I know you're not sleeping," Shoz said softly, dropping down to his knees by her shoulder. His fingers brushed her throat.

"Go away," she hissed. His fingers raised a tingle along her spine. The coil inside her tightened. So did her fingers, around her purse.

His hand slid down to her chest and over one of her breasts. "Waiting up for me?"

"No!" She knocked his hand away.

"I'm going to prove you a liar," he said silkily, slipping one arm under her.

Lucy pressed away from him. "Joanna will wake up!"

"She'll enjoy the show," he said, nuzzling her ear.

"You are wicked! Depraved!"

Shoz laughed. "Sainthood is boring. Besides, there's room in hell for both of us." He licked her ear.

Despite her anger, delicious spirals of sensation filled Lucy. "Stop! You'll have to rape me, and I mean it!"

"Okay."

Lucy froze when he gathered her closer in his arms as if to lift her. He nibbled her throat. Unable to look at what she did, she flicked open her purse and groped for the derringer. His arms tightened around her and he stood up, lifting her to her feet. She pressed the little pistol into his diaphragm.

His arms went still around her, he became motionless.

Lucy felt a surge of triumph—mitigated with fear at her daring. "Let me go."

Shoz laughed. The sound was soft, menacing. He dropped his hands and took a step back. "Nice toy."

Her temper soared. "It's not a toy—and I happen to be an expert marksman. But at this distance, no one could miss."

"Markswoman," he said softly.

"What?"

He grabbed her wrist so quickly she hadn't even seen him reaching for her, forcing her hand down and the gun away from his person. Lucy cried out, dropping the pistol. "Did you really intend to shoot me?" He was amused.

She was furious with his apparent amusement, and with her failure to shoot him. Riled and dismayed, she watched as he retrieved the gun and emptied it of bullets. Shoz picked up her purse and inspected it for more ammunition. Satisfied, he tossed it aside. She didn't have any more bullets or any more places to hide them, and he knew it. He was smiling when he handed the pistol back to her.

She felt like smacking that smile right from his face. She contemplated the idea with relish, but got no further than that when he abruptly lifted her into his arms—and began to carry her away.

"Put me down!" she gasped.

"Not until we finish what we started," he said flatly.

Lucy had no intention of finishing anything with him. She struggled wildly and futilely as he walked away from the camp. And when she spoke, she meant every word. "When I get back to the D&M, I'm going to tell my grandfather you raped me, you son-of-a-bitch!" she cried. "He's one of the most powerful men in Texas and he knows everybody—the governor, senators, even the president of the United States! They'll hunt you down and lock you up and throw away the key!"

He froze. "Let me guess. Your granddaddy is Bragg himself."

"That's right!" she shouted. "You will be finished, finished!"

Shoz cursed and abruptly put her down. Lucy almost collapsed, then backed away, panting. "You little bitch," he said. "You'd do it, too, and not because I slept with you, but because I won't fawn all over you."

She didn't answer.

He smiled harshly. "Don't worry," he said. "I'm not going to touch you. You aren't worth it."

7

Never had Lucy seen such a welcome sight. "Paradise!"

"And not a minute too soon," Shoz muttered.

They were all astride the mules, Shoz in the lead, Lucy and Joanna riding double. The terrain had changed, the parched plains giving way to rocky hills, more green than brown, the trees larger and lusher now. They were passing the first of Paradise's outlying whitewashed homes, most of which were surrounded by white picket fences with roses creeping up to gaily painted mailboxes. Ahead, the road turned in to the town's wide, dusty main street, appropriately called Bragg Avenue.

Lucy, who had learned to ride in Central Park at the age of four, sat in front of Joanna, who clung to her from behind. She sought out a soiled handkerchief with one hand, made a sound of dismay at the sight of its wretched state, then used one tip to blot her face. What she wouldn't give for just a few of her creams and powders! She tried to arrange her hair single-handedly, realizing this was a far cry from her fantasy of a grand entrance in a shiny new roadster, dressed impeccably in silk and velvet. It was one of the few times in her life that Lucy prayed no one would notice her.

They were on Bragg Avenue now, passing low-fronted stores with cheerfully painted hanging signs: Joe's Eatery, Full Breakfasts One Dollar; Hirsch Laundry While-You-Wait; the Barber Shop, Free Shave with Bath and Cut: Rooms for Rent, $2.50 Per Night, Breakfast Included. The Livery, owned by the giant blond Swede Olaf, was just up ahead. "We will get off at the livery," Lucy said evenly. Her gaze wasn't particularly friendly.

He smiled. "You can keep the mule. And we'll let bygones be bygones."

Lucy looked at him contemptuously. "I don't want your mule. We'll rent a carriage." She pulled on the reins, dismissing him from her mind and her life. Joanna slid down, then Lucy dismounted.

He sat watching for a moment. Lucy shook out her skirts briskly, touched her hair, smoothed her jacket, and flashed Joanna a smile. "Almost home," she said.

At that point, voices could be heard from inside the barn. Two men came strolling out, a big blonde and a lean, wiry cowboy. Lucy's face brightened. "Olaf! Billy!"

Both men stopped to stare, quizzically. Lucy sailed forward, radiant. "Hullo! How are you? It's so good to see you!" She had known Olaf since she was a child, and Billy had always been infatuated with her.

Olaf's mouth dropped. "Miss Lucy? Is that you?"

Lucy halted.

Billy gaped. "Lucy?!"

"Of course it's me," she cried, brushing at her skirts. "You don't recognize me?"

"Of course I do," Billy said very quickly, rushing to take her arm. "What *happened* to you?"

"Are you all right, Miss Lucy?"

"Yes, yes," she cried dramatically, leaning against Billy.

"Oh, it was so awful! Our automobile broke and we had to walk, leaving our bags, and we were stranded in the wilderness with no food!" Shoz snorted. "I don't know how we made it here, truly I don't!"

Both men turned to look at Shoz and the mules.

He saluted her. "It was nice knowing you, too." He turned away, spurring his burro into a trot.

"Who is that?" Billy asked.

"We met him this afternoon," Lucy lied. She had spent a good hour developing her tale when she knew they were close to town. "Fortunately, he had an extra mule, so we asked him for a ride, and of course, he chivalrously agreed." She gave Joanna a warning look.

"You must be exhausted," Billy said, his arm protectively around her. "But how is it that you two are alone?" For the first time he noticed Joanna.

"Mrs. Seymour became ill the day we left," Lucy said.

"Come on, I got a wagon out back, I'll take you straight to the D&M."

"Leave the wagon," Lucy said. "We'll take Olaf's nicest buggy, and you can pick up the wagon another time."

Billy did not argue. An hour later they were driving up the curving road to her grandparents' house. It sat on a hill slightly above all the whitewashed barns and paddocks and bunkhouses, with commanding views. Thoroughbred weanlings raced them as they trotted up the drive. Wildflowers grew along the road, big shady oaks guarded the house, and potted purple and yellow petunias were on the front porch. The house was a two-story, sprawling affair, freshly whitewashed like every other structure on the ranch, the shutters green, with numerous brick chimneys and a veranda that ran around three sides. Under the biggest oak in the yard was a white swing for lovers. Her grandfather had built it for Miranda, when she was pregnant with their second child, Lucy's aunt, Storm.

Lucy let Billy help her out of the carriage, barely able to restrain herself from leaping out. But then she could hold back no longer. She raced up the porch steps and threw open the solid front door. "Grandma! Grandpa! I'm here!"

Her grandmother appeared, her eyes wide. Her dark hair,

frosted with silver, was coiled in a braid around her head.
Once again Lucy marveled at Miranda's elegant appearance,
despite the apron she wore and the flour covering her hands.
Her delicate features still seemed handsome to Lucy, hinting
at the beauty she must have been. "Lucy! Oh, Lord, Lucy!"

They embraced. Lucy was much taller than her diminutive
grandmother, and even though she needed to be held by her
after the trauma of the past two days, it was as if she did
the holding. Miranda drew back. "Child, where have you
been? Derek and I have been frantic!"

"It's a long story, Grandma," Lucy said, somewhat tear-
fully.

"Did I hear Lucy?" her grandfather shouted, striding
into the foyer. As always, he made a grand entrance, filling
up the room with his presence more than his size. "Lucy!"
he shouted, wrapping her in a bear hug.

Lucy couldn't help it; in her grandfather's protective embrace, she started to cry.

"What happened?" he demanded, holding her at arm's
length so he could stare into her eyes. His eyesight was as
keen as a hawk's.

"Don't be mad," she moaned. "It was just an idea, that's
all, to buy a car and drive to Paradise! But the roadster
broke down and we were stranded and had to walk until
this man came and had an extra mule. Oh, Grandpa, it was
awful!"

"I want to know why Mrs. Seymour is still in New York
and why the hell you weren't on the spur yesterday
morning!" Derek yelled. He was mad from the terrible fear
her disappearance had caused.

Lucy wept now, her nerves finally shattered. Her grandfather was not as easy to get around as her father. This last
realization made her cry harder, in actual self-pity. She
would have to face him and his shrewd questions, sooner
or later, and if he ever learned the truth . . .

Miranda glared at Derek and pulled Lucy into her arms.
"There, there, dear, you need a hot bath and hot food.
Joanna, come in, come in. Forgive us our manners."

Joanna, who had been hovering in the open doorway,
moved inside. "Hello, Mrs. Bragg. Hello, Mr. Bragg."

"Call me Derek," Derek shouted. "Billy!" He bellowed. "You come with me, I want a word with you."

"Yes, sir." Billy nearly saluted, following the leonine man into his study, where Derek shut the massive double doors with a bang.

Miranda took the girls upstairs, settling them in adjoining rooms. "I'll have Billy bring up your things," she said, briskly turning down the white lace sheets of the four-poster bed. The room boasted pink and white pinstriped wallpaper, thickly upholstered furniture in embossed wine damask, delicately wrought tables and chairs from England, a brick fireplace, pine floors, and a thick multicolored Oriental rug that was predominately red. The bed was all white lace and ruffles. Miranda plumped the pillows, walked into the spacious pine-floored bathroom, and began to run the tub.

Lucy thought about her bags and all of her best clothes, most of them purchased exclusively for this vacation, undoubtedly stolen by now. "We don't have any bags," she said, wiping her eyes. "We had to leave them in the auto." She didn't want to think about their adventure, or about *him*, but unfortunately, she did.

"Then you'll just have to buy a new wardrobe," Miranda said cheerfully.

Lucy almost brightened. She usually adored shopping. Her smile was wan, however. "I'm sorry about all the tears, and about the awful mess we got into."

"I know," Miranda said, patting her shoulder. "First a bath, then some food and rest, and then we can talk about it."

Lucy quickly calculated that she had a few hours to get her story straight and tight. She smiled at her grandmother, then turned—and glimpsed herself in the mirror. "Oh my God!"

"Lucy!" Miranda reproved. She was a fairly observant Catholic. "Into that bath!" She hustled out.

Lucy stared at her reflection—and wanted to die.

Never had she looked like this in her entire life. And her only thought was—why had he even wanted to touch her?

She looked like a dirt-poor washerwoman, her clothes gray with dust and spotted with stains. Her hair was even

dirtier, a tangled rat's nest despite the sagging and ludicrous
coil atop her head. Worst of all—her beautiful face was
shiny with sweat and smudged with dirt. She was no beauty.
She was ugly!

"Oh God," she said again, sinking into a plush club
chair.

It didn't seem fair. It didn't seem fair that after all she
had been through, she had to bear this final humiliation.
That tramp had seen her looking like this, and she supposed
she should be grateful that he hadn't been his normal nasty
self and commented upon it. Thank God she would never
have to see him again.

8

Shoz took the best suite at the Paradise Hotel. He ordered
a five-course dinner and a bottle of French brandy, soaked
in a steaming tub, considered a whore, and got drunk instead. He slept until midmorning the next day.

Because of the brandy, he slept deeply, unlike the previous two nights, when he'd tossed about restlessly, due to
his unrequited lust for Princess Bragg. He wasn't exactly
used to being so aroused over one female. Yes, this one
did have an ungodly body, and he guessed she was attractive
when cleaned up, but he'd had many beautiful women,
mostly beautiful women, the most beautiful in the world—
and it didn't make much difference to him. He'd always
preferred making love in the dark.

Besides, he didn't like her type, not at all. And he knew
her type intimately, too intimately. They were eager to jump
into bed with him, but should they pass each other on the
street, these *ladies* would pretend not to even know him.
They were sexually fascinated by him, more so, he sus-

pected, because he was taboo to their society, being three-quarters Apache, than because he was appealing and vigorous in bed. Almost all were married and didn't give a damn about their wedding vows. Oh, he'd had enough of her type long ago—seven years ago, to be exact.

He wanted to stop the terrible train of his thoughts, because they were sure to disturb him, but he couldn't. He could still see Marianne Claxton lying on her dressing table where he'd pushed her down, in the black corset, legs spread, panting for it even while she was afraid he'd murder her after taking her. They'd been lovers for an entire year, beginning midsemester of his final year at law school, and she not only had sent him up, she'd set him up, and after he'd escaped prison in upstate New York, she thought him capable of murder.

Shoz's anger simmered, as always when he thought of Marianne and the damn phony trial and prison. But a part of him, deep inside, wept a little, too. Not because he'd just hung his sign on the tiny cubbyhole of an office he'd rented, *S. Savage, Attorney-At-Law*, but because his dreams had started dying way before that, when he'd left the ranch where he'd been raised in southern California.

Being morose first thing in the morning was not good for his digestion, or his mood, and he cursed the Bragg girl for stirring up memories that were usually dormant. Breakfast consisted of coffee and one swig of last night's brandy to chase away the throbbing above his temples.

Business demanded his attention. It was a bright, hot day, no surprise. He strolled leisurely down the boardwalk, taking in the sights of the freshly painted little town. The awning over the druggist was bright red. The general store boasted gold lettering half his size stenciled on huge windows, a red and white striped candy-cane light stood sentinel outside the barber shop. There was something about this town that disturbed him; it was too clean and too fresh, the kind of place where people moved to raise a family. It was too idyllic. He could almost stay awhile. But this kind of place wasn't for him—and it never would be.

At the post office he sent a telegram to his buyer in Houston. He told the clerk he'd be awaiting the reply at the hotel, then went and had a haircut and shave. He returned to the hotel expecting a response to his telegram; there was nothing. His buyer was not at the designated hotel in Houston.

This was very bad news.

Shoz sent another telegram, this one to Havana, Cuba.

He would not receive a reply until that night or the next morning. He refused to worry. The deal was firm, but obviously something had arisen and the sale would have to be postponed. He hoped, fervently, that his buyer hadn't wound up in one of Cuba's dark Spanish dungeons. This was a distinct possibility, and then the deal would be delayed indefinitely or even canceled until someone else could be found to take his place. Hopefully his buyer was not in prison and he would arrive in Houston soon, so the sale could take place as scheduled, in a few days.

It wasn't that he minded sitting on the stolen guns. He did not feel like killing time in Paradise. His instincts warned him to evade its strange allure. This was not his kind of place. Nor did he relish riding back to Death Valley and then returning again.

At the hotel he sat down to a late lunch in the refined dining room amidst white linen, crystal goblets, and ribbed columns supporting high ceilings. The restaurant was considered the finest in town. He'd just dug into his plate of roast beef when they walked in. *When she walked in.*

He put his fork down without taking a bite.

They hadn't seen him. Despite the hour, the restaurant was crowded with business lunches and groups of women while he sat unobtrusively in a corner with a view of everyone. He stared, his senses spinning.

He had misjudged the princess. She *was* a princess, a spectacularly beautiful princess, and he could not take his eyes off her.

He didn't notice what she wore, nor did he care, some bronze-striped dress with a matching parsol. What he saw was her face, her perfect oval face with its sheer ivory complexion, dominated by her too full mouth and her too blue eyes. She was a heart-stopper, all right, and he wanted her.

She had sat down with an old, elegant woman and Joanna, laughing and chatting nonstop, enthralling her audience, regaling them. He smiled. Maybe it would be amusing to spend a few extra days in Paradise. After all, they'd never finished their business, had they?

He recalled what she'd said. That he'd have to rape her if he wanted her, and that she'd set her Bragg family and the law on him. He didn't doubt that she would, not for a minute, not if she was angry with him. And she was angry, because he wouldn't play the role she'd assigned him and every other male she laid her eyes on. She was spoiled and self-absorbed and used to getting her own way one hundred percent of the time.

The last thing he needed was the law—or her powerful family—breathing down his neck.

But he liked a challenge; some even said he liked danger. He knew he could seduce her, make her want it, take her willingly. He could play the role she wanted him to play—temporarily. There would be a risk, of course, the risk that when he left her, she'd cry rape anyway and he'd be hunted down. The question was if the risk was worth it. If she was worth it.

He didn't have to think about it for very long. All his senses were alive, keenly tuned like those of a hunter. He watched her. She was his prey now. He enjoyed the feeling, and it was very sexual. After a moment she stopped talking, looked around with confusion, and saw him. She froze.

Shoz smiled and lifted his wineglass. She gritted and put her nose high in the air before turning her head aside. He sipped.

He left before they did, deliberately walking past their table. His gaze remained on her as he stalked her, and he savored every second. Her shoulders were stiff. He knew she knew he was approaching. He could sense her fear— and her anticipation. He paused when he was abreast of her and she could see him. "Hello," he said, very politely.

Lucy gave him a bare, rude glance. "Hello."

Joanna smiled shyly. "Hello."

The elegant old woman stared. "And who are you, sir?"

He smiled at her. She didn't soften, but he persisted. "I escorted these two young ladies to town."

Miranda's stare hardened.

Lucy reached out to touch her hand. "He's the one with the mules, Grandma. The one I told you and Grandpa about."

"Yes, I see. Thank you, Mr. . . . ?"

"Shoz Cooper," he said, using the alias he had assumed seven years ago when he had escaped prison.

"Thank you, Mr. Cooper."

He eyed Lucy. He wondered what she had told her grandparents. Nowhere near the truth, he suspected. Otherwise this proper little woman would not be sitting here saying thank you—not if she knew the two girls had been unchaperoned with him for two nights.

Lucy twisted to face him. "I see you haven't left town?" she said, all sugared vinegar.

"I'm enjoying the weather," he said. He saluted them and strolled on.

At the front desk he asked for any messages. A reply to the telegram he'd sent to Havana hadn't come yet. "It's urgent," he told the clerk, giving him a dollar. "Please have me notified the moment it arrives."

"It's urgent that you leave," Lucy hissed from behind him when the clerk had disappeared into the office.

Shoz leaned an elbow against the counter, amused. She was red. "Hello, princess," he drawled, low and suggestive.

"Don't call me that!"

"Whyever not?" His gaze roamed over her. "You are a princess—no, a goddess."

She was oblivious to his flattery. "I want you out of here!"

"Oh, you do?"

"Why are you here?"

"I don't think that's your business."

"When are you leaving?"

"That's none of your business either."

"You bastard!" She gave a worried glance over her

shoulder toward the dining room. "Are you going to make trouble for me?"

"Only if you ask for it." He smiled at his double entendre.

"I'm warning you!" She raised a white-gloved fist at him.

He grabbed it. She went rigid. His hold was firm, unyielding, but not at all painful. He pressed her small hand against his chest and he stared at her.

She stared back, and for one moment, his heart pulsed against her palm.

"Let's make peace, Lucy," he said, low.

She yanked her hand from his with an inarticulate cry, gave him a look of utter disbelief, and fled.

"Lucy, are you all right, dear?" Miranda asked.

They were sitting in the smaller of the house's two living rooms, the cozy one with the walls papered in a multicolored tree-of-life design, the furniture plush and deeply upholstered in gold and forest green, the carpets thick underfoot. They were waiting for Derek before going in to dine.

Lucy had been very quiet ever since leaving Paradise that afternoon. She attempted a smile and a nod. "Yes, Grandma, just worn out, I guess."

"I hope you're not sick."

Lucy didn't answer, she was too immersed in her thoughts. Why was that no-good drifter still in town? What was he up to? The sooner he left, the better for her in all respects! She wanted to forget what had happened, desperately, and if he remained, there was always the chance of someone finding out the truth!

She must, at all costs, prevent this.

There were two truths, and two lies. She had told a convincing falsehood to her grandparents—that Shoz had come upon them only during the day that they had arrived in Paradise. She had not let them suspect that they had actually spent two whole days and two whole nights in his company. Only Joanna knew the truth.

She knew both truths. That not only had they spent two

nights with Shoz, Lucy had allowed herself to be somewhat compromised by him.

Shoz knew both truths, too.

Lucy trusted her friend absolutely. She trusted him not at all.

Derek had spent a lot of time shouting at her for her foolishness, and then he had sent some men to rescue her car and any surviving luggage. Lucy felt she had gotten off easily, and was very grateful. If either truth were known, however, she wouldn't get off so easily, she would be tarnished or completely ruined. In either case, Lucy was certain Shoz would wind up with one of Derek's bullets somewhere in his anatomy.

Not that she cared, really, if he was shot, although it did seem a bit extreme.

She resolved to take matters into her own hands.

The following morning, Lucy cajoled Billy into driving her into town for a so-called shopping trip—without Miranda. It wasn't really unusual for Lucy to go to Paradise without her grandmother, and this morning they departed without her knowledge. She wished she could also go without Joanna, but she needed her. Better Joanna be privy to what she was doing than Billy, who would try to accompany her everywhere if she were without her friend.

They left Billy at the saloon after convincing him he would be bored watching them shop. Lucy's pace was brisk as she headed for the hotel with Joanna in tow. "What is going on, Lucy?" Joanna demanded. "You're going to meet *him*, aren't you!"

Lucy was stunned, but only slowed fractionally. "Joanna, it's not what you are thinking!"

"You are using me so you can meet with him," Joanna said steadily.

"It is not a lover's tryst."

"I don't believe you."

"Trust me," Lucy said, placing her hand on her friend's arm. "Please, Joanna, I need your trust."

Joanna finally nodded. Both girls entered the large lobby of the Paradise Hotel. "Where would he be at this hour?" Lucy asked nervously.

"It's only nine o'clock," Joanna said. "He's probably still in his room." She gave her a sidelong glance.

"I can't go up there!"

Joanna said nothing, while Lucy fretted. She grabbed her friend's arm excitedly. "You distract the clerk. Ask him to . . . ask him for a map. Ask him where Pete's Peak is, if it's nice for a picnic, and how to get there. I'll run upstairs—just for a minute."

"How do you know which room he's in?"

Lucy smiled. "He was asking for his mail yesterday—and the clerk looked in box 525. That's the suite Grandpa puts his best guests in on the top floor. Go now, Joanna!"

Lucy watched Joanna approach the clerk and edged toward the newly installed elevator. Soon they were in a conversation—but the man was facing her. Lucy eyed the ceiling. Was Joanna stupid? She had to get him to turn away—and then he did, going into the back office. Lucy banged the button, the doors opened, she threw a look at the desk where Joanna stood alone, staring at her, and she leapt into the elevator. The doors closed just as the clerk returned—and she didn't think he'd seen her.

Her heart was jumping madly in her breast.

The Governor's Suite. It had been called that ever since the governor had first stayed there over thirty years ago. Lucy was surprised Shoz would even have the money to afford such accommodations. Then she thought, uncharitably, that maybe he didn't—maybe he'd skip town without paying his bill. She knocked.

He opened the door immediately.

He wore only his snug, faded jeans, the belt and snap open. His chest was bare and damp. His gaze widened.

Before he could speak or even invite her in, Lucy rushed past him. "Close the door!" she cried. "Before someone sees us!"

He closed the door, grinning.

9

Shoz leaned against the door with his thumbs stuck in the loops of his Levis. His teeth were very white in his wide grin.

Lucy was trembling. She stood only a few feet from him, and the suite, which was large, seemed close and confined. Suddenly the two of them seemed very alone. It was eerily intimate and highly disturbing.

For a moment she forgot her resolve, forgot why she had come, and wanted to flee.

Why didn't he put on his shirt?

It was very difficult to concentrate on the task before her when confronted with his damp, shiny bare chest and hard belly. Her gaze dropped to the white threads of his denim fly and what was so suggestively and barely constrained there. His jeans were indecent. He was indecent.

Shoz's smile faded and his gaze became strained. He levered himself off the door with a slight curse. "I didn't think it would be so easy," he said. "Come here, princess." His voice was husky, without any antagonism or hostility.

Lucy was mesmerized by the sound, and by the proximity of his near-naked presence, yet somehow she realized what was happening. He had misunderstood everything! His hands were surprisingly gentle as they curved possessively around her shoulders, then they tightened. "I like how you look at me," he murmured.

She had been staring at his mouth. She looked into his eyes and saw them smoldering. Her own chest was tight, her own heart racing, and there was that throbbing need she recognized—and did not want. *This man did not like her.*

He had said so, he had made it very clear. This man had used her. This man might betray her.

He was a bastard.

"No!" She wrenched violently away.

For a moment, surprise showed in his eyes, then the corners of his mouth tilted up. He stalked her. "Playing hard to get?" His tone was teasing, but she only heard the words.

"Hard to get?" She laughed shakily, scooting around the back of the sofa as he lazily followed her. "I've got news for you, Mr. Cooper—I am one woman you are never going to get!"

"Is that so?" He had backed her up against the bed and he was laughing; Lucy didn't find it funny, not at all. "Then what are you doing here? Couldn't stay away, could you?"

His arrogance infuriated her, and she dug into her reticule and found the note and slammed it against his bare chest. "I'll show you what I'm doing here!"

He caught her fist and held it. "What's this?"

"Money."

For a second he was still, then he smiled again, this time without any mirth. He tightened his hold and she gasped and dropped the note. "Money matters later," he said. "We have old business to conclude first." He yanked her up against him.

Her bare hand was pressed between their bodies, and the skin of his chest was like a smooth silk-and-steel wall to her touch. He had her anchored by the small of her spine. One of his hard legs had become jammed between both of hers, so that she rode him, and the hardness of a rapid erection ground against her hip. Lucy tried to press away, but her movement only fit her more snugly against him, only made her ride his thigh higher.

Her palms, pushing frantically against his chest, tightened into fists. She pummeled him furiously, turning her face away to avoid his kiss. His laughter was soft on her ear, yet it sounded cold and angry, and then she felt his tongue there.

Hot spirals of pleasure swept through her; she went very

still. "Good girl," he crooned. His hand slipped to cup one buttock, his tongue delved lazily.

Lucy closed her eyes, just for a moment allowing herself to feel the thrill of what he was doing. His mouth moved to her neck with practised expertise.

"And you," she heard him saying as he rubbed her buttock languidly, "didn't have to pay for it. Usually I give it for free."

Her eyes opened.

His breath was hot on her neck. "But in your case, I'll make an exception."

His hand insinuated itself up between her legs.

His controlled voice, his methodical passion, the way he was touching her with cold calculation, began to dim the fires he'd raised, enough so that she could think. So that she could think that something wasn't right, something was more than wrong. He palmed her, his fingers fluttering over her. Despite the jolt of sheer pleasure, Lucy wrenched free of him and spun away, putting the sofa between them. She stared at him in confusion, breathlessly.

He was panting. A slight sheen of sweat covered his torso, and the sunlight pouring through the open drapes made his skin glisten. He wasn't excited, not at all; he was furious.

The desire he'd kindled died quickly. Lucy clutched the back of the sofa.

"You little brat," he snarled. "At least the other rich bitches don't play power games, at least they have a few shreds of decency left."

"What are you talking about!"

"But if you want to pay for it, baby, go right ahead. I'll even make it worth your while, how's that?"

She gasped.

"You want to play games? You want me to chase you? You want to be raped?" He was so mad, he would happily take her by force. Never, ever, had he been so insulted in his life. And he had not a doubt that she'd done it on purpose—to put him in his place.

"Touch me again," she managed, "and I will scream down this hotel. You are disgusting! You are crazy! In fact, right now there's nothing I would like more than to see you thrown in jail!''

This silenced Shoz. Dark, horrible images of another prison and another time flashed through his mind.

Lucy was clinging to the couch. She released her hold. "I did not come here to be pawed," she said stiffly.

"No? Then what the hell did you come for? And what the hell is this for?" He bent and picked up the check. His hand shook.

"That is my personal check," Lucy said shakily, gulping air. How could he have thought she was offering to pay him for . . . for . . . his body!

He waited, staring.

"My banker's draft," she added. He was starting to frighten her.

He looked at it. "A thousand dollars." His gaze was ice. "I guess I should be flattered." He barely got the words out.

"I didn't come here for . . . for . . . your body! I didn't come here to pay you to . . . to . . .''

"To fuck?"

"You do that on purpose!" she cried in frustration, the horrible word shocking her anew even though she fought for calm. She took a long breath. "The check is to insure your silence."

He looked at her. "My silence."

"That's right." She tried to smile; it was horribly difficult.

"From gigolo to con artist." He crumbled the bank note.

"What are you doing!" she cried, panicked.

"Princess, you're not so smart. Why, a crook like me has no honor. You think I won't cash this in and then speak up?"

She paled. "You wouldn't! Even you couldn't be so low, like a . . . like a . . .''

"Like a snake?"

"Worse!"

"Like a breed?"

She had no answer.

He regarded her. Lucy tried to gaze steadily back. She

forced a smile. "I know you can use the money. So that's settled. Now you can leave town."

He smiled derisively.

Lucy edged toward the door. "You have the money. So I suppose you'll be on your way?"

He didn't answer. Her back touched the door and her hand closed over the knob. "Well?"

"Your money always buy you everything?"

She blanched. "I'm not buying anything, I'm just—"

"Forget it," he said, with one bitter laugh.

Gladly, she did. Between him and the question, she was thoroughly unnerved. "Can you leave tonight? Tomorrow?"

After a long pause, he said, "I *can* leave."

Relief swept her. Warm, wonderful relief. "Good!" she cried, smiling brilliantly. "Good! Then—" she laughed nervously "—good-bye!"

His gaze was pale gray and enigmatic. She turned the knob, flung open the door, and fled. In the corridor she had to remind herself to walk, not run. She had done it. She had chased that bastard out of town.

10

He paced the room, from the double French doors overlooking the wrought-iron balcony to the canopied bed with thick velvetine drapes. Still clenched in his fist was the crumpled bank draft.

"Brat!"

He couldn't really remember when he had ever been so angry. He was having lovely visions of wringing Lucy Bragg's lovely neck.

Did she think she could pay him off? Run him out of

town with a few lousy dollars? He smiled. She had another thing coming.

However, he did have business to attend to and he was going to leave town as soon as he could transact it, and not because she'd commanded him to. He'd have to think up a proper farewell for her.

He unfolded the draft. He'd been so mad when she'd first handed it to him, mad and disappointed, thinking she was trying to get what she wanted and show him he was inferior by paying him like a prostitute. He'd jumped the gun—why did she make him particularly edgy? Why did he seem to dislike her even more than all the others? His thoughts bothered him, and he tried to dismiss them.

Still, this payoff was no less insulting than the other one. What did she think he was, some kind of total bastard who enjoyed violating virgins and then ruining their reputations? Did he really come off as such a heel? He had to admit that once or twice he had felt a bit bad, a bit guilty, for being so nasty to her. She seemed to bring out the worst in him, and he didn't know why.

She was going to contribute to a revolution, he decided wryly. Then he changed his mind. It was too noble for him, much less for her. She'd contribute to something far better, a gift for Carmen, something French and black and wicked. The idea gave him immense satisfaction.

But of course, he would not do it. He could not keep the money, much less spend it on Carmen; as soon as it was convenient, he would return the check.

He threw on a new shirt he'd bought yesterday, a soft blue cotton. Soon after, he was trotting down the stairs. The clerk called out to him before he'd taken a foot off the final step.

"Mr. Cooper," he said. "We have just gotten your telegram."

Shoz came forward eagerly. His expression went bleak, however, as he skimmed the reply he had been awaiting. His buyer *had* been delayed in Cuba—and a new buyer would not be able to meet him for several weeks.

Shoz crumpled the telegram. He could not leave the guns, even buried as they were, for a few weeks. Government agents had been attempting to break their operation for the past six months, and Shoz was well aware of it. So far, he had eluded them, but he could not count on his trail being entirely cold. He had had a very close call with the last shipment he'd sent to the Cuban rebels from Corpus Christi. Federal agents had staked out the docks and tried to prevent the ship with its cargo from leaving. Fortunately, they hadn't arrived earlier—to prevent the steamer from being loaded. A gun battle had ensued. Shoz had lost one man, with three casualties. They'd inflicted as much damage as they'd received, however, which wasn't particularly good. Shoz's criminal record was becoming too damn long. It was one thing to be wrongly imprisoned for a theft he hadn't committed and to escape successfully; it was a helluvanother to have a gunfight with the federal government. Things could not have gotten worse.

Until, maybe, now.

He had to stay close to the guns so he could check on them periodically. He couldn't afford to have them stolen from him, or uncovered by the Feds. Which meant he wasn't going very far.

Sometimes, like now, he got the uneasy feeling he was digging himself deeper and deeper into a grave—one with his tombstone at the head.

But he was tough and he was smart and he was real close to the border. Fate just hadn't smiled kindly upon him. But he could play the hand being dealt—and win.

Which meant he could hang around Paradise—and if he dared to face it, he wasn't exactly in a rush to leave.

Very willingly, he recalled how eager a student Lucy Bragg had been when he'd folded her hand around his stiff erection. He grew inflamed. He wouldn't mind sticking around. In fact, because she had ordered him to leave, tried to pay him to leave, he would enjoy staying.

However, he needed a cover. He couldn't just loiter in the hotel for a month. That required some serious thinking.

Despite the setback in his business affairs, his mood was suddenly, surprisingly, good, better than it had been in days. He strode out of the hotel into the sweltering heat. He was filled with the anticipation of both the hunter and the hunted, the skin prickling on the back of his neck. At the same time he had a warning instinct—that if he did stay, there was going to be trouble.

He wrote it off to the threat of government agents and his staying in one place for so long. His instincts had nothing to do with the titian-haired Bragg girl. After all, how could she be dangerous for him? He would have to remain alert and wary of any newcomers arriving in town.

Shoz pushed open the screen door of Joe's Eatery. The café was mostly empty as it was already midmorning. Two flannel-shirted loggers sat at one table, two teamsters at the counter. They looked like they'd been on an all-night bender. Joe, short and thin, and his nephew, Little Joe, were waiting on the customers.

As he took a seat at the counter, he was regarded by everyone, and not because he was a stranger in town. Shoz was used to it. There was no mistaking he was mostly Indian, and he'd encountered these kinds of half-curious, half-wary looks his entire life. He was used to it—but not complacent about it.

He ignored everyone, ordering steak and eggs and coffee. Yet his senses were alert. And, unfortunately, one of the drunk teamsters tried to pick a bone with him. Sometimes it happened, sometimes it didn't. Shoz had learned when he was six to be ready for a fight, always.

"Thought all the Injuns in these parts were locked up on that reservation in Tularosa," the big redhead said loudly. "Hey, Jake, ain't that so?"

"Yip," Jake said. He was even bigger than the redhead. "Maybe he's escaped."

Shoz set his whiskey down and stared at them. He knew he could kill them both, if he wanted to. But right now, killing wasn't in his plans. He didn't want the attention. "You accusing me of something?" he said, very softly.

A group of cowboys had entered, spurs clinking. Shoz's gaze swept them reflexively, lingered on the old white-haired man just for a moment, then returned to his adversaries. The red-haired one was saying, "Maybe we are. Maybe we should take you to Fort Bliss and see if there's a reward posted."

Shit, Shoz thought. Just his luck. He should be smart, he should make a humble response, soothe the redhead's ego; in other words, eat dirt and diffuse the situation. Instead, he smiled meanly. "Why don't you try?"

"That an invitation?" Red asked.

"No," Shoz said, "this is." He tossed his coffee all over the man's broad chest.

A shocked silence filled the café.

Shoz was already moving. They were going to fight with him, that was inevitable. He preferred to be on the offensive. Before the redhead could recover from his astonishment, Shoz hit him with a powerful driving right in the abdomen. The teamster gasped—but only flinched.

It wouldn't be quite as easy as Shoz had thought.

He hit him in the face. The redhead took a step back, then caught Shoz's arm as he was about to deliver another blow. He was very strong, and the two men were suddenly grappling, and then they went sprawling on the floor.

Shoz felt a stunning blow to his eye and knew he'd have a helluva shiner—if he didn't lose his eye. He jammed his knee into the man's groin. The redhead collapsed. Shoz rolled on top of him. Without mercy, he threw his fist at his head. A booted kick from behind lifted him clear off the floor, and he went face-first out the screen door.

He was already on all fours and then upright, just in time to meet Jake, diving on top of him. They went flying backward into the dust of Bragg Avenue. A crowd began gathering from all the adjoining stores. Someone calmly requested the sheriff, and someone else said, "Sure thing, Derek."

With a little luck and a lot of agility, Shoz wound up on top and began pummeling Jake. The teamster went limp. With a roar, Red grabbed him from behind, locking him in a bear hug and trying to break his ribs. Shoz used his arms to break free, whirling and striking out blindly at the same time. He could barely see, there was too much blood. He connected with the man's jaw, but it only rocked him back. An instant later, Shoz received a blow in the midsection that knocked the breath right out of him and propelled him halfway across the street.

Jake followed him. An undercut caught his chin, rattling every tooth he had. He blinked at stars. The teamster grabbed his shirt, dragging him upright, fist poised. Shoz blocked the blow and kicked Jake as hard as he could in the kneecap.

Quicker than the eye, Shoz had withdrawn his knife from his boot. Red backed up, panting, Shoz stalked him, grimly. And then Jake delivered a stunning blow to the back of his head, and his world went black.

First he felt the pain.

There was the ungodly throbbing of his eye and jaw, and the back of his head seemed to be shattered. He heard voices. Lots of them, but they sounded far away and were unreal. The pain absorbed him. His head swam. He felt like throwing up.

The voices became louder and began to sound as if they belonged to a part of this earth. He became aware of the hard ground beneath him, and the hot sun beating down upon his face and body. He felt sticky wetness on his face, and when he licked his lips, he tasted blood.

"He started it, Derek," someone was saying. "The breed started it, I seen the whole thing!"

"Yeah, the Injun attacked old Red here! He's crazy, maybe he's rabid!"

"Calm down," an authoritative voice said. "Billy, Joshua, put him in the wagon."

Shoz fought to regain consciousness as he felt himself being lifted carefully. He tried to protest. He felt panic. He was helpless, and he knew what kind of justice awaited him—the color was white. He desperately tried to get a grip on his world. He struggled to open his one good eye.

"You gonna throw him in jail, boss?"

The question echoed. Shoz froze, but his gut twisted and his pulse began hammering. *He would not go back to prison*! He pushed at someone as he was laid down in a wagon.

"No one's going to jail for a little fistfight," the man said. "Not when Red Ames and Jake Holt are the two worst rabble-rousers around here. I've warned them twice not to start up in Paradise, and I won't warn them again.'' His voice was hard, without a stitch of compromise in it. ''Besides, I heard the whole thing.''

''Billy!'' he called sharply. ''You and Joshua get these two fixed up. Then you escort them out of town. Kindly inform them their contract with the D&M is terminated. Got that? They are no longer welcome in Paradise!''

''Yes, boss!'' came a chorus.

Shoz did not relax. What about him? He knew better, he had learned his lesson long ago in New York. He finally opened his one good eye and found himself sprawled on his back among sacks of supplies, gazing up at the cloudless sky. The sun made him blink.

He pushed himself up on his elbows. It was no easy task.

The old white-haired man came to stand in front of him. ''You okay, boy?''

Shoz smiled, a mean smile. ''I'm just fine—boy.''

The man froze, then held back a grin. But the many crow's-feet along his amber eyes deepened. ''I'm kicking seventy-nine, *boy*,'' he said. ''And in a few more days, it'll be eighty.''

Shoz sat up, wiping blood from his face. ''And I'm thirty-five,'' he said. ''No one calls me boy.''

This time the man laughed. ''I do,'' he said. ''And you're in no shape to fight me.''

Shoz suddenly felt stupid. He'd been ready to fight with this old man, a man of eighty. He forced himself to relax. ''No one calls me boy,'' he repeated firmly.

Derek shrugged. ''You want a doctor? My *boys* will drive you over. Your eye needs a stitch or two.''

''I don't need a ride,'' Shoz said, levering himself off the wagon. He almost fell, but managed to stay upright by holding on, hard. He steadied himself.

''Pride's only for the young,'' Derek said, watching him. ''And for the foolish.'' His smile was very engaging. ''Pretty foolish to attack *both* Jake and Red. The two together must weigh in at over four hundred pounds—and they aren't fat.''

''They wanted to fight,'' Shoz said, more interested in remaining on his feet than in the conversation. He didn't know why he even bothered to answer the old man.

"That's a good reason?" He laughed again and turned away. "My offer stands. You can get a lift over to the doc's—you need it."

"I don't need a ride," Shoz gritted, releasing the wagon.

He was okay, he told himself. He took a few breaths, until the dizziness and nausea cleared. He knew they were watching him, not just the old man, but half the town. He couldn't have announced his presence in town more loudly if he'd tried. He found that he'd twisted his knee in the ruckus, as he limped toward the sign hanging a block away, bright hand-painted green letters reading, "Dr. Jones/Remedies for Everyone/Surgeon on the Premises."

Thankfully, he made it without fainting, and more thankfully, Jones was in. Shoz sat on the wooden operating table while the doctor, a chubby, friendly little man, cleaned him up, chattering nonstop.

"Could hear the hullabaloo all the way over here. Said to myself and to the wife, God rest her soul, they're at it again. Must be that wild Red Ames, saw him come to town earlier. When Red and Jake's in town together, I spend all my time fixin' people up. Now, Sarah, God bless her, she used to help. Still, I always get the feeling that she's up there, beaming down on us."

The front door opened and closed, bells jangling. Shoz winced as the doctor dabbed alcohol on his eye. "How is he?"

Shoz couldn't turn his head, but he recognized the voice of the old man who'd called him "boy" and wouldn't back down.

"Strong as a mule," Jones said cheerfully. "Reminds me of you fifty years ago. How about some laudanum before I do some fancy needlework?"

Shoz jerked when he realized Jones had abruptly changed the direction of his comments and was addressing him. "No," he said. "Just do it."

"It's your skin," Jones said cheerfully.

Shoz gritted as the doctor gave him three neat, small stitches just above his right eye while the old man watched. "There," Jones said. "You can breathe."

"Didn't stop," Shoz said. It was a blatant lie. He was sweating like a pig.

"See you, Doc," the old man said as he left.

"See you, Derek," Jones called to the swinging front door. "Give my best to Miranda."

"Who was that?" Shoz demanded sharply.

"Derek Bragg, who else?"

"Who else," Shoz muttered. And then he straightened, as a thought pierced him like lightning. He had the solution to his dilemma.

He needed a cover to stay in town. Derek Bragg had surprised him, proving himself to be a fair man without apparent prejudice. After all, he had sent the two teamsters packing, when Shoz had expected to be thrown in jail, if not strung up with a rope around his neck. He could not loiter in Paradise doing nothing except guarding his guns for the next month.

But he could remain in Paradise if he was working for Derek Bragg.

11

Dr. Jones had instructed Shoz to remain in bed for a few days. Despite his aching head, eye, and jaw, Shoz had smiled. "Get me the right woman, Doc—and I'll stay in bed a week."

"I want you to rest," Jones said, unamused. "You took a serious blow to your skull, young man, with the butt of Jake's pistol."

Shoz decided one day in bed couldn't hurt, even without a woman. The next day he felt fine, with only a slight headache that came and went. His left eye was closed completely, however, mostly black and a bit blue. It was a helluva shiner. His jaw was sore and swollen, also mottled purple, but at least he hadn't lost any teeth.

He traded in his two mules for a small bay gelding that didn't look like much but would have a lot of grit and stamina if the Arabian ancestry he saw in the horse's head and lines proved true. He reached the D&M around noon.

Asking for Derek Bragg, he was directed to the main house, which was set slightly above the other buildings on a shady hill. He noticed everything. Every building was whitewashed and maintained to look fresh, clean, and new. The stock Bragg kept was excellent, especially the racing blood for sale back East. Shoz's one weakness was horses. The house itself was inviting and homey despite its size, with flowers everywhere and curtains peeking from all the windows. His gut constricted. Although the D&M was much larger and more modern, it reminded him of his father's ranch in southern California—it reminded him of home.

And it had been a long time since he'd been there.

Too long, but that was his own fault, because he had put off returning again and again. Not because he didn't miss his family, but because he didn't want his parents to know the truth about his life, about him, and be so very disappointed.

Better to let Jack and Candice think he was someone else, someone better.

He dismounted, resting against his bay for a moment, and he wondered where she was. The thought was irritating, mostly because he couldn't pretend indifference even to himself, and also because right now his head hurt, his stomach was upset, he felt weak and not at all like a man. He didn't want her to see him like this.

He walked up the porch steps and used the brass knocker. Derek Bragg himself answered, his surprise brief. "I have the feeling you're looking for me," he said, his mouth almost curved into a smile.

"I am," Shoz said. "Shoz Cooper. I'm looking for work."

Derek's brow lifted, then he gestured at Shoz to go inside. "We'll talk in my study."

Shoz followed him into a grand foyer with high ceilings

and a curving oak staircase. The floors were pine, waxed to a high shine. The walls were fresh and white. He caught a glimpse of himself in a big, ornate silver mirror and hastily removed his battered Stetson.

"Sit down," Derek said, once he'd closed the double doors behind them.

Shoz sat, hiding his relief.

"Drink?"

There was a mug of coffee steaming on the large mahogany desk. "You have something stronger than coffee around here?"

Derek poured them both whiskeys. "Doc tell you to take a ride in the heat today?"

"I'm fine," Shoz said. "You look like you can always use more men around here."

"You know cattle? Horses?"

"Yeah."

"You don't look up to work to me."

Shoz hesitated. "I need the job," he said stiffly. It was a lie. But even the lie was hard to say because of his pride, and if it were the truth, he'd never, ever say so.

Derek studied him. "Where are you from?"

Shoz was startled. "Southern California."

"I've been out to the West Coast. My daughter Storm and her kids and their kids live in the San Francisco area. Your family from around there?"

Shoz shifted. "No, Bakersfield."

Derek leaned back in his chair. "Rancher?"

"I was raised on a ranch," Shoz said. "If that's what you're getting at."

"Your family still there?"

"Yeah."

Derek smiled. "You don't give much, do you, son? Tell me about them."

Shoz stood, angry. "What is this? Do I have the job or not?"

"I want to know what kind of man I'm hiring." Derek was unruffled.

"My father's name is Jack. He built the Gold Lady with his own two hands, starting right after the Civil War. I have a half-sister, Christina, about my age, and three half-brothers. She married some Russian prince or something and lives in Saint Petersburg. My brothers, last I heard, are still at the ranch." The words came out hard and fast like rapid gunfire.

"Your mother?"

That did it. "My mother is an Apache squaw and I don't know where the hell she is, maybe behind some pretty stockade fence, maybe dead. You about through?"

To Shoz's amazement, Derek chuckled. "Guess we have something in common, son. My ma was an Apache squaw, too, Mescalero."

Shoz blinked, but quickly recovered. "I was raised by my stepmother, Candice. *She* is my real mother," he said, stiffly, not understanding why the hell he was volunteering more information to the nosy bastard.

"Okay." Derek smiled, rising. "I can always use a good hand around here." He grabbed Shoz's hand and shook it. "Wages are at the end of the month, fifteen dollars to start, all you can eat. Find yourself a bunk in one of the bunkhouses. Ask for Jim. He's ramrod around here."

Shoz nodded. He had his cover. But he didn't feel relief, more like he'd been worked over with brass knuckles. His head throbbed.

"Glad to have you at the D&M." Derek smiled.

Shoz found the foreman in the broodmares' barn after some searching, finally being directed by one of the stable boys. Jim instructed him to set his gear in the cabin with the red door, which was only half-full. He was given a generous lunch by Wally, one of the two cooks, and then set to fixing a loose section of fence in one of the paddocks.

He didn't protest. He'd come too late to ride out with the other hands; it was already midafternoon. He began inspecting the section of fence, then took out the three split rails. It was hot. Sweat poured down his body, even interfering with his vision, poor as it now was. He removed the standing post, which was loose, and set about digging a new hole.

After ten minutes he was acutely dizzy and his head hurt like the devil. Maybe Jones had been right. He paused to strip off his soaking shirt and dunk his head in the trough of water between two blooded mares. It was clean and cool. He paused to croon to the pretty little chestnut and scratch her ears. Then he started digging again.

He heard her laughing, first. He hadn't heard her laugh before, but he knew it was her, and every nerve in his body stiffened. He froze, spade jammed hard into the ground. Her laughter stopped abruptly.

He straightened and turned.

Lucy, almost a virginal vision in lacy white cotton, faltered beside her grandfather.

Their gazes locked. He clung to the spade. Shit, he thought. She would have to appear now, just in time to witness his weakness.

He would not, he vowed, reveal any.

So he stood even straighter.

It was a shock.

Seeing him standing there was a terrible shock.

Lucy had returned from Paradise yesterday confident of her victory, confident that she had chased him from town. Her victory hadn't come cheaply, but her secret was more important than money. She knew she should be ecstatic.

But she wasn't. Her mood was restless. That night she could not sleep. Reading did not help. She kept seeing him as she'd last seen him in the Governor's Suite, his face handsome even when enraged, his body with its sheen of sweat as carefully and perfectly sculpted as a Michelangelo statue. She began to eat imported chocolates from Switzerland, but they failed to satisfy her, too, and she gave them to the tiger-striped cat. The next morning, exhausted, she went to help Miranda in the kitchen.

At home in her parents' New York mansion, there was a head chef and many assistants who would be shocked if she ever entered their domain. Here her grandmother liked to cook, even though she had plenty of help. Lucy hadn't set foot in the kitchen at Paradise since she was thirteen or so. When she was a child, they had baked cookies and cakes together. Her mother did not cook, being too busy with politics and social work, but she had joined them, too, and it had been a merry trio. Those days had passed, of course, but Lucy found herself wishing today could be spent in just the same way.

She ignored her grandmother's surprise and offered to help. Fetching items from the icebox and mixing bowls of ingredients gave her something to do. Anything to keep busy.

The Duryea was being fixed in town and would be ready later that day. Lucy was looking forward to having her automobile back; she and Joanna could drive about the ranch, or even into Paradise. After finishing in the kitchen, still feeling restless and vaguely dissatisfied, she dressed in something cool and white and wandered downstairs. Derek invited her to join him in inspecting the broodmares down at the foaling barn. Lucy agreed.

Halfway there she froze, thinking her eyes were playing tricks on her. It couldn't be. It was. It was him.

He nodded politely.

And then she saw his face. Lucy gasped. What had happened to him? He looked like a prizefighter! He looked terribly hurt!

Lucy realized that she was staring, but so was he. She looked away quickly, aware of her grandfather asking him if he was okay. The image of his terribly discolored eye and jaw remained. But there were other images, too, competing ones—his leanly sculpted chest, slick with sweat, his thighs braced in the snug, faded jeans as he leaned on the spade. Those thoughts were not welcome, and stubbornly she shoved them away. What was he doing here?

"You sure you're okay, Shoz?" Derek was asking.

"Fine."

"Why don't you take a break."

"I'm almost finished," Shoz said, lifting the spade. He lost his balance slightly but recovered it.

"Take a break," Derek said. "Go lie down in the bunkhouse. You wind up with a fever and you're no good to anyone."

Shoz smiled sarcastically. "Yes—sir." One cool gray eye met Lucy's. She abruptly turned to her grandfather. Yet even as she asked, her mind was racing ahead. He shouldn't be here, he shouldn't be anywhere near Paradise. He had said he was leaving. "What happened to him?"

Shoz was slowly taking his shirt off the fence and putting it on. As he walked away, Lucy's gaze followed him. "Grandpa?"

"He was in a fight yesterday with two ironheaded louts. One of them took the butt of his six-shooter to the back of Shoz's head."

"Is he all right?"

"I don't think so," Derek said. "He looks mighty pale around the gills to me. I'll send Miranda down to check on him. Come on, honey."

Lucy followed her grandfather into the cool, stone-floored barn. She shouldn't be worried about him; his health was not her business. What should concern her was why he was still in the county—and why he was here at the ranch. She wanted to know just what Shoz was doing working at the D&M, but she didn't dare ask. And if he was up and working, he couldn't be seriously hurt, and the look in his good eye had been unmistakable.

"Isn't she a beauty, Lucy?" Derek asked, eyeing a gray Anglo-Arab mare. "She's in foal to Thunder." There was pride in his voice. Thunder was his oldest and most prized—and proven—stud.

"Yes," Lucy said automatically. "Grandpa, who is that?"

"Who?"

"That—cowboy."

"Just a new hand."

"When did you hire him?"

"Just today."

"Why did you hire him?"

"He said he needed a job. I like him. You know the D&M is the main source of employment in the county. What's your interest, Lucy?"

She flushed. "None, of course! It's just that—" she shuddered dramatically "—he looks so mean! He looks like a thief! Or worse!" It was hard to believe that for once, someone had pulled the wool over her grandfather's eyes.

Derek laughed. "He's no thief. I'm a good judge of

character, and I can tell you that. He's just a hothead is all, and a proud one. Don't you worry."

Lucy frowned. The situation was insufferable. She had paid him to leave town, but instead he was working at her grandparents' home. He must be fired, and immediately. "I don't know, Grandpa. Maybe this once you're wrong. Maybe you shouldn't have hired him."

He was amused. "Leave the running of the D&M to me, sweetheart. Being as no one else in the family has shown any inclination to do so! Nick is running that earldom he inherited from Miranda in England, Rathe's built up Bragg Enterprises from New York to Hong Kong, Brett's got hotels across the country and shipping across the world. You want to run the D&M, Lucy?"

Lucy squeezed her grandfather's hand. She heard the disappointment in his voice, even though he was trying to make light of it. Everyone in the Bragg family knew he'd built the D&M for Miranda, and had one day intended to pass it on to their children. But none of them wanted it; they were all too involved in their own affairs. Likewise, Nick's eldest son would inherit his estate, his second son was studying the law, and his other children were girls, while Brett's two boys were already grown men running his shipping and hotel interests. Her own brothers were too young yet to really judge, except for Brian, the oldest, who seemed to be heading for medical school.

"Well," she said, slyly, "I'm a city girl myself, Grandpa, but I do have five brothers, and even though Daddy has more than enough of Bragg Enterprises to go around, I'm sure he wouldn't mind one of the boys taking over here."

"And I'll be a hundred," Derek said gruffly.

"Probably only ninety, Grandpa."

Lucy lifted the hem of her skirts and ran.

Derek was preoccupied in the south paddock, and this was her chance. She was going to find out why he was here. She had a terrible suspicion. No one must see her, of course, but all the hands were still out on the range. She darted onto the porch of the whitewashed bunkhouse with the bright red door and paused, panting. She heard footsteps and froze.

The door opened, and she came face-to-face with Wally.

"Miss Lucy!"

"Wally!"

"Howdy, gal. What are you doing down here?"

Lucy thought fast. "Grandpa asked me to come and check on the new hand, to see if he needs anything. He's hurt."

"Yeah, guess so. He's inside." Wally gestured and waddled off.

Lucy took a breath. Then, trembling, she stepped inside.

With five bunk beds pushed up against the walls of the house, ten cowboys could bunk here comfortably. A round table with five chairs was in the center of the room, an iron stove with two more chairs in a corner. Another corner housed a sink and mirror, and a bathroom with showers was to the left. All the hands ate together in a communal dining room in another building. The D&M had about fifty men and boys employed on the premises. This did not include the help up at the house, or those employed in the iron mines, the freight lines, the oil well, or in the many Bragg-owned businesses in town.

Any concern she might have had for her enemy's injuries vanished the moment she saw him.

He was grinning. Like a lion licking his chops. Shoz sat at the table, his booted feet kicked up on the top, a cigar in his mouth, coffee in his hand. He'd obviously heard her outside. He set the mug down.

Lucy saw that they were alone. He didn't look ill. She glared at him and slammed the door shut, advancing toward him. "What are you doing here!"

His feet hit the floor with a thud. "Hello, princess. Real sympathetic woman, aren't you?"

"Go to hell!"

"I don't doubt I will. No tender inquiries about my poor battered face?"

"None! How dare you! How dare you!" Lucy cried.

"I dare pretty much what I please, Miss Bragg."

His snide tone wasn't lost on her. "How dare you get a job here! I told you to leave town!"

He caught her hand and his smile reappeared. Slowly, oh so slowly, he pulled her toward him, and then she was in his lap.

"Let me up!"

His arms went around her, holding her flush against him, her legs dangling over the side of the chair. She wore pretty little orange booties with a dozen pearl buttons. "Nobody tells me what to do," he said, as if she weren't struggling wildly.

"You took the money!"

He stared at her mouth.

She stopped wriggling. Her heart pounded against her breast. "You want more."

"Yes," he said softly. "More, a lot more." His hand slipped into the nape of her hair, which was pinned up. Abruptly the huge mass came spilling down. Lucy didn't move. Beneath her buttocks, she felt him—all of him.

"But not money," he said.

His tone was low and sexy. His gaze was utterly compelling, mesmerizing. It took a great effort for Lucy to tear herself free of the spell he'd cast, but she did, lunging to her feet.

She stumbled away from him. "You have such audacity."

He smiled, enjoying his power. "You'd like it if you let yourself, honey."

It was a battle, and she had almost given him a victory. "And what if I tell my grandfather that you grabbed me?"

"And what if I say you came here, looking for me—and that we're *old* friends?" he replied coolly.

There was no mistaking what he meant. It had been her horrible suspicion all along. "That's why you're here, isn't it? To blackmail me. Isn't it?"

He squinted at her, his bruised face not revealing anything.

"There's no other reason for you to be here," Lucy accused. "You're a monster. A despicable, low-down monster."

"You didn't seem to think so the other night. Not the way you were carrying on."

He would, of course, bring up that one damn indiscretion; he had not one shred of decency. She glanced wildly around, but no one was outside listening; they were still alone.

"You seduced me!" she cried. "I was upset, stranded, without a protector—and you seduced me!"

"And you liked every moment."

"I want you off of this ranch."

"I'll bet you do."

"How much more do you want?"

He kicked back the chair furiously. Lucy jumped backward. She rushed for the door when she realized he was coming after her. The look on his face told her she was in dire jeopardy.

"I don't want your goddamn money!"

She rushed outside.

"Run!" he flung after her. "Run as far as you can, Miss Bragg! But it won't be far enough, and you damn well know it!"

12

Shoz had moved to his bunk. He'd taken the upper one even though the bottom one was free, because he didn't want his ability to move to be restricted. Now he sat on his bed, back against the wall, one knee up, listening to the sounds of the ranch hands outside approaching the bunkhouse.

The door opened and the men started filing in. Six of them, mostly young cowboys between the ages of eighteen and twenty-two. They all regarded him openly, with more than unabashed curiosity, as if looking at a rare reptile in a zoo. Shoz steadily stared back. No one said hello. He hadn't expected them to. Instead, they all exchanged "what's this?" glances.

If he were white, they'd have said hello and offered him smokes and whiskey and invited him to join in the game of cards that was now about to start at the center table.

He had another headache. It wasn't a good feeling, not being in the best of shape, knowing he could not handle a situation the way he normally would. Not that there would be trouble here. He knew a man like Bragg made rules that were not broken. The men might not accept him or like him, but they wouldn't start anything.

It was unnaturally quiet in the bunkhouse. The hands, all six of them, began a game of five-card stud, pulling up an extra chair from in front of the stove. The lone chair left there seemed annoyingly symbolic. Shoz lay back on his bunk, hands beneath his head. He wondered how a man like Derek Bragg could be related to a spoiled brat like the princess.

"Hello," Miranda said, smiling, stepping within. A tray was in her hands with a big bowl of steaming soup, a cloth napkin, silverware, and a covered breadbasket. Shoz could smell the chicken from across the cabin. A Mexican woman followed her with a plate of cookies—he could smell them, too, still fresh from the oven.

A chorus of greetings came from the cowboys. Miranda looked from them, seated around the table, to Shoz, who was now sitting up on the bunk. She turned to the young woman behind her. "Maria, put the cookies down for the men, and thank you."

Maria did so and left.

Miranda approached Shoz, inspecting him from his head to his toes, not critically, just thoroughly. Shoz stiffened in astonishment when he realized what was happening. She had come to bring him soup!

"Hello," she said. "Derek didn't tell me that the new hand was the man who gave the girls a ride."

Shoz just looked at her.

"I brought you some homemade soup; it cures just about everything." She smiled warmly and set the tray down on the lower bunk. "Would you mind coming down here, young man? I want to look at your eye, and more especially your head.''

Shoz blushed. It had been years since he'd done so. He slipped off the upper bunk, still dwarfing the tiny woman. ''I'm fine, ma'am,'' he said awkwardly.

She was already gently probing the back of his head. He winced. ''Oh my, what a lump. You will not work for a few days,'' she said. There was no question that that was an order, one Shoz knew was not refutable.

But he tried. ''Ma'am, really, I'm fine, aside from having a small headache. I can pull my weight around here.'' He flashed her his rare, disarming smile.

''If you are too proud to stay abed, you can help me up at the house with some *very* lightweight chores. Don't argue with me, young man,'' she said as Shoz began to protest. ''Even my husband knows better than to argue with me,'' she added softly. ''Turn your head.''

He did. Her touch was as soft as the petals of hothouse flowers. Shoz didn't move while she touched his face, inspected his eye, and clucked with regret. It had been so long. She was treating him exactly the way his own mother would, and for some unfathomable reason, it brought a lump to his throat.

She picked up the tray and pushed it into his hands. ''Now. Eat the soup, all of it, get into bed and rest. Tomorrow report to me at the house at nine, no earlier. I will tell Jim you'll be working for me for a few days.'' She patted his arm and turned away.

She said a few words to each of the cowboys before she left. Shoz gazed after her.

''Someone's got it made, don't they?''

''Yeah, a little tap to the eyeball an' you get to laze around the big house all day! Want to give me a shiner, Lew?''

''Laze around the house all day! What I wouldn't give to be up there next to Miss Lucy!''

At least two groans greeted this remark.

Shoz was expressionless. He set down his tray, walked over to the table, and reached between two of the men for a cookie. He popped it into his mouth and chewed it with relish. Then he took another one. "You want a shiner," he said, "I can give it to you. No problem." He smiled, his good eye as cold as steel.

Thereafter they ignored him. Which was just as well. He ignored them, too.

"Lucy, why didn't you tell me Shoz was the one who brought you and Joanna to Paradise?"

Lucy swallowed. How had he found out! She had been summoned by her grandfather, and now she darted a glance at Miranda. "It didn't seem important," she said lamely. Had Shoz revealed this information? She was sure he had, just as she was sure that he was playing with her like a cat with a mouse. Why else would he be here if he didn't want money?

"What are you hiding?" Derek asked. "Today you acted like you'd never seen the man before."

"I didn't say I didn't know him, Grandpa." Lucy flashed a smile. "I just didn't tell you because it didn't seem important. But really, you should know, he's one of those vagrant tramps, not at all the sort you should employ here on the ranch."

"You should not judge people like that, Lucy," Miranda said firmly. "Especially not a man who was nice enough to give you a ride when you desperately needed it."

Lucy's mouth was set in a firm line, but she said nothing. How was he worming his way into their esteem? It was unfair—it was incredible!

"If he was unemployed, it wasn't his fault," Derek said. "This depression has been ruining hundreds of thousands of good, honest workers. And honey—" he patted her arm "—now he's got a job, so you can't go calling him a tramp."

Lucy managed a weak smile.

"What do you think of Shoz, Derek?" Miranda asked.

"I think he's stubborn as a mule with mettle made from steel. I think he's got a chip on his shoulder bigger than all of Texas. He sure as hell has too much pride for his own good. And I'm sure he's one hard worker."

Lucy turned away, toying with some porcelain and bric-a-brac on a side table.

"They don't accept him, you know," Miranda said. "They were all playing cards and he was sitting by himself, looking so proud and so alone."

Derek frowned. "I can only make the rules, sweetheart, I can't change men's minds."

"I hate prejudice," Miranda said fiercely. "And hypocrisy. They condemn him—while every one of them knows you are half-Apache yourself."

"It's because I look white," Derek said easily. "Besides—" he grinned "—I pay their salaries."

Lucy decided she just couldn't listen to any more. "Would you mind? I'm going upstairs to read."

Shoz trudged up to the house the next morning just before nine. He'd been up for hours, but hadn't dared go sooner, for fear of disturbing Mrs. Bragg. He had his hands jammed in his pockets, feeling foolish. The sun beat down on his back, blazingly hot already, and humid. It was going to be a bitch of a day.

He knocked on the front door and was greeted by Miranda herself.

"Prompt," she remarked, her eyes twinkling. "Good morning, Shoz. How did you sleep?" She was already moving briskly down the hall, and he followed, remembering to take his hat off just in time.

He said, to her tiny back, "Fine, thank you, ma'am."

She pushed through the door to the kitchen, where lunch was already being prepared for the family. Maria was drying the breakfast dishes, another girl was cutting up a chicken. "Coffee?" Miranda asked.

"I already ate, ma'am."

She shoved a bowl of pea pods into his hands. "Then you can shell these," she said, moving to a dicing board, where she rapidly began slicing carrots.

He blinked. Shell peas? She wanted him to shell peas? He felt foolish enough, and now he felt all of ten or twelve. She glanced at him. "You do know how, don't you?"

"Yes, ma'am," he said, hanging his hat on a peg on the wall. He began shelling peas.

Everyone worked in silence, Maria humming a pleasant tune. It was quiet and comfortable and comforting in the kitchen. Miranda reminded him of his mother, although they were nothing alike. Candice was much younger, for one, and tall and voluptuous and blond. But it went beyond the physical differences; Candice was softer, gentler. It didn't matter; he got the same warm feelings from Miranda that he got from his own mother. It was very disconcerting, yet very soothing, too.

Miranda finished dicing and left the kitchen. Shoz kept shelling the peas, somewhat clumsily. When he heard a gasp, he looked up to meet Lucy's surprised gaze. All he could think of was how idiotic he felt to be caught shelling peas.

Lucy glanced at Maria and Anna, then stepped closer, furious. Her voice was barely a whisper. "What are you doing in *here*?"

He gestured to the bowl. "What does it look like?"

Lucy looked over her shoulder toward the open doorway where her grandmother had disappeared. Both Maria and Anna were now regarding them with avid curiosity. "Come outside with me," she ordered in a low voice.

Of course, the two maids could hear every word. "*Anything* you *want*, Miss Bragg."

She hurried to the back door, then held it open, making sure he preceded her. In the backyard she grabbed his arm and dragged him behind some bushes.

"Can't wait to get me alone?" Shoz grinned. "Can't wait to continue where we left off yesterday?"

Her hands flew to her hips. "You know I can't wait for you to ride out of Paradise—and out of my life!"

"Am I in your life?"

"*Oh!* You know I didn't mean it that way!"

"You did," he stated, his eyes smoky. "You sure as hell did."

"Think what you want—you will anyway," Lucy cried. "First you stay in town, then you come to the ranch, now you're in the *house*! What are you doing? What do you want?''

Shoz smiled. ''Better control that red temper, princess, or someone will hear you, and you're going to have a lot of explaining to do.''

She clenched her fists. She knew he enjoyed annoying her, that he did it on purpose, and she should refrain from taking the bait. ''What do you want?''

''You know what I want.''

She looked at him. His low, sexy tone did just what he wanted it to do, it sent a tingle along her spine and raised some vivid, hot memories. She took a breath. ''Did you tell Grandpa that it was you who brought me and Joanna to town?''

''Now, why would I do that?''

''Someone did!''

''Take my advice, princess, and calm the hell down. The only one who's going to reveal your deep, dark secrets is you, yourself.''

She looked at him.

He jammed his hand in his back pocket and came out with a folded note. ''Here.'' He shoved it in her hand. ''Something you seemed to have forgotten in the Governor's Suite a couple of days ago.''

Lucy glanced wildly around, afraid someone had heard. She looked at the paper; it was her banker's draft. And when she looked up, he was gone, striding back into the house. The screen door banged shut behind him.

13

Leon Claxton stood on the outside platform between two railroad cars as the locomotive slowly chugged into Paradise, blowing its horn.

He was arriving as scheduled one week before Derek Bragg's surprise party. Had he not wanted to spend most of his two-week holiday with Lucy, the rest given over to the journey, he would have traveled with his parents next week in the luxury of the private Claxton car. But he did want to be with Lucy, and his parents would not arrive until the day before the party, like most of the other out-of-town guests.

Leon was smiling with anticipation. He was tall and lean, with broad shoulders, and he cut a dashing figure in his dark, expensive suit. He was blond and blue-eyed, and most women found him very handsome. His face was oval, his features perfect and patrician—he had inherited his mother's superb looks. Lucy had once told him that he was the "epitome of elegance." He had liked that. He had liked that a lot.

Lucy. His heart quickened. He could see the train station ahead as they approached. It had been too long since he had last seen her. He had been very annoyed and had not bothered to hide his feelings when she decided to go to Paradise ahead of her family with the chaperone. It was hard to believe, even now, that she would prefer this cow town to his company.

However, the love and loyalty she felt for her family was commendable, and it was one of the reasons she would make a perfect wife for him. The others were her beauty and sensuality, not to mention his own lust, but Leon was clear-headed enough not to make too much of that. There were other beautiful, enticing women in the world, equal to Lucy in every way. Except one. None of them were Braggs.

Right now Leon might be stuck in the grimy job of Roosevelt's assistant police commissioner in New York, but it would not continue for long. The job had been his own choice. He had decided to leave the foreign service and his post in Madrid, begging a leave of absence. His father had arranged the appointment to Roosevelt. Roger Claxton was one of the most powerful senators in the United States, and one of the most politically shrewd. His father was friends with the young Roosevelt, but not out of the goodness of his heart. He knew a winner when he saw one.

Leon respected and admired his boss, even if he thought that Roosevelt was too idealistic at times. Fortunately, his idealism was mitigated by his shrewd practicality. Like his boss, Leon had jumped on the McKinley bandwagon, as had most of corporate America, including his father and the Braggs. Teddy was campaigning and working actively for McKinley's election over the populist Democratic nominee, Jennings, and he had recruited Leon. Leon knew Teddy expected a "plum" after McKinley's election, and so did he—although being younger, he did not expect as high a position. But it was another important stepping stone. His future was coming along nicely, but that wasn't enough. He was going to add the power of the Bragg family to his arsenal, and he was going to go places quickly, indeed.

Leon was only twenty-six, but he was very impatient.

Which was why he clutched an three-carat diamond ring in his pocket. No woman, and certainly not Lucy, who loved beautiful and expensive things, could resist the flawless ring he carried with him. Not that he thought she could resist him. He had everything and he knew it—looks, charm, charisma, power, breeding, wealth. He hadn't proposed to anyone since his wife's death in Madrid. She should be quite flattered. He intended to court her all week, and after the party, before he left, he would propose.

He saw her. He waved. She waved back gaily.

* * *

Lucy was exhausted. She had had another sleepless night. Her insomnia was getting worse, not better. She waved at Leon with a bright smile. She felt a bit guilty because she had not thought about him once since she had arrived in Texas.

That was strange, now that she realized it. Leon had been her favorite beau by far for the past few months. They had had a lot of fun together, attending balls and soirees, horse races and sailboat competitions, and everyone had said how well suited they were. Lucy had sort of assumed that one day he would propose and one day she would accept. After all, next year she was graduating, and it wouldn't do for her to become a spinster, and she certainly would not find a more suitable fiancé than Leon. Lucy had always accepted her parents' unspoken rule that the man she married must have certain qualifications—social status and wealth. Of course, she would fall in love with the man she eventually chose to marry. For a while, she had been merrily in love with Leon. Or close to it. She had found his career exciting. Although he now worked in New York City, he assured her he would be returning to the Foreign Service soon. Lucy had easily imagined herself the wife of an ambassador and living in Paris or London or even Rome, three of her favorite cities. That had soothed her when she had faced the fact that one day she would marry, and marry someone like Leon—if not Leon himself. She wasn't particularly ready to wed and raise children and become a Society hostess, so she preferred not to dwell on those responsibilities that awaited her after graduation.

Yet she hadn't even thought of Leon once in the past weeks. Well, she supposed that would soon change. He was here in Paradise now.

She stifled a yawn. She must not allow Leon to see her like this and think she was bored. Yet she was desperate for a good night's sleep. Thoughts of *him* kept her awake at night.

He'd worked up at the house for three days, during which time Lucy did her utmost to avoid him. Yet it seemed she always knew exactly where he was and what he was doing. She only had to glance out the parlor window to see him returning from the smokehouse with a side of beef, his strong legs stretching taut the fabric of his jeans. Or she'd be in the library, searching for a book, and she'd hear him whistling tunelessly in the living room, as he put back up the heavy drapes Miranda had taken down to clean. She couldn't escape him even in the privacy of her bedroom. She heard him in the hallway outside, helping the maid shift furniture so the floorboards could be dusted.

And each time she heard him, she visualized him, lean and dark, proud and arrogant, every sinew outlined in his damp shirt and his tight jeans.

And she waited for blackmail.

Surely that was why he was here.

There could be no other reason. She didn't believe that he didn't want money. He was toying with her, playing a cruel game, although she could not fathom why. Any day now he would make his demands in return for his silence. She lived in anxiety. And worst of all, she had no doubt that he knew her innermost thoughts, for whenever they came face-to-face, she could see the smug, knowing look in his eyes. He knew damn well how he was racking her nerves, and he was enjoying it.

The insomnia dated from that very first day she had found him working at the ranch. The Texas nights were so hot and so humid that under normal circumstances it was difficult to sleep. But nothing was normal now. Images she did not welcome taunted her, teased her. Images of Shoz demanding blackmail money, images of his hard body in his tight jeans, his torso naked and slick and wet. Images of his mouth. She would toss and turn, the damp sheets twisting around her, her body consumed with its own blazing heat. She could remember the feel of him that one heady night in the desert when they had come together in wild abandon; his body hot, slick, and hard beneath her hands, his weight warm and heavy on top of her, the power coursing through him which, ultimately, he had not been able to restrain. The feel of him, the scent of him, the look of him . . . Lucy could not bear her memories in the heat and dark of these endless nights.

Last night had been like the others, only worse. The air

was so thick and wet, her cotton nightgown was like a second skin, damp and opaque. Even the sheets were annoyingly wet. She had padded barefoot to the open window to try and catch a breath of air—to try and escape her fantasies. To her shock, she saw him standing in the front yard by the swing, clearly illuminated by the moon and the outside porch lights. He was shirtless, his back resting against a tree, his cigarette glowing. No doubt he had the same intention as she, or did he? His was staring directly at her window, directly at her.

Suddenly realizing that if she could see him, he could certainly see her, Lucy hastily drew back. It was a long time before she slept at all.

The train was slowing. The noise was deafening. Leon was smiling and calling to her; Lucy smiled back. She suddenly thought of what she had done with Shoz, and she was stricken. If Leon ever knew, he would drop her like a hot potato, but that would not be as bad as witnessing his incredulity and his disgust. The latter would be withering. Tension suddenly tied her in knots. What if he found out? And next week her family would arrive, not just her parents and brothers, but everyone—Uncle Nick and Jane and their children, Aunt Storm and Brett and their children and grandchildren. And everyone knew her so well, especially Nicole; someone would guess . . .

Panic hit her sharply. She knew she must not let it show. Especially not now, because although Leon had only courted her these past few months, he knew her well enough, and he was very astute. He would miss little, if anything.

He jumped agilely from the train, taking her in his arms. "Lucy!"

Her smile was tremulous. "How was your trip?"

He didn't answer. He was pulling her into his embrace and kissing her soundly. Lucy stiffened reflexively, although Leon had kissed her many times—and she had always enjoyed it. This time she didn't enjoy it; how could she? Her predicament had just become a near-crisis, and Shoz was laughing at her in her mind's eye.

"What's wrong?"

Lucy managed a smile. "Leon, everyone will see!"

"I know," he said, smiling and chucking her chin.

Lucy pulled away. He had never kissed her in public before. She was uneasy. Now was not the time for Leon to become serious.

They returned to the ranch in the Duryea, with Lucy driving. Leon admired the car, now as good as new, but was skeptical of Lucy's ability to drive. "I've gotten quite good," she retorted. He seemed to find it rather amusing to be chauffeured by a woman.

Lucy halted the automobile in front of the house and climbed out without waiting for Leon's help. He raised an eyebrow at her as he came around the front of the car to take her elbow. "Am I forgetting that we're now in Texas, or are you forgetting you were raised in New York?"

It was a rebuke, and Lucy found it annoying. She gave him a look, and saw his surprise. But he did not apologize—as any gentleman should after receiving such a glance from Lucy Bragg. Lucy was somewhat put out.

She couldn't help noticing that he made no effort to retrieve his luggage from the Duryea's backseat. Was he right about the differences between New York and Texas? In New York no gentleman would handle his bags. Yet this wasn't New York, it was Texas, and here even her Uncle Brett, the most elegant gentleman she knew, handled his own luggage.

Miranda came out to greet them, wearing a simple blue skirt and shirtwaist and an apron—which she was drying her hands on. Leon was gallant, of course, and very proper, but Lucy was stunned to realize that he was shocked to see her grandmother in an apron and so obviously coming from the kitchen.

They entered the cool, spacious foyer. "Lucy, why don't you show Leon to his room?" Miranda said. She poked her head into the open doorway of the large salon. Lucy saw over Miranda's small shoulder that Shoz was there, standing on a ladder, fixing one of the windows. Her heart flopped and sank.

"Shoz?" Miranda asked. "Would you mind bringing some luggage in from Lucy's roadster?"

Shoz's cool gaze moved from Miranda to Lucy to the man standing beside her. Lucy could feel her cheeks flaming. Beside her, Leon moved impatiently. Shoz's lips curled, not exactly pleasantly. Lucy almost expected him to turn on her, one finger pointed, and tell all. Of course, it was only a horrid moment of fear, and he did no such thing. He stepped off the ladder. Lucy turned brightly to Leon. "Right this way."

Leon smiled back.

She led him upstairs and down the hall. As was correct, he was not staying in the same wing as she. This particular guest room was decorated in warm red tones with dark oak furniture and many Persian rugs. She moved across it to open the window. "You have wonderful views of the Pecos and the hill country. You can even see some mountains on the horizon."

He came up behind her, crowding her. Lucy jumped when he gripped her arms. "Darling, why are you so nervous?"

"Me?" she asked, her voice a higher pitch than normal. She cleared her throat. "I'm not nervous—just excited is all."

"Excited to see me?" he murmured, his hold tightening.

Lucy could not say no. "Of course," she said, striving for a light tone of voice. "It's been weeks."

He smiled, pulled her up against him, and before she could protest, his mouth claimed hers.

Leon's mouth was warm and firm and coaxing. Lucy had allowed herself, in the past, to be seduced into accepting his tongue. She had always preferred his kisses when they were closemouthed. Now she had no intention of allowing him such liberties, and she kept her lips firmly glued together.

Something heavy hit the floor with a thud! Lucy was intent on keeping her mouth closed no matter how hard he tried to pry past her lips, while he was intent on attaining her surrender. Both heard the noise but did not react. Then there was another thud, this one more forceful. Leon froze and lifted his head; Lucy jumped free of his grasp.

Shoz set the third bag down even more resoundingly and left without even a glance in their direction. As if they were invisible. But of course, he had seen them standing right there in the middle of the room.

"That was outrageous!" Leon gasped, staring after him. "Who the hell does he think he is?"

Lucy hurried to the door and did not reply. It was a harbinger of the disastrous week to come.

Every time Lucy turned around, it seemed like Shoz was there, lurking in the background. She took Leon for a morning ride, and there he was, fixing the fence in the south pasture. In the hottest part of the day, they sought the shade of the swing beneath the big oaks, and he was there, too, painting the porch railing. She and Leon could not even stroll in the moonlight without crossing his path.

Yet he ignored her. He did not spare them a glance, not ever. Lucy's feelings changed from confusion to disappointment to displeasure. Severe displeasure. What was she, invisible?

Perhaps it was fortunate that Shoz always seemed to appear when he was not wanted. One afternoon Lucy, Leon, and Joanna planned a picnic at Pete's Peak, but at the last moment Joanna pleaded a headache. Lucy and Leon went alone. Lucy spent the entire first hour fighting off Leon's kisses, finally succumbing to them out of sheer fatigue. In this case, his will was stronger than hers. But when his hand ran down her waist and then up and over her breast, she leapt to her feet, absolutely drawing the line then and there.

Leon apologized. "I'm sorry, Lucy, but we haven't had a minute alone all week. I'm going crazy for your kisses!"

His smile didn't work on her. "That wasn't a kiss," she said hotly, "that was groping." She chose that moment to remember having been the willing partner to a lot more than just groping not so long ago, and her color increased. Leon took it as a sign of her ire.

"I am sorry, truly. Now come back here." He patted the blanket where he sat.

"I had better not, Leon." Now that she was free, Lucy had no intention of getting caught in his embrace again.

Somehow, he no longer held the appeal he once had—and she knew why. Under her breath she cursed Shoz for ruining her interest in the best beau she had ever had. Because until Shoz had come along, she had found Leon utterly fascinating: charismatic and handsome and quite perfect.

She was really angry because even now there was no comparison between the two. Leon had everything and in abundance, Shoz had nothing. Leon was gorgeous—Shoz was rough. Yet envisioning them together, Leon's perfect looks seemed faded and almost delicate, while Shoz's dark features seemed dangerous and irresistibly virile.

"Lucy," Leon was saying, "do you think it was easy to get Joanna to agree to fake a headache and stay behind? What's wrong with you? Come here."

Once Lucy might have been flattered at the effort he had expended to get her alone, but she wasn't now. She was furious. "I think we had better go back, Leon."

Thereafter, Lucy made it a point not to be alone with Leon. Joanna was invited everywhere with them, and Lucy made sure she came. If Leon knew what she was contriving, he gave no outward sign. Lucy was certain he knew, but was gracefully bowing to propriety, for despite having schemed to picnic unchaperoned with her, he was a born gentleman and he did know better.

And then, finally, the day dawned. The day of her parents' and family's arrival, the day of Derek's eightieth birthday.

Lucy was tense with excitement—and anxiety. If the truth would ever be discovered, it would be now.

Lucy was up with the sun, but stayed in her room, because to do otherwise would most definitely arouse her grandfather's suspicions. She was trembling with excitement. At the moment, her fear of discovery was overwhelmed by the joy of the impending family reunion. At eight o'clock, as planned, the ranch foreman came up to the house and interrupted Derek's breakfast. The fence had come down in the north pasture and all the blooded mares and foals had gotten out. Derek left immediately. In actuality, the stock had been moved early that morning to a different location, and her grandfather and the cowboys would spend the next six or seven hours trying to track down the escaped animals. By noon everyone would have arrived and the party would be set up.

Lucy ran downstairs to await the arrival of her parents and brothers, her aunts and uncles, and especially her cousins. Already wagons were rolling in from town with the supplies and food and decorations for the party. The men were already digging the barbeque pits out back and setting up rows upon rows of picnic tables. Lucy was soon occupied in the kitchen with last-minute chores.

She was up to her elbows in lemons when a familiar voice cried her name from the doorway. "Miss Bragg!"

Lucy shrieked and whirled. "Lady Shelton!"

The two cousins ran into each other's arms. "I'm so glad to be here!" Nicole cried.

"I'm so glad you're here!" Lucy said. Nicole was her Uncle Nick's eldest daughter, a stunning, exotic beauty so much like her father—tall, dark-haired, gray-eyed, with a golden complexion and high, high cheekbones. She had just turned twenty-two that May.

"What are you doing?" Nicole laughed, eyeing her disheveled appearance. "Is this my cousin or some imposter?"

Lucy grinned. "I'm a disaster, I know."

Nicole was unfazed. Although her appearance was usually impeccable, it was a shocking contrast to her behavior—which rarely was. She was one of Lucy's favorite people in the entire world, and they had been partners in crime more often than not. "I've never seen you in your shirtsleeves before," Nicole laughed. "Change that awful outfit and put on something utterly wicked!"

Chatting nonstop, the two girls ran from the kitchen. Lucy screeched to a halt in the foyer, which was crowded to overflowing with her entire family. Everyone was talking a mile a minute, hugging, laughing, crying. It was chaos.

Her father, Rathe, was embracing his older sister, Lucy's aunt, Storm. She was a tall, handsome, formidable woman, equally at ease in the backwoods as she was in her Nobb Hill mansion. Lucy had had a secret crush on her husband, Brett d'Archand, when she was a child. He was tall and dark and dangerous-looking, and so very elegant in his tailored black suit. He was pumping her Uncle Nick's hand. He was Lord Shelton, the Earl of Dragmore. He had one of his arms wrapped around his unbelievably gorgeous, petite blond wife, the famous actress, Jane Barclay, who was trying to wrest herself free to hug Lucy's mother, Grace. Years ago in New York, the two had become best friends, or so they said.

Then there were her cousins. Brett's sons, Stephen and Lincoln, and their wives were surrounding and embracing Miranda, who was crying. Their six small children were racing around the room shouting like Indians with a gangling shepherd puppy, which seemed to be dragging one of them on a leash. Lucy's youngest brother, Colin, age eight, was racing with them, whooping the loudest of all. Her brothers Brian, Greg and Hugh were trying to catch the younger ones and restrain them. Mark was suspiciously absent. Lucy didn't have time to think about this, though, because Nicole's brothers, Chad and Ed, and her younger sister, Regina, rushed forward to envelop her in big bear hugs.

Over Regina's shoulder, Lucy caught her father's glacial eye. *He knows*, she thought, panic knifing through her. He knows about Shoz!

She went white, meeting his stern, disapproving gaze—and then realized that he could not possibly know about Shoz! Her knees almost buckled. Regina gave way to Stephen. She hugged him, filled with relief. Daddy was only angry because he'd found out she'd gone to Texas without Mrs. Seymour!

Things began to quiet down. Not much, but a bit. Lucy said hello to everyone, avoiding her parents. Her mother had also given her a sharp "we're going to talk" look. "Where is your brother, Mark?" Nicole asked.

Lucy was about to reply that she didn't know when he appeared from outside, stepping into the crowded foyer. Something was in his arms, something furry, something yowling. He released it. The oversize puppy barked and lunged. The cat screeched and ran. Chaos reigned again.

* * *

All the guests could not possibly fit into the house to hide in order to really surprise Derek. At noon everyone was milling outside, chatting and renewing acquaintances, or making new ones. Over a thousand people from coast to coast had turned out for Derek's eightieth birthday, and they took up most of the grounds behind the ranch house.

Ten huge barbecue pits were already fired and smoking. The band was tuning up. Giant caldrons were already simmering with chili, and bartenders were serving everything from martinis to cream sodas. Cowboys in denims and hats mixed with ladies in silks and parasols, their husbands in white or navy sack jackets and linen trousers; children played hide-and-seek noisily, grandfathers sat smoking pipes and watching, their wives eating and gossiping. Shortly after one, Derek Bragg rode in.

On a platform boasting the flags of both the United States of America and the state of Texas, Nick, Storm, and Rathe stood, grinning happily. Nick raised his hand, and the crowd shouted, "HAPPY BIRTHDAY, DEREK!"

Derek rode up to the platform, eyes wide, as if stunned beyond belief. Watching by the side, Lucy bit her lip. "What the hell is going on?" Derek roared.

"SURPRISE!" A thousand people roared back.

Derek's hand went to his heart and Lucy gasped. Then she realized her grandfather was hamming it up. He slid from his mount and was practically dragged by his sons onto the platform. Derek was grinning, but protested. "I don't know what the hell is going on here," he said into the megaphone. Everyone laughed and Nick appropriated the speaker.

"Father," he said, "I'm happy to enlighten you." He grinned. "You gave me the perfect opening. All of these people have traveled a helluva distance to honor you on this occasion, the day of your eightieth birthday. They've come not just out of friendship, but out of respect. No one man symbolizes more what this country and this state stand for.

"You were born in the mountains in a shack in obscurity. Yet today you have become one of the most powerful men in this state and in America. And everything we see here—" Nick gestured "—was created with your own two hands, with your own sweat—with your own blood and guts. You are a testimony to the success of the American pioneer through courage, integrity, and perseverance against the worst odds. Against the odds of foreign powers, like Mexico, whom you fought against to liberate this land, just as you fought against the Comanches, to civilize it, and most of all, against the brutal and unyielding land itself. Your success is not just your own. It is the success of this state and this country. The greatness of Texas and America would not have come about without the ambition and courage and dedication of men like yourself.''

Lucy hollered and cheered with everyone else, tears streaking her cheeks. Next to her mother and Aunt Jane, Storm held her grandmother, who was both smiling and crying at the same time, her rapt gaze on her husband. Lucy thought that Derek's face looked a bit red when he took the megaphone from Nick.

"Thanks, son." He coughed. "I think enough's been said for the moment. I only want to add my thanks to everyone here, and everyone who couldn't be here but wanted to come. And to my family. To my children and their children, to my wife. It's for them that I did all of this, not for anyone else." He paused when thunderous applause greeted this. He grinned and leaned forward. "Now let's have a fiesta!"

Shoz stood in the shade of a tree, leaning against it, arms crossed, and eyed the guests.

To one side, hundreds of steaks were being barbecued on ten huge grills, and a dozen vast pots were simmering with beans. A score of picnic tables were cheerily draped in red, white, and blue bunting with the words *Happy Birthday DEREK* stenciled across the top of each one. One was set up just to serve hundreds of fresh rolls, thousands of ears of corn on the cob, fresh salads, desserts, and punch, sangria, lemonade, and coffee.

Guests milled everywhere, easterners and locals mixing with the hired hands. To the other side, a Spanish band was playing, and already couples were whirling across an area covered with sawdust and marked off by bales of hay. Shoz had to admit, the Braggs knew how to throw a party.

He took his time inspecting the ladies. There were more than a few pretty faces and alluring bodies in the crowd, but he was disappointed when he realized no one could compare to Lucy Bragg. He knew where she was—he'd known all along. She was impossible to miss.

She wore a low-cut flame-red dress that left her shoulders completely bare, her hair hanging loose in riotous titian waves. She was dancing enthusiastically with Billy, who'd finally claimed her from that easterner. *That easterner*. For a moment Shoz stared at him, while he stared in annoyance at Lucy and Billy.

Shoz disliked everything about the man, from the tips of his polished shoes to his impeccably starched shirts. He disliked the man's casual elegance, his blond good looks, his background, breeding and wealth. All of it showed, and if he'd shouted to the heavens who and what he was, it couldn't have been clearer. He was Lucy's equal in every way.

They made a handsome couple.

One day, they'd make the ideal man and wife.

Shoz did not care. Why should he? Lucy was nothing to him but a passing distraction. In fact, it was amusing the way she struggled so hard to be proper with Leon—when she hadn't been proper with him at all. He wondered how Leon would feel when he took his wife and found out she wasn't a virgin. Shoz uncharitably felt satisfaction at beating the man on that one score. Leon would not be pleased; in fact, Shoz was a good judge of character, and he suspected he would be downright ugly about it. The man might have been born with a silver spoon in his mouth, but he was cold and ambitious, not soft at all. He laughed as he thought about warning Lucy to fake her virginity on her wedding night.

He stared again at Leon. It was the utmost irony that he was Marianne's son. When he had first seen Leon, he had thought there was something familiar about him. He knew Marianne adored Leon, from the few conversations they'd had when they'd been lovers, and he knew she wanted him to attain vast power and wealth. Undoubtedly she approved of Lucy Bragg for her son. Shoz felt even better about having taken what Leon wanted so much. Even though his interest in Lucy had nothing to do with revenge, the coincidence, of who her beau was, was damn nice.

If he really wanted to, he could pluck the plum right from Leon's grasp. Too bad he wasn't such a bastard. He didn't have it in his character to publicly ruin an innocent girl, no matter how much he would love to avenge himself on Marianne Claxton.

He watched Lucy. She was laughing while she danced, her red skirts twirling to reveal a lot of lovely leg and immodestly high heels. She was reveling in the physical release.

He had been watching her for hours. He wasn't surprised that she should dance like a gypsy. He'd already touched on her passion for sex, and now she was dancing with the same wild yearning, the same abandon. And he knew that she knew he was watching; she had known it all night. Her sensuous movements were for him, and if she intended to arouse him, it was working. He had never wanted her more.

He made up his mind. No more games. He wanted her and would have her, regardless. Tonight. He would just make sure no one would ever know—nice guy that he was.

And then, then his gaze swept past a woman, a slim blond woman, exquisitely dressed, flashing jewels, with an exquisitely proportioned body. It couldn't be. Just because Leon Claxton was here . . . His gaze shot to her again.

Marianne Claxton stared back at him.

And Shoz was thrown completely back through the gates of hell.

14

He was born in the Dragoon Mountains of Arizona in the summer of 1861. His natural mother was a Coyotero Apache and his father's second wife, the first being Candice. His father was known as Jack Savage to the white men and El Salvaje to the Apaches. A half-breed of unknown origins himself, he had been captured by Cochise as a young boy and adopted by a Coyotero couple. Although he had left his clan and later married a white woman, Candice Carter, he'd returned to Cochise to fight with him when the Apache Wars began.

Shoz was born in those first brutal days of the war. His full name was Shozkay, after his father's brother, one of the war's first casualties. When his father took Candice and their daughter, Christina, to California to start a new life, he took Shoz as well. Shoz's mother remained behind in the Dragoon Mountains with her people.

Shoz grew up on their ranch outside of Bakersfield with his half-sister and three other younger half-brothers. Candice was the only mother he remembered. It was a distinct shock to learn that she was not his real mother. Jack explained it kindly when he was seven, wanting him to know the truth—and to be proud of his own heritage. His father told him not just about his natural mother, but about her people, and about Cochise and their battle for survival. He vividly described what it was like to live in that time, to ride with Cochise. He explained it in such a way that the young Shoz was proud to be who he was, and the hurt of discovering that Candice wasn't his real mother passed quickly.

He grew up working the ranch alongside his father and

his brothers. His family was very close, and he and Christina were like twins, having been born only months apart. In the school they attended in town, he was quick to defend her honor—and she his.

The prejudice began when he and Christina went to school for the first time. On their third or fourth day, Christina came to him crying. The school bully, a big twelve-year-old, had called her "squaw." Shoz didn't exactly understand why it was an insult, but he knew it was intended as such—and he was incensed. He got a black eye for his efforts to defend Christina—and so did she when she tried to help him in his losing battle.

He didn't lose too many battles after that, learning that when you go up against someone twice your age and twice your size, *anything* goes. Shoz learned to fight mean, and dirty, if need be.

Children can be cruel, and epithets like redskin, Injun, and breed were occasionally flung at him until he quit school at sixteen. No one ever dared to insult Christina again, though, or his younger brothers, because they quickly learned that while Shoz might smile indifferently when they insulted him, his fury knew no bounds when his family was the target of their taunts.

But it wasn't bad, just the infrequent and callous harassment of an occasional bully. In general, his family was well thought of in Bakersfield, and respected. Shoz knew most of the townspeople by sight, at least, and was known to help the old widow Calder across the street or earn a penny and an apple from Mr. Dickson for sweeping up at the general store.

When Shoz was eighteen, he left home to make his own way. It was one of the hardest things he'd ever done in his life. His father understood and didn't try to hold him back, although his mother wept so much, Shoz almost changed his mind. He wanted to travel, see the land, experience more than what Bakersfield offered. His first destination was the land of his people, the land of the Chiricahua.

He drifted through the territory, hoping to find out if his mother was alive, only to be caught up in the final assault being made by the U.S. Army on the last free Apaches, led

by Geronimo. He joined Geronimo, after having proved his
courage and his ability to fight. He was incensed by the
army's methodical slaughter of the Apache—incensed by
the conditions on the few reservations he'd seen—and sickened by the Apache's vicious response. They burned and
raped and maimed. In his father's day, no Apache would
ever rape innocent women or kill innocent children. He left
them with no regrets, just with the horrifying memories time
could not erase.

He rode the range throughout most of central Texas, once
even joining one of the last drives up the Chisholm Trail.
He drifted into Memphis. He had been learning hard, bitter
lessons. On the trail he was accepted grudgingly by other
men, but only after he had proved he could work harder
than anyone. In the big cities, he found he was considered
socially unacceptable by just about everyone. The only work
he could find was of the lowest sort, fit for children or the
aged and infirm, with the lowest of wages. He was considered taboo by the women he approached. It didn't stop any
of the latter from sharing his bed, but only in the utmost
secrecy. Should he pass a lover in the street, she would
pretend not to know him. He soon despised their hypocrisy.
He despised them.

It was worse in St. Louis, where he was stared at as if
he were a freak. He began to see white women as conquests,
vehicles for his pleasure, nothing more, to be used and
discarded at whim. His attitude hardened with a quality of
deliberate vengeance. They were his payback for the insults
he'd withstood from their white brothers and fathers.

At twenty, Shoz realized he couldn't drift endlessly, he
had to make a decision to do something with his life. He
returned home and announced he was going to go to a
university and study the law. His parents were thrilled. Jack
encouraged him to apply to the top schools back East. He
was accepted by Columbia University on a partial scholarship, and began his freshman year when he was twenty-
one in 1882.

New York was not like St. Louis. New Yorkers prided
themselves on their liberalism and their avant-garde ways.
It was all bullshit. Shoz bitterly realized he'd been accepted

because he was an Indian, not because he'd done well on their entrance exams. He was the token redskin, to soothe the board's guilty consciences for their innate bigotry and their government's systematic genocide of his people.

He was determined to match their disguised contempt and even outstrip it. He excelled at his studies despite having to work part-time. He proved not just his equality, but his superiority to his white classmates by graduating number two in his class—and screwing more New York ladies than all his classmates combined.

The summer before his last year at New York Law School, he began seeing Marianne Claxton. She was a beautiful married woman who was a born slut. Their appetites were well matched. His own prowess was becoming legendary in certain circles.

Marianne had a little maid named Bettina, plump and lush and very interesting. One day Marianne caught Shoz and Bettina in her own bed. Bettina promptly wound up unemployed. Shoz stayed where he was—in Marianne's bed, soothing her ruffled feathers.

That night, in his small apartment above Vincenzo's Ristorante, the police came and showed him a search warrant. In his own trousers they found a ten-carat diamond ring. He was arrested immediately, and held without bail.

The trial lasted less than two working days. Justice was swift. Marianne testified that it was her ring. Bettina testified that she had, indeed, had an affair with him and that he had been in the house. Shoz declared himself innocent. As far as Bettina went, he admitted to having slept with her, "among others." And he looked right at Marianne.

She denied it, of course. But he'd made another mistake. Her husband was Roger Claxton II, a very powerful senator as well as the ancestor of a founding New York family. Claxton came up to him after he'd sullied his wife's name. "You just signed yourself into prison, boy," he said.

His sentence was seven years without parole.

In the fall of 1889, Shoz was incarcerated. Seven months later he escaped.

* * *

Shoz strolled toward Marianne, never taking his eyes from her.

She stood absolutely motionless except for the mad fluttering of her hand-painted Chinese fan. Her eyes were wide and blue and fixed upon him.

He smiled. "Hello, Marianne."

The hummingbird movement of her fan increased. "Shoz." Her tone was husky, a tone he knew so very well.

His gaze swept her crudely. "I wonder who's luckier because of this chance meeting, you or me?"

She didn't seem to understand, or didn't try to. "How are you, Shoz?"

He sneered. "Even better than the last time."

This innuendo didn't escape her. Two tiny patches of color appeared on her delicate cheeks. Her eyes smoldered. "What are you doing here, of all places?"

"I work here. And you, Mrs. Claxton? What brings you out West? You never struck me as having a fondness for anything other than ballrooms—and bedrooms."

The two pink stains on her cheeks darkened. "My son Leon is enamored of Derek Bragg's granddaughter. Shoz. I am sorry, so very sorry."

"Really? Then why don't you set the record straight and tell the truth."

"I can't. You know I can't. How could I! I'd be ruined!"

He wanted to strangle her. "See you *around*, Mrs. Claxton."

"Wait." She touched his arm, and didn't remove her hand.

He turned.

"Shoz," she said, low and breathless.

Unbelievable, he thought. He'd treated her like the bitch she was—and she still wanted more. He wondered if he should give it to her—and realized he'd lost all interest. "Enjoy the party, Marianne," he said.

"Wait!" She grabbed him. "We must talk!"

"Talk?"

"Please! Meet me in an hour and we—"

"If you think there's going to be a repeat performance of the last time, think again."

Her eyes flared with anger. "I think you'll be interested in something I have to say. Try this word for size: blackmail."

His lips curled up at the corners, but she had his complete attention now.

"I'm sure," she said, her gaze drifting down his denim-clad hips, "Derek Bragg would love to know exactly whom he's hired."

The curl of his lips increased. He took her arm and propelled her roughly forward. Marianne stumbled. He moved her through the crowd until they had rounded one of the barns and were alone. He pushed her up against it. She stared at him, her breasts straining against her low bodice.

"Do you want it now, or later?"

"Shoz," she protested, all innocence now.

He caught her face between his hands and held it, frightening her. "Don't you ever threaten me."

She couldn't speak, although she tried to.

"Go ahead, tell Bragg; see if I care. But find your fucking somewhere else." He released her.

Her eyes blazed with fury. "You son of a bitch."

"The gutter becomes you, Marianne," he said.

He was about to leave when, from behind them, a soft voice said, "Hello, Mother. I saw you coming out here and wondered what you were doing."

Shoz turned to glimpse a younger version of Marianne, a blond, blue-eyed vision who had to be her daughter. The girl gave him a very pretty smile. "Hello." Her voice had that same distinct well-bred tone.

He nodded.

"Shoz is an old friend, dear." There was tight exasperation in Marianne's voice as she introduced her daughter, Darlene.

"From New York, Mother?" There was the very faintest hint of scorn in her tone. "Are you from New York, Shoz?"

"No."

She smiled prettily again. "I didn't think so." She laughed softly.

She would be an easy conquest, and he knew it—and a boring one, but he could positively feel the heat of Marianne's wrath, so he asked her if she wanted to dance. When Darlene agreed, her big blue eyes never leaving his face, her laughter soft and coquettish, he heard Marianne actually hiss.

"I am so hot," Lucy declared, fanning herself.

"Can I get you something, Miss Lucy?" Billy asked.

She batted her eyes at him. "I would love a glass of that wicked red punch. The one spiked with alcohol."

"I'll get it," Leon said quickly, but annoyance was in his tone. He stalked off.

Billy glared after him. "How about some cake?"

"Punch and cake; why not?" Lucy said gaily. When Billy departed, Lucy turned to Joanna. "Who the hell is that!"

Joanna, demure in a pale pink dress next to Lucy's flaming red ball gown, followed her gaze. "You've met Darlene," she said. "Don't you remember?"

"No, I don't," Lucy said sourly, although now she did recognize Leon's sister. With open fury and a murderous scowl, she watched Shoz and Darlene make their way through the crowd, hips bumping, heads bent together. "What a pasty white skinny blonde!" Lucy declared.

"I think she's beautiful," Joanna said.

Lucy glared. "She has the figure of a twelve-year-old!"

"You're jealous."

Before she could deny it, Nicole appeared, wrapping one arm around Lucy's waist. She looked almost sinful in a yellow off-the-shoulder Mexican blouse with wide crimson and gold silk skirts. She wore huge gold hoops that touched her bare shoulders. Lucy thought she looked exotic—like a wild gypsy. "Who is Lucy jealous of?"

"I am not jealous," Lucy said.

"You don't look very happy on Grandpa's birthday," Nicole accused. "And what a party! Who has the figure of a twelve-year-old?"

Lucy frowned, but her gaze found Darlene and Shoz again. Nicole followed her gaze. Joanna answered. "Darlene Claxton."

"Don't worry, Lucy," Nicole said. "She's pretty, but next to you, she's nothing. Who is that?"

There was no question about to whom Nicole was referring, and Lucy was shocked by the surge of jealousy she felt. "He's not for you, Nicole."

Her cousin looked at her quickly. "He's not my type! He reminds me of Daddy and Uncle Brett!" She shuddered dramatically. "I am not stupid. I have no intention of ever getting involved with a strong man. In fact, I have no intention of ever marrying at all."

Nicole's words were more than theatrics. Not only was she headstrong and rather wild, she had failed dismally during her first few Seasons in London—even before the scandal that had erupted shortly afterwards. It was a bit of an embarrassment as her younger sister Regina had already had several offers and she had not as yet made her debut.

"So," Nicole said slyly, "who is that?"

"He is just some riffraff that Grandpa hired," Lucy answered irritably. She did not want to discuss Shoz with Nicole. Her cousin would soon guess everything.

"Really?" Nicole teased. "He is very handsome—in a rugged way."

Lucy was saved from responding by Leon's return. "Leon!" She smiled widely. "Thank you!" She took the punch and drained half the cup.

"Careful, Lucy," Leon warned, disapproval in his tone.

"Why?" Lucy asked. "You know the conventional bòres me." She finished the glass, following Shoz and Darlene with her eyes. They were standing much too close, and it was the height of bad taste.

Leon took the glass from her. "How about another dance?" He lowered his voice. "Before you become cooked."

"I'm too hot," Lucy stated. "Nicole will dance with you, won't you?" Now that Shoz was no longer watching her, she didn't feel like dancing. Earlier he had been watching her, and she had been dancing for him. It had been exhilarating.

Nicole wouldn't let Leon off the hook, and reluctantly he led her out amongst the twirling dancers. Billy returned with a few assorted desserts, and Lucy took a bite of each. Shoz and Darlene had disappeared. Her vexation was intense. She searched the crowd. Where were they?

"Do you want some more punch?"

"What?"

Billy repeated the question, and Lucy nodded. She knew where they were, she knew what they were doing. She had no doubts on that score. Not that she cared; in fact, it was the utmost relief to finally have him direct his vulgar attentions at someone else.

She was standing alone. Joanna had abandoned her, and Billy had gone for the punch. She thrust her hands on her hips. She shouldn't spy, but . . . she was going to see what *they* were doing.

Joanna didn't mean to spy.

Lucy was involved with her suitors, as always, so she wandered off, trailing after the dark, handsome Shoz and the flirtatious Darlene. She wished she could flirt like Darlene. Not like Lucy. She never imagined she could ever be anything like Lucy, not in any way. Lucy was too bold and too vibrant. But Darlene was a bit pale and gentle and somewhat demure, not so different from herself. If Shoz liked her . . .

But she wasn't like Darlene; she wasn't blond with a perfect petite figure. She didn't know how to flirt, and she would die before even trying. And he didn't like her, not even a little. He was barely aware of her existence. He only had eyes for Lucy—and now Darlene.

She wondered what it felt like to be in his arms, the way Lucy had been.

Joanna realized she was following just Darlene, that Shoz was nowhere in sight. Where had he gone to? A moment ago they'd been together. But there were so many people now, it was getting so crowded, that he could be anywhere. She found herself standing behind Darlene, and was about to say hello.

"Mother!" Darlene exclaimed, no longer so demure. "Mother! Why haven't you ever introduced us before!"

Joanna stepped back a bit, not really meaning to listen. But she did.

"He is not for you, Darlene," Marianne Claxton said, her blue eyes blazing with fury. Joanna caught a glimpse of her and was stunned by the depth of passion she saw, by the raw jealousy and hatred she saw on Mrs. Claxton's face. She assumed it was directed at Shoz, although it appeared to be aimed at her own daughter.

"Why not? Because he's a cowboy?" Darlene asked contemptuously. "Or because *you* want him?"

"You listen to me," Marianne said harshly, grabbing her daughter's gloved wrist. Darlene gasped, but Marianne yanked her close. "Listen to me! That man is not for you! He is a dangerous criminal!"

Darlene pulled her hand free. "What are you saying?"

"I am saying that he is an escaped convict, Darlene. He is a felon—wanted by the law."

It was late; soon it would be midnight. The fiesta was in full swing; there must have been at least a thousand people reveling in the moonlight. It wasn't easy to find them amongst the crowd. Lucy's determination grew, and with it, her suspicions. If Shoz and Darlene were not among the partiers, where were they?

They weren't dancing or among the group still enjoying the barbecue. The night was thick and hot, and the air petal-soft. The wild strains of the Spanish band followed Lucy everywhere. She grabbed Maria. "Have you seen the new hand? Shoz?"

Maria shook her head.

Lucy turned away, frowning, then caught a glimpse of Darlene dancing with one of her friends. A wave of relief washed over her. They weren't together. It didn't really concern her, yet Lucy couldn't stand the idea of Shoz throwing her over for one of her peers. But if he wasn't with Darlene, then who was he with? And where was he?

Lucy left the party and began heading for the stables and the bunkhouse, partially on instinct but mostly propelled by mulish determination. She would search everywhere if she had to. Walking between two whitewashed barns, she left the sounds of the music and laughter behind. The night air was wet and still. A fine film of perspiration covered her body; her bare shoulders and chest gleamed.

And then she saw a dark figure leaning against the paddock adjoining the studs' stable. She didn't have to see clearly to know it was him—and he was alone. Her pulse quickened. He was smoking, his cigarette glowing each time he lifted it to his lips.

Lucy paused when she could see him, her breasts already heaving. "Hiding?" she demanded sarcastically. "Or waiting for someone!"

He tossed the cigarette and ground it under his heel. "Oh, I've been waiting for someone, all right."

"I knew it! Which lover are you waiting for, Shoz? Darlene? Someone else? Who!"

"You."

She stepped back abruptly, blinking.

"I was wondering how long it would be before you'd come looking for me."

"I am not one of your lovers."

His teeth showed white. "No? Maybe my memory's playing tricks on me, but I seem to recall one night not too long ago—"

"Don't you ever bring that up again!" she cried angrily. "As far as I'm concerned, nothing ever happened!"

"You've got a convenient way of looking at things, princess. Come here. Parties bore me."

"You didn't look so bored an hour ago."

"Jealous?" He grinned.

"Never."

"Come here. I want to work on your status—make you my lover."

His hand came out to grab hers. Lucy stiffened as he pulled her forward, fast. She came up squarely against his hard, warm body. Without any conviction, she pressed her hands to his damp shirt and almost pushed away from him. Instead, she became still.

"Hello, princess," he murmured, running his hands down her back.

"Shoz."

"No more games," he said, and he caught her face in his hands.

The feel of his warm, rough palms cupping her face was wonderful, and so was the strangely warm look in his eyes. "I don't want to play games either," Lucy said softly.

The expression in his eyes softened. "Then tell me," he said, "tell me it's been as hard for you as it's been for me, these past weeks; tell me, Lucy, tell me now."

"It's been as hard for me," she said unsteadily. "Shoz—what's happening?"

"I don't know—I don't care."

Lucy was not prepared for his onslaught. He kissed her, hard, fiercely, a man spending passion long pent up. And she clung to his shirt, kissing him back just as wildly.

In the thick heat of the night, anything was possible.

Marianne paused, squinting in the darkness. She had seen Shoz come this way, toward the barns, but the area ahead of her seemed deserted. She flung a glance over her shoulder, to glimpse the last of the dancers doing a wild two-step. Then she lifted her skirts and hurried forward.

She had no intention of ceasing her search until she found him. She was obsessed. It was fate that he should be here where she was. She knew it.

And she would get her way. She was afraid, oh yes, but the fear heightened her lust. When he finally took her under coercion, he would be rough, and so very powerful. Marianne could not wait, she had to find him, now.

She stopped by the corner of one barn when she saw the lovers ahead of her, their backs to another barn, in a torrid embrace. Instantly her suspicions were aroused, and just the thought that he might be with another woman—even with her daughter—fueled the fury pulsing in her veins. She hurried forward and ducked near stacked bales of hay. Not that she needed to hide. They were too involved to notice anyone.

Clouds broke, spilling moonlight. Marianne gasped. It was him, that bastard, and he was with Lucy Bragg. The thought of murder leapt into her mind.

She wanted to kill them both.

* * *

Leon Claxton was looking for Lucy, and he was angry.

Angry and frustrated. Texas was not his choice of vacation spots, and the past week had barely been tolerable. Lucy had made a point of keeping Joanna at her side, depriving him of any opportunity to be alone with her. On the surface she remained the same, but Leon sensed that she was tense and nervous. Why? What was she hiding? Why was she suddenly too proper to sneak away with him for his kisses?

He didn't like it. He did not like it when things did not go as he intended.

He also did not like that cowboy, Shoz. The man actually had the balls to be contemptuous of him, Leon Claxton. He hadn't said anything, but Leon felt it. And like any man worth his salt, Leon sensed the cowboy's interest in Lucy—sensed that they were adversaries even though it was impossible to think that Shoz might compete with him on any level, for anything, much less for Lucy. Still, when the man was around, Leon was intensely aware of Shoz, and he sensed that the man, Shoz, was just as aware of him. And Lucy was aware of him, too.

Leon sensed that as well.

He wasn't worried. Just angry and annoyed.

Even more so tonight. Lucy was flirting left and right, and Leon did not appreciate it. He wanted some time with her to reaffirm their relationship. When she left the crowd of the party, Leon seized his chance. He followed her.

And then he saw her in someone else's arms.

They had both created their own world, in which the only existing force was the need to physically merge.

Lucy clung frantically, straining against him, every inch of her wedged and pressed as close as possible to his body, his heat. Shoz had her buttocks in his hands, had her lifted and pressed against his groin, had her riding him. Later, he would wonder how he'd ever had the mental coherence to understand what was happening.

Something clicked in the back of his mind. Voices, a cry of pain. From within the stable. A horse's agitated snort.

Hooves stomping in frenzy on stone. And then the gunshot.

He thrust Lucy behind him and against the barn, straining to listen. His body reflexively shielded her.

"What?" Lucy cried.

"There was a shot," he gasped, panting.

"I didn't hear anything." She was trembling, and he could feel it.

And then the door to the barn was flying open, horses and riders galloping out. Lucy shrank against the wall of the barn as a horse swept by them, his flank actually grazing Shoz. Comprehension came a moment later.

"That's Grandpa's stud!" she shrieked. "They're stealing Grandpa's stud!"

Shoz moved. He darted into the barn. One light was on, illuminating the old groom lying facedown in blood. Shoz dropped to his knees and found his pulse. He'd been shot in the back and was dead.

Then he saw the horse, riderless and saddled and ready to go, near the dead man. He grimaced; it was obviously an inside job—the old groom had been one of them but had been murdered at the last moment by the avaricious rustlers. He leapt on the horse and went thundering out of the barn.

He heard Lucy's cry of shock as he swept past her, but did not stop. He was too intent on following the thieves with Bragg's prized stallion. He wasn't positive, but now he remembered how big they both were—and he wondered if it was Red and Jake.

And there was another retort. Instantaneously Shoz felt the searing in his back, and realized he'd been shot.

From behind.

15

Dawn broke, shading the sky pink and gray. Lucy hadn't slept all night. She sat in the kitchen with a mug of coffee in her hand, still in the flame-red dress from the night before. Joanna and Nicole sat with her, having kept vigil with her since the theft of Derek's prize stallion. Her aunt Jane and Regina had stayed up for a while, too, but they had long since gone to their rooms and to bed.

She wondered if he might die.

She felt sick.

Miranda and Grace came into the kitchen. Lucy leapt to her feet. "What's happened?"

"The posse's getting ready to go out," Grace replied. "The sheriff's just arrived."

Sheriff Sanders had been at the party, as had almost everyone in town. When Shoz had been shot, Lucy had run for her father, and for help. Shoz had been taken inside, tended by Doc Jones, but had been too weak to answer more than a couple of questions, already fighting unconsciousness. Sanders had also questioned Lucy. She had told him they had been talking outside the stud barn when the robbery had occurred. That Shoz had *run* after the thieves, on foot, and then been shot. Sanders had questioned others, too, but no one else had witnessed the horse stealing and shooting. Doc Jones had shortly thereafter produced the bullet. It came from a small derringer such as those favored by ladies. This only added confusion to the unfolding drama. Had a woman shot Shoz? If so, why? And who had it been? Most of their guests had already gone to their accommodations and homes for the night, and it was impossible now to search and question everyone, looking for the handgun. Sanders had left a few hours after midnight, to get a couple hours sleep before attempting to track the thieves in the light of day.

"How is he?" Lucy managed as her mother put a comforting hand on her shoulder. She wanted to be in the guest room where Shoz, semiconscious and in pain, had been placed hours ago. But she didn't dare. She'd already used up all her excuses for going there. He had water and blankets and had been dosed lightly with laudanum by Doc Jones.

"He's sleeping," Grace replied, squeezing her shoulder. But her mother's gaze was too intent and too questioning, too astute; Lucy looked away.

"Jones says that normally he wouldn't worry," Miranda said, "being as Shoz is strong as a bull, but after that crack on the head, he's afraid the shock will be too much. The gunshot itself isn't too bad."

Lucy was white. Nicole was staring at her.

Joanna asked, "He might die?"

"Hush," Grace scolded. "Of course he won't die." Again, she looked at her daughter.

He might die, Lucy thought miserably. She knew she shouldn't care, but she did. She was sick. Even sicker because she knew something nobody else seemed to have noticed, something she should have told the sheriff and hadn't. *He was one of the thieves.*

He had come tearing out of that barn right after the others. No one could saddle a horse so quickly. The horse had been ready and waiting for him. Just like he had been ready and waiting for his partners at the barn when she had found him. He was one of the thieves, and maybe he had even murdered the poor old groom.

Lucy clutched herself. She had to tell her grandpa and father, soon. But why couldn't she?

Derek barged in, looking grim, with Nick and Rathe at his side. Brett and Storm were right behind them. The hawk-faced sheriff was on their heels with two deputies, Chad, Brett's two sons, Stephen and Lincoln, and the two eldest of her brothers, Brian and Greg.

Sanders was speaking. "I thought that the sorrel that we found out in the paddock all saddled and riderless belonged to one of the thieves. That he'd been shot and fell off and the horse drifted here.''

"So did I,'' Derek said shortly.

"But there was no body.''

"They could have taken the third thief with them,'' Nick pointed out.

"Maybe,'' Sanders said. "But then again, we did find someone shot, didn't we?''

"But with a lady's pistol,'' Rathe said. "And that doesn't make sense.''

"That might have nothing to do with the horse theft,'' Brett said. "It might be completely independent.''

"Not likely,'' Sanders said. "But possible.''

"That tip you got has to be checked out,'' Derek said, walking right on through the kitchen. Everyone was on his heels, but Rathe grabbed his sons, preventing them from following. "Haven't you two had enough excitement for tonight?''

"Pop,'' they protested in unison. "He's going to question Shoz, isn't he?'' Brian, the seventeen-year-old, demanded.

"He is, and you two are turning in for a few hours sleep.''

Lucy leapt up, ignoring her brothers as they informed their father that they wanted to ride with the posse. She rushed after her grandfather.

"Grandpa, what's happening?''

"Go to bed, Lucy,'' Derek said, dismissing her as he headed for the guest room in the back of the house.

"No one thought to check the brand,'' Sanders was saying, right behind Derek. "Not until I got this anonymous tip.''

"How long will it take to get a reply?''

"We'll have a wire later today.''

Derek threw open the door to the guest room. On his stomach, Shoz blinked at them blearily.

Sanders put a restraining hand on Derek. "Now, that tip could just be some stupid prank. After all, a kid delivered it and slipped right out of my hands before I could get him to tell me who had sent him.''

Derek nodded, his eyes on Shoz, who gazed back at him

steadily if not groggily. "You're going to answer some questions, Shoz," Derek warned.

Alertness soon replaced the unfocused haze in Shoz's eyes.

"What's happening?" Miranda demanded, pushing past Lucy. "What are you doing?"

Derek made to silence her, but Sanders responded. "Sorry, ma'am," he said. "But I was recently tipped off, anonymously, that Shoz here is an escaped felon from New York State."

"I don't believe it," Miranda said.

Lucy gripped the bedpost, hard.

"Maybe he was one of the thieves. He was shot in the back, ma'am. Men who are fleeing get shot in the back. We found a D&M horse out in the pasture, saddled and riderless. But no body. Maybe that horse was waiting for someone? Looks like it was an inside job, and maybe Shoz was the man on the inside."

Miranda was angry. "You are basing your very serious accusations on an anonymous tip that he is a wanted man. This could prove to be false! Lucy said he was pursuing the thieves on foot when he was shot!"

"That's what she said," Sanders admitted. "But maybe he was running to the horse. That D&M horse was out there for a reason."

"This poor boy was shot in the back. And what about that?! He is too hurt to be questioned. You are convicting a man before he is proven guilty!"

Derek, who was furious over the robbery of his favorite stallion, whirled on his wife. "Explain to me the D&M horse, Miranda. Why in hell was a D&M horse used tonight if not by the thieves on an inside job? If Shoz is innocent, then he'll be free. But with his alleged record, we can't *not* ask him questions!"

"I am sure the thieves took the third man with them, Derek. Let this man sleep in peace!" Miranda shot back.

"We can't wait, ma'am," the sheriff said. "Not if we ever want to get that stud back."

Derek turned on Shoz, who had rolled onto his side to

watch them. "You a wanted man, Shoz?" he demanded. "You steal my horse?"

Lucy realized her cheeks were wet with tears. "Sheriff Sanders?"

"I didn't steal your horse," Shoz said, low. Sweat streaked his face, but he stared at Derek unflinchingly. "I tried . . . I tried to stop them."

Lucy wiped her eyes. He was lying, and she knew it. "Sheriff?"

Sanders looked at her. So did Shoz. She could not meet his gaze. She could barely breathe, much less speak. "What is it, honey?"

She took a gulp of air. "I—I didn't tell you exactly what I saw."

Derek had relaxed; now he whirled. "What?"

Shoz made a sound. His eyes blazed.

"I was looking for Shoz—to talk to him. It took me a while to find him." She was crying. Grace handed her a handkerchief. Her father had come into the room to stare at her; everyone was staring at her. She knew she had to tell the truth—but why was it ripping her heart out to do so? "He wasn't at the party. He was alone. At the barn."

Everyone waited, silent and grim. "Go on," Derek said.

She darted a glance at Shoz. His eyes blazed hotter than hell. She looked away, dabbing at her tears with the linen. She couldn't tell the rest of it, she couldn't.

Rathe put his arm around her. "Tell us what happened, honey," he said, very softly and very gently.

"Two riders came out of the barn with your stud," Lucy cried. "Shoz ran inside—and a second later, he came out, too, on the saddled horse—and he galloped after them."

A stunned silence fell, then Rathe broke it. "Honey, you said he ran after the thieves."

"I didn't tell the truth," Lucy managed, crying.

Derek looked at Shoz, long and hard. Sheriff Sanders gestured to his men. "Cuff him."

Shoz's eyes widened, and he weakly started to push up onto all fours. But then a deputy was shoving him down, another one yanking his hands behind his back, forcing him face-first into the pillow. Gleaming steel cuffs were snapped on.

"You are under arrest, boy," Sanders said, "and be warned, we got long, stiff sentences for horse thieves in these parts."

Shoz tilted his head up so he could stare back at the sheriff. Coldly, expressionlessly. "I've lived through hell once, Sheriff," he said. "I can live through it again."

PART TWO

THE LOST ANGELS

DEATH VALLEY, MEXICO

16

Lucy knew she shouldn't go.

Ten days had passed since Shoz's arrest. He had remained at the house the first few days, under guard, until he was well enough to be moved to the Paradise jail. Lucy had not gone near him; she had not dared.

She would never forget the look of hatred in his eyes after Sheriff Sanders's deputies had cuffed him—and it was directed at her.

The horse theft had provided an unpleasant and abrupt ending to the party. However, none of the out-of-town guests had been inconvenienced by it, as all had their plans to continue on afterward and were able to do so. Derek had decided that none of his guests need be detained for questioning as far as the shooting was concerned; Sanders agreed and concentrated on the local population.

Leon's departure was a relief. He left immediately after the party, as he had intended. He had been cool and distant when they parted, but Lucy had barely noticed.

Derek's stallion had finally been found. The posse had tracked the two bandits north into the Llanos Estacado and east to Abilene. Thunder had been recovered from a businessman who had bought the stallion from two men who fit the descriptions of Red Ames and Jake Holt. Most of the posse had returned to Paradise. Brett's two sons had returned to San Francisco with their families, unable to leave the D'Archand empire unattended. But Derek, Nick, Rathe, and Brett had continued on. Unable to find Red and Jake or two other men resembling them in Abilene they had just returned a few days ago.

Shoz was in jail awaiting trial. The reply to Sheriff Sand-

ers's inquiry had come back affirmative: Shoz was wanted
by the New York State authorities for escaping the state
penitentiary seven years ago. He would be tried first in the
Paradise County court for horse theft and maybe even murder; if found guilty, he would serve time in the Texas State
lockup before being returned East to finish his sentence
there.

It was so unbelievable.

Lucy knew she should not go to see him.

She had heard that he was better. He was still confined
to bed, but each day he got up for fifteen minutes or so to
exercise, under supervision. Doc Jones had prescribed the
routine. Everyone had been waiting for Doc to give the go-
ahead to move him to Odessa, where the county court sat.

Tomorrow they were taking Shoz to Odessa.

And it was her fault. There was no reason to feel guilty,
but she did.

No matter how often she reminded herself that he was a
felon, and that he had betrayed her grandfather by accepting
employment from him and then stealing his horse—and
maybe even killing a man—she felt guilty for her part in
turning him in. Lucy believed in justice, of course, but she
wished it had been someone other than herself who had
revealed that he had been working with the thieves.

She tried not to brood. It was difficult being at the D&M
with all the women of the family—they were all too sensitive
and too aware. Eyes. Lucy was always feeling their eyes
on her. Her mother, her grandmother. Her aunt Storm. Even
her aunt Jane, who was so sweet and kind, who seemed to
bring sunshine into the room with her whenever she entered,
gazed at her with worry. And then there was Nicole.

"What is it?" she demanded the day they'd moved Shoz
to the Paradise jail. "What is wrong with you!"

The two girls were clad in knickers and tailored shirtwa-
ists after a game of badminton. They were sipping lemonade
on the back veranda. No one else was around. As usual, it
was unbearably hot.

Lucy looked at Nicole. What would her dear cousin say
if she knew the truth—all of it? Lucy had the insane urge
to tell her everything. But she would be shocked. Lucy

herself was shocked whenever she dared to dwell too precisely upon her memories and the facts. She had let an escaped convict make love to her.

"It's him. I know it's him." Nicole's voice was low. "Lucy, don't. Don't think about him. You said it to me and I'll say it to you: He is not for you!"

"Of course not," Lucy said with a weak smile. "Can you imagine me bringing someone like that home to Daddy—even if he weren't a crook?"

"No, I can't."

"It's not what you're thinking, Nicole." Lucy set her glass down. "He hates me."

"It doesn't matter," Nicole said firmly.

"You know," Lucy said, her voice shaky, "he isn't entirely responsible for what he is. He's a product of his background, his environment. Maybe his father was a drunk who beat him. My mother says—" her voice cracked "—that most of the down-and-out are born into very bad circumstances with three strikes against them."

"You're starting to sound like Grace," Nicole said with a slight smile. "Lucy, what's between you two?"

Lucy inhaled. She looked at her cousin. She looked around; they were completely alone. "He kissed me—more than once."

Nicole wasn't shocked. Instead, she sounded wistful. "I've never been kissed, not even once."

Lucy stared at her gorgeous cousin in shock.

"Did you like it?"

She flushed. She leaned close. "Yes, that's the worst part; I did, I really did!"

Nicole left her wistful thoughts behind. "Lucy, just forget him. If he wasn't a thief and a felon, I would ask if you loved him. But he is a very bad sort."

"Of course I don't love him! I actually dislike him immensely." At Nicole's wide-eyed surprise, she blushed again. "I can't explain it. I just wish I hadn't been the one to see him riding out of the barn; I just wish I could find out more about him, what he did in New York, and why. Maybe he was starving! Maybe it was food he stole, or maybe he was homeless, and maybe it was blankets! Nicole, maybe it was the depression that made him an outlaw.''

Nicole squinted. ''Lucy. The crash wasn't until ninety-three, and he was incarcerated in eighty-nine.''

Joanna appeared, and Nicole adroitly changed the topic. But the subject wasn't over for Lucy, far from it. She felt compelled to go see him. She fought the compulsion for the next week. But then the family was notified that they were moving him on the morrow to Odessa. It was now or never. There was so much about him she didn't know, and she was suddenly determined to unearth the whole story. And she had been the one to put him in jail, so to speak. The least she could do was appease her conscience by checking on his health before he was transferred to the county seat. Lucy commandeered a horse and buggy, and alone, she drove to Paradise to see him.

Her parents would be furious if they knew, she thought nervously. Yet nothing could deter her now. For the outing she had dressed with care in one of her finest tailor-mades, a navy skirt and matching jacket with wide leg-o'-mutton sleeves. A straw hat shaded her flushed face, and a wicker basket was tucked by her hip—carefully packed by herself. She was bringing him his noontime meal.

Lucy cracked the whip, and the dappled mare trotted smartly into town. It was hot and humid and she was damp beneath her traveling suit. She parked the buggy right in front of the jail. There was no point in trying to hide her visit from anyone. The deputy on duty would know, of course, so the sheriff would know, and sooner or later all of Paradise would know, including her family. No matter. She would deal with that problem when it arose.

She entered the sheriff's office. A big ceiling fan circulated the thick, wet air, doing little to alleviate anyone's misery. The deputy, a tall, young man with a droopy mustache, shot to his feet. ''Miss Bragg!''

''Why, hello, Fred; how are you this fine day?'' She was gay.

Fred stared stunned at the basket she carried, no doubt thinking it was for him. ''Why, uh, fine, Miss Bragg, and you?''

"Very well, thank you. I decided the prisoner needed a proper lunch," she continued, ignoring his surprise. "How is he?"

Fred recovered. "Real quiet. Stays in bed and doesn't say anything. You can't go in there with him, Miss Bragg."

"Whyever not?"

"Well—" Fred grew redder "—he's a dangerous criminal, that's why."

"Pooh! He stole a horse, is all! Have you forgotten that this 'dangerous criminal' escorted me and my friend to Paradise when our automobile broke down? We spent half a day with him, and no harm befell us!"

"Well, yeah, but really . . ."

"Fred, do I have to ask the sheriff for permission to bring the prisoner lunch and some good cheer? Are we barbarians? To treat a man not yet judged guilty in a court of law as a leper, or worse? As some crazed dog, not to be allowed human kindness and company?

"Besides—" Lucy smiled prettily "—Grandpa said it was all right." It was only a white lie, she told herself, and it was an effective one.

Fred gave in, crimson. Lucy hadn't known she had so much of her mother in her. She guessed that going to all those women's suffrage and Negro rights rallies as a child had had its influence on her. Fred pushed through the door to the prison in back.

It was just a hallway, with two cells on each side. Shoz was the only prisoner, and he was lying on his stomach, his head on his arms. He didn't move at the sound of the heavy door closing. But when Lucy followed Fred down the short corridor, her heels clicking loudly on the cement floor, Shoz turned his head to look at them. His gaze widened—and then it narrowed.

"You've got a visitor," Fred announced. He paused. "You sure you want to go in? You can just leave him his lunch if you want."

"I'm going in," Lucy said firmly. "Grandpa said—"

"Okay." Fred sighed. "You got a knife in there?"

Lucy was looking at Shoz, who hadn't taken his gaze from her. Slowly he sat up, swinging his legs to the floor.

There was such contempt on his face, she was almost ready to change her mind and run out of the jailhouse.

"A knife?" She was confused and forced her attention back to the deputy. "Oh, why, of course there is a knife."

Fred requested it, and Lucy handed him a silver dinner knife from Tiffany's. Fred unlocked the cell and let her in. "Behave yourself," he admonished Shoz.

Absolute silence greeted her.

Lucy entered, biting her lip. She was suddenly so nervous. And she was very aware of Fred standing behind her, just outside the cell. "I brought you some home cooking."

"How nice."

She fumbled with the basket. "A roasted chicken and corn muffins and—"

"I'm not hungry."

She looked up. Their glances held. His seared her. "Shoz . . ."

"Feeling guilty?"

"I had to tell the truth!"

"The truth? Oh, you didn't tell the truth, lady, not by a long shot."

Lucy was taken aback. He would still feign innocence? Could he be innocent? No, she had been there, she knew exactly what she had seen. "Shoz, I didn't come here to argue."

"Why did you come? To gloat? The little princess happy with her revenge?"

"No!"

His fists clenched. "Go on home to your powerful daddy, princess. Just go."

"It wasn't revenge!" she cried.

"If it wasn't revenge, then why were you so quick to accuse *me*? Why the hell didn't you ask *me* what I was doing?"

"I know what I saw! You were waiting at the barn—the horse was saddled and waiting for you! I had to reveal what I knew; can't you understand?"

Shoz stared. "What you think you knew."

"What are you saying?"

A hard expression crossed his face. "Forget it."

Lucy recovered with effort. "I've brought you lunch." He laughed.

"I know you probably haven't had a decent meal," she said, sitting on the end of the cot, placing the basket on her lap. She opened it. Her heart was pounding heavily and fast. It had been a mistake to come. She was more upset than ever. She was feeling more guilty than ever. And she could feel the heat of his body, even though she had left a decent space between them. And she could feel his anger.

"Deputy or no," Shoz said, low, "I am about a second from throttling you if you don't get out of here."

Lucy froze. She believed him. He hated her, but of course, he wouldn't see her side of things. He was barely restraining himself from doing some kind of damage, no matter that he was sick. She couldn't swallow; fear choked her. He hated her. He wanted to hurt her. He would hurt her, too, if she pressed her luck. She shifted, about to rise.

And the movement made something in the basket glint.

Too late, Lucy remembered there was also a carving knife in the basket for the roast chicken. Swiftly she reached to snap shut the lid of the basket.

But he saw it, too, and he was faster.

Shoz's hand was already inside, gripping the knife. He looked at it, and then, for an instant, an endless instant, while they were both frozen in time, he looked at her—and Lucy saw the intent in his eyes.

She screamed, rising.

He was quicker, also on his feet, the basket flying across the floor and all its contents spilling. And then his arm was around her rib cage, so tight and hard, he forced all the air from her lungs in a gasp, and the knife was at her throat.

"Don't move," he snarled. "Or I'm going to slit your pretty white throat."

17

"Don't move," Shoz repeated.

Lucy froze. Her entire body was pressed against his. His grasp was steel, his arm hurting her breasts, his breath against her ear. She could feel the tip of the knife against her throat, and she was afraid.

"Jesus," Fred gasped, gun in hand. "Let her go!"

Shoz smiled. "You might be a good enough shot to hit me," he said, "and not Lucy, but I doubt it."

Lucy gave a little cry. Fred went even whiter, and Shoz jerked on Lucy to remind her to be still.

"Let me warn you," he said coolly, "I'm Apache through and through. You fire, and this blade is going right through her jugular vein."

Lucy moaned. The pressure of his arm increased, cutting off the sound and her minute attempt to struggle.

"Jesus," Fred said again, sweat dripping down his brow.

Lucy pleaded with him. "Don't do it! Fred, don't, please, don't!"

Fred was unsure, and it showed.

"Drop the gun," Shoz ordered, moving forward with Lucy still in front of him, her body almost entirely shielding his. He hustled her through the cell doorway, Fred backing up until he was against the bars of the opposite cell, but still holding the gun. "Drop it!" Shoz commanded harshly. "Drop it, right here, at my feet!"

"Shit!" Fred cried.

Lucy felt the increasing pressure of the blade at her throat, then the pricking of pain, and she gasped. The knife had cut her skin, and she felt the moisture of her own blood. "Drop it," she begged. "He cut me, drop it!"

"Oh my God," Fred gasped, and he dropped the gun.

Suddenly Shoz threw Lucy aside, so hard she went stumbling to the floor, while he lunged for the gun. He was so swift, he had it pointed at Fred a scant instant later. Lucy was on her hands and knees at Shoz's feet, panting. "Hands up!" Shoz said.

Fred complied with alacrity. Lucy sat on the floor and felt her neck. There was no outpouring of blood. She wiped away the moisture—and saw nothing but sweat.

Shoz grabbed Fred, throwing him into the cell. With his gun pointed at Fred's chest, Shoz said to Lucy, "Come here."

Lucy froze.

"Come here!"

She got up, her heart pounding. He was going to lock her in the cell with Fred. He was going to lock them up and escape!

Wildly her gaze swung around, searching for a weapon or something to hit him with. Yet even as she did so, she knew it would be futile and foolish to attack him while he was watching her and waiting for her.

She came slowly, her mind desperately seeking a means of escape, a way to thwart him. No solution presented itself. With a low growl of impatience, he grabbed her arm, yanking her forward. The gun he aimed at Fred never wavered. Lucy cried out at his manhandling. He ignored her, delving into the breast pocket of her jacket. He took her handkerchief and forcefully stuffed it into Fred's mouth. Then he shoved Fred onto the bunk.

Lucy, of course, edged away, until her back made contact with the iron bars of the cell.

Shoz jammed the gun in the waistband of his jeans, grabbing the sheet from the bed and jerking it off. Swiftly he cut the linen into strips. Lucy understood—he was going to tie them up. Fred was immobilized with fear—and at Shoz's elbow anyway. Too close to do anything, but . . .

Lucy knew she had to act, and act now.

But how? There was nothing to hit him with. Wildly she glanced around, her gaze scanning the spilled contents of the picnic basket, the roasted chicken, a few plates, the scattered muffins and napkins. And then in the corner of the cell only four feet from her, she saw the lead crystal pitcher that she'd brought filled with lemonade. She pounced.

Shoz had already bound Fred's wrists behind his back and was rapidly wrapping a linen strip around his ankles. As hard as she could, Lucy swung the jug down on his head.

Instinct made him duck and turn before she made contact. His hand found her wrist, forcing her to release the pitcher. It hit the floor with a crash and broke. Lucy cried out in despair and pain as he forced her to her knees. "Sit!" he commanded, and turned back to Fred.

Acting on pure instinct, she leapt up and fled instead, hearing his curses behind her. She ran down the hall and threw open the door to the sheriff's office. She heard him ordering her to stop. She heard the metal clanging of the cell door being shut. She was through the sheriff's office, and she heard his footsteps behind her.

She grasped the front door, flinging it open hysterically. She opened her mouth to scream. No sound ever came out. He grabbed her from behind, hauling her back inside, slamming the door shut, and clamping his hand over her mouth. She bit him as hard as she could.

"Dammit!" he yelled, and then a strip of linen was stuffed in her mouth.

Lucy fought him every step of the way. He dragged her with him back through the office, taking Fred's rifle, which was propped up against the desk. Because he was, apparently, still injured, it was a real contest. He pulled her, while she was braking as hard as she could. They were both panting hoarsely, and sweat dripped from his brow onto her cheek.

At the door to the jail cells, he stopped, jerking her body up even closer to his, so he could snarl in her ear: "Either you start moving, or I'm going to hurt you."

Lucy moved. He propelled her and she ran. She didn't doubt for a moment that he'd hurt her; she sensed he was at the limit of his patience. They ran into the prison. Fred was hog-tied and gagged and locked in Shoz's cell. Lucy expected Shoz to throw her inside with him. She was stunned when he hauled her out the back door instead, into the shadows of the alley outside.

Wild thoughts went screaming through her mind, impossible ones. Why hadn't he left her behind, in the cell with Fred? Where was he taking her? She stumbled as they raced down the alley, away from Bragg Avenue with its steady stream of carriages, buckboards, and passersby. He held her upright. Hysterical fear filled Lucy. She realized he was going to use her as a hostage to help him escape from town. There was no other explanation, was there? A hostage . . . a hostage . . . The word was imprinted on each hard beat of her heart.

But surely he would let her go as soon as he made good his escape! Wouldn't he? She looked back toward Bragg Avenue, where there were so many people going about their business, all oblivious to the drama being played out in the small, shady alley between the false-fronted buildings. If only someone would notice them!

They ran down the length of the alley until they came to the next street. They paused behind some garbage cans, waiting for a dray to pass, regaining their breath. Across from them was a smith, a metalworker, a tailor, and a German cabinetmaker. So was a horse, saddled and tied in front of the blacksmith's.

"Just my luck," Shoz said.

Lucy darted a glance at him, to see if he was being earnest or snide, but she could not tell. She understood, though. He would steal the horse, the one, single horse, so this was where they would part. From here he could escape without her. She would only slow him down; she would only be a liability. Her heart soared, and if she hadn't been gagged, she would have shouted in relief.

The dray passed. With a half smile, one hard but triumphant, Shoz darted across the street—and dragged Lucy with him. Before she knew it, he had thrown her on the bay gelding and was leaping up behind her. And then they were galloping down another alley—and out of town.

They did not slow down or stop until they had put a few hills and gorges and a good ten miles between them and

Paradise. Lucy tried to protest at first, which was no easy feat with the gag; before she could remove it, he had tied it in place. He ignored her. If they hadn't been going so fast and his grip on her hadn't been so firm, she would have tried to leap off. Her mind was in a frenzy. Why had he taken her with him? Why had he abducted her? Why?

It did not make sense. He should have left her in town. He could go faster and farther alone. He no longer needed her. Unbidden, the sarcastic words he'd hurled at her in the cell echoed in her mind: "Happy with your revenge?"

Revenge. There was no other logical explanation. And revenge wasn't logical. It was a deed of passion. It was horrible, it was ugly, it was terrifying. He was an escaped convict, a horse thief, an accomplice to murder—or maybe even a murderer. Lucy was trembling.

An hour later he urged the lathered bay into a stream bed. They had been heading west. He jumped off, pulling Lucy down as well. She nearly collapsed in his arms.

He pushed her away from him with a hard, uncompromising expression on his face. She caught herself from falling again and looked at him. Their gazes met. He was pale beneath his bronzed skin, his soft blue shirt completely soaked and sticking to his skin. Lucy stood beside him, knee-deep in the stream, despairing and afraid to move. Yet his gaze was steady, not the gaze of a crazed killer seeking vengeance.

He didn't make any moves toward her. Her heart slowed, and some of the stiffness left her shoulders. Cautiously, her hands unsteady, Lucy reached for the gag. This was the first chance she had had to remove it since he had bound it. As she fumbled with the knot, her eyes never left him. Her heart sank when he abruptly grabbed her hands, but he only turned her around and deftly released the gag.

Lucy took great big lungfuls of air, aware of him behind her, aware, for just a moment, of his thighs brushing her buttocks before he stepped away. And then she was cupping the cool water in her hands and pouring it into her mouth. Never had she been thirstier in her life.

When she was sated, she splashed her face and looked for her kerchief to dry herself, only to remember that he had used it to gag Fred. This made her straighten slowly, stiffly, listening for him behind her. He was utterly silent—she could only hear the horse blowing softly. Lucy turned so she could look at him.

He was watering their mount, stroking the bay's sweaty neck. He lifted his gaze to catch her staring, and she abruptly turned away. Her soaking skirts were heavy around her legs, and she regretted the layers of clothing she wore. She pretended not to look at him but knew that he was filling their canteen. This moment of respite had done much to calm Lucy's shattered nerves. She had to face him sooner or later. There was a question she must ask—no matter how much she dreaded hearing his answer.

"You ready?"

She moved about awkwardly to face him, dragging her skirts with her. His tone was weary, and he was leaning against the bay's flank—as if too tired to stand upright without support.

Lucy stared. He had been shot ten days ago. How long could he keep up this pace? Would he kill himself? If he was very weak . . .

"Don't start thinking," he said. "Or planning."

"Where are you taking me?"

He levered himself off the horse and took her arm and the horse's reins, leading them downstream. "I advise you to shed that skirt, princess. Let's go."

He hadn't answered; instead, he was pushing her forward, into the shallower water by the bank. Still, it came to mid-calf, making it impossible to walk with her skirt and petticoats twisting around her ankles and calves. She stumbled forward, and then balked. "Please, Shoz! I have a right to know!"

He paused and leaned against the horse. "Why did you take me?" Lucy cried. "It doesn't make sense!"

"Damned if I know," he muttered. He was sure that taking her with him was going to prove to be a big mistake.

"What?"

"Let's just say you're my ticket out of here."

"You're already free! Leave me here! I'll just slow you down! Please! You don't need me anymore!"

For the past half hour he had been asking himself what the hell he was doing abducting Lucy Bragg. He should have left her in Paradise, and he knew it. She would slow him down. Yet he hadn't exactly been thinking when he'd abducted her, he had been acting. With an instinct, a primitive, territorial instinct as old as time.

He saw her white face and her stricken blue eyes and told himself he was an utter jackass if he let himself feel sorry for her. There was only one person he should be thinking about, and that was himself. He was a fool. Her being a pretty piece was no reason for him to abduct her, nor was revenge, not when the stakes were so high. His life, his freedom. He should leave her here. He could probably escape the posse that was certainly being formed this very minute. If he weren't weak from the gunshot wound, he knew without a doubt that he could escape across the border. But he was weak, and he did have doubts.

"Let me go, Shoz," she was saying. "It's not too late to let me go!"

"I'm taking you with me to the border," he decided abruptly. Just in case the posse caught up with him on this side of the Rio Grande.

"The border! Mexico? You're going to Mexico?"

"I sure as hell don't mean Louisiana."

"And then you'll let me go?"

He eyed her. Her face was wet with sweat, her hair mostly up, but a few tangled knots had come down to straggle around her face. She was wet up to her armpits, her jacket open—he had to enjoy just for a moment, how her shirt clung to whatever newfangled contraption she wore beneath it. Too bad he wasn't in better shape. Too bad they were in such a rush. Too bad. Despite the betrayal, despite her lies, despite her revenge—he wouldn't mind finishing their business, and taking some of his own revenge.

But his back hurt like hell.

"Yes," he said. And knew he was more than just a fool. Not for making the promise, but for feeling regret.

"Yes!" she echoed, stumbling on her skirts for the hundredth time.

Quick as a wink, he had the carving knife in hand—and

he sliced off her skirt and petticoats at the knee.

She gasped, staring down at her white-stockinged calves and at the delicate lace ruffles of the hem of her drawers just below her knees.

"Let's go," he growled. He'd seen her legs before. Still, they were great legs.

She looked up at him, her eyes wide and stunned.

"Just walk," he said, pushing her on.

She walked.

And his mind was made up. He would keep her until they got to Mexico and had crossed the border. She would be his insurance, his ticket to freedom. And then he would get rid of her. Send her home, or to the nearest town. But until then, she would keep the Braggs and half the Texas militia from stretching his neck. She would be a bargaining chip if they managed to catch him.

He hoped.

Her safety, for his freedom.

18

They hadn't stopped to rest, not once.

Since they had left the stream bed hours ago, they had trekked across rock flats and through narrow desert gorges. The going had been so rough for a while that they had both walked, Shoz pushing on ahead of Lucy, leading the horse, Lucy stumbling after him. Now, hours later, it was twilight. They were both astride the horse, and had been for some time, heading south through an endless stretch of sage-studded desert. For the first time, Lucy glimpsed a stand of saguaro.

She felt anew the welling of despair. They had been traveling since midmorning; surely the posse chasing them would never catch them now. They were far from Paradise, far from the ranch. The Mexican border must be very close. And when they crossed it? Would he really leave her? And what about tonight? Were they ever going to stop?

She couldn't go on. She just couldn't. Her body was bruised; every part of it ached. She knew that if she did dismount, she would barely be able to walk. "Shoz! We have to stop—I can't continue another moment like this! I need a rest!"

"Soon."

Lucy gripped the pommel, hard. She had exercised the utmost self-discipline and until now hadn't asked him to stop, not once. But now her pride was in shreds. She was hot and sweaty, sticky and oh so dirty, but mostly, she was exhausted and she desperately wanted to rest. On impulse, she suddenly threw her leg over the pommel and slid to the ground.

To her horror, her knees gave out and she collapsed in a heap in the sand.

The horse kept going, as if Shoz were oblivious to her disappearance. A few yards past her, he pulled to a halt. Lucy looked up at him with a stifled sob. He sat very still, slouched, gazing down at her. For the first time in hours, she saw his face and his eyes, and she was shocked. There was no interest in his expression there, nothing vital at all. There was only blank indifference as he regarded her, and he was whiter than a sheet. She had ceased sweating at sundown, but sweat poured off his face, actually dripping from his chin.

He looked ill.

Lucy forced herself up.

He made a sound, and turned the horse slowly around. The bay plodded back to her. Lucy bit her lip.

"Get up," he said.

Lucy stared. He was ill, most likely with fever, and she was almost certain she could escape—either on foot or, later, by stealing the horse. She hesitated, filled with the immense possibility confronting her.

"Lucy."

She gnawed her lip, then approached. "Let's stop," she said. "Please."

He nodded once and slowly slid off the gelding. He paused there, leaning against the animal's flank.

Lucy trembled. He was hurt; he needed rest and someone's care. It was obvious. But her chance for escape was imminent. She didn't go to him.

He tied the horse to a stunted mesquite. Lucy watched, not moving. He uncinched the girth, pulled the saddle off, and its weight as he placed it on the ground nearly brought him down on top of it. He slid down beside the tack, leaning back on it. His gaze found hers.

Lucy stood very still, wetting her lips. This was her chance. She was a good rider, and as a child, she'd ridden bareback every summer, so the lack of a saddle was no deterrent. She would jump on the horse and head north, straight north.

And leave him here alone, on foot, too sick to even move, much less walk.

He would probably die. Lucy doubted the sheriff would find him, not the way he'd kept to stream beds and rock flats, not the way he'd swept their trail clean with brush. She was certain the sheriff would never track this man, who seemed to be well versed in the art of hiding his trail. Instead, he would stay here, alone, and die.

Just for a moment his gaze was lucid as it searched hers, and Lucy was certain that he knew she was thinking about escape. But then he dropped his head, eyes closed, and began to sleep.

Now she could go.

She didn't.

In that precise moment, she made up her mind, more the fool she. She could not leave him alone, on foot, to die. She could not. He was a thief, yes, and maybe a murderer, but there hadn't been a trial and there hadn't been a conviction. To use Nicole's words, he was "a bad sort," but he was a human being. There was no doubt in Lucy's mind that she was crazy not to take advantage of his condition, but she just couldn't. He had abducted her, but he hadn't hurt her. Besides he had said that he would let her go once they crossed the border—and the border had to be less than a day's ride from here. Tonight she could not leave him alone.

She dropped to her knees beside him, studying him and reaching for the canteen. "Go easy," he said.

Taken by surprise, she almost dropped their precious water. His eyes were still closed; he appeared to be asleep. Lucy flushed. To think she had almost abandoned him, sure that he was incognizant of his surroundings.

"No water until tomorrow," he added without moving.

Lucy handed him the canteen. He took it and drank a few sips. Lucy removed it from his hands and took a long drink. She touched his forehead to check his fever. His eyes flew open, startled. He was warm, but she couldn't be sure if it was a low temperature or not, and that in itself was a good sign.

She rummaged in the saddlebags, found a few tins of beef and beans and some jerky, and forced him to accept the latter. He ate without interest, his eyes closed, but she ate hungrily. All the while she watched him. He slept deeply.

Exhaustion overcame Lucy, too. She stretched out beside him, on her side, her cheek on her arm. The ground was hard and uncomfortable, and without a blanket or pillow, she was sure she would never be able to sleep, especially when she began to worry about her family, and how they must be reacting to her abduction. But she was so fatigued, sleep came instantly. Some time later she woke up, cold and shivering. A thousand stars glittered overhead, an owl hooted, and she could hear Shoz's even, deep breathing beside her. She was still exhausted, and without giving it much thought, she crept close to him and curled next to his big body, almost but not quite touching him, just for his warmth. This time sleep did not come so easily.

Shoz woke up when the sun was almost high in the sky, with Lucy in his arms.

He blinked. Her body was spooned into his, her buttocks nestled in his groin, and his arms were around her, his mouth against the nape of her neck. What the hell! He searched his mind, trying to remember just what they had done last night. It took him a moment to become fully awake. They hadn't done anything—he had been exhausted from the long, hard day. It was just that he had never woken up with a woman in his arms before, and the assumption had been automatic.

She felt good. He craned his neck to look at her. He should have smiled, or even laughed, but he didn't. She was a mess. Miss Lucy Bragg had a propensity for looking better than any woman he knew—or worse. Now was one of those times when she looked as bad as a woman could. She was dirty, from the tip of her nose right down to her pretty little stockinged feet.

But somehow, she was sexy as hell. Worse, she felt sexy as hell.

He was aware of the beginnings of arousal, meaning he had slept well and replenished his body's strength during the night. If they didn't have such a long day coming up . . . He sighed. If he messed with her now, he would be in a helluvalot more trouble than he already was.

It was a grim thought. The first thing the Braggs would want to know when they got Lucy back was if he had touched her. Lucy wasn't a liar. She wouldn't cry rape out of spite, and he sure as hell wasn't going to give her a better reason. As tempting as she was, he'd keep his hands to himself.

As he got up, thoughts came rushing back to him. One demanded priority, and as he saddled and fed the horse, he turned to look at her, this time with no need to disguise either the interest or the curiosity he was feeling. Last night she could have left him. Either on foot or with the horse. But she hadn't.

He inhaled sharply. His heart was beating as hard as if he'd run a race. Why hadn't she left him? Because she was afraid to try and return to Paradise through this desolate land alone? Lucy might be a spoiled princess, but she had grit, obstinacy, and she also had courage. Her grit was real, although mostly untested; her determination was like a mule's, what little he'd seen of it; but her courage came from ignorance and naïveté. She wouldn't consider the hardship of traveling north without him for a moment, she would just do it, spurred on by desperation and determination. Fear of hardship wouldn't stop her from escaping him.

Then why?

He finished saddling the horse and eyed her. The question was too immense; there were possibilities that actually caused a roiling in his gut. *Damn! Damn* her! He decided he didn't care why she hadn't left him, there were many possibilities. Maybe she couldn't ride bareback, maybe she'd just been too damn tired. Or maybe from this particular trial and tribulation, she had learned some common sense and was afraid of riding north alone. Hell! What did he care anyway?

He poked her with his booted toe. "Get up."

There was a faint reponse, the fluttering of her lashes, a groan.

He poked her again. "We're riding out, Lucy."

She blinked at him. He had to admire her calves, being given a birds'-eye view. He saw the moment she became fully awake. Her blue eyes widened with total awareness and she sat up. She looked at him very, very warily. Then she stiffly got to her feet, biting back a moan—but he heard it anyway. She shook out her tattered skirts. "I need to freshen up."

He knew what she meant. "Go behind that stand of saguaro," he directed. "And be careful."

She nodded and walked away. Shoz began erasing the signs of their camp with a big piece of brush. She was surprising him again. A good night's sleep had done a helluvalot to calm her. He was appreciative; he didn't need to be burdened with a hysterical woman right now. It seemed like they had attained a wary, if temporary, truce.

Night had fallen. Lucy sat with her arms around her knees, and her short skirt pulled carefully over her legs, watching him. He had made a small fire, and the smell of the meat and beans he had cooked was almost too much to bear.

Today had been even longer and more grueling than yesterday. Lucy was too tired to move. Shoz was also exhausted; she could see it in his every movement, she could see it in the drawn lines of his face. But he wasn't as bad off as he had been last night—she could see that, too. The man's resilience was amazing.

She couldn't go another step, much less ride; her body was screaming in protest, her muscles were tortured, and she was starving. She could fend off sleep only until after the meal. She suspected that waking up tomorrow would be a whole lot harder than it had been today.

He picked up the pan and brought it to her, their glances meeting. In anticipation, Lucy had to smile; he smiled, also. He sank down beside her. "Sorry we don't have any china, princess."

"Next time," Lucy quipped, making him regard her steadily. She quickly looked away, unnerved for some reason. His hostility was easier to bear than such a direct, searching look.

He handed her the fork that had been in the saddlebag along with the tins, taking the spoon himself, and they both ate ravenously, from the same pan.

When they had finished, Shoz took the pan to the stream and filled it with water. Lucy felt a twinge of guilt. She didn't know how to cook, but . . . he was doing everything. She hadn't helped at all.

She watched him carefully as he set the pan full of water on the fire, which he stoked higher. He let it boil. After a few minutes he removed it and emptied it, dousing the fire thoroughly. With his toe he kicked apart the charred embers, burying them with dirt. Then he stuck the pan into the saddlebag.

Lucy vowed to remember everything he had done.

He returned to sit next to her. Suddenly Lucy became aware of the intimacy between them—and the potential. They were both alone and awake in the middle of the night in the middle of nowhere. Unlike last night, when Shoz had been so exhausted that he had immediately gone to sleep. Her heart began to race. Instead of remembering his abducting her yesterday, she recalled the week he'd been at the ranch, in a series of rapid, vivid images. Shoz shelling peas in the kitchen, so big and dangerously masculine among the women there, and looking as if he felt ridiculous. Shoz standing on a chair pulling down drapes, in his tight, worn Levis. She remembered being unable to sleep, night after night, because of the humidity and heat, tossing and turning, her nightgown sticking to her body. She remembered going to the window and seeing him there on the lawn by the swing, smoking, the tip of his cigarette glowing, as he gazed up at her window.

"Sheriff Sanders make any progress on his investigation?"

"What?" He'd broken into her thoughts.

He repeated the question.

"They found the stud in Abilene," Lucy began, but he cut her off.

"I know about the damn horse. A man was shot—who happens to be me—but the whole goddamn town is up in arms about your granddaddy's horse."

Lucy stared at him, realizing how horribly right he was. "No. Not that I know of."

"You see anyone that night when you came to meet me?"

Lucy didn't bother to correct him—she hadn't been on her way to meet him, just searching for him. "No one. But someone else must have seen what I saw, and thought you were one of the thieves. People in Paradise don't like horse stealing much."

"Try again." His tone was mocking. "If some good Samaritan shot me thinking I was one of the thieves, then why didn't he—or she—come forward and claim the deed?"

Lucy looked at him. He was stretched out comfortably on the ground, his hands resting under his head, propped up on the saddle. His shirt was open, his dark skin glistening from his throat to just above his navel where it was exposed. Lucy wished he would button it. "I guess someone was afraid to come forward."

"Damn right."

His tone was so hard that Lucy stared at him. "You know who did it, don't you!"

"I've got a good guess."

"Who?"

His mouth curled. "Your boyfriend's mama."

"Marianne Claxton!"

He eased back on the saddle.

"You're insane!" Lucy stared at his chiseled profile. "Why would she shoot you?"

He grinned at the night. "We were friends in New York. Let's just say it ended badly—and we both hold mean grudges."

"Friends in New York!" Lucy was stunned. It was a long moment before she could assimilate this information. "You mean . . . lovers?"

"Why are you so shocked? Didn't know sweet, proper Marianne has an appetite her husband can't satisfy?"

Lucy was trembling. Shoz and Marianne . . . The thought was terribly upsetting. Marianne was beautiful, but she was older than he was! And in New York! "When were you in New York?"

"Seven years ago."

He didn't offer any more information, and Lucy did not want to know anything else. She was having enough trouble absorbing what she had already learned. At least their affair had been a long time ago. But if Marianne had shot him, passions still ran deep. Did he still love her? "Maybe you're wrong."

He didn't look at her. "Maybe."

"I don't think she would shoot anybody. And a lot of women carry small guns; even I have one. Even gentlemen carry them."

He lit another cigarette. "Where *is* your gun?"

"My gun?"

"Your gun."

"You don't think that I . . ." She stopped in midsentence, too stunned to continue.

"I know you didn't shoot me, princess, even if you wanted to." He grinned. "It wasn't on your person—anywhere."

She felt like slapping him. He would remind her of how his hands had been everywhere, even up under her skirts. "I suppose my gun is where I left it, in the drawer of my bureau." Her tone was cool.

"Don't get all huffy. You were having fun. What do you mean, you think it's in the drawer? You see it that day?"

Lucy had to think. "I put it away when we arrived. I haven't touched it since."

Silence greeted her words. The minutes passed and a shadow crossed the moon. Lucy thought about Shoz and Marianne. It had ended badly. Did he hate her? Marianne Claxton taking a lover—taking Shoz as a lover—it was unbelievable. She was so elegant, the perfect senator's wife.

"Why didn't you take off last night, princess?"

"What?"

"You heard."

Lucy hesitated, groping for a response. "I thought you were dying," she finally said.

He still didn't look at her. "So?"

She looked away, at the stars. "It just didn't seem right," she said lamely. "To leave a dying man."

He turned onto his side. "Come here," he said gruffly.

She lifted her gaze slowly to his.

He wasn't smiling. His face was implacable. He was also much too close for comfort. The night was suddenly very still. "Come here," he repeated, and he pulled her into his arms.

"What are you doing?" Lucy cried, struggling, yet her pulse was racing wildly, her nerves tingling, her skin flushed.

"It's cold."

She was on her back and he was on his side, cradling her. One of his legs covered hers. Impossible yearning swept over her. "Please don't."

"You didn't mind sleeping with me last night," he said, his breath warm on her neck. Delicious tingles ran through her.

"Last night?"

"Last night," he murmured, the sound husky, and she felt his lips on her neck. "You do remember last night, don't you?"

While her body abandoned itself to the rush of wondrous sensations, to the need and desire rising so blatantly, her mind frantically sought to recall last night. Last night? Had something happened last night? Had she slept through it?

His mouth touched the delicate skin of her throat. Lucy

gasped, her last coherent thought being that this was wrong, absolutely wrong, she must not allow this, and while he nibbled there, she felt his hand close over her breast. His palm made lazy, sensual circles. Lucy's eyes closed and she lay very still, letting him touch her.

A moment later she became aware that his hand had paused, that his mouth had paused. Lucy could hear her own harsh breathing and the pounding of her heart. She was afraid to move. It wasn't possible, was it? Very cautiously she turned her head to look at him. "Shoz?"

There was no response. Incredulous, she saw that he was sound asleep. Her head fell back down. She expelled a long, shaky breath of relief—mingled with frustration.

19

Ahead was the Rio Grande.

Lucy wasn't sure how she felt. It was midafternoon and gruelingly hot. They'd been riding at a moderate pace since sunup, without a break. She knew she was very lucky to have her straw hat, and wondered how Shoz could bear to go bareheaded in the heat. He'd cut off one of his shirttails and tied it around his forehead to catch the perspiration before it dripped into his eyes.

They paused on a rise, mounted on the bay. Lucy's heart was pounding. She sat in front of Shoz, as she had whenever they rode, and he had one hard forearm braced around her waist. Sometimes she could feel his breath on her nape, and it was disturbing.

He, too, was silent. What was he thinking?

Was he going to let her go? She thought that promises didn't mean much to an outlaw like Shoz. But he had to let her go. She had to return to Paradise, to her family, who, by now, were probably sick with worry. She had to return. They had reached the border and she had served her purpose. There was no reason for him to take her any farther.

"The Rio," he said, spurring the bay forward.

Lucy was afraid to ask him if he'd keep his word. Afraid of his answer—afraid of a no. Yet was a tiny secret part of her afraid of a yes? Was it possible she could be so foolish?

They cantered into the shallow river. Her stockings had been so torn, she had shed them this morning, and the water splashing up on her barely clad legs was a delight. Lucy clung to the pommel, while Shoz gripped her even more firmly, his body rocking hers with the motion of the horse.

It reminded her of last night. Despite her exhaustion, it had taken her hours to fall asleep. The feel of Shoz's hard, hot body had agitated her and kept her awake. If she hadn't faced it last night, she had to face it today. He had a potent magnetism, and she wasn't unaffected by it. Despite who he was and what he had done, she found him very attractive. If Lucy dared to allow her mind free rein, she would remember the one time they had made love and how unbearably exquisite it had been.

To harbor some kind of feelings for this sort of man was not just wrong, it was shocking.

But her feelings, her little tendresse, if she labeled it such, did not matter. If he kept his word, she would never see him again. Which was, of course, for the best.

The bay scrambled up the far bank. They were in Mexico.

Shoz let the bay drink and then they continued on. Lucy could not get the question out. The longer they rode on, away from the border, the more her sane self grew frightened and upset. Over an hour later, Shoz reined to a halt in the elongated shadows of a stand of huge saguaro. Lucy knew by now that this meant a rest break—or was this where he was leaving her?

She slid off the horse, and deliberately began brushing off her skirts. Was this where they would part? This had to be where he would let her go—it had to be.

He slipped off and drop-reined their mount. He looked at her.

She bit her lip. "Are you going to let me go now?"

His very pale gaze, almost silver in the bright, hot light, held hers steadily. It seemed an eternity passed before he answered. "There's a small town two miles from here."

So he was going to let her go after all!

"Thought me a liar, did you?" His tone was sarcastic.

"No, I . . ." Lucy trailed off. This was as it had to be, and she was glad. Except for that tiny secret part of her. That part of her was confused, even disappointed. Here they would part and never see each other again.

She stared at him standing in front of her, his shirt open almost to his belt buckle, his dark skin slick and shiny. Her gaze drifted to his compact hips in the skin-tight denim. She stared at the white threads of the faded denim of his fly, just for a second. Lucy looked away. He grabbed her shoulder and spun her roughly around.

"Damn you!"

Lucy gasped but didn't move, because he was gripping her shoulders so tightly. Why was he angry? And how come she wasn't frightened at all? He was only inches from her, and she found herself staring at his sensuous mouth.

He cursed and pushed her away from him, pacing restlessly. This time there was no mistaking her disappointment. She had wanted him to kiss her. Ridiculously, her feelings were hurt. Of course, why would he want to kiss her now? Lucy knew she did not look pretty; she was very dirty and remembered only too well how she had looked the last time she had been stranded in the wilderness. She walked to a pile of rocks and sat on a boulder. Her joints ached, and her bare feet were sore in her shoes. She watched him standing with his back to her, his legs braced hard in his jeans. She wondered what would happen to him.

Would he eventually be caught and sent back to prison? Or would he meet his fate at the end of a hangman's rope? Lucy shouldn't care, but she did. She did not want to see him incarcerated, despite Derek's stolen stallion, and she suddenly knew that he had not killed the groom. She felt relief.

He whirled. "You're boring holes in my back."

Lucy managed a laugh. But she didn't look away from him. Her gaze was steady and searching.

It only made him angrier. "Stop looking at me like that, Miss Bragg!"

His snide tone in addressing her hurt her again. "I'm sorry." She stood up.

"Let's get the hell out of here. We've wasted enough time as it is."

He took the bay's reins. Lucy watched him try to stretch, as if to ease the discomfort in his back. The bandage Doc Jones had put on the bullet wound was a visible wad beneath his shirt.

She came forward with determination then. "Shoz, let me look at that."

"Why?"

"Because you're leaving me and you'll be alone and it should be looked at."

He eyed her, then sat down on a rock, unbuttoning his shirt. He pulled it off.

He *was* a magnificent man, Lucy thought, momentarily mesmerized by his sculpted, muscular body. She forced her thoughts elsewhere and unwrapped the binding carefully. It was dusty and dirty on the outside, and when she pulled the gauze packing off, she was glad to see that it was clean on the inside, except for some stains from the antiseptic. The wound was scabbed and apparently healing well. There was no sign of infection.

"It looks good," she said, tossing the bandages to the dirt. Her hand lingered on his shoulder. It felt like smooth, silky hot steel. "Does it hurt?"

"Not now," he said, standing abruptly. "Let's go. The sooner we get to Casitas, the better."

He didn't care that they would never see each other again. But of course, he wouldn't. Lucy reminded herself that he was a lawbreaker, a criminal, apparently a hardened one. He hadn't hurt her, but that was not a good enough reason for her sympathy, and just because she didn't want to see him locked up or hung didn't mean she should forget the facts. They were not here on a picnic. He had abducted her, he was using her.

But the bottom line was that in a few minutes she would never see him again.

They rode to Casitas, and Lucy was aware only of him, of him and her dangerous thoughts. He was the most attractive man she had ever met. The feel of his body behind hers was erotic and sexy. They were never going to see each other again. They had already done it once. And no one had found out.

What she was thinking was wicked, depraved, shocking.

But she *wanted* his kisses, his touch. She wanted his lovemaking more than she'd ever wanted anything, more than the Duryea or anything else. Lucy had never been denied anything she wanted so desperately. It was wrong, but no one would ever have to know.

As another mile passed, she feebly attempted to argue herself out of her intentions. She only succeeded in deciding once and for all to do as she willed and not give it another thought. Having made the decision, she felt a soaring excitement, and she was filled with determination.

"I can feel your thoughts racing," he growled. "What's going on in that red head of yours?"

"I've just been thinking," she said, shifting to look up at him. "About you."

He stiffened. His arm pulled her hard against his torso. His lips actually brushed her ear. "Thinking about revenge, princess? Thinking about me at the end of a rope?"

"No," she said, softly. "No."

He had reined in abruptly. "What kind of game are you playing?"

His arm had tightened so much that she gasped. "I'm not."

He relaxed slightly, but she could feel his torso, stiff and taut against her back. He was very still, and the bay moved restlessly beneath them. "I don't think I've been misreading your signals," he finally said. His arm tightened and he forced her to twist around so he could see her face. "Am I?"

Lucy's heart was pounding wildly, and for a moment she couldn't speak. She could feel it, a rock-hard erection pressing against her hip. What should she do now? "Shoz, I . . ." She didn't know what to say. She waited for him to kiss her.

"I'm not misreading your signals!" he said, furiously. Lucy was stunned by his anger. "Is this what you want, princess?" he sneered.

His horrible tone hurt her and brought sharp tears to her eyes. She didn't have time to dwell on it, however. He kissed her. Hard, hurtfully, violently. There was nothing nice about it, and Lucy protested, her hands going to his shoulders, trying to push him away. It was like trying to budge a boulder.

He was bruising her mouth terribly, and just when she thought she couldn't stand it, everything changed. His mouth went very still, and she thought he cursed. And when he kissed her again, it was whisper-soft and barely there, a teasing touch of his mouth, as gentle as he had been rough before. A burning need sparked in Lucy's veins.

His hand was caressing her side as he kissed her. She clung to him, strained for him, mated with his tongue. Such fierce need stabbed her, she felt faint.

The bay snorted. Shoz went still. Lucy whimpered and kissed his jaw. Shoz's big body went hard and stiff and he suddenly grabbed a handful of her hair, stopping her. "Enough."

It was like being underwater and coming up for great gulps of air. Lucy inhaled, watching him. He watched her back, his gaze blazing. "You would tempt a saint," he said roughly. "And I'm not a saint."

"I know," Lucy said.

He grimaced. "What in hell are you up to? What's your angle?"

Lucy blushed. This was much more difficult than she had imagined. How to entice him delicately? She touched his cheek. "Shoz, we're never going to see each other again."

His eyes widened. "So this is your way of saying goodbye?"

Her color deepened and she nodded.

"Just what in hell are you asking for? Do you know what you're asking for?"

"We've already done it once."

He didn't say a thing, he just stared.

"And no one found out then. They won't find out now."

"Got this all thought out, do you?"

"Yes."

"No crying rape to Daddy?"

"Of course not. I would be ruined."

He slipped off the horse, bringing her with him. Lucy found herself in his arms, thigh to thigh and chest to chest. "If you wanted it, why in hell didn't you just say so," he said roughly. Lucy couldn't respond. He'd clasped her buttocks and lifted her against his huge arousal. His body pushed her backward, against a tree. His mouth was already devouring hers.

Lucy clung to his broad shoulders while he kissed her and rubbed himself against her. She heard him curse, gasping. She herself could barely breathe, could barely stand up. His body rocking so suggestively against hers was nearly unbearable, and Lucy found herself grasping his buttocks to anchor him closer. One of his hands was suddenly under her skirts and between her legs, beneath her drawers. He rubbed her there, slickly, fast, opening her thighs by pressing one of his own between them.

"I hope you're ready," he said hoarsely. " 'Cause I sure as hell am."

Lucy barely digested his words, because his touch was both heaven and hell. He grabbed one of her legs and wrapped it around his waist. She didn't understand—not until he was thrusting hard and deep into her. She cried out in surprise, but he ignored her, lifting her other leg so she was riding his waist, her back against the tree. She clung to his shoulders. He pounded into her. Her cry had changed into a soft keening.

In her mind, and maybe she did utter her thoughts, she begged him for release. She begged him for more. In her ear he murmured something indistinct, encouraging, a promise. She felt his palm pressing down on her swollen mons, and then nothing mattered, because she was exploding like the Fourth of July fireworks.

"God," he groaned, burying his face in her neck. Lucidity was rapidly returning, and Lucy felt him convulsing inside her. She was also aware of her back pressed hard against the tree, her nails digging into his shoulders, her legs locked around his waist. He relaxed against her, leaving her, and then he let her feet slide to the ground.

Lucy found she couldn't stand and she sank to the ground, regaining her breath. When she looked up, she saw him staring down at her, one shoulder against the tree, as he zipped up his fly. He didn't smile. He just stared.

Lucy stared, too, limp, exhausted, sated. His expression was impossible to read. She looked for condemnation or contempt, but did not find it. She really couldn't believe how they had done it. She wasn't sure, but it seemed more shocking than the last time. And—even more stunning.

A rough smile curled his mouth. "Don't look so surprised. That's been coming for a long time."

Lucy looked away. In one way, physically, she felt completely satiated. But in another way, an indefinable way, she did not. Inside her, there was an elusive yearning.

He levered himself off the tree. "I'm real sorry we wasted the past few weeks fighting, princess, real sorry." Then he smiled. "But that was really good. I sure as hell couldn't have asked for a better good-bye."

His words jerked Lucy right back to reality.

He scowled at her expression. "Come on, get up. There's no way in hell we can dally around here—as much as I'd like to. Or have you forgotten? I'm a wanted man, and we're not far enough from the border for comfort. For my comfort. I want to make Las Casitas way before dark."

Before dark. All of reality intruded. Slowly, Lucy got to her feet.

20

He was angry.

Angry and frustrated; in fact, he felt downright mean.

There was no reason for his mood, and he damn well knew it. If anything, he should be feeling pleased as all hell; after all, he had gotten what he'd wanted, and he'd wanted Lucy Bragg for a long time. He wasn't used to waiting for what he wanted, just like he wasn't used to his near-infatuation, or should he say obsession? It was just lust, but that didn't matter. He'd just satisfied his lust, so she should be out of his system and his mind, right? Well, she wasn't. Far from it.

He was sorry he had taken her hostage, sorrier still he hadn't let her go hours before at the Rio Grande, or even sooner, outside of Paradise. He was sorriest of all that he had just banged the hell out of her.

His body was taut with tension. Fortunately, the foolish girl had not tried to initiate any conversation as they rode toward Casitas. It was fortunate because he would have bitten her head off.

She acted hurt. He swore, not caring if she heard. He had never promised her roses, and if she thought a roll in the sack meant something more, then she was a fool.

Like he was. Because what he kept remembering most vividly wasn't her naked body or her passion, oh no, it was how she'd touched him once, on his forehead, two days ago, to see if he had a fever. As if she cared.

It had been a very long time since a woman had cared about him.

And the traitorous thought intruded, again: *Keep her. Don't let her go.*

He was insane!

Shoz wrenched the bay to a halt, the horse protesting with a snort. Instantly he was contrite, relaxing the reins and stroking the animal's neck. The rangy mustang had the courage of the finest, purest-bred racer. He crooned softly in Apache.

Ahead, in the dusty twilight, a few adobe huts and smoking chimneys were visible. Not a soul stirred on the wide, dusty main street.

"This is Casitas?" he heard her ask tremulously.

"Don't worry," he responded. "They've got a telegraph. And a hotel. Of course—" he wanted to be nasty "—it's not what you're used to, princess."

She didn't answer, but he felt her stiffening in reaction to the cruelty in his tone. Good, he thought savagely. Good! Do I give a damn if you hate me? He swore to himself that he didn't.

Abruptly he lifted her and set her on the ground without dismounting himself. He stared at her.

"You're leaving me here?" she croaked, her gaze anxious.

His gaze was derisive as it swept her. "You can't go in to town like *that*."

Automatically she crossed her arms over her bosom, to little avail. She wore her navy jacket open, as it had lost half its buttons during their run from the law. Her shirtwaist and underclothes were plastered indecently to her. And then there was her knee-length skirt and petticoats, and her long, sleek calves and ankles were utterly nude.

She'd taken her hair like a rope and knotted it, with the tail hanging long and loose over her shoulder. She was a far cry from the Society princess of Paradise and New York. She was the sexiest thing Shoz had ever seen.

Her temper ignited and sparked. "You're the one responsible for my clothes!" she shouted, tears forming in her eyes. "Or should I say, my lack of them!" She brushed angrily at her eyes.

He relaxed insolently in the saddle. "Having regrets, are we?"

"Yes! No!"

"Make up your mind."

She took a deep breath. "Yes." There was a challenge in her expression.

He chose to ignore it. "Wait here. If someone comes for God's sake, hide in the cactus, okay?"

She glared at him.

He ignored the look and wheeled the bay, cantering to the village. Was she really regretting what they'd done— at her invitation? He chastised himself for being such a fool. Of course impulsive Miss Lucy was having second thoughts about what had happened. Now that she was stuffed full with what he'd given her. He was angrier than ever. He didn't want to believe it.

He slid off the bay in front of a building slightly larger than all the others in town. It was a saloon. There were a few rooms in the back for rent. Usually the whores took their clients there, but occasionally a weary traveler would rent one for a night. He took note of the four horses tied to the hitching rail in front, not liking so large a crowd in attendance. He walked in.

The floors were wood planking, covered with dust and grime. There was a long bar and a few rickety tables. Smoke hung in the air. The place smelled of refried beans, un-washed bodies, cigarettes, and sex. The owner, Fernando, was a big, fat Mexican. As always, he was behind the bar, drinking tequila. A villager Shoz recognized, a middle-aged reed-thin peon, was at the bar with him. The four riders sat at one table.

When he walked in, silence descended.

Shoz went to the bar. He'd already taken stock of the four riders. They all wore crossed bandoliers, carried their rifles, and had knives on their persons. They were banditos, typical ones, dangerous ones. How could he leave Lucy here?

He couldn't. Not alone. Fernando couldn't protect her, wouldn't even try. She'd be raped no matter what kind of dress she wore, raped again and again until she died.

Damn! His frustration increased. He couldn't leave her here, alone, waiting for her family to come and fetch her. And there was no way he could spend the night with her here, guarding her. Not when they were so close to the border. Casitas was not a safe hiding place. There was no other town near by on this side of Death Valley. Unless he went out of his way to drop her off somewhere else, he'd have to take her with him. And he had no intention of going out of his way. It was too dangerous. His only intention was to seek the safety of his impenetrable hideout. Which meant he was taking her to Death Valley.

The Braggs could search high and wide, but they'd never discover them there in the eastern Sierra Madres. Never.

Lucy's reunion with her family would have to wait. When it was safe, he would send her down to one of the towns on the Gulf, or even escort her himself. The decision made, Shoz felt all of the hot tension draining from his body. He didn't dare question why; after all, he was, as usual, reacting to the spin of Dame Fortune's wheel.

With the money he'd taken from the deputy in Paradise when he'd trussed him up, Shoz bought and downed two whiskeys, sheer heaven. He and Fernando went into the back to discuss business, and when Shoz left the saloon, he had a revolver tucked into his belt, a stiletto knife in his boot, a rifle and a small sack of supplies in one hand. The four riders watched him leave intently.

Lucy wasn't where he'd left her. His exasperation was light, despite the urgent need to get going. Where was the chit? Had she finally decided to run away? Her sense of timing stank!

The thought struck him that some cutthroat had found her, or a rattlesnake. He plunged through thick stands of cactus to find her, unable to call out her name, well aware that his heart was thundering from fear, not fury. He pulled to a halt. Very intently, he listened to the descending night.

He could hear, far away, the yelping of a pack of coyotes. Closer, he heard the softest, slightest movement, something softly brushing stone. He whirled, but only chased an opossum into hiding.

Had she run away from him? Alone, barely dressed, fled into the Mexican wilderness? Or had some damn bandit found her? A feeling of helpless outrage assailed him and he clenched his fists. He urged the bay on, into an expanding circle.

Periodically he stopped to listen. And then he heard her—soft gasps. Maybe pain. The gun in his hand, he galloped toward the sound, and some dozen yards away, he burst through an outcropping of boulders. He found her with her back against one, sitting on the ground, alone—crying.

His first thought was that someone had hurt her, and his rage foretold murder. He was off the bay, about to grab her, but she had seen him and risen to her feet, wiping her eyes.

"What happened?"

Her glare was directed at him, full force.

"What in hell happened?" he demanded, releasing her.

"Nothing."

He stared, unable to believe her words, not when she was crying, hidden here, and it had taken him half an hour to find her. "You're lying. Why are you lying? What happened?"

"Nothing!" she screamed.

Shoz stepped back. He had told her to hide if she saw someone, but apparently she had been hiding from him. And crying. He told himself he didn't care, didn't give a damn, damned if he did. "Why are you crying, Lucy?" The problem was, he knew why she was crying, and secretly he hated himself.

"Why am I crying?" She laughed hysterically. "You kidnap me and drag me across half of Texas and all the way into Mexico and you ask me why am I crying?"

"You weren't crying yesterday."

"No." Her mouth trembled. "I wasn't crying yesterday."

Another image of her touching his forehead swept him, followed by a flashing remembrance of their recent love-making. "If you play with fire," he said harshly, "you risk getting burned."

She stared at him. Her chin lifted. "Don't flatter yourself."

This he could handle. Her fighting anger was infinitely

preferable to her hurt and tears. "Get up," he said, mounting.

She held out her hand and he swung her behind him. He urged the bay into a canter, for the first time heading east.

Lucy clung to him. "Where are we going?" she gasped. He could feel her full breasts against his back. "Casitas is back there!"

"Unless you want a fate worse than death, I can't leave you there—and I sure as hell don't dare spend a night so close to the border."

Lucy's mind froze—then it began spinning. "What are you saying?" she cried. "I don't understand!"

The bay plunged into a rocky gorge. "There were four outlaws back there, and frankly, my dear, they wouldn't give a damn who you are just as long as you're a woman. Understand?"

"Oh," she said faintly, her mouth touching his ear as she bumped against him.

He wanted to put distance between them and Casitas, and he pushed the bay, hard. Yet intent as he was, he waited for her unspoken question, and then it came. Tremulously. "If you're not leaving me there, then where are you leaving me?"

"I'm not."

"What?! But you said you were going to let me go!"

"Give it up. You're staying with me."

21

The ground shook beneath the hundreds of galloping hooves, the sound filling the air like thunder. A mass of horses and riders raced across the hot Texas desert, toward the Rio Grande. Almost as one, the cavalcade turned slightly and slowed, coming to a rolling halt.

"The Rio."

Rathe turned to his father, his blue eyes blazing. "We can't stop now—we lost too much time as it is."

Derek Bragg, Nick, Rathe, Brett, and Storm rode in front of the fifty-man posse with Sheriff Sanders and four Texas Rangers. They were an imposing, frightening lot. They were all identically clad, even Storm, in dusty leather chaps, worn boots, wet cotton shirts, bandannas knotted at the throat, and battered Stetsons pulled low. Everyone packed hardware, and lots of it. Rifles were in their scabbards, six-shooters strapped to their thighs. Derek carried a bowie knife—and so did his daughter.

But it wasn't just their sheer number or their cumulative firepower that was so frightening. It was the aura of power, rage, and determination that would make anyone hesitate to cross their path.

Fortunately, Fred had been discovered just an hour after being tied up and locked up in the prisoner's cell. Lucy's disappearance had not been noted yet, and might not have been remarked upon until much later if Fred had not been found so soon. He garbled the entire story. Immediately a posse was formed, and within two hours of Lucy's abduction, the fearsome group had ridden out.

Unfortunately, the consensus was that Shoz would ride directly south for the border, and that was how they had gone, looking for his trail. They hadn't found any sign by that afternoon. They had to backtrack all the way back to Paradise. The man was canny. He'd actually followed one of the Pecos River's tributaries west, first, to throw them off the scent. They knew this for sure because, late in the day, Nick had found sizable pieces of Lucy's skirt and petticoats clinging to the branches of a bush by the bank. Apparently they had been cut off and tossed aside. This obviously meant that, for the moment, they were walking downstream. Rathe had nearly been out of his mind.

A terrible argument had ensued. Would their quarry ride west into the New Mexico territory? Or was he trying to confuse them? Would he head south after all?

At this point, the Rangers they had wired joined them. The posse split up. Half went west, led by three Rangers, the rest headed directly south for the border. Each and every Bragg believed with his gut instinct that the outlaw would run for Mexico, and they all rode south together.

Now they had reached the Rio, almost a full day later. They hadn't found another sign of the outlaw and Lucy since the one by the creek yesterday. They were relying on instinct and common sense, and without hard evidence proving that they were on the right trail, frustration rose hot and hard among them all.

"We can't stop," Rathe repeated. "Not now."

His brother, Nick, astride next to him, laid a comforting hand on his shoulder.

"It'll be dark soon," Derek said flatly. "We won't be able to do much in the dark."

Brett moved his blowing stallion forward. "We can't let them get into those mountains," he said.

Everyone looked southeast, at the jagged mountain peaks etching the dimming mauve-hued sky. They looked ominous and forbidding. The eastern Sierra Madres. Up until now, they had been riding though hill country, then desert. But once a man got into those mountains, he could hide forever.

"We must find another sign," Storm said firmly. "And we must find it soon."

Clark Wade, the captain of the Rangers, gave orders to fan out on foot, very, very carefully. This was the moment when they had to find a sign of where Lucy and Shoz Cooper had crossed the Rio—if indeed they had come this way. But time was against them, in more ways then one. The outlaw was ahead of them, and would soon escape into the twisted guts of the Sierras, if he had come this way. And soon it would be dark, too dark to find any trail. Everyone felt the powerful urgency to work fast.

It was Rathe, spurred on by desperation, who found the one barely visible track in the loam by the river's bank. The water had eroded most of it, but to an expert—and many of these men were just that—it was the mark of a horse's hoof, one that was heavily burdened—carrying the weight of more than one man.

"It just could be them," Sanders said. "The horse he stole was small, like this one."

"Or it could be a pack mule," Clark Wade said.

"It's them," Rathe spat. "I know it! Let's go!"

Holt turned to Derek unhappily. "I'm sure you know that we can't cross that border."

"I know."

"Even ten years ago, we could have done it, but not in these days, in these times."

"Have the Pinkertons meet me in Casitas," Derek instructed. "It's six or seven miles south of here. If we're not there, have them wait. I'll send word, or we'll come."

Wade nodded and gave Derek, who was an ex-captain of the Rangers himself, a salute. He signaled to his men and they broke from the group, riding east.

"You know I can't go any farther either, Derek," Sheriff Sanders said. Then, uncharacteristically, he cursed.

"Get back to Paradise, reassure the women."

Rathe grabbed Sanders's arm. "Tell Grace not to worry. Tell her I said everything will be all right."

Sanders nodded, knowing he was being asked to lie, and knowing he would do it.

"Let's go."

The posse split up again. The sheriff and his deputies and the men from town who had volunteered out of respect for the family turned to head back to Paradise. A few dozen other riders remained, those whose allegiance was stronger.

Many were cowboys who worked at the D&M, others were close family friends. Some were just plain decent folk outraged that something like this could happen to this family, in their town. The Braggs led all of them across the Rio Grande and into Mexico.

He had lied after all.

Lucy sought refuge in the hot anger that swept her. Anger was better than the hurt and disappointment that had filled her after their lovemaking. Her fingers dug into his shoulders as they cantered through two buttes, leaving Casitas farther and farther behind. And with it, his broken promise. "You said you were going to let me go!"

"Shut up," he said, as the bay scrambled up a twisted path that would begin their ascent into the mountains.

Lucy didn't think. She was too consumed with emotions for logic. She acted. She let go of his shoulders and slid backward off of the horse.

The fall hurt. It momentarily knocked the breath out of her. It had jarred her neck hard, but she'd landed on her side, saving her head from any injury. Furious desperation fueled her. She heaved herself to her feet. And then she ran.

She heard his shout behind her.

She crashed through wiry brush, leaving the trail to scramble down a rocky slope into a gorge. She tripped and fell with a cry. She rolled once, twice, helpless to stop, stones and roots digging into her, scratching her, and then she came to a stop in a heap on the flat floor below.

"Lucy!"

Fear laced his voice. Shoz didn't hesitate, he forced the bay over the side of the gorge, riding him for hell. The animal scrambled and slid down the steep slope, kicking up a wake of debris. Before they got to the bottom, Shoz was leaping off. The horse lost its footing and went down with a cry. Shoz didn't lose his, and he ran to the inert figure lying facedown, sprawled in the dust.

Panic knifed him, but as he knelt beside her, his voice was calm and controlled, and his hands were steady and gentle when he touched her shoulders. "Can you hear me?"

Lucy's voice was faint. "Yes."

"Are you all right? Did you break anything?"

Still facedown, very aware of his hands probing her, Lucy tried to determine her condition. It was hard to tell if she was all right, her entire body hurt like hell, but it had started hurting two days ago, and she couldn't distinguish her previous aches from her current ones. She sat up; he helped her.

Now he cursed. "Goddammit! That was the stupidest thing I've ever seen!" His grip on her tightened.

"You lied!" she cried. To her horror, tears welled in her eyes. She was in a very fragile state, and it had nothing to do with her physical agony. Lucy sought control. What did it matter that he could so intensely make love to her and then so casually prepare to leave her? She should have known better than to expect anything from him! But she had been naive, so naive, and this time the hurt was worse than the first time. At the least, couldn't he have given her a tender smile? Couldn't he have even acted like their parting would bother him?

But their near parting hadn't bothered him, and he wasn't nice enough to even pretend that it would. Just like he wasn't nice enough to hold her and kiss her and tell her she was, well, special. Or even to lie, and say he'd miss her. He wasn't nice, he was a bastard, and she had been so utterly stupid to give in to her attraction to him.

"Why are you crying?" he said, grim. "I seem to be asking that question a lot."

"I'm not crying," she said fiercely. "I want you to leave me here. I know that promises don't mean much to a man like you, but . . ."

He scowled, and she was glad she'd succeeded in irritating him. "Didn't you hear me, Miss Bragg? Those men back there would have raped you if I left you there. And you wouldn't have enjoyed it, believe me. Now, get up."

Lucy let him help her up only because he didn't give her a choice. Then he left her standing there, trembling, aching, bruised, and went to their mount. The bay was blowing softly. He was also lame.

Shoz cursed, stroking the animal's neck. Lucy felt a rush

of guilt; the poor animal had given himself heroically to them, and his injury was her fault. "What are we going to do?"

"We're going to walk," he said shortly.

Lucy gasped. Her feet were killing her. She knew she could not possibly walk. "I can't!"

"Oh yes you can," Shoz said, ridding the bay of the rifle, bedroll, and saddlebags. The horse would wander back to Casitas, or be found by a farmer. Shoz was looking at her expectantly, and he held out a hand.

She balked. "I can't."

"I hate to tell you this, Lucy," Shoz said, "But those men in Casitas are thieves, and I have no doubt they're riding this way right now, looking for me as a victim. Now, let's go."

Every step was torture, but Lucy ignored the pain and stumbled to him. He took her hand and pulled her up the slope. Lucy knew she would have never made it without him. They didn't stop once on the path, they started to run.

It was the longest ten minutes of Lucy's life. He half dragged her as they raced up the narrowing, twisting path, up, always up, and she tripped and stumbled repeatedly. Although he carried their supplies and the rifle, he never let her fall. His arm became a clamp around her waist. Now he was dragging her; only his strength and determination kept her going. Lucy knew that soon, no matter what he did, unless he carried her, she would drop in her tracks.

"Good girl," he muttered, suddenly leaving the path and hustling her through large boulders. The opening was so narrow, Lucy would have never attempted to enter, but he gave her no choice. He pushed her ahead of him and through. Before Lucy knew it, he was propelling her from behind, pushing her upward, forcing her to climb the mountainside between rocks. Just when she was going to give in and beg him to stop, he shoved her into a narrow fissure.

It was twilight. The sky was crystal gray, edged with purple, and very soon it would be dark. In that last moment of light, Lucy could still see. Shoz was wet with sweat, breathing hard, but his eyes were as hard as diamonds, and determined. "No matter what," he said, "don't move."

Lucy's eyes widened, then he dumped their supplies down at her feet and was gone.

Fear was immediate. There had been no mistaking the urgency of their flight into the mountains. They were definitely running from someone. What if these outlaws found them?

Lucy had a terrible image of Shoz hurt or captured and herself a prisoner at the mercy of dark, shadowy, menacing men.

She shoved it away, inhaling deeply, trying to calm her taut nerves. She was shaking, and not just from their recent flight. If they hadn't been running so hard just now, she would have questioned if there really had been such dangerous bandits in Casitas. After all, she hadn't seen them. Shoz had seen them. And she didn't trust him.

But they were on the run, and she was deathly afraid. Yet she hadn't seen these outlaws, had she? What if it wasn't outlaws chasing them? What if they were running from someone else?

Lucy leaned back against the cold stone of one rock wall. It was a terrible thing, not to trust Shoz, but he was her abductor, only her abductor, nothing more. And she could not fool herself and say she knew him; she didn't know him at all. Maybe they weren't on the run from Mexican bandits; maybe they were running from the law.

Lucy was exhausted. She couldn't think anymore, she didn't know what to think. Only one thing was clear. Earlier, she had been the biggest sort of fool to invite his attentions. And now, now she was here, hidden, so no one could find her. And Shoz was somewhere out there, and he wasn't alone. Someone was out there with him, someone who had been chasing them, and maybe it was her family.

And there was nothing she could do except wait.

22

He had known that they would be followed; he had been certain of it. It had only been sheer, hardened instinct. And he was right.

Shoz crouched on the rock ledge above the narrow trail that wound up toward the plateau's rim. The going was bad enough in daylight, and worse at night. It was slow and rough and too easy to break a horse's leg. Yet the bandits moved fast, surely and quietly. Only their mounts made any noise. There were four of them. It was no coincidence that they, too, were on this trail.

He hated wasting four bullets, but didn't have much choice. Shoz fired. He fired rapidly, hitting the two leaders, winging the third, and missing the fourth rider completely. One of the leaders fell from his horse and off the side of the hill, down into the gorge where Lucy had been. He was probably already dead, if not dying. The other leader also fell from his mount, but rolled away, returning Shoz's fire. The third began to shoot up at Shoz, too, from the cover of a tree. The last one fled.

Shoz had the complete advantage, as he had known he would. It was why he had chosen to stop where he had—and it wasn't the first time that he had used this exact place for an ambush—or the fissure above to stash something or someone. He knew these trails better than the back of his own hand.

From his position above the bandits, he could pinpoint them, but they couldn't find him. Being careful not to waste his ammunition, he took very careful aim before returning their fire. The remaining light worked in his favor. A few moments later, utter silence descended upon the hillside.

Very cautiously, Shoz climbed down from the rocks to the trail below. He checked the three men; they were all dead. Shoz relieved them of their weapons and ammunition belts and went to their mounts. All three horses were grazing by the side of the trail. Being well trained, for obvious reasons, they had remained where they had been drop-reined during the brief gunfight.

Shoz chose two and sent the other galloping back down the trail. He led them up the trail to a higher point, one closer to where he had hidden Lucy. He left them to get her. He found her wide-eyed, white, and shaking.

Her fear halted him in his tracks and drew a powerful and strange reaction from him—an impulse to reach out and hold her, comfort her. Of course, he didn't.

"It's all right," he told her gruffly. "We'll hole up for the night in a cave not far from here."

He reached a hand into the narrow space to help her out. She shrank back from him. "Who was it! Who was it! Are they dead?"

"It was the bandits from Casitas," he said, perplexed. Then he went rigid, his gaze narrowing. Understanding hit him unpleasantly. "You thought I lied, Lucy? You thought, perhaps, it was someone else on our ass?"

Lucy released a breath, her palm covering her chest in the vicinity of her heart. "It was really the bandits?"

Her lack of trust sickened him. He knew he shouldn't expect more, but foolishly, he had. "It wasn't your family." He reached in and yanked her out. She stumbled against him with a faint cry. Her body was warm and soft and she was trembling. He distanced himself immediately and grabbed her elbow.

She leaned heavily upon him as they made their way back to the trail where he'd left the horses. He had no delusions about her feelings for him, and he knew if it weren't for her poor physical state, she wouldn't even touch him. Did she now condemn him as a murderer, too? Why had he even cared to save her from those cutthroats?

And he had cared, as much as he didn't want to admit it. The thought of Lucy at their mercy had filled him with the hardest determination imaginable not to let it happen.

So much for his foolish heroism. She didn't appreciate it, and she never would. Just like she didn't appreciate his not abandoning her in Casitas.

"Horses," she said, a soft yet relieved sound. She moved toward one; he stopped her.

"We have to go on foot. It's not far."

She whimpered.

As they led the horses off the trail in another direction, Shoz couldn't help but be aware of her stumbling behind him, of her soft gasps. He steeled himself against the sympathy he could too easily feel for her.

Five minutes later, they reached the cave. It was big enough to accommodate the two of them and their horses, and it was hidden from the outside by trees and boulders, making the entrance difficult to discern. Once inside, Shoz led the horses to a space apart, untacking them. He didn't look at Lucy, but knew she had collapsed on the hard stone floor with another one of those inarticulate little cries.

He lit a candle he had received with the rest of their supplies from Fernando and set it down. It cast long, dancing shadows upon the rough walls of the cave. Outside, the night was very still and very quiet, making their world within seem closed and detached and almost unreal—like a separate universe. He was very aware of Lucy. He fed and watered the horses; then, a blanket and canteen in hand, he approached her. She was so tired, she barely looked at him, until he spoke. "Let me see your face."

He dropped the blanket by her side, for her to sit on. He reached for her chin. She twisted away stubbornly, anger filling her blue eyes. "Don't touch me."

His mouth tightened. "You bruised your cheek in the fall. Let me look at it."

She stiffened, but allowed him to tilt her face toward him. The candle barely provided enough illumination. Shadows flickered across her face. It was a light abrasion, full of dirt, and Shoz cleaned it with water and a strip of his shirt. She didn't make a sound.

"Let me look at the rest of you," he said.

"I'm fine!"

"Your elbows and knees are scraped."

She sighed, a sound that was suspiciously like a moan, and held out her arms. He cleaned all the abrasions methodically, with detachment. Her knees and shins were sunburned as hell, redder than tomatoes. When he touched her leg, she winced. "Tomorrow we'll find some salve," he said, feeling sorry for her despite his best intentions to remain aloof.

"What do you care?"

"It's three days from here to Death Valley," he said angrily. "And damned if you're going to cry and moan and slow me down."

She lifted her chin. "Then leave me here."

"I'm not leaving you here," he gritted. She waited, but he refused to explain. Leaving her would be murder—she couldn't possibly survive.

"You're going to hold me for ransom, aren't you? It was all a big lie, that you'd let me go at the Rio Grande."

He'd had no such intention, but madder than ever, he said, "Maybe."

She absorbed that. "And then will you let me go? They'll pay you, you know. My father will pay you anything."

His smile was twisted. "That right? Honey, I'd be ten times the fool if I let you go. After that, I'm going to sell you south—to a white slaver."

She gasped, becoming whiter than death.

He was so mad, he forgot himself and grabbed her and shook her. "You listen to me, you damn fool! I don't want any goddamn ransom! I wouldn't touch your daddy's money with a ten-foot pole! I only want my damn freedom! As soon as I can, I'm going to set you free. If I could have, I would have happily left you in Casitas—but I'm just not the damn bastard you think I am, to leave you to be raped by those bandits I killed. I had no choice but to bring you with me. But as soon as I can, believe me, as soon as possible, the sooner the better, I'm going to drop you in a village where you'll be safe until your daddy can come for you. It's just that right now, my priority happens to be me— and my safety. So first we go to Death Valley, where I can't be found. You got that, Miss Bragg?"

She grabbed the blanket and wrapped it around herself. She didn't say anything.

He turned away, shaking. Then he whirled around. ''I'd give you my word, but that wouldn't be good enough for you, would it?''

She was always surprising him. She surprised him now. ''I'll take your word.''

''You have it.''

He found the other bedroll and shook it out, ignoring her. Why in hell had he gotten so upset? Why did she have this power over him? He pinched out the flame of the candle. No other woman, not Marianne, not even Carmen, pushed him so far. In fact, with other women, even a selfish bitch like Carmen, he was always detached, always in control. More disturbed than ever, and secretly, very secretly, afraid, he lay down. He was exhausted, but he was much too agitated to sleep.

Rather than take all the rooms behind the dirty saloon, they preferred to make a camp just outside the village. But the night was endless and Rathe couldn't stand it, not when he was filled with such fear for his daughter. And it didn't matter that his father had tried to reassure him, time and again. Derek was convinced that he was a good judge of character and that Shoz Cooper would not hurt Lucy even though he had abducted her. In fact, now that he had his stud back and was calmer himself, he found it hard to believe that Shoz was even a horse thief. The man who had bought Thunder in Abilene had now identified Red and Jake conclusively as the thieves. Warrants were out for their arrest. Derek found it very strange that Shoz would join forces with the two thugs he had slugged it out with. And if he hadn't been one of the thieves? Maybe desperation had motivated him to use Lucy to escape jail, a last resort of no choice. Rathe had coldy pointed out that his police record was a hard fact. Derek had no answer to this.

Most of the posse was asleep, snug in their bedrolls around the two campfires. Rathe stood, pulling on his boots. He could not stay there, tossing and turning and thinking.

''Where are you going?'' On the ground beside him, Nick

sat up, speaking softly so as not to disturb anyone.

"I need a drink."

"I'll come with you." Agilely, Nick was on his feet.

"Thanks." Rathe needed the company. And his older brother was solid and reassuring and someone he could lean on.

Their father was asleep, but Nick stooped to tell Brett where they were going. D'Archand hadn't been sleeping; he had been talking quietly with his wife, who was curled up next to him. "I'll come with you," Brett said. "I don't like the look of that town."

Storm raised herself up on an elbow, a question in her eyes. He kissed her forehead. "Stay and get some sleep, darling," he said huskily. "Your brother shouldn't go alone."

"Be careful." The smile she gave him was very, very soft, a look reserved exclusively for her husband. No matter how often they had seen it, it always surprised her brothers, who still saw her as the tough tomboy she had been when she was a girl.

The camp was only a short walk from the main street. The village was black as pitch, except for the saloon. It was lit up brighter than a Christmas tree.

The threesome stepped within. The saloon was empty except for one table of poker players, including the owner, whose name, they had learned earlier, was Fernando. The village had already been taken by surprise with their arrival; now no one gave them much of a glance. Fernando did not get up to serve them. But a woman who might have been his daughter did.

She had been sitting alone at a back table, nursing a whiskey. She sidled behind the bar. She was plump, dark, and not particularly clean. It was obvious from her low-cut blouse and her breasts, bare and quite visible beneath, that she gave the patrons more than just liquor.

"What do you want?" Her English was heavily accented.

"What do you have?" Nick returned wryly.

"Don't ask," Brett said. He winced. "Give us the local rotgut."

Rathe said nothing.

They drank in silence, his brother and brother-in-law attempting to make small conversation but failing dismally. They ordered refills. The woman was pouring them when the sound of the thundering hoofbeats of a lone rider made everyone stiffen and listen. A moment later a dark, very disreputable type came staggering into the saloon, shouting in Spanish.

Fernando rushed to him. At the same time, he saw the three strangers standing at the bar and he went silent. Giving them a wary glance, he let Fernando take him to a corner table.

"What was he saying?" Nick asked Brett, very low.

Brett spoke Spanish fluently; he had been born in Mazatlán. "He said they were attacked and their leader is probably dead. He said the bastard was waiting for them. That's all."

"Is it possible?" Nick asked.

"It must have been that damn Shoz!" Rathe cried in a furious whisper.

"You're really jumping the gun," Brett said. "Relax, be calm, and let me handle this."

"And try to pretend indifference," Nick added.

The three men sipped their drinks while the woman brought the frenzied rider and Fernando a bottle and two glasses. She sat with them and listened until the rider obviously had no more to say. Fernando left him to join the others, the little drama apparently over. The woman got up and left the man nursing his drink alone, returning to the bar.

"More?" she asked.

Brett leaned forward with a smile. His teeth flashed white. The cleft in his chin deepened. His dark eyes were magnetic, alluring. His gaze slid over her breasts. "Only if you'll join me, querida."

23

The sun had barely risen when Billy found the gauze bandage, tossed carelessly aside, at the foot of an ancient saguaro about two miles from Casitas.

The night before, Brett had learned that the frenzied rider rode with three other companions, all of them rather dangerous. They had followed a lone traveler into the mountains to rob him. The traveler had ambushed the four bandits, killing and wounding everyone but the man who had returned hysterically to Casitas that night.

The barmaid had been garrulous when prodded flirtatiously by Brett—up to a point. When it came to the identity of the traveler, she refused to say a thing. Brett gained the impression that she knew him, or at least had seen him, from time to time.

There was no proof that this man was Shoz Cooper, and he had appeared to be alone. First thing that morning, they had fanned out in a wide circle, searching for his trail. Now they had found the bandage, and this time, other signs as well.

The horse's small, deep hoofprints were visible, and so was an imprint from a lady's shoe. Most important, a strand of red, curling hair was caught on the bandage's adhesive.

"He's gotten careless," Brett said.

"Or he's tired," Nick returned. "Very tired."

"Or—" Brett's look was sharp "—he's very confident." They exchanged glances and looked at the hot, arid mountains looming before them.

Two hours later, they found the horse, completely tacked, grazing on a rocky hillside, lame. "They're on foot," Rathe shouted, exultant.

187

The posse spurred their mounts into the mountain country, following a trail showing signs of recent use.

And then they found the three dead bandits.

Lucy awoke, wishing she hadn't.

She was aware that every part of her body was stiff and sore, and she was afraid to test it by moving. She was also afraid to test him, so she didn't open her eyes, but feigned sleep.

It gave her a chance to prepare herself for the day confronting her, and for the man awaiting her.

The events of the past few days seemed jumbled and distorted, even wildly exaggerated. Like a bizarre nightmare. But it was no dream; the hard floor of the cave testified to her actual presence here, somewhere in the foothills of the Sierra Madres, with a convicted criminal—her captor.

It was strange, but even when she had accused him of lying about his intention to let her go once they made the Rio Grande, she hadn't really meant it. She had been lashing out at him out of hurt more than fear, hurt and disappointment. Today she felt saner, calmer. She was the naive fool for inviting his attentions, and then secretly harboring some hope for affection. She had known who he was from the very beginning—he was a mean, selfish bastard. And from the very beginning she had even suspected his unsavory background, and then it had been confirmed. Yet despite how well she knew him for what he was, despite the fact that he had abducted her and then failed to release her in Casitas last night, when he had given her his word that he would free her when he could, she believed him.

There was also no point in doubting him. It would only feed her hysteria, which probably lurked not too far from the surface, and she didn't need that.

She could not lie around pretending sleep forever, so, reluctantly, Lucy opened her eyes, looking for him. The light was dim and gray in the cave, making her think that it was very, very early. Turning her head, she saw that her only company was the two horses. His blanket was neatly rolled and tied to one of the saddles. Lucy turned her head the other way, and with a start, saw that outside the cave, the light was bright and yellow and harsh. It was not the crack of dawn, far from it.

She sat up. Her back shrieked in protest, and she found she could barely move her neck. It was stiff as a board after her fall into the gorge yesterday. When she straightened her legs, she emitted a groan. Her knees were scabbing and objected to the movement fiercely. Oh, God, she thought. How was she going to survive this day?

How was she going to survive him?

He had overslept, despite his firm intention not to. After making his way out of the cave, Shoz paused in the sunlight, calculating that it would soon be nine. They had lost three or four hours already, and he wasn't pleased.

He carefully scrambled down the rock slope, then jumped off a boulder onto a deer trail. He followed that to the edge of a cliff, and there he raised field glasses to his eyes.

There was no movement south of them, nor east, just the tortured, twisted terrain of the arid mountain landscape. He gazed west, toward Casitas, and made out the sleepy village—nothing unusual there. The mountain they were crossing blocked his view of the north.

Nimbly, easily, he left the cliff, following the scrappy trail west until it veered sharply upward. He left it to cut across a granite rock face. A moment later he stepped between two massive boulders to peer down on the trail below, the trail he and Lucy had taken from Casitas—the one where he had left the three corpses.

He froze. Just for an instant, and then his heart thundered in his ears. Below him the posse milled. Half of the men were on foot, inspecting his handiwork and looking for his sign. He instantly recognized his boss, Derek Bragg, and Lucy's father, Rathe. He watched for only a moment more, and then he slid away and hurried back to the cave.

They had to move, and they had to move fast. He could not rely on the Bragg's being unable to discover where he'd left the trail, but he was sure, if they did find the spot, it wouldn't be within the next hour or so. He was too skilled, he'd eluded too many pursuers. But that didn't cut down on his need for haste. Every second counted, and while an hour from now, he might be an hour, or more, ahead of the law, right now he was practically sitting in their lap.

And then it flashed through his mind—now he could free her.

Now was the propitious moment to leave Lucy Bragg behind, within shouting distance of her family. *There was no excuse not to leave her behind.*

Yet his cunning mind found more than one. If he left her behind, ungagged, her shouts would bring the Braggs—and he wouldn't have the head start crucial for his escape. If he left her behind gagged and tied, or didn't tell her her family was so close, she might never find them—and would eventually succumb to the fate this barren, harsh land dealt to green intruders.

And even if he could immediately figure out a way of freeing her and gaining a head start, the law was too close for comfort, closer than they'd ever been before—even closer than that time in Corpus Christi, because now they were practically in his own backyard. How did he dare relinquish his best bargaining chip, just in case he failed to elude his pursuers? Because there was no way he would ever go to prison again.

In his mind he continued to roll the dice, and the same number kept showing up—and Lucy's freedom wasn't it.

He burst into the cave. She was sitting where she'd slept, and she glanced at him. He began tacking their mounts, efficiently, quickly, but without apparent haste. "Get up," he said, keeping his voice dispassionate. "We've overslept and we're leaving."

Lucy got to her feet and a low moan escaped her. He looked at her sharply, pulling a cinch tight, and saw tears in her eyes. She was hobbling. "What's wrong with your feet?"

"I think I have blisters."

They didn't have time for this. Knifelike fear pierced his gut, but he pushed it away. "Later, Lucy."

She jerked her gaze to his. "What is it?"

"We're getting out of here," he said, leading the horses forward. He grabbed her arm and brought her with him.

"Is someone out there?"

It was on the tip of his tongue to tell her that more bandits had pursued them, but he didn't. Their glances met and held, hers wide and vulnerable, his dark and shadowy. He couldn't lie to her. "You want me to hang, Lucy?" he asked very softly.

Her mouth opened, but the reply wasn't immediate. "No."

"Then let's go."

Lucy bit her lip, her heart pounding madly. They stepped out into the bright, hot sunlight. The law was back there, and she knew it.

She should scream, shout for help, alert them to their presence. So why didn't she?

She stared at Shoz, who was leading the horses along a very narrow, barely discernible animal trail. He was a bastard, but she didn't want him to hang.

He hadn't hurt her; how could she hurt him?

His hands last night, healing her, had been very gentle.

Lucy swept all thoughts away, especially such inappropriate ones, and stumbled after him. She only prayed she wouldn't regret her decision.

"Take off your shoes."

It was an order. They had stopped for the night after another endless day. The first half of it had been spent mostly on foot, climbing with the horses up impossibly steep, narrow, rocky trails, descending down equally impossible slopes squeezing through nearly impassable passes. Then they had cut onto a well-used deer trail, and they had ridden hard and fast, up, always up, higher and higher into the Sierras. Now they had made camp by a stream of mountain run-off, and Lucy sat tiredly by their saddles, unable to move.

She was also unable to protest when, after she did not respond, he took off her shoes for her. "Jesus!"

Lucy held back a whimper, and almost afraid to look, she did. Her feet were a sorry sight, covered with the raw spots of broken blisters and a few new swollen ones, too. She lifted her gaze and found Shoz staring at her, with surprise and compassion.

"You never said a damn word," he said.

"Would you have stopped?"

He frowned and helped her to the stream. Lucy let him clean her feet. "No shoes tomorrow," he said afterward, declining to answer. "We'll wrap your feet in cloth. Give me one of your petticoats."

She looked at him.

"I want to wash it. You want to wrap your feet in filthy linen?"

She turned her back on him, blushing even though he'd seen much more than her petticoats, more than any man should ever see. She tugged down one of the slips from beneath her skirt and handed it to him. He left her without a word.

Like the night before, his hands were gentle when he cleaned her feet, and it was incongruous with the hard, roughman he was, Lucy reflected. Was it possible that there was more to Shoz than the mean, mocking facade he presented?

Lucy was uncomfortable with her thoughts, and she found herself staring at him. They hadn't made a fire, but they ate stale bread and tinned meat. He seemed to concentrate very hard on the tin of beef in front of him. Lucy tore her gaze away. But she was like the foolish moth, he the flame. She looked at him again. What desperado cleaned and cared for a woman's blistered feet? It didn't make sense.

"Why didn't you scream, Lucy?" he asked suddenly, his glance sharp and penetrating.

Lucy was taken by surprise. She wanted to look away, but he held her gaze and wouldn't let it go. "I believed you when you said you would let me go once you are safe."

He didn't make a smart, sassy retort. He just stared. "Why didn't you shout for help, Lucy?"

He would not let her off the hook. Obviously if she had screamed, she would be free now, if all had gone in her favor. She fidgeted uncomfortably.

"Why!"

"All right!" she shot back. "You are a mean bastard, but you don't deserve to die! You may be a horse thief, but I'm sure you're not a murderer." She instantly thought about the bandits he had chased away last night—or killed. But that had been self-defense.

"I'm not a murderer," he said, his gaze unwavering. "I'm also not a damn horse thief."

Lucy stared down at her food. He still insisted that he was innocent, but she knew positively what she had seen. She didn't want to talk about it; it was too upsetting.

He made a sound of disgust and got to his feet. He disappeared into the night. Lucy was left with a sky full of stars and a raw ache in her heart.

24

Death Valley.

It was dry and hot deep in the bowels of the constricted valley. They had spent the last two days crossing an arid desert mountain range. The trails they had followed had been narrow and rocky and very dangerous, ascending steep inclines, again and again. At times they had attained dizzying heights. Too often, one slip would be anyone's last, into deep, bottomless gorges that snaked alongside them, granite cliffs soaring over them on the other side. The morning of their third day began their descent. It had taken hours, and it had been equally treacherous, slippery, and rocky. The going was dusty and got worse as the altitude lessened. It had been hot up in the mountains when they were trapped between giant cliffs that blocked any breeze and sucked in the heat, but at other times, on an open mountainside, it had been warm and even pleasant. Now it was hot, hotter than Texas, hotter than anywhere Lucy had ever been.

She had the feeling they had descended deeper than any human being had a right to, and it was eerie. It was like being funneled into a pit, or into the guts of the earth, with no way out. Lucy glanced up at the high, sheer rock walls looming over the valley, dominating it completely, so high and so overpowering that she couldn't see their tops or the sky. Of course, that was only because they were riding so close to the cliffs, she told herself hastily. She wasn't re-assured.

She wondered at the valley's awful, ominous name. Death Valley. It wasn't so different from parts of Texas, was it? Just hotter. Stunted, gnarled brush, brittle sage, and hot, hot white sand dominated it—and those damn towering walls. But maybe that was it. Maybe it was the walls, locking you in, forever, trapping those who entered, killing them . . . She dared to glance at Shoz.

He heard her exhalation and twisted in the saddle to look back at her. He must have sensed her unease, or read it in her eyes, because he pulled up to wait for her to come abreast. "I get a funny feeling every time I return here," he said.

"You do?" She was nearly panting.

"Like this is my damn grave." He glanced at the towering walls.

That wasn't what she wanted to hear. "That's silly."

"You're right. I think there's a feeling everyone gets when they come down here, and it has something to do with the valley's elevation. We're below sea level."

Her eyes widened. So they were in the very pits of the earth, in its very depths. So it was a place no human being had a right to be . . .

"Don't look so frightened; it's not like we've died and gone to hell." His lips twisted at a private, and bitter, joke.

"But it's unnatural," Lucy said, looking around uneasily. No wonder the valley was so still, so lifeless. There weren't even any trees. No wonder it was called Death Valley. How could anything live here? Or anyone?

He didn't respond. They rode on in silence. Lucy was relieved when they left the proximity of those threatening walls and she found that she could, indeed, see the sky.

Relieved, she let her thoughts turn again, as they had done so often, to her captor. He was riding ahead of her, easily, as if the kind of journey they had made had been merely an outing in the park. His resilience and power amazed her. She herself was a weary, aching wreck.

Last night, their second after leaving Casitas, he had wanted to make love to her. He hadn't said so, and he hadn't suggested it. But Lucy had sensed it from the moment they had dismounted to make their camp. She had felt his eyes on her, repeatedly. And when she had caught his gaze, his had been keen and interested.

Lucy had not been interested. Not very much, anyway, and not because of the hurt she had felt after they had made love outside of Casitas. Time, the eternal healer, had made those feelings start to fade. And she had learned her lesson, yet that wasn't it, either. Of course, one sensual look like the one he had given her made her insides flutter. Yet nothing, at that moment, could compete with her aching body and its need for rest. She only wanted to collapse on the ground and nurse her sore feet and her bruised body. When she stretched out her legs, the scabs broke, again, and she groaned.

He'd fixed their meal in silence while she dozed, not really sleeping. She could feel his eyes, hot, boring into her; she could feel his need, his desire. It was tangible, taut, like a wire stretched between them. He was compelling, his sexual magnetism so strong, it reached out to her across the space of their camp while she lay aching and half-asleep.

He had the decency not to approach her, except to hand her the plate of food he'd prepared. Yet after she'd eaten, she dreamed that he held her while she slept, touching her arm, her waist, stroking her hip, her breast, and it was erotic. It was also very real.

This morning, remembering, Lucy had been grateful for his consideration. Yet refreshed after a good night's sleep, she just might have been the tiniest bit disappointed. She was certainly surprised. Knowing Shoz, she would have expected him to have no consideration at all and at least to try and seduce her, mocking her in the process. But he hadn't. Maybe she didn't know him as well as she thought she did. Or maybe he hadn't wanted her as much as she thought he had. Both thoughts were disturbing.

Lucy was diverted from her reflections when she thought she distinguished man-made shapes ahead. She blinked. Was she seeing things, or were there Mexican-style adobe buildings ahead? Was there a village there? As they came closer, she saw with relief and joy that there was a group of buildings. She could make out numerous corrals, and slightly set apart, one larger house that most definitely ressembled a ranch house.

They rode past a wide, flat river. A few groups of stubby trees graced its path intermittently. The sight of the creek, the few trees, and the grassy banks was uplifting. Lucy actually smiled.

A group of sturdy young women was doing laundry. Youngsters were racing around, playing and teasing one another, while toddlers sat near their mothers, making pies in the sand. The women paused, shading their eyes to watch them pass, expressionlessly. They were all Mexican, dark-skinned and dark-haired, wearing loose, soft white blouses and plainly colored skirts. All their chatter had ceased. Even the children had stopped their games to halt and stare silently. Lucy stared back curiously. She called to Shoz, riding ahead of her. "Is this a village?"

"You might say that."

His answer annoyed her. She also sensed, for the first time in days, that she was no longer the focus of his attention. That was annoying, too, and perversely, she said, "Is this a ranch?"

This time he did glance at her, and laughed. "No."

She hadn't thought so. This was either a village, long since lost and forgotten deep in the Sierra Madres, where Shoz holed up, or it was a hideout. But if it was a hideout, why were there so many women and children there?

The big house was placed near the wide, flat river, and was graced with several taller, nearly lush trees and the welcome shade they provided. It was like stumbling unexpectedly upon an oasis in the middle of an African desert. The house was immensely inviting, although there was nothing outstanding about it—except its location in this godforsaken place. It was one level of rectangular yellowish adobe, the roof wood. A corral was not too far from it, a few fine-looking horses within. On the other side of the corral were a dozen other smaller houses, sheds and shacks.

Just as Shoz halted in front of the house and dismounted there was a screech and a woman in vibrant colors rushed out, flew across the few paces separating them, and launched herself right into Shoz's arms.

Lucy was shocked.

He let her cling and jabber breathlessly. She spoke a heavily accented English. "Where have you been, querido! It has been so long! We feared you were—oh! I dare not say! *Caro mio*, what happened? Are you all right?" She was actually clutching his face.

Lucy was shocked. All the time that he had been chasing her, he had a woman, this woman, here, waiting for him! She was frozen in the most rigid and furious disbelief that had ever gripped her in her entire life.

The woman was shorter than she was. She had a thick mass of tight black curls that came to her shoulder blades. Lucy thought it looked like a bird's nest. She couldn't see her face. The woman was clad in a shocking orange blouse, short-sleeved, which she wore off both shoulders. The material was thin and filmy and hung to full breasts. She wore a black and silver woven belt to accentuate a very tiny waist. She wore an even more shocking pink skirt, over what had to be another skirt, this one turquiose. On one arm was a dozen silver bangles, and when she turned slightly, Lucy saw one large hoop earring.

She looked like a whore, Lucy cried inwardly. And then she saw her face.

Something inside her seemed to die. She was the most exotic creature Lucy had ever seen. Her face was a perfect heart shape, her skin dark gold, her eyes big and black, long lashed and very seductive. Her cheekbones were high, her nose straight and proud. Her mouth was perfectly shaped and enhanced with red rouge. The woman stared back at her, just as stunned.

"Who is this!" she screamed. And a string of Spanish followed.

Even though the woman looked like a veritable gypsy, was undoubtedly a whore—his whore—and had no breeding, even though Lucy could not possibly stoop to compare herself to this woman, she had no doubt that she looked atrocious while this woman was so unbearably beautiful. Lucy was suddenly so tired, overwhelmingly so. She slid off the horse.

"Shut up, Carmen."

Carmen stopped her frenetic flow of verbiage.

Shoz took her chin in his hand. "She is my hostage."

Carmen stood angrily, eyeing Shoz and eyeing Lucy, her bountiful bosom heaving. "Damn you!"

"Has it been too long?" Shoz asked very softly. "Have you forgotten your English? She is my hostage."

Carmen beat a hasty retreat, but a moment later, she was back in his arms, crooning, pressing against him. "*Caro mio*, what can I do? What do you need? Want? Tell me, darling." She stroked his face.

The woman was most definitely a whore. She was practically rubbing her breasts all over him.

"Food, hot, good food," he said, glancing at Lucy. "A hot bath. And some whiskey."

"That's all?" she asked, sliding her hands under his worn shirt.

He didn't smile. "That, too, later." He pushed her away. Just as he did so, there was a child's shriek and the pounding of running footsteps. Lucy saw, with more shock, a young, black-haired boy leap right into Shoz's arms. The child was screaming. "Papa! Papa!"

And Shoz was beaming as he whirled the youngster around. Never had she seen such a smile on his face. It came from his eyes, from his heart, from his soul. The child clung to him. He was about six years old, small and dark— dark like his father. Like his father and his mother.

She could not watch. Suddenly she felt sick. He and the child were chatting happily, but she did not listen to what they were saying. Shoz's joy—his love—was evident. She stumbled to the corral. She could not cry, not now, not with that woman watching her. That woman. Was she his wife?

Lucy leaned against the fence. The answer was obvious enough.

25

"I have something for you, *niño*," Shoz said. His tone was gentle. They were still outside, in front of the house.

"What?" the child asked excitedly. "For me?! A present?"

Shoz smiled and went to the bay, removing an object from the saddlebags. Lucy watched. She knew what it was. He'd been whittling at nights, whittling a rearing horse. Now he knelt again to hand it to his son.

His son.

The pain was vast.

Carmen shot her a malicious look.

"I know it's not store-bought," Shoz said, "but next time I'll get you some new toy soldiers, I promise."

"A horse!" His son began jumping around. Shoz laughed and ruffled the boy's short, black hair. "Have you taken good care of your mother while I was gone, Roberto?"

"Sí, Papa." He had stopped dancing and was very solemn. "Just as you said."

"Bueno." It was soft. He turned to Lucy. "Come on."

The look she directed at him was mutinous, incredulous, and despairing all at once. She found, for the first time in their relationship, that she was completely at a loss, unable to respond to him, too tired to fight. She came, and he went into the house. Lucy followed, as she was apparently supposed to do.

"What are you doing?" Carmen ran after them.

Shoz ignored her, walking through a living area with a couch, two chairs, skin rugs, and a very cozy adobe fireplace. A short corridor led off the room. There were two doors facing each other, and a third at the end of the hall, between them. This he opened, directing her in.

Lucy saw a single bed, a scarred table and lamp, a very small bureau with washing utensils. There was one large window, shuttered. The room was dark and dusty. Were the shutters nailed closed? Now she understood. This was to be her prison.

She is my hostage, he had said. He had only spoken the truth.

"This is your room. Carmen will bring you clothes and soap, and I'll have a tub brought in." His gaze swept over her.

"You mean my prison," she mocked.

"No, I mean your room."

"Am I confined here?"

"Do as you please." He turned and left.

Stunned and just for a moment distracted, Lucy stared after him. From within *her* room, she could see down the corridor into the living room. Carmen was staring, waiting, with her hands on her round hips. Lucy stared back. She expected to see Shoz walk into her arms. He didn't. He opened the adjacent door and disappeared inside.

When she heard him moving around, heard his boots hitting the floor as he took them off, Lucy leapt up and slammed her own door shut. Then she sank on the bed, uncertain. She was trembling. She just sat there, waiting for her own reaction to the worst crisis in her life to set in.

No tears came. She was either too exhausted, physically and emotionally, or she was becoming too hardened. She took a few breaths. *How could he!* All the time that she had known him, there had been Carmen, here, waiting for him. Carmen and his son. She was so hurt—and so mad.

At least now she knew where she stood.

Not that it mattered. He was a bastard and a thief and a felon. And married. Oh God. She shouldn't care, not at all, but faced with Carmen, she did! He had made love to her, twice. He had used her. And it had been obvious from the way he had treated her afterward, but she hadn't wanted to see it. Oh, why had she been so foolish—why was she still so foolish?

She breathed deeply to calm herself. Was she a prisoner?

He had said she could do as she pleased. Lucy didn't believe him. Abruptly she got up to see if the wood shutters were nailed shut. They weren't. When she opened them, sunlight streamed into the room. She had a wonderful view of the broad, sluggish river, but it was ruined by the immense yellow walls of the valley towering over it on the far side. She shuddered, thinking about how they were lower than the sea, about how those walls, from this angle, looked like the giant jaws of a trap. She quickly turned away.

At least now she knew what she wanted to do—what she would do. She would bathe and wash her hair as soon as they brought her bath, and don fresh clothes. And burn these rags as soon as she could.

Lucy sat on the bed in the sunlight pouring through the window. She would dearly love to jump out of all her filthy clothes, but she didn't dare. She tried not to think while waiting for the clothes Carmen was supposed to bring, and for her bath. But the minutes stretched into what surely must be an hour, and no one came.

Lucy went to the door and leaned against it, listening for sounds in the house. She didn't hear a thing. She unbolted her door and opened it a crack. The door to the room adjacent to hers, where he had gone, was closed, no sound coming from within. Lucy walked into the living room, for the first time looking around. It was dusty, even dirty in the corners, and quite untidy. A violet scarf had been left on one chair, an empty tin full of crumbs on the couch. Dirty, unwashed cups with encrusted coffee sat on the low wooden table. A pair of high-heeled shoes was on the rug, a comb on another table, a pot of rouge on top of a pile of old Sears catalogs. On the other side of the room was a heavy wooden table with two long benches on either side—and one chair at its head. It was covered with dirty dishes and glasses. Lucy heard women's voices and turned to see the entrance to the kitchen.

She went and stood in the open doorway.

A big, heavy older woman and Carmen were obviously hurrying to prepare a meal. Vegetables, both fresh and tinned, flour, meat, and pots and pans lay out upon the counterspace and the big, rough worktable that dominated the room. Both women stopped what they were doing to turn and stare at her.

Lucy let them get their fill even though their inspection would have made her uncomfortable in the best of circumstances. She feigned haughty indifference, which wasn't exactly easy when she could imagine how awful she looked—when she could even smell her own sweat. The older woman smiled and went back to work. Lucy watched the highly visible progression of Carmen's rage. It started with malice and became full-blown fury. She was holding a cleaver, and she whacked it as hard as she could on the table. Lucy jumped.

The thought flitted through her mind—this woman is capable of hurting her enemies, and you are her enemy. Be careful. But she said, "Shoz said you would give me clothes. And where is my bath?"

Carmen smiled nastily. "The men are emptying the tub now. Not too soon. You stink!" She wrinkled her nose. "And that ugly red hair!" she added in Spanish.

"At least my hair isn't a nest for rodents," Lucy said calmly—in fluent Spanish. She had learned the language as a child during the summers she had spent in Paradise.

Carmen's eyes widened, then she stomped over, pushed Lucy rudely aside, and marched through the house.

Lucy followed. When Carmen flung open the door adjacent to hers, to the room that was apparently Shoz's, she felt her heart sink yet again. So they shared a room. Somehow, she had stupidly hoped they slept separately, with Carmen in the room across from his.

Lucy stood in the doorway to their room, her face impassive. Her heart was pounding ferociously. Shoz was lying on the bed, shirtless and freshly washed, his hair still damp. He sat up. Furiously Carmen flung open an armoire. Lucy refused to look at him, but she knew he was looking at her.

Carmen was muttering angrily as she shoved through her clothes, once, twice, three times. She whirled, her skirts twirling to show all of her calves. She opened her mouth to speak, but no sound came out as she saw Shoz regarding Lucy.

She grabbed his arm. "Why do I have to give her my clothes?"

"Because I said so."

Carmen turned sullenly and yanked out a brilliant orange blouse, one Lucy knew would look awful with her red hair. She threw an ugly brown wool skirt on top, one much too hot for this climate. She smiled in triumph. "Take it."

Shoz got up, moved her aside, and went through her clothes. Carmen screamed and ranted; he ignored her. He finally removed a green blouse that Lucy knew would do wonders for her coloring. A red petticoat followed, and then a rainbow-hued print skirt. He went to a bureau and opened a drawer. This time Carmen was trying not to jump up and down. "You cannot give her my beautiful silk drawers from Paris!"

"Why not? I bought you the stuff." He calmly took out a pair of gorgeous white, sheer, short, lacy *things* and added them to the clothing on the bed. "Sorry, princess, but Carmen doesn't wear chemises, camisoles, corsets, bust bodices, or any of those other things you ladies seem so fond of."

"Of course not," Lucy said stiffly. "She wouldn't." She took the clothing and, head high, turned her back on him. She might be a mass of overwrought nerves on the inside, but outside she would be all aristocratic disdain and dignity. She was Lucy Bragg from the Braggs of New York and Texas, and damned if she would let anyone forget it.

Lucy entered her room, closing the door behind her. She was trembling again. She walked to the bureau and grimly surveyed herself in the round mirror hanging on the wall. It was a mistake to do so. She was not surprised at what she saw, she was beyond that. Yet she was taunted with Carmen's exotic—and erotic—image.

Lucy knew she had never looked worse, but what did it matter in this hellhole? Her face was sweaty, dusty, grimy. Her hair hung in the one ponytail, knotted the best she could. Tendrils were escaping riotously everywhere. Her cheek was bruised from her fall into the gorge. She shrugged out of her ripped jacket, letting it drop to the floor. The shirtwaist followed, then everything followed, until she wore only her thin chemise and shortened skirts.

Now she appeared as indecent as Carmen. Lucy cocked one hip out and placed her hand on it, then thrust her chest forward. Her breasts were firm and full, straining against the thin chemise, molded precisely by the fine, expensive fabric. Her nipples were visible, darker shadows, now becoming hard and pointed. Lucy eyed the size of her waist, a tiny twenty-one inches on her five foot eight inch frame. With her broad shoulders and full breasts, it looked even smaller. She felt a small surge of satisfaction. Carmen didn't have anything that she didn't have. She was merely a slut to show it off, while she, Lucy, was a lady born and bred—and much more than that, she was a Society heiress. She gave her reflection a reassuring smile.

"Put some clothes on."

Lucy whirled to meet Shoz's angry expression. She froze; his glance settled on her barely clad breasts and then he picked up her jacket and threw it at her. Lucy saw a man's leering face behind him, and she hastily held it in front of her. Shoz gave her a hard look and stepped aside so that two dark, dusty men could bring in an old wooden tub.

The two men looked unsavory, like the worst sort of outlaws, and Lucy pretended they were invisible. She was clearly visible to them, however, for they eyed her lasciviously, as if they could see through her skirts and the jacket she held so protectively over her bosom. Then Shoz called out an order, and they dropped their gazes as they put down the tub and strode out, quickly enough.

They had frightened her in a way Shoz never had. Lucy lifted her wide blue eyes to his.

He kicked the door shut. It reverberated like thunder cracking right overhead. Lucy jumped. "This isn't Paradise!" he shouted.

"No, it's not, is it?" To her horror, she heard her voice crack, for she was suddenly so close to tears. Lucy sat down on the bed, the jacket slipping to her lap. She didn't look at him. She struggled for control. She would die and be damned before he would know how upset she was—and why.

"Lucy . . ."

The intensity of his tone made her look up. His gaze was riveted to hers. She was held there against her will for an endless moment, while inside she wanted to scream at him for being a bastard and a liar and for having a wife. His gaze slipped. Lucy recovered, shielding herself with the jacket once more.

He recovered, too. "Don't flaunt yourself—not here!"

"Flaunt myself?" She was on her feet. He would accuse her of flaunting herself when his wife paraded around without chemise, corset, or anything else?

He pointed at the jacket she clutched to her nearly naked chest. "I can control my men—usually. But not if they're given unholy provocation."

"Unholy provocation!" she screamed.

"Or were you flaunting for me?"

She threw the jacket at his head. He caught it and tossed it to the floor. "You conceited ass," she said, hitting him as hard as she could right across the face.

It felt so good. It had nothing to do with his accusing her of flaunting herself; it had everything to do with his having a wife. He was stunned. For a second he just stood there, in disbelief, the crack of the slap echoing between them. Suddenly realizing what she had done, Lucy backed up, but her legs hit the bed, and she sat down, hard.

She didn't stay sitting for long. He jerked her up, against his body, and she could feel every muscular inch of him, from the tip of his toes to the jut of his chin. "You bitch," he said, and he kissed her.

Lucy did not want to be kissed. His mouth was very hard and very aggressive, but she refused to open hers. He was very hard, and equally aggressive; Lucy tried to twist her body away from intimate contact with his. He wouldn't let her. He clamped down on her buttocks and kept her pressed against his hot, hard erection.

Fortunately, and Lucy knew it was fortunate because damn him, he still had power over her, one of the men knocked on the door, calling out. Shoz went still; Lucy went still. He was panting; so was she. He set her away from him, his grip hard and bruising. Then he found her jacket and shoved it at her. Lucy grabbed it and scooted as far from him as she could get.

The man entered with two buckets of steaming water, his partner behind him with two more buckets. Shoz strode out as they filled the tub. His strides were long and hard, and she heard his door adjacent to hers slam closed. She didn't move. The two men grinned at her and left. Lucy raced to the door and shut it. Thank God it had a bolt; she threw it down.

She leaned against the wall, trembling. Anger, fear, and even arousal coursed in her veins, the emotional jumble nearly overwhelming. It was a long time before she was calm enough to shed her clothes and bathe.

26

It seemed as if Lucy had sat on her bed with her knees drawn up and cradled in her arms for a small eternity. Her hair had dried, and outside, the sun was completing its descent.

Lucy didn't know how she felt anymore, so she had stopped thinking. Her thoughts had only been tortured and confused. Not thinking was a relief. Instead, her back against the wall, facing her bolted door, she sat like a zombie in an exhaustion as emotional as it was physical. She turned her head slightly to watch the sunset through the open window. She found that she couldn't see it. Of course. The light outside was dimming rapidly, but the monstrous walls of this dead valley monopolized her view. Soon it would be dark.

The delicious aromas of spicy stews and fried tortillas began wafting into her room. Lucy sat up straighter. Nothing had ever smelled so wonderful. What she wouldn't give for a good meal. Thinking about food was also a relief; it gave her a new focus. Would she be summoned? She waited a few minutes, the aromas becoming stronger. And then there was a knock on her door. It was the old woman. *"Señorita,* come to eat.''

Lucy hesitated, more to fortify herself with strength than with uncertainty, then stood and went to the door. She slid the bolt and walked out.

Carmen, Shoz, and the little boy sat at the big table, with Shoz at its head.

Her heart sank. The three of them were eating and had apparently just started. Now everyone paused to regard her. Lucy looked away before she could meet Shoz's gaze. There was no fourth place set for her, and even if there were, she could not join them. She would not. But was she to eat in the kitchen like a maid? It was one blow after another. The thought occurred to her that she could take a tray to her room; then she reminded herself that this was not New York. They undoubtedly did not even possess trays around here, and even if they did, they would surely think she was sulking. The kitchen seemed to be the only alternative. She started that way, but not without glancing once more at the cozy scene.

''Who's that, Papa?''

''Her name is Lucy. Where are you going?''

She froze in her tracks. She turned slowly to face him. ''I'm going to get some food.''

''The food is here on the table. Linda, bring another plate.'' He began eating with the absorption of someone long denied adequate fare.

Carmen gasped and began protesting angrily to the indirect invitation. As if Lucy would accept! ''No, thank you, I prefer to dine alone.'' She hurried into the kitchen.

She wanted to hit something or someone, she wanted to weep. As if she could sit there at that table with them— with him and his family.

But of course, she did neither. Instead, she inspected the pots and pans, found a plate, and helped herself to hefty servings of everything. There was a stool by the worktable, which hadn't been cleaned. Lucy sat down there. Grimly she took stock of the situation: eating at a meat-stained worktable covered with bits of flour and raw vegetables in the kitchen, like a servant. While that criminal dined like a king, outside—with his whorish wife and his son. She picked at her food, no longer quite so hungry. Somehow, through all of this, she would have to maintain her dignity. It seemed to be all she had left.

Carmen came in, shooting her snide looks, carrying the dishes from the table. Lucy ate, ignoring the other woman, listening to Shoz telling his son it was time for bed.

"Papa, it's early!" Roberto protested.

"I'm going to bed, too," Shoz said. "If you want me to tuck you in . . ." It was a bribe and Roberto readily agreed.

Tears misted her eyes. Lucy kept her gaze down, not about to let Carmen see anything. With the little boy, his tone was warm, teasing, and gentle. She imagined him tucking Roberto into bed, and it brought an unbearable ache. She couldn't eat anymore. She heard Shoz saying good night, a door closing—then another one closing.

So he was going to sleep early, too. Lucy didn't want to think beyond that. She didn't dare,

Carmen threw an apron at her. "You did no work," she said, hands on her hips. "You clean everything. I'm going to bed." She smiled, tauntingly.

Lucy drew herself upright. "I am not going to clean this kitchen!"

"Shoz said you are to help me. Did you help me today? No! So clean up here!"

Lucy didn't move. Her heart was thumping. "Where I come from," she said distinctly, "we have fifty servants to cook and clean. Fifty! I have never cooked in my life, I have never cleaned in my life. And I never will! That," she added, "is for your class of people."

Carmen's black eyes widened. "Stupid bitch!" she cried. Before Lucy could move, she had grabbed Lucy's thick braid and was wrenching it roughly. Lucy gasped from pain and tried to free herself. She stopped all her efforts, however, when she saw the knife Carmen held an inch from her scalp.

No one in her life had ever abused her physically before. It was a shock.

"I will cut it off," Carmen hissed. "You won't be so pretty then, will you? So do as I say!"

Lucy didn't respond, genuinely frightened. Carmen was volatile in a way Shoz was not. Lucy was afraid the woman would cut off all her beautiful hair. And then do worse. Carmen released her. Lucy was trembling.

"Now I am going to bed," Carmen announced, emphasizing the last word with a smug look. She smiled and walked off.

Lucy sat at the dirty table and pushed her plate away, trying to recover. Her hands shook. Such abuse was too much to bear! That woman had been a scant instant from severing her braid from her head! That woman, his wife! She was a monster! But what could she do?

Lucy heard a door closing. A rush of memories assailed her, all of them of her and Shoz, his hands and mouth devouring her. She imagined what was going on that very minute behind his bedroom door. She saw him touching Carmen, kissing her, holding her naked buttocks while he thrust himself into her. Lucy screwed her eyes shut. She couldn't handle imagining such a thing, not now!

But her imagination was uncontrollable; all she could seem to think about was the two of them together. Abruptly Lucy lunged to her feet and ran from the kitchen. She had to escape this house, she had to escape them! She rushed onto the front porch, stumbled down the steps, and did not pause in her wild run until she had reached one of the trees by the creek. She leaned against it, panting. Her face was wet, from her own tears.

Was it only a few hours ago that he had held her, kissed her? But that had been because she had slapped him. Still, he had kissed her and he had wanted her; there had been no doubt of that. With his own wife in the very same house. It was shocking, but she was no longer shocked; it was disgusting, but she wasn't disgusted. She just couldn't bear it. She had to face it. She was hurt and angry, as if *she* were the wife betrayed!

If only she could escape more than this house. If only a real escape were possible.

It wasn't. Lucy would never even attempt it. Even if she could escape this damn valley, she would never find her way out of the Sierra Madres and to civilization, never. She was going to have to remain here, a semiprisoner, his hostage, until he set her free. She realized that despite his lies and his betrayal, she still believed that he would keep his word and release her as soon as it was safe to do so.

Lucy wiped her eyes, realizing it was only a matter of time. And time was something she could survive. She was young and she was strong, and if she could just get her wild emotions under control, she would cope and do it well. She must remind herself frequently of the actual facts: She was Lucy Bragg, he was an outlaw. She did not want him, they did not suit each other, they would never suit each other. Carmen suited him. Perfectly.

He stared out the window into the night. He was gripping the sill, but he couldn't see much, because he had chosen the bedroom facing west—the one facing the major entrance to the valley. Oh, he could see the darker outline of the ragged rim of the valley, and if it were daylight, he would have a view to its very end. But he couldn't see her.

He had heard Lucy leave the house, and he knew by listening acutely that she had rounded the other side to go toward the creek. He pictured her running, Carmen's gypsy skirts billowing around her, revealing lots of long, sexy leg.

"Caro?" Carmen slithered from the bed and came up behind him, pressing her naked breasts against his bare back. He still wore his jeans, and with her hand, she gripped him through the denim. He was full and turgid, but not because of her. He was aroused because he wanted Lucy.

"You miss me," she said, satisfied. She kissed his shoulder, then bit it. He flinched.

She rubbed the length of him expertly. "Come to bed."

He was insane—either that or obsessed. He turned abruptly, removing her hands. "Later." He shoved past her, and barefoot, headed for the bedroom door.

Her eyes went wide. "Where are you going?"

Shoz wasn't a liar. "Outside."

"Why!"

He could have lied, he could have said he was going to relieve himself. He didn't, he opted for silence. Carmen's scream made up for it. "You bastard! You're going to her!"

He didn't answer.

Shoz listened intently to the quiet of the house, to the stillness of the night. He went to Roberto's room and very quietly pushed the door open. Roberto was afraid of the dark and slept with a small gas lamp burning. Despite these modern times, electricity and running water had not come to much of Mexico—much less Death Valley.

The boy was sleeping peacefully, and Shoz backed out silently. He was disturbed as he left the house, and he admitted it. On the porch he paused, gripping the post rail, searching the darkness by the river with his eyes. There was not a sound to disturb the thick, hot stillness of the pitch-black valley. There was no movement; not even a leaf quivered. It wasn't the first time he'd gotten an eerie feeling of unreality, standing outside in the heavy quiet of a night like this. But tonight there was more than that. He felt lonely. It was an old feeling, one he was not comfortable with and did not like. Not at all.

He made out her form after a second pass, because she was leaning against a tree, almost merged with it, giving it a grotesque shape. He hesitated.

He had never been faithful to Carmen—just like she wasn't faithful to him. They had been together for five years, and it would have lasted only five days—if it weren't for Roberto.

Thinking about Roberto made him clench up inside. There was no precise parallel, but Roberto reminded him of himself in a way. He made him think about how lucky he had been that his mother—Candice, the woman who had raised him—had loved him as if he were her own son, so much so, he'd never known the truth until told. Roberto had a real mother, but Carmen had none of Candice's love to give to her son. Shoz identified with the boy strongly, even though there was really nothing similar in their circumstances. Shoz had had a doting father—who had raised him with a loving stepmother. Roberto had a selfish, self-absorbed mother, and legally he had no father at all.

It had been almost five years now since he'd started up with Carmen, and more important, five years since he'd first mussed up a tiny toddler's black head. He knew he was Roberto's anchor, his rock, and something of his hero. Shoz hoped fervently that the day would never come when Roberto would find out the truths about him and become bitterly disillusioned.

On his part, he and Carmen had stayed together because of Roberto and convenience. Carmen and he had a very unusual, mutually self-serving relationship. In bed, they satisfied each other; outside of bed, he paid little attention to her. As long as Carmen was the queen of his bedroom, she did not care. Carmen knew nothing of his affairs, and didn't suspect that he knew of hers. She didn't know of his affairs because he was away from Death Valley often, and she always stayed behind. He had never taken any of the women in the valley, because none of them were very desirable, and Carmen pleased the hell out of him—and any man, he suspected—in bed. And he had never brought another woman here, either.

But now Lucy was here.

Which was why he was so disturbed.

He hadn't believed he had any decency left, but maybe he did. Why else would he be hesitating on the porch like a schoolboy? He owed Carmen very little, if anything. He used her, she used him. But she did live in his house, and they had spent five years together, even if they'd been apart as often as not. He didn't care what she did, because he didn't care about her, but if she did something under his nose, she would be testing his tolerance. Just as she would be enraged if he took Lucy now.

It was unbelievable that he was even hesitating to go after her. He could not remember a time when he had wanted a woman and refrained from pursuit—and conquest.

Maybe it was time to get rid of Carmen. It wasn't a new thought, and the argument against it was old and well-worn: he would never abandon Roberto.

This time he asked himself another question. What if he

managed to get Carmen to leave, without taking Roberto? He had never considered this before. He considered it now. Carmen would screech and scream and holler, but if he wanted her gone, she would ultimately go. He knew his own will, his power. He imagined he could pay her off handsomely and she would willingly, even gladly, leave her son. But what kind of life would Roberto have without a mother, even one as selfish and self-centered as Carmen?

Soon Lucy would be gone, too. He imagined coming "home" to this valley with only Roberto to greet him, and Linda. He imagined going to bed, night after night, alone. He supposed he could occasionally find release with one of the village women, if he was really in a bad way. At the moment the thought disgusted him. Eventually he might find another woman to take Carmen's place in his life, but he doubted it. Their relationship was too unusual. Again he thought about returning just to Roberto, and to an empty bed. The feeling of loneliness that had gripped him earlier gripped him again.

He didn't want to come home to this house without a woman waiting for him. Carmen only provided an illusion of the family he needed, a shadow of what his parents had and what he'd once, foolishly, assumed he would have, but he desperately needed that illusion anyway.

He stared out into the darkness. His groin had eased; now he should go back into the house, back to Carmen. Lucy wasn't for him anyway. But he didn't move.

He stayed on the porch staring at her even though she was nothing but a blurred outline. He stayed thinking and remembering, until he was aching and hard again. He stayed until he had her scent, and was crazy because of it. He stepped off the porch, shoving all his doubts aside.

Lucy was an illusion of what he needed so desperately, too. And then it occurred to him that in another time and in another place, she wouldn't be an illusion at all.

27

Lucy hadn't heard a single sound in the godforsaken night, so when he touched her shoulder, she jumped with a cry.

"I didn't mean to frighten you," Shoz said.

It was one of the blackest nights Lucy had ever experienced, the sky heavy and dark, unlit by any stars, with the giant rock walls of the valley leaning in on them, somehow making the night even darker. Yet in the murky blackness it was impossible to decide where the sky ended and the cliffs began, and Lucy had finally gotten the fantastic impression that the two had merged and were hovering over her like a low, overburdened ceiling, threatening to cave in.

Shoz was a relief because he was real and human, yet he was the last person she wanted to be with, too. She could barely make out his form, much less his expression. Only his teeth, glimmering brightly when he spoke, and the sheen of his eyes. She stepped back. He was like an apparition, adding to the unreality she had been experiencing. He was her own private demon come to taunt her. "What do you want?"

"I want you, Lucy."

His voice was low and sexy, and her name on his lips in such a tone could have had a magnetic effect upon her. The pull was there, mesmerizing. But she was truly affronted, with his wife within calling distance, his little boy in a bedroom whose very window looked out upon them, a stone's throw away. If he hadn't had a wife, if they had been alone on this night in this place in this time, Lucy might not have resisted him at all. "What about her!"

Shoz wanted to kick himself for not exercising restraint and attempting a more subtle, seductive approach. But he was never subtle around Lucy. Since they'd first met, she had brought out his worst side. Not that he had ever been a saint with other women, far from it. "Lucy," he started, wanting to amend the breach he sensed was widening rapidly.

She turned her head away, but not soon enough. His gaze was very acute, and he thought her eyes shone with tears. Because he had been unsuccessfully debating that very same question—what about Carmen?—for a good part of the evening, he did not have a ready response.

"Leave me alone."

He couldn't. If he could have, he would have. He stepped forward, crowding her, and although she backed up, he reached her and caught her arm. "You wanted me the other day, when you thought it was good-bye."

"I was a fool, and I did think it was good-bye!" She tried to twist away, but he wouldn't let her.

He had broached a topic that was very important to him, too important, one he normally would have never addressed. But on a night like this, inhibitions fled. "Why, Lucy? I had made up my mind to leave you alone, but you wanted me. You asked me. Why?"

He had her other arm now, too, and he was so close, she could feel his heat. "Let me go!"

"Tell me," he whispered.

She tried to wrench free, but with a bit less determination. He was too close, too male. Too exciting. She could feel the heat emanating from his body, and she could smell his scent, tobacco, sweat, leather—and man. Her body was starting to tremble, from despair and desire. "Please let me go."

"Not until you tell me why you encouraged me, Lucy."

Her temper erupted. "Because I'm just not a decent woman, am I? Because I wanted—" she hesitated, wanting to be crude, wanting to wound him "—sex. We'd already done it, hadn't we? So what would one more time matter? I wanted to try it again, and I certainly couldn't do it with someone from back home! Most importantly, I would never see you again, and no one had found out about the first time, and they wouldn't find out about this. So I was safe. So I could do what I want, then say good-bye and never have to see you again.''

He released her now and stepped away from her.

He remained unmoving, and for an instant, Lucy regretted everything she had said. Then his lips curled, his teeth gleaming. ''What if I tell you that this is also good-bye?''

His tone was very dangerous, but only his words registered. She gasped, staring at him and trying to discern if this was a lie. ''What?''

''I'm leaving tomorrow.''

''You're leaving?''

''That's right. No one will ever know, Lucy. Your little secret will be safe with me.'' He didn't move toward her. He leaned against the tree, his pose relaxed, one knee bent and his foot braced against it. But his eyes never left her.

''Where are you going? When are you coming back? What about me?''

''Where I'm going is none of your business. I'll be back in ten days or so. After that, I'll find the time and the place to let you go.''

''I want out of this hellhole! I want you to take me with you! You promised you'd set me free after we got here!''

''I'm not going to a garden party. I have every intention of keeping my promise to you when I get back.''

''You bastard.''

''Not very original.''

She knew there was no use in arguing, that he would never change his mind. Silence filled the moment between them, and Lucy folded her arms tightly against her breast.

''Where's my good-bye?'' he drawled contemptuously.

''Never again.''

''Never? Never's a long time, Miss Bragg.''

''I mean it.''

''Why?'' His voice was mocking. ''No one will know. Why, we can pass each other on the street in New York City someday and I won't even tip my hat. Promise.''

''You disgust me!''

He shoved himself off the tree. His teeth flickered white

again. "The feeling's mutual, princess. Enjoy the night. I intend to." And without a look back, he walked away.

And Lucy didn't have a single doubt where he was going, and to whom.

Although he didn't make a sound as he entered the house, his strides were hard and coiled tight. He exercised the utmost will not to slam the front door behind him as hard as he could.

She was just like all the others.

She was exactly like all the other *ladies* he'd fucked, the ones who would suck him off in the bedroom and look through him as if he were invisible should they pass on the street. And he despised her, even more than all the others, even more than Marianne.

When he walked into the bedroom, Carmen hurled a glass at him. He ducked and it hit the wall, just missing him. "Don't you come in here!"

He wasn't in the mood for this; he wasn't in the mood for her. "This is my bedroom. You don't want my company, then get out."

She sat still. She wore French lingerie, sheer, black, revealing everything. Her eyes were wild, her breasts heaving. But Carmen knew him well, and she was shrewd. She studied him for one more moment. "What happened?"

He didn't answer, stripping off his jeans. He was glad he hadn't laid her, because the last thing he wanted to be was Miss Bragg's private stud for her sexual experimenting.

"You didn't make love to her," Carmen said.

To get her off his back, he admitted it. "No."

"You don't want her?" She watched him the way a cat does a mouse.

He smiled meanly. "I don't care for frigid bitches in my bed, Carmen, especially not ones who will run to Daddy crying rape. I don't need that on my head, either."

Carmen was too clever to be fooled, and sensed everything. She was also too clever to reveal what she understood. "Who is she? Who is that little nobody who gives herself such airs?"

"I used her to break out of jail and took her as a hostage.

As soon as I can, when it's safe, I'm freeing her.'' He would be a fool to reveal Lucy's identity to Carmen. He didn't trust his mistress for a second.

"For a ransom?"

"No ransom." His gaze was impatient. "I didn't kidnap her, and I'd prefer not to have kidnapping added to my record."

Carmen thought about this while he climbed into bed. He tried not to think about Lucy, the snobby bitch, because if he did, he would get so angry that he would never sleep. Instead, he thought about something else that had been preoccupying him lately.

Would the guns still be there? Would the guns still be buried near Geoffard's Hanging Tree? There was a good chance that they would. Shoz could not leave such a cache indefinitely. He couldn't afford to lose them should they be unearthed; he had a deal to finish. He had decided to take all of his men to retrieve them except for two, whom he would leave behind to guard the stronghold and Lucy. It would only take ten days to bring back the weapons if all went well. They would pack them out on four sturdy horses. He would be very cautious and clever about entering Texas again, and fortunately, the guns were not buried in Paradise County. Once back across the border, he would stop briefly to send a telegram to his contact to rearrange another sale.

He knew it was dangerous to go back to Texas, but he didn't have much choice. Besides, he'd be going with a small, fast army. If they had to, they'd fight and then run. It wouldn't be the first time, unfortunately.

By now, he imagined they were getting pretty desperate for the guns down in Cuba. What had started as a small uprising against the yoke of the Spanish government, led by someone named José Marti, seemed to be heading for a real war. If the quantity of arms they were requesting was any indication. Shoz didn't know much about it and didn't particularly care. He doubted like hell they'd succeed against one of the world's strongest powers. But as long as they kept paying cash, he'd keep supplying them with guns and whatever else they needed.

Carmen snuggled next to him. Shoz had lost absolutely

all desire, but he thought of that bitch outside turning up her nose at him, so when Carmen started stroking his belly, he did not remove her hand. She was very skilled, and she knew exactly how to please him.

She slid down his body, kissing and biting him, her fingers like magic on his testicles, until she was cradling him with her big breasts. Carmen teased his shaft with her lips and tongue until he was painfully rigid. Shoz had ceased to be aware of her. Instead, he was thinking about the Bragg princess. He imagined that it was Lucy sucking him like this, against her will, helpless to resist; he imagined that he was forcing her to kneel before him, forcing her to rub her face all over his shaft. Only, hot bitch that she was, what began as coercion ended with her whimpering in pleasure and need.

With a growl, he tossed Carmen on her back and plunged into her. It was over in moments and he rolled away, panting. As always, the physical release seemed to be just that and nothing more. It had never bothered him before. But now, it did.

He did not feel satiated. He did not feel satisfied. Foolishly, he thought of Lucy again.

Carmen's hand stole over to his hard chest. "You missed me," she purred, pleased with herself.

The last thing he wanted was more of her attention. He stopped her hand. "I'm exhausted."

"What?"

"You heard me. I'm leaving early tomorrow."

"What!?"

He turned over, away from her, not bothering to explain. He had explained more than enough for one night.

The Braggs had taken over the entire saloon for their headquarters. Fernando had been handsomely paid for the use of his premises, and hadn't been seen since. The decision to remain in Casitas had been made three days ago, the day they had found the lame horse and the three dead bodies on the trail leading up into the mountains.

It was obvious that the killer had been in the boulders on the plateau above the trail, ambushing the bandits from this

vantage point while they were traveling unsuspecting below
him. They weren't certain it was Shoz Cooper, but they
knew he and Lucy had come in this direction, because of
the stolen horse they had found earlier. It certainly could
have been Shoz Cooper, and if it was, he was proving to
be a very cunning adversary. For it had taken several hours
to find Shoz's trail after that.

But they had, and sometime later they had found the cave
with the recent droppings of two horses. They had also found
Lucy's shoes.

Late in the afternoon they picked up their track on a deer
trail. But soon it disappeared, and no amount of searching
in the past few days had recovered it.

Shoz Cooper had vanished into the Sierra Madres with
Lucy Bragg.

Now the night was still and dark, the town asleep, except
for the saloon. Within, fifty men drank and played cards
and passed the time. Another fifty men were camped just
outside of town, preferring sleep to liquor and gambling.
The ranks of the posse had been swelled by the arrival of
fifty private Pinkerton agents just that morning. Everyone
was waiting for their orders.

One of the back rooms, the largest one, had been rear-
ranged hastily to serve as a command center. A solid old
wooden table served for conferences, surrounded by a dozen
rickety chairs. Another table held an enamel pot of hot
coffee, chipped mugs, several bottles of whiskey, and
chipped glasses. There were seven people in the room.

Storm sat next to her brother Rathe to comfort him. He
was unshaven, thinner, and gray with despair. The dark
circles beneath his eyes testified to all the sleepless nights
he had endured. Storm kept her palm on his forearm. Yet
he was sitting straight and tense, his blue eyes keenly alert.

Everyone was keenly alert—Brett, near the wall, his
hands jammed into the pockets of his dungarees; Nick,
straddling a chair across the table from his brother and sister;
Derek, standing next to him, his fists clenched. In the center
of the room was the focus of their attention. He called
himself Lloyd.

He was tall and whipcord-lean in a dusty brown suit and

worn boots. About forty years of age, he was nondescript except for his shrewd, penetrating blue eyes. He worked for the United States government.

The connection between this man and Shoz Cooper had been made by the chief of the Pinkerton office in New York, whom Derek had contacted by wire to hire the detectives. It was a fortunate coincidence, really. The New York bureau chief recalled a conversation he had had a year earlier when based in Washington, D.C., with a friend of his who was an ex-Pinkerton and now worked for Uncle Sam. In that conversation, the name Shoz Cooper had come up. It was the alias of the man his friend's bureau was hunting. His real name was Shoz Savage.

"What?" Rathe said, stunned.

"I know just about everything there is to know about Shoz Cooper—the name he's been going by these past seven years—because I've been hunting him this past year—all three hundred and sixty-five days of it."

"Since when is an escaped felon convicted for burglary so important to the federal government?" Brett asked. More research had been done during the past few days, and another detail had come to light—the nature of the offense he'd committed in New York.

"Since he started selling stolen army rifles to the rebels in Cuba."

A moment of silence greeted this bit of news as everyone struggled to digest it.

Lloyd continued. "The first thing I want to do, Rathe, is assure you that Cooper is a smart mercenary, but in no way a typical criminal. I have not a doubt that your little girl is safe. He's not a murderer, so you can rest at ease. Although I cannot understand why he would steal a horse. That is bothering me; it doesn't fit.

"After interviewing the Paradise deputy, I'm more convinced than ever that he merely used your daughter to escape, and kept her as a hostage to insure his success. Things have been getting a bit too hot for him lately."

"You haven't reassured me. I won't be reassured until I have Lucy back, safe and sound and—untouched," Rathe said fiercely.

Lloyd said nothing on the last matter, although Storm turned to him. "He did rescue the girls when their auto broke down."

Rathe said nothing.

Derek cut in. "We got word from the Abilene marshall today that Red Ames and Jake Holt have been arrested. We'll know that story soon enough."

Lloyd continued. "Let me fill you in on a few facts. Cooper's real name is Shoz Savage. His story begins in New York. He attended Columbia University on a partial scholarship, paying the rest by himself by working part-time. He also worked his way through New York Law School." Storm gasped in surprise. Lloyd ignored it. "If he ever did anything dishonest then, we have no record of it. But after graduation, just after he opened a private practice, he was caught stealing a large diamond from the employer of a housemaid he was seeing." He looked at Storm. "Excuse me." He wasn't apologetic.

"Why would he steal at such a point in his life?" Storm asked.

"It was a helluva diamond. Maybe he just couldn't pass up the temptation. A nice little egg like that could have set him nicely on his feet. What does it matter? He was tried and convicted—he was caught with the ring in his pocket.

"Seven months after his incarceration began, he escaped. He was working on a chain gang and overpowered two guards, stole one of their guns, and forced them to unlock his manacles. After tossing the key to the other inmates, he took off, and did not come to my attention until last year."

Lloyd paused briefly, his gaze touching everyone in the room. "As you probably know, our government is very concerned with the recent events in Cuba. It's a mixed deal. A lot of American property is at stake. Our citizens have some fifty million dollars invested in that island, and that doesn't include the cash value of our annual trade. Right now we have sixteen million dollars of claims filed against the Spanish government for property damage and loss and even downright dispossession, but they turn a deaf ear. That's another story anyway. We're also a democracy, and it's a fact that an American can't look the other way when an entire people are savagely oppressed. There's also strategic considerations. Cuba's in our backyard.''

"Get to the damn point," Rathe erupted. "I know more about fucking Cuba than you ever will.''

"Yes you do, don't you, Rathe? You and your family are major investors, aren't they? Maravilla, railroads, freight depots, warehouses, shipping, ports, you name it.''

"Half of the board of the Manhattan Bank has major assets in Cuba," Rathe snapped.

"Exactly. That's why we are so concerned, as I said. That's why when guns began to reach the rebels in Havana, I was brought in.''

"And Shoz is running some of those guns," Nick stated.

"Shoz is running most of those guns. He's been doing it very successfully for the past year. He's clever. But we almost caught him a few months ago in Corpus Christi when he was sending out a shipment. Unfortunately, he and his men escaped." The agent was grim for the first time. "Nevertheless, I can offer hope, and a lot of it. We have an informer in Santiago.''

Everyone sat up straighter except for Rathe, who was on his feet. "How in hell does that affect me? I don't give a damn about Cuba right now!''

"I understand that your daughter has priority, Rathe, believe me, I do. But we have a common interest, wouldn't you say? In apprehending Shoz Cooper.''

"I take it you are going to make us a proposition?" Nick asked dryly.

"Damn right. We're going to work together. That is, you're going to do my work for me, in Mexico, where I have no damn authority and no right to be.''

Six pairs of eyes shifted and met and turned back to Lloyd. "I don't think anyone here objects to breaking a Mexican law or two," Brett said. "I certainly don't.''

"Good, but let's make sure we understand each other. I will tell you everything you need to know, but if your path ever crosses that of the Mexican authorities, you're private citizens acting on your own.''

"We've played this game before," Derek said. "Go on.''

"The rebels are awaiting another shipment of guns, desperately," Lloyd said. "There was a delay recently when one of their men was caught by the Spanish authorities and executed. He had met Shoz Cooper three times this past year on Texas soil to buy the guns and ship them to Cuba. It's only a delay. They are sending someone else to take his place—soon. When they set up the new deal to make the transaction, we will know exactly where it will be, and when. And Shoz Cooper will be there."

Rathe lunged forward. "And we'll be waiting for the bastard."

"That's right."

"I'm going to kill him," Rathe said.

28

The door opened and hit the wall with a bang. Startled out of a sound sleep, Lucy practically bolted out of the bed. Bright morning sunlight was streaming through the windows. Realizing she wore nothing but her drawers because of the heat, Lucy clutched the sheet to her neck, expecting to see Shoz in a temper.

Carmen stood against the door. She wore a flaming red blouse and a black skirt with a another gold one underneath. There were pink combs in her hair. "Get up!"

Luck blinked. "Pardon me?"

"The sun is up. Who do you think you are? Everyone is already working. Get up!" She strode out.

Lucy debated defying Carmen; after all, who was she to tell her what to do? Then, as exhausted as she was, she decided it wasn't worth fighting over, not with that volatile woman. Besides, judging from the sunlight pouring into her room, and the oppressive, wet heat, she had already overslept. She rose, washed, and dressed quickly.

In the kitchen, Carmen and the older woman were rolling tortillas. "Finally!" Carmen cried. She shoved a rolling pin at Lucy. "Linda will show you how to do it."

Lucy found herself holding the pin and thinking that this was patently unfair. "I'm not doing this. I haven't even had my breakfast yet!"

"The royal queen hasn't even had her breakfast!" Carmen mimicked. She seemed ferociously angry. "Did you hear that, Linda? You are our prisoner," she said to Lucy. "And you do as we say. As I say."

Lucy had had enough. She put down the rolling pin. "I am not *your* prisoner. And I am going to eat breakfast." Even if I have to make it myself, she added silently. This was in itself a major concession.

She had forgotten about last night, sleepy as she still was. Carmen grabbed her ear, shocking and hurting her. "You didn't clean up last night, did you? Today you sleep until seven. Now you don't want to work? Do you want me to give you to the men?"

Lucy wrenched free, her ear throbbing, her heart pounding, her eyes wide. "How dare you!" Her tone broke. The memory of Carmen almost cutting off her braid with a knife last night came rushing back to her. And now she had mauled her. That another person should touch her so, should willfully hurt her . . . She was speechless.

"Start work!"

Lucy just stared, stunned and shaken. This woman was mad, she decided. Mad and dangerous. God! She didn't want to go to Shoz, but she knew she needed protection from this witch. "Where is Shoz?" She started for the door at a run, but Carmen's answer brought her to a halt.

"He is not here." There was pleasure in her tone.

Lucy whirled. "What do you mean? You make it sound as if he has already left!"

"He has! He has gone with most of the men." Slyly she said, "But he left two. To guard you. His instructions were clear. You are his prisoner, *puta,* and you are to help me. If you disobey me, you answer to me."

This could not be happening to her, Lucy Bragg. To be kidnapped by Shoz was one thing. To want him was another.

But to be left here, *a prisoner*, at the mercy of his violent wife . . . "When will he be back?"

"Ten days. Maybe even two weeks."

Ten days . . . two weeks. Now she recalled him saying so. How would she survive? Lucy didn't have a chance to consider her new dilemma. Carmen warned, "If you do not start making tortillas, I am going to let Pedro and José have you. I mean it."

Lucy did not doubt her. Tears of rage, frustration, and even despair welled. She reached for the rolling pin she had set down, and accepted the dough Linda handed her. How could this be happening? How could Shoz have left her here alone? Moments later, she was up to her elbows in cornmeal.

After an hour or so, spent mostly sipping coffee and eating buttered bread while dispensing bossy orders, Carmen left. Lucy worked numbly alongside Linda, now chopping vegetables. She tried not to think; it was better not to think.

It was with surprise that she realized Linda was holding out a hot cup of coffee. Lucy accepted it gratefully. It was very strong, black with the barest amount of sugar, but it was delicious. She sipped it with relish, watching the older woman, who regarded her as well. Linda seemed old enough to be Carmen's mother, and time had not treated her well.

"Thank you for the coffee."

"De nada."

"Is it really so early? It's so hot—I thought I woke up late."

"Carmen woke you after the padrone rode out—just after seven."

Lucy clenched her fist. She didn't know who she was angrier at, Carmen for making sure Shoz was well and gone before waking her, or Shoz, for leaving without a goodbye. She remembered how Shoz had wanted to say goodbye last night and felt herself flushing. She had done the smart thing in refusing him, the only thing. Had he gone to Carmen? It shouldn't upset her, but it did.

Lucy was determined to have some answers as long as Carmen was gone. "Have you been here long?"

"Many years."

Lucy set the cup down. "As long as Carmen?"

Linda nodded. Lucy felt her heart sinking. "And Shoz? He, of course, has been here with you for many years?"

"Of course. All this is his. He is the boss, the padrone."

"Why did he go? Where did he go?"

The big woman shrugged. "I do not know where he goes. You ask a lot of questions about him, señorita."

Lucy shrugged to hide her interest. "He kidnapped me. And Carmen? Is she—always so—emotional?"

"Carmen is Carmen."

How apt. Lucy finished the coffee, glancing out the window. No sign of her new tormentor. At least in Linda she had some sort of ally. Was Carmen also so "emotional" in bed? So volatile? Lucy imagined she was. She was probably exactly how Shoz liked a woman to be in bed. The thought was unbearable.

"What are you doing?" Carmen cried from behind her.

Lucy jumped and spilled the coffee. It was hot and it burned her hand, but she stepped back when she saw the other woman's fury. "Stop wasting time! You are not here to drink coffee!"

Lucy put the cup down, and wiped her hands on a rag. "Why do you hate me so?" she asked, looking at Carmen directly. "I've done nothing to you." It was a lie—she had slept with her husband.

Carmen snorted. "I do not hate you! You are nothing, nothing to me. And nothing to him!"

Lucy lifted her chin high. "Thank God. I don't want his interest. My beaux come from Society, from big brick mansions with acres of green lawns, from good families with breeding and background; they are not criminals hiding in some godforsaken place like this."

Carmen mimicked her. "My beaux! You think you're better than us, do you?" She laughed, eyeing her contemptuously. "Where are your fifty servants now?"

"He has given me his word—he is going to release me soon."

"And until he does, you stay away from him," Carmen warned. "Unless you want to be his plaything, his whore. Is that what you want, *puta*?"

Lucy knew what *puta* meant, and she flushed, because of what she and Shoz had done. "I told you, I have absolutely no interest in him."

"I don't believe you," Carmen said shrewdly. "All women look at him—but he is mine. I have been with him many years—and I will stay with him many more!"

"I'm sure you will," Lucy said, eager to end this conversation, which was making her uncomfortable.

"Just remember this the next time he looks at you," Carmen hissed. "For him, you are something new, a new toy, like he brings Roberto."

Lucy couldn't find a response, because she was afraid that Carmen had spoken the truth.

Carmen smiled cruelly. "If you sleep with him, it is as his whore. For a while he will enjoy you, then he will toss you away." She turned on her heel. But in the doorway she paused, triumphant. "And then he will return to me. He always returns to me."

The morning was endless. It was so hot. Sweat covered Lucy's body with a fine film, making her clothes stick wetly to her skin. Since last night, she had decided not to put her hair in a braid, afraid it would be too accessible to the willful Carmen. But now she could not stand its unrestrained mass on her back, and she coiled it on top of her head. She had rolled tortillas until her arms ached, chopped vegetables until she cut her thumb, and baked bread until she was red in the face from the heat of the oven. She was so hot and so tired, and she was no longer even hungry.

Around noontime, Linda told her to place a plate of fresh tortillas and a bowl of beans on the table. Lucy obeyed without question. When she was instructed to bring a pitcher of lemonade to the table, a terrible inkling occurred. Linda then handed her two plates, napkins, and flatware, and Lucy froze in her tracks. "This is for Carmen?!"

"Sí, for her and *el niño pequeño*."

Lucy shook. She was dropping with exhaustion—and here she was *setting the table* for that other woman? For his wife? "I won't do it."

Linda studied her mutinous expression, took all the items

from her, and placed them on the dining table in the next room herself. In the kitchen, Lucy clung to the worktable. Her heart was thundering. She had to make a stand, didn't she? She was not going to be a maid to that woman; it was intolerable.

Some moments later, Carmen and Roberto entered, the little boy very quiet compared to the day before. Lucy wondered if it was the heat, or if he missed Shoz.

Lucy and Linda sat in the kitchen while Carmen and Roberto ate in silence in the other room. Hunger gnawed at her. She had barely eaten in days, and had had nothing at all today. Anger began a slow simmer. Carmen called out for more lemonade.

Lucy looked at Linda. Linda shrugged, stood, and waddled into the other room. Lucy sat very still, dreading a confrontation. But it was not to be avoided.

"You don't serve!" Carmen shrieked. "Where is that bitch? Where?" Something was slammed on the table.

Lucy sat unmoving while Linda returned with the empty pitcher and handed it to her. Lucy didn't get up. She knew she had to fight this woman, she had to, but she was afraid. What if Carmen did give her to the two men left behind to guard her? Lucy thought Carmen would enjoy letting them rape her, was probably waiting for the right opportunity, and even looking for an excuse to let them have her. God! She got up, filled the pitcher, and reluctantly brought it into the dining room.

As she was leaving, she caught Roberto's eye. He was regarding her curiously. The solemn expression on his face almost made her heart stop. That poor boy is lonely, she thought with a pang. She remembered how he had appeared yesterday, the sheer joy on his face when he'd seen that Shoz had returned.

Back in the kitchen, Lucy found herself straining to hear Carmen—to hear a mother's love for her son. But Carmen did not speak except to chastise Roberto for not eating his food—only then to tell him that if he wasn't hungry, he could go. The little boy escaped the house at a dead run.

When Carmen left, Lucy and Linda cleared the table. Then, in the kitchen, they sat down to their own meal.

When they were finished, they washed all of the dishes and then Linda told her it was time for a short siesta. "Only one hour, señorita," she warned. "Then we must start preparing the supper."

One hour sounded like heaven. Lucy stumbled into her room, shutting the door and dropping the bolt. Was this how she would pass her days? In the kitchen, slaving over meals for Carmen? With that terrible thought, she fell into a deep sleep.

Lucy grew used to the heat.

Several days passed. Lucy rose just after the sun, spent the entire day in the kitchen with Linda except for a siesta, served Carmen and Roberto lunch and dinner, and was finished with her duties shortly after sundown when the kitchen was clean and tidy. The past few nights she had been too exhausted to do anything other than sink into bed and fall instantly, deeply asleep.

Tonight she wasn't exhausted, although she was tired. She slipped outside to sit by the river, hoping to find the night cooler and less oppressive by the water's edge. It wasn't. There was no breeze, just the still, wet heat. But tonight she detected different sounds by listening intently. The faint whirring of an annoying mosquito, the whickering of a horse in the remuda, and farther away, maybe, just maybe, she heard a lone wolf howl. She counted the days.

Three days had passed since Shoz had left. In one week he might be returning. Or in ten days.

If he was not delayed.

What did she care, anyway?

She stroked a blade of grass and thought about the dream—the very disturbing dream—she'd been having when Carmen woke her up that morning. It had stayed with her all day. She and Shoz. Naked and entwined, making love deliciously, languidly. It had been very exciting and very real. The strangest, most disturbing part wasn't that she had awakened unbearably aroused. It was that in the dream they had been laughing while they were making love, laughing.

Shoz had only made love to her twice, if she counted

that first abortive time when her new automobile had broken down and Joanna had found them. Both times he had been very intense and strained. She could not imagine him making love to her, or anyone, with such carefree abandon, with such lighthearted playfulness. What did she care, anyway?

She told herself that she didn't. It was just a foolish dream. How he made love was not her business, it was Carmen's.

When would he return? It was amazing how one could change one's feelings so completely. When they had arrived in the valley and she had discovered Carmen's existence, Lucy had hoped never to set eyes on him again. Now she prayed that he would return as soon as possible. Her heart seemed to skip at the thought. He would fix her awful situation and put that horrid Carmen in her place.

A kind of status quo seemed to have been attained, with Lucy doing her duties and Carmen smugly satisfied. The woman enjoyed forcing her into servitude, and it was hateful. The past few days Lucy had been too tired even to think anymore, but tonight she felt a lot of resentment, and a lot of anger.

How could Shoz stand her?

There was only one answer, one terrible answer; he found her so gorgeous that he could not see what she really was. He wouldn't be the first man to be blindly in love.

Lucy got to her feet. The pleasure she had found in the evening was shattered by reality. She made her way back to the house and slipped quietly inside.

And came face-to-face with Carmen.

Carmen stood in the living room in a yellow dress with a gold shawl over her shoulders and a red scarf tied around her curly black hair. The two women stared at each other. "Where have you been?" Carmen demanded.

"I was sitting by the river—if that's all right with you," Lucy retorted.

"Alone?"

"Alone? Of course alone? Who would I be with—the coyotes?"

"Maybe you were with Pedro."

Lucy actually recoiled. "Pedro!"

Carmen seemed satisfied and stalked past her and out of the house.

Lucy turned to watch her, wondering where she was going, but the night swallowed her up. How strange, she mused, then decided that the other woman, like herself, was seeking some coolness in the evening. She wouldn't find it.

She paused when she passed Roberto's door, noticing that it was ajar, and that a light came from within. Wasn't it late for a little boy to be up? Gently she pushed the door open. "Roberto?"

He was lying in bed but not sleeping. He looked so sad and forlorn that it tore at Lucy. "Are you all right?"

He sat up. His eyes were very big and black. "Sí, señorita."

"Can't you sleep?"

He shook his head, his sober gaze glued to her.

"Why not? It's not still too hot for you, is it?"

Again he shook his head. "I don't like being alone at night," he finally blurted out. "Papa is gone, I saw your door open, that you were gone, and Mama went out . . ."

Lucy felt a real urge to strangle Carmen. Surely that woman knew her son was afraid of being left alone at night! "Well," she said cheerfully, "I'm here now, and I'm going to bed. I'll be right next door."

His smile was small, but glad. "Sí, señorita."

She moved forward to turn out the lamp.

"No! Papa lets me keep it on!"

Lucy hesitated, then smiled. "I didn't know." She looked at him, wanting to offer him something, some comfort, because he seemed so lost and lonely. Lucy touched his head, her fingers lingering there among the silky softness for a moment. "Do you want me to bring you some warm milk? It will help you sleep."

This smile was shy. "Sí, señorita."

Lucy returned his smile with one of her own and went to heat some milk. When she brought it to him, she sat at his side while he sipped it, telling him that she had five younger brothers, the youngest almost his age.

"Really?"

"Really."

"I wish I had a brother—or a sister."

Lucy tensed but smiled anyway. "I'm sure you will. Now—" she took the empty glass from him "—go to sleep. I'm right next door. If you need me, come and get me. It's all right. I don't mind being woken up."

"You don't?"

"Not at all."

"Mama would smack me if I ever walked into her room," he declared. "She told me I must never, ever go in at night."

Lucy was appalled. She understood, though—Carmen didn't want her lovemaking interrupted, that witch! "I am not like your mother," she said calmly. "Call me if you need me." At the door, she paused. "Good night, Roberto."

"*Buenas noches,* señorita."

29

"Linda, how do you make cookies?"

Linda looked at her quizzically. It was the morning of another hot, humid day, the sun blazing in its intensity outside. "Cookies, señorita?"

"Yes, for Roberto."

Linda beamed. "I will show you, señorita. It is easy."

Lucy smiled back. "But I don't think we should let Carmen know." She glanced over her shoulder, but the woman was not eavesdropping from the doorway. "I have a feeling she would not like my baking cookies for her son."

"It will be our secret," Linda said.

Carmen was still sleeping, so the two women whipped up a batch of sugar-coated cookies, using expensive white flour. She was sleeping uncharacteristically late, for she had been up every morning before Lucy in order to wake her up pounding rudely on the door. Lucy had not slept soundly last night. She had thought about the lonely little boy for a long time—and his hard, self-contained father. In the end-less hours of the night, when thoughts, like magical dragons, metamorphosed and grew and took on unreal proportions, she had been struck by a terrible insight. Any man who showed such affection to a small, quiet boy was not a com-plete and hopeless bastard. There was a deep, hidden well of sensitivity, compassion, and even love within Shoz. It was the most awful, frightening thought she had ever had.

Just because he loves Roberto doesn't mean he will ever love you, had been one of her last lucid thoughts before drifting off. Besides, he loves Carmen, doesn't he?

Lucy had woken up after midnight when Carmen came in none too quietly, her heels clicking, cursing when she knocked into a table. She had wondered briefly at the hour and then turned over to toss restlessly again. The night passed in a strange collage of dreams with one key player—Shoz.

After lunch had been served and the table cleared and Lucy was free for a siesta, she baked the cookies, with growing anticipation. She put them in a small basket and went looking for Roberto. She found him fishing at the river, quite some distance from the house. The pole he held was made of shiny blue aluminum, most definitely store-bought. His eyes brightened when he saw her.

"What a beautiful pole," Lucy said gaily. "Wherever did you get that?"

"Papa bought it for me in Texas," Roberto said proudly. "Last year—for my birthday."

This disturbed her. She was reminded of all her mental rampaging last night—of her crazy conclusion that Shoz was not such a tough bastard. She smoothed out her skirts and sat down. "Want to share some cookies?"

"Cookies!" It was the magic word.

As Roberto scrambled over, all shyness forgotten, Lucy smiled. She didn't mind missing her siesta at all. It was worth it, just to see such pleasure on his solemn young face.

The days crept slowly by, much like the flat, sluggish

river. Lucy discovered calluses on the pads of her fingers. A few days later she noticed that her ivory skin was the palest, softest gold. There were riotous blond highlights in her hair. She eyed herself critically, and decided she looked quite exotic. As exotic as Carmen?

Would Shoz like the changes in her appearance?

She shoved such inane, inappropriate considerations away. She still spent most of her time in the kitchen with Linda. Many days now she had forgone her allotted siesta to sit by the river—or swim. She only dared the latter in her clothes, which dried quickly enough, and when she was certain her two guards were otherwise involved. They spent most of their time playing cards and drinking aguardiente, with a seemingly limitless tolerance.

One afternoon Lucy made a shocking discovery, one that drastically affected her relationship with Carmen. Not tired enough to nap, she strolled along the river and stumbled upon Carmen and Pedro, as naked as newborn babies. There was nothing innocent about what they were doing, however, and Lucy beat a hasty retreat. They were too involved to notice her.

Did Shoz know? Her pulse was pounding. Did Shoz know his wife was an adulteress? Lucy was sure he did not. Something like excitement filled her, and she paused, leaning against the side of the house, her body taut and tense. Shoz was not the type of man to let his wife cuckold him. Absolutely not. He didn't know. What should she do?

Lucy knew it was wrong, un-Christian, to be glad that Carmen was such a snake. But she was glad. Of course, she could never snitch, no matter how much she despised her, no matter how much the woman pushed her. Still, one day Shoz would find out. She imagined his fury. It would be terrifying.

Because Carmen and Pedro were occupied, Lucy decided to take a swim. She had just entered the water when she heard a noise on the bank. She whirled, ducking underneath. Even though she wore a blouse and her petticoat, she knew they revealed much more than was allowable. She was surprised to see Roberto, hesitating by a tree.

She smiled. ''Hullo.'' She had made several attempts to

become his friend, but the little boy was shy, and although he'd eaten the cookies with her several days ago, he'd merely mumbled a "yes" or "no" to her queries and run off. Now he sort of smiled. There was loneliness in that smile, and it pierced her. She thought he looked wistful, and an idea struck her. "Do you want to swim with me, Roberto?"

His face brightened as if hundreds of electric lights had gone off, and he beamed, coming forward. "Sí, señorita!"

"Do you know how to swim?" Lucy asked.

"Sí." He nodded vigorously. "Papa taught me. We swim together all the time."

"Take off all your clothes except for your underwear," she instructed him. He complied readily and was soon wading in to paddle around her. Lucy smiled and splashed him. He laughed and ducked under the water, coming up like a porpoise blowing air.

They paddled around and played like two children. Lucy was pleased to see that Roberto was truly enjoying himself. She thought that they should do this more often, and decided to find some other activities that they could share. That was when Carmen screamed at them from the bank.

Lucy dropped to her neck in the water instinctively, but Carmen was alone. "What are you doing?" she shouted. "Get out, Roberto, get out this instant!"

Roberto scrambled to obey, all the joy going out of his expression, which became solemn and closed. "Put on your clothes," Carmen cried, pointing at his shirt, jeans, and moccasins. "You left them in the dirt!" She turned her wrath on Lucy as Roberto struggled into his clothes. "You! How dare you!"

Lucy stood up, the water cascading off her. The other woman stared at her body, growing angrier, her eyes narrowing. "How dare I what?" Lucy asked calmly. "Take a swim? Invite Roberto to join me?"

"Shut up! He's my son—not yours! I didn't give him permission to swim, do you understand?"

Lucy had never hated anyone as she hated Carmen. She walked out of the water and paused to face her. "I understand. I understand that you do not deserve the appellation of mother.''

Carmen blinked, clearly not comprehending exactly what Lucy had meant. "What did you say? Speak plain English!''

"You do not deserve to have such a sweet little boy,'' Lucy flared.

Carmen glowered and stomped her foot, then, in a huff, she grabbed Roberto's hand and ran to the house, dragging her son with her. Lucy watched them go. Inwardly she hurt for Roberto. But what could she do? Roberto was Carmen's son.

She had just towel-dried her wet clothes and hair and put on her skirt when Carmen reappeared—with a bundle of bright clothing in her arms. She threw the bundle at Lucy, and it fell to the dirt. "You want to swim?'' She sneered. "Fine! You can swim while you do this!''

Lucy looked at what was obviously Carmen's gaily colored clothes. "What is this?''

"Laundry!''

"You expect me to do your laundry?''

"Do it, *puta*.''

Lucy stared at the other woman. She was fed up, as fed up as she had ever been in her life. "No,'' she decided, "I won't do it.''

"What!''

"I'm not going to do your laundry, Carmen,'' Lucy said furiously. "You have washerwomen here who do laundry. I am not a laundress!''

Carmen was shocked at her refusal, but only for an instant. Her hand swung out, but Lucy was ready, and she ducked, backing away.

"I'll give you to the men!'' Carmen shouted.

Lucy's heart stopped, then it sped on. "No, you won't,'' she cried, much more bravely than she felt. "Because if you do, I will tell Shoz about you and Pedro!''

Carmen blanched.

Lucy knew she had just achieved a small victory, her first. Her elation was tempered by anxiety, however, and she backed away waiting for Carmen's reaction. Carmen was so angry, it was fearful to behold; she was apparently incapacitated with her rage. Lucy seized the moment and hurried back to the house, expecting Carmen to chase after her at any moment. She didn't. Once inside, Lucy leaned against the cool stone wall. Her heart was thundering. Would her threat work? Or would Carmen retaliate?

Yet dinnertime arrived, and nothing had happened. Roberto appeared for his meal precisely at seven, anxiety in his gaze. Lucy reassured him with a smile. Fifteen minutes passed, and Carmen was late. Lucy decided to serve Roberto anyway. She hoped Carmen was sulking, although she doubted it. Roberto began eating with gusto.

Carmen finally appeared, her mood black and foul. "Why does he eat without me?" she cried. Before anyone knew what she was doing, she had swept Roberto's plate off the table and onto the floor. "Go to your room!" she screamed at him.

But Roberto was already up and running away, into the sanctuary of his bedroom. The door slammed closed.

"How could you!" Lucy cried, never more shocked in her entire life.

Carmen advanced on her clenched fists. "If you say one word, I will kill you!"

Later, Lucy never knew how she stood her ground, but she did. She didn't move, she didn't retreat, she stood there as Carmen stalked forward, until they were nose to nose. Her heart was pounding in her ears.

Carmen spit out something incomprehensible and dropped onto the bench at the table. Lucy felt quite weak—and terribly relieved. Her threat had worked; she and Carmen had a standoff. Then she became aware of Linda cleaning up the mess on the floor. Abruptly she came to life.

She hurried into the kitchen to serve Carmen. As soon as she had done so, she prepared another plate for Roberto, and, tension rearing again, she headed for his room. Carmen only looked at her in disgust. "You spoil him."

Lucy breathed easier and knocked on his door. There was no reply, so she walked in. He sat on the bed, very solemn, hands clasped in his lap. When he saw her, he looked relieved. "I brought you your dinner," she said softly.

"I'm not hungry," he said, searching her face. He was

such an intense little boy. Then he looked at the plate, and his stomach growled.

"Shall I keep you company while you eat? Tell you a story about my brothers?" Lucy asked, sitting beside him. His eyes went wide, and while he ate, she told him a story.

That night, Lucy could not sleep. She was too wound up from her various confrontations with Carmen. She was still amazed at her own daring, at her bravery, but now, being calmer, she was also feeling somewhat triumphant. It felt good to be able to hold her head up, it felt good to fight back. She realized, with a start, that never in her life had she really had to fight for anything!

She'd always had everything. Money, food, clothes, servants, gifts, beaux. Everything had been given to her upon her command on a silver platter. Even men! Every man she had ever wanted had fallen all over her, admired her, even loved her. Except, of course, Shoz.

Her heart tightened. He should be back any day now. It was impossible to deny how much she anticipated his return. Just as it was becoming impossible to deny other feelings as well. Other traitorous, dangerous feelings, Lucy thought sleepily. But she would deny them, she would as long as she could . . .

The next morning, the incidents of the day before overwhelmingly fresh in her mind, Lucy baked another batch of cookies for Roberto. "He is a good boy, no?" Linda asked.

"He is a darling," Lucy said, then stopped stirring the batter. "Linda, how can Carmen treat her son that way? How? It's too awful!"

Linda shrugged. "She should not be a mother, that one. She is too selfish and vain."

Lucy had forgotten they were cousins. It was hard to believe, Linda being so steady and patient and placid— completely the opposite of Carmen. Or had she just learned to accept reality? Lucy stared out the window at the corral. Before she had come to Texas this summer, the reality she knew had been so different from the one she lived in now. Never had she dreamed that this kind of life existed. Now her former life seemed so very far away—and even unreal.

"Shoz should be back soon," she heard herself say. She looked at Linda. "Will he return as he promised? Is he sometimes late?"

"Sometimes," Linda said. "Sometimes there are problems." She watched her. "*Niña*, you are going to make more problems for yourself if you are not careful."

Lucy blushed. Was she so transparent? "He is my captor. I want my freedom. Only he can give me that." She was stunned at her own words, stunned because they were lies. She hadn't thought about her freedom in days; she had only thought about his return.

After lunch, which Carmen did not appear for—and Lucy had a good idea where she was, and with whom—Lucy presented Roberto with the tin of warm cookies. He was thrilled, and he ran off with his treasure clutched in his hands. Lucy decided to take a siesta, not wanting to go anywhere near the river today.

Linda had left the house to go to her own cottage, and Lucy had last seen Roberto taking the cookies and racing outside. She was alone in the house, and the privacy was vastly pleasing. It was so hot and sticky, worse than ever, and she could not sleep, not even naked on top of the sheets. She pulled her damp clothes back on, wondering how anyone could live in such a miserable climate. Death Valley should be more appropriately named Hell Valley, she thought sourly.

She had nothing to do. She had never been much of a reader, so the books she had glimpsed in Shoz's room did not interest her overmuch. She would love a swim, but wanted to avoid that witch and her lover. Frustration soared with the temperature. It was so damn hot!

Barefoot, a state she found herself in constantly these days, she stepped from her room into Shoz's. It was only the second time she had ever been within, and she felt his lingering presence. Of course, that was nonsense. Still, there was something comforting about the stark room with the rough, heavy, masculine bed and bureau. Too bad signs of Carmen were everywhere, her dirty clothes on the floor, jewelry, powders, and rouges on the bureau, a scarf left on the mussed-up bed. Abruptly Lucy turned away.

There was a bookcase against one wall, but to her dismay, all the books seemed to be textlike, encyclopedic volumes, not novels or poetry. She came closer and pulled a tome from its place and was shocked to find *Bennet's History of Law; the Anglo-Saxon Tradition.* She pulled several other books down. Shoz had a collection of books dealing with jurisprudence! There was everything from actual case decisions to legal philosophy. She was stunned. It made no sense. And there was certainly nothing for her to read—not that she'd wanted to, anyway.

She moved out into the hallway, lost in thought about her strange discovery, then into the living room. She stopped, surprised to see Carmen lolling on the couch, thumbing through the Sears catalogs. Carmen glanced at her, then ignored her, and reached into the tin for a cookie.

For a cookie.

She was eating Roberto's cookies.

Lucy froze, staring at the tin, staring at the cookies. She strode forward. "I gave those to Roberto!"

Carmen looked up. "So?"

"You took them from him!"

"So? Make him more."

Lucy didn't hear. For the first time in her life, she understood the expression "to see red." She did see red, and she pulled the tin away from Carmen.

Carmen gasped, leaping to her feet.

"These are for your son," Lucy cried before she could speak.

Carmen grabbed the tin, but Lucy would not relinquish it. "Give it to me! You can make him more!" She yanked the tin out of Lucy's grasp, and most of the cookies flew onto the floor, breaking.

Lucy could not make him more, because they did not have any more white flour. She saw the cookies on the floor and something inside her snapped. With an outraged cry, she smacked Carmen as hard as she could across the face.

It felt good.

Carmen hit her back, just as hard.

Lucy was only stunned for a moment. With another cry, something like the war cry reminiscent of her Apache forebears, she flew at Carmen, knocking her backward and onto the couch. She grabbed her hair and pulled hard. Carmen howled.

Lucy was on top and knew immense satisfaction—until she saw Carmen's long, painted nails flying for her face. She felt the stinging and knew she'd been scratched, and she released her hold to jerk back. Carmen took advantage cruelly, grabbing Lucy's breast and twisting it painfully.

Lucy cried out and tried to break away from the other woman. She fell on the floor, Carmen on top of her, still wrenching her breast. Lucy went motionless, tears of pain coming to her eyes. Carmen, recognizing victory, gave a satisfied snort and rolled off. Lucy lay panting, her breast throbbing, her cheek stinging. Oh God, she thought! What had happened? How had she wound up fighting physically with Carmen?

"Don't you ever try that again," Carmen said, panting. "You're lucky I didn't take a knife to you!"

Lucy sat up. Her hair had come loose and she tossed her head. She would not show Carmen that she had been hurt— or shaken by their fight. Oh no, never!

Carmen stood, brushing off her skirts. The look she threw Lucy was dark, but it lacked its normal smug character. Lucy got to her feet slowly after Carmen had left, gingerly rubbing her breast. She undoubtedly had a hell of a bruise. It had been worth it—just to wipe that smug expression off Carmen's face.

A standoff had been reached. During the next few days, Lucy did her duties. Although she did not provoke Carmen, and in fact was careful not to, she did not let the other woman push her around or bully her. Carmen sensed the change, and retreated to her own sphere, eating the meals Lucy cooked and served with Linda. Lucy did not swim again with Roberto, and there was no more white flour, but she spent an afternoon churning fresh ice cream for him— with immense satisfaction. And every night she told him a story about one of her brothers' various hell-raising escapades, sitting on the side of his bed while he was tucked in. Carmen knew, feigned superior indifference, and went her own way. Lucy was sure her trysts with Pedro continued, now at the midnight hour.

Two weeks had passed since Shoz had left. With every new day that came without his return, she grew perturbed and angry with herself for counting so faithfully the days that had passed. She was no longer really angry with him for leaving in the first place. Instead, there was worry. What if something had befallen him? Linda would not say where he had gone, if she knew, and Lucy was not so stupid as to ask Carmen. What if the law had found him? What if he had already been jailed—even hung? She had to fight such desperate thoughts. Shoz was not in jail, he was not dead! But oh, it was so very clear—she was deathly afraid now for his safety, and every passing day increased her anxiety.

It was unbearably hot, just before siesta time. Lucy had stood in front of the oven for the past hour, and she was flushed and wet with sweat. Her thin blouse and skirt were sticking wetly to her skin, and her hair was falling down around her face. Only Linda was in the house with her, working by her side. Lucy heard the horses and knew he had returned.

Her heart leaped into her throat. Her spirits soared high, excitement pervaded her. She fumbled to wipe her hands quickly on a rag, trembling. She heard the door slamming, she heard his booted footsteps. She flew to the kitchen doorway, and there she froze.

He stood in the middle of the living room, filling it with his immensely magnetic, sexual presence. As usual, he wore tight, faded Levis and a worn, soft cotton shirt. His clothing was damp and clung to every lean muscle he possessed. He packed a low-slung gun on his right thigh, and his Stetson was pushed back far enough that she could see his eyes. He stood without moving and he stared at her.

His eyes were silver, and a flame leaped in them the instant he saw her. Lucy couldn't move or even breathe, trapped by his gaze. For a long moment they just looked at each other, gray eyes pinning blue. Shoz had returned, and now there was no escaping what she had known for so very long. There was no escaping the awful truth. Somehow she had fallen in love with the son of a bitch.

30

Shoz stared back at her, unable to move.

The seconds ticked into minutes. Still, neither one of them moved.

It had been a long two weeks, the longest of his life. Because shortly after he left Death Valley—and Lucy—he had to face a terrible truth, which had stayed with him from that moment on. His lust for Lucy had turned into something much stronger, it had turned into an obsession.

She had been on his mind night and day, invading his thoughts at the most inappropriate times. The bitterness of their last argument had faded, crushed beneath the heavier weight of his obsession. So what if she considered him beneath her? Here they were on his territory, here they were equals. Tossing restlessly at night, hot and hungry for her, his pride seemed meaningless. There were other times when it was the most important thing in the world—because it was all he had left of the man he'd once been. But not anymore.

He didn't like being obsessed. He didn't like it at all. He could write it off to unrequited lust, but secretly, fearfully, he remembered the last night he'd been in the valley, a night hotter and quieter and more unreal than most, when one could shed one's inhibitions like a snake its skin. And somewhere deep inside himself there existed the young man who had gone East to go to the university, full of hope and eagerness and ambition. That young man had believed in love, and he would have looked at a woman like Lucy with more in mind than just a tumble in the grass. Unable to escape his deepest inner voice, his most potent needs, Shoz was angry.

A part of him had counted the days before returning to the valley. Another part of him had dreaded going back to that hellhole—and all it stood for. But the part of him that foolishly still held on to a piece of the young man, and the part of him that was randier than a stud bull, that part of him couldn't forget that Lucy was there. He had to remind himself that she was not exactly waiting for him. He had to remind himself that he had abducted her and he had brought her there against her will. She was his hostage, not his woman. She would never be his woman. The most he could aspire to was a few hot interludes of lusty lovemaking.

And what about Carmen? That conflict had wracked his mind repeatedly, too. He had made no decision as far as Carmen was concerned, he only knew that he wasn't ready to send her away and face the valley alone. Soon, very soon, he would give Lucy her freedom. Carmen would be the one waiting for him when he returned to Death Valley; Lucy would be in the Bragg mansion in New York City, dressed in the finest clothes and the most expensive jewels, being courted by boys of her class and background.

He had to free her soon. Urgency had been factored into the equation, in the form of her powerful family.

It had been a shocking discovery to find out that the Braggs had a private army of some one hundred men, half of them Pinkerton agents, based at Casitas. Having espied their presence before riding into the town, Shoz had arranged a secret meeting with Fernando and gotten all the pertinent details. He had never been pursued like this before in his life. He was uneasy. Very uneasy. He was sure they could not find Death Valley, but he'd never faced such a formidable foe before, and he would be a fool not to harbor doubts. It had been simple enough to backtrack with his men into the mountains and cross the Rio at a safe distance from Casitas, retrieve the rifles, and return to Mexico. But he hadn't taken an easy breath until they were swallowed up by the Sierras again.

It was crucial to get the Braggs and their army off his back. The need to free Lucy and free her soon was overwhelming. He had become obsessed with her, but until he freed her, he would have to maintain the status quo. She would return to her family safe and untouched, not crying rape or anything else. He didn't need to increase their wrath or their desire to capture him.

But logical reasoning didn't change everything. It didn't change his unholy obsession. Seeing her again for the first time was like being struck by lightning and living through it. It seemed like a small eternity passed before he could take his eyes from hers.

When he did, it was to drink his fill of her, really look at her. It quickly became a form of torture. Her thin blouse clung damply to her, revealing every curve she had; even the skirt clung and outlined her long, graceful legs, and where they veed between her thighs. His gaze lingered too long where it shouldn't, with an ambition of its own. It had been a long two weeks, long and hot and celibate, and his body was responding to the sight of Lucy with fierce intent.

"Shoz," she said weakly.

His heart seemed to be thundering strangely and he almost stepped to her to take her in his arms, heedless of two weeks of rationalizing.

"Papa!"

Shoz smiled, whirling, to capture Roberto as he catapulted into his arms. Hugging Roberto, he had a chance to gain some control. He held the little boy hard. How he'd missed him. Carmen ran breathlessly into the house.

"Shoz, *caro! Caro mio!*" She grabbed his arm, beaming.

Shoz didn't have to look to see that Lucy had gone. He hugged Roberto harder. How was he going to handle this hellish situation?

He put the boy down and found Carmen in his arms, clinging. She was soft and female, and his body was still hot and aroused. This was something that could not go unnoticed by Carmen, and it did not. "Querido," she purred, shifting herself to press fully against him. "You have missed me." Her palms slid to his buttocks.

His head still swam with images of Lucy.

Shoz pushed Carmen away, and she pouted. He reached for Roberto, taking his hand. "Come outside," he said, smiling. "I have something for you."

Roberto glowed. "Another present?"

Shoz grinned, nodding. He had been a fool to ride into Eagle Pass to buy the boy a gift, but he'd wanted to give him more than another whittled animal. He could have been caught and hung. Yet he had done it without thinking twice. He led Roberto outside, and produced a bulky, wrapped gift from his saddlebags. Roberto seized it eagerly, ripped off the paper, and produced a pair of beautiful green and black lizard cowboy boots. "Oh, Papa!"

"I think it's about time you had those, don't you?" he said softly.

Roberto shed his moccasins, stumbling in his haste. Laughing, Shoz helped him put on the shiny handmade boots.

Lucy watched from the window, her heart in her throat, tears in her eyes. The scene was so touching and she found that she wanted to share it with father and son. Which, of course, was impossible. Carmen belonged with Shoz and Roberto, not her. The lump she was choking on increased. How could she have let herself fall in love with him?

For just a second, Lucy had thought he was going to embrace her. But he hadn't. His look had been blazing in its intensity, scorching her with promise. As if he had been as excited to see her as she was to see him. Or had it merely been a damn leer? She wiped her eyes. She had probably been seeing what she had wanted to see. How could she be so foolish to have fallen in love with such a man? With a married man?

She watched him help Roberto pull on the beautiful new boots. Lucy bit her lip until it bled. He wasn't so rotten. He was kind and gentle with his son. But he would never be kind and gentle with her; she was certain of it. To hope so was idiotic. Why did she keep forgetting about Carmen?

Carmen had come outside, and Lucy almost laughed bitterly. Carmen stood behind Shoz, and she was mad as a hornet, gloweringly jealous of her own son. Oh, why couldn't Shoz look at her, and see what a bitch she was? She didn't look beautiful now.

But that, of course, wouldn't change anything. Marriage was forever.

"*Por Dios,*" Linda muttered.

Lucy whirled. She had forgotten that Linda was there, and she was horrified to be caught with her emotions so openly displayed. She wiped her eyes with the back of her hands.

"Crying gets you nothing, *niña,*" Linda said kindly.

"Of course." Lucy had to glance back outside at the scene in front of the house; to her dismay, Shoz had handed Carmen a gift as well, what looked like a vivid striped shawl. She was screeching in happiness and throwing her arms around him. Lucy turned away.

"How much do you want him, *niña*?"

Lucy blanched. "I don't want him. I despise him, I do. Besides, he's married to Carmen."

Linda stared at her, then chuckled.

"What's so funny!"

"Carmen is not el padrone's wife, *niña.*"

"What?"

"Carmen only lives here. She is not his wife."

As Shoz walked back into the house, his glance strayed to the open kitchen doorway. He hesitated, his strides slowing, as he saw Lucy. His pulse seemed to deafen him. She froze, staring unblinkingly back. Shoz realized he had halted in midstride. The tension coursing between them was so hot, it was like a live electric wire. Shoz thought that she looked as if she had been crying. The tip of her nose was pink.

Carmen broke the moment, running in, her shawl knotted around her waist over her longer skirts. She ordered Linda to heat water for his bath. Shoz moved on, into his bedroom, his blood thick in his veins. He stared out the window without seeing anything.

Ten days from now, he had to be in Matamoros. He had rescheduled the sale of the guns. He decided in that moment that after the sale, he would free Lucy.

He would return to the valley and take her immediately to Nuevo Laredo. There. It was settled.

He thought about her standing hot and flushed in the kitchen—in his kitchen. He thought about the Braggs with their powerful army camped at Casitas. He would not go back to prison. Not ever. If it came down to that, he would try to escape, no matter how foolhardy, even risking a certain death in the attempt. Death was preferable to prison. Never would he serve time again.

He blocked out the painful, vicious memories.

Carmen entered, her look sultry and inviting. She pulled a big tub out from behind a screen. "Soon you will have your bath, querido."

He wished she would go away.

"Darling," Carmen murmured, sitting beside him, her hand slipping into his open shirt and across his flat, taut belly.

"Not now." He removed her hand.

"I don't understand you, *caro*."

"There's nothing to understand. I'm hot and tired and hungry. It's been a damn difficult trip. There's an army of Pinkertons after me, Carmen. I've got a helluvalot on my mind."

Carmen started. "An army? But why?" Comprehension flashed in her eyes. "Because of her?"

Shoz turned away.

"Who is she!"

"A rancher's daughter."

Carmen squinted at his back, her own thoughts racing shrewdly. "They won't find us here, will they?"

"I don't think so."

She grabbed his arm. "If she is so important, she is dangerous! You must get rid of her!"

"I intend to."

"Soon!"

He gave her a look.

"I'll get your bath. We'll eat early." Carmen walked out.

She was placing flatware on the dining room table when he came in. She froze in the act, not lifting her head, although every sense she possessed was intently attuned to him. She knew he had stopped in the hallway, and she could feel him watching her. Her heart was thudding heavily.

Carmen wasn't his wife.

Carmen was only his whore.

Lucy wet her lips nervously and straightened. Her glance met his. For a long moment they just stared at each other. It became unbearably, thickly hot in the room.

Roberto came running through the front door in his new boots. ''Papa!'' He screeched to a halt and did a little dance, showing off his boots.

Lucy turned away as Shoz complimented his son on his fancy footwear. His son. Roberto wasn't his son—Shoz wasn't his father.

It was unbelievable, and she was still reeling from the shock—and the joy. Linda had told her that he had been with Carmen for most of five years, and Roberto had been almost one when he had met her. He wasn't his father, and it made their relationship even more touching. He wasn't a rotten bastard at all. Or at least, he had a kind, compassionate, and loving streak within him.

Lucy prepared the platters of food for the table with Linda, listening to Roberto chattering with more animation than he'd shown in all of the past two weeks. She listened to Shoz. To his voice, gentle and warm and teasing. Rough and baritone and sexy. He might want the world to think he was a complete bastard, but he wasn't. He was proving it more with every moment. Oh, he had his moments, granted, and he had his record, but . . . but he wasn't as bad as he would have her think. Not by any means.

She was still too shaken and unsettled to have thought any further. She heard their chairs scraping back as they sat. Carmen hadn't appeared yet, but the food was hot and Lucy didn't care. She entered carrying two platters of tortillas and rice and found herself staring at Shoz. She just couldn't keep her eyes away from him. His gaze darkened visibly in response.

She smiled at Roberto and complimented him on his boots. He beamed, squirming. This time when Lucy returned from the kitchen, she carried their plates, each boasting a fat steak. She set Roberto's down. Why did she move between father and son to serve Shoz? The desire to serve properly had nothing to do with it. As she set his plate down, her hip brushed his elbow, her arm his shoulder. He swiveled to stare at her.

She was still leaning over him, withdrawing her hand from the plate, when her breast bumped his shoulder. For a moment she didn't move, their gazes locked together.

"Lucy tells me stories at night, Papa," Roberto interrupted. "She has five brothers!"

Lucy straightened and moved away. She was aware that it took Shoz a moment to recover and respond with something nonsensical. The front door slammed and Carmen flounced in, taking her place beside Shoz and across from Roberto. Lucy grimaced, but returned with her plate and set it rather abruptly down. Liquid from the meat splashed over the rim onto the table. Lucy was aware of his eyes, always upon her.

"She is a clumsy cow," Carmen cried, making certain Lucy could hear as she walked away. "Do you know she sits and does nothing all day? She refuses to help me and Linda!"

In the kitchen, her hand reaching for a pitcher of lemonade, Lucy paused. Of all the lies! Lucy had never worked harder in her life, and she had the calluses and dried hands to prove it! Since she had arrived, it was Carmen who loafed all day—except when she was flat on her back. Lucy marched back into the dining room with the pitcher in hand.

Carmen scowled at her. "Spoiled. She thinks she's better than we are!"

Lucy poured Roberto a glass of lemonade. Her heart pounded in her ears. Shoz calmly told Carmen to shut up. Lucy could feel his gaze again, but didn't care. She walked over to Carmen, and instead of pouring the lemonade in her glass, she poured it straight into her lap—without any pretense.

Carmen screamed, bolting to her feet.

Not stupid, Lucy stepped back and out of reach. "Oh, goodness me! Look what I did! Oh, I'm so sorry!"

Shoz laughed.

"You bitch, I'll kill you!" Carmen screamed.

Still smiling, Shoz exchanged an absolutely warm glance with Lucy. "No you won't," he said. "It was an accident."

Lucy started to smile, too. She had been impulsive. She had poured the lemonade without thinking, just barely restraining herself from pouring it on top of Carmen's head. Her new knowledge had given her added courage. But she hadn't expected Shoz's laughter, nor had she expected him to defend her.

Carmen stomped off to change. Lucy returned with a plate for herself and seated herself beside Roberto. The look she gave Shoz was long and direct. He was no longer laughing.

31

Dinner was an awkward affair.

Although Roberto sat between Shoz and Lucy, mutual awareness vibrated tangibly between them. Lucy could not eat. She could feel his gaze upon her. Likewise, when she did look up, her gaze was drawn to him. And then there was Carmen, sitting directly across from her, scowling and trying to kill her with murderous looks. When she wasn't shooting daggers at Lucy, she was leaning against Shoz, stroking his arm and flaunting her possession. Curtly he finally told her to cease and desist, that he was trying to eat. After which she sulked and again stared maliciously at Lucy.

Lucy's heart had become lodged in her throat by the time the meal was over. She began clearing the table while Carmen huffed off to the bedroom. Shoz and Roberto went outside to inspect a pregnant mare. Lucy began rinsing the plates in the sink, using the hand pump. She dreaded the passing of every moment. Soon it would be dark. And then what?

Then Shoz would return, tuck Roberto into bed, and join Carmen in their bedroom.

She paused, leaning against the cool iron sink, gripping the edge of the basin hard. God, she could not bear the thought. She couldn't! She could not stand to be here another moment under these circumstances!

Some time later the scenario she had foreseen occurred. Shoz and Roberto returned just as the heavy curtain of night blackness fell over the valley. He took Roberto to his room, and when the little boy was settled in, he crossed to his own room. Lucy listened to his quiet footfall and to the door gently closing.

She felt sick. She was quivering with nerves. "Sit and rest," Linda advised. "I'll finish the dishes."

They were almost done, but Lucy could not abide doing nothing and giving her mind the leisure to dwell on the two of them together. "No, you go. I'll finish up here. I would rather be busy." Her voice broke.

Linda patted her hand, removed her apron, and slowly ambled out. Lucy found herself staring into the living room, straining to hear something. The house was very quiet.

And then there was a scream and the sound of something heavy hitting the wall or the floor. Another one of Carmen's furious shrieks sounded. Lucy heard glass shattering. Another silence descended, this one pregnant with another imminent eruption.

Lucy didn't have long to wait. She heard a door slam hard against the wall and then Carmen was flying past her and out into the night. One short glance at her face told Lucy that she was enraged.

Lucy was standing in the kitchen doorway, gazing tensely after Carmen. She sensed his presence behind her. Turning, she saw him standing in the hallway where it connected with the living area. He stared at her. For a moment, Lucy couldn't move. Neither did he.

He went back into the bedroom. Lucy returned to the kitchen. She was trembling as she finished tidying up.

Lucy carefully extinguished the gas lamp. She started for her room, but her steps slowed when she entered the short hallway and came abreast of his door. It was still open and she faltered, her gaze drawn irresistibly within.

He was sitting in bed, a heavy book in hand. When he felt her gaze, he looked up, saw her, and put it down.

His eyes were gray and intense and mesmerizing. He wore only his tight, faded Levis. His feet were bare, the jeans unsnapped but zipped. His sleek bronze torso was covered with a thin sheen of perspiration.

He looked incredibly male and incredibly virile in that heavy, masculine bed, lounging against its white sheets. Lucy swallowed and drifted past his doorway with an effort. When she was within her own room, she closed the door and leaned against it, breathless.

Lock the door, an inner voice said.

Lucy had bolted her door every night since Carmen had barged in the day Shoz left. Tonight she did not.

She had only a lantern and she lit it. Feeling hot and dazed, she walked to the bureau to wash, a nightly ritual. She observed herself the way a stranger might. The skin of her elegant, high-cheekboned face was golden, and it made her large eyes a vivid sapphire blue, almost purple. Her blouse was very damp—and very indecent. Although she had long since found a chemise, the two thin layers of cloth clung to her breasts as if she were naked. Was this how he had viewed her? There was a constriction in her belly, between her thighs.

She let down her hair and shook it out. A golden red mane, it came to her waist, thick and heavy. She thought she appeared exotic and erotic; she liked how she looked.

She glanced at the door, then back at the mirror. She removed all of her clothing. She had never really bothered to look at herself before, but now she stared at her naked body: at her full breasts, one of them sporting a purple bruise from Carmen, and at her small waist; at her slim, curving hips and her long, long legs. At her womanhood. She touched one of her breasts and was rewarded with the hardening of her nipple. She blushed at her shameful behavior and dropped her hand.

She washed herself by hand and sponge as she did every night and every morning. The water was cool and pleasant on her skin, making it tingle sensually. Tonight her sponge bath took twice as long as usual, tonight her hand moved very slowly over her body. Tonight her every nerve ending was overly sensitized. She told herself that it was the heat.

Again, she looked at the door.

Standing naked in the middle of the room, her gaze rivetted there, listening, she lifted the mass of hair from her neck, seeking cooler air against her skin. Then, with a sigh, she dropped it and moved to the bed. She knew that tonight she would never be able to sleep. She sat on the thin, lumpy mattress, her back against the wall, and stared at the door.

It opened. She had known it would.

Shoz appeared, framed in the timbered doorway. Lucy sat up straighter. He kicked the door closed with his bare foot, never taking his gaze from her, and dropped the bolt. Lucy gripped the edge of the metal bed.

"This time," he said, "we're going to do it right."

Lucy tried to reply, but couldn't.

"Lucy?" His glance returned to hers, only to be drawn again in a rapid perusal down her body. "If this isn't an invitation, you'd damn well better say so, and fast."

Lucy opened her mouth. Only air came out. With a shaking hand he had unzipped his jeans, and his penis sprang out, hugely erect. He was shoving the pants down his hard, compact hips, stumbling over them. When he stood again, he was completely naked, lean and hard and sleekly bronze, powerfully male.

He strode to her. Tiny warning bells were sounding. Lucy Bragg, you are going to get into trouble and you know it!

"Well?" he asked, his hands on her shoulders, forcing her down onto her back. "Last chance."

Lucy gulped. He was straddling her, a knee on each side of her hips, and his hands, large and rough and callused, pinned her shoulders to the bed. She looked at his mouth, parted slightly, and her gaze swept relentlessly down his sculpted body to rest with fascination upon his thick, stiff manhood.

Shoz cursed. "Saints be damned," he said, and he kissed her.

Knowing him, she hadn't expected a tender kiss, and she didn't get one. Starved, he crushed her mouth with his, forced her lips open, and mated fiercely with her tongue. Lucy found the curls at the back of his nape and gripped them hard.

He released her shoulders to crush her breasts, to mold them. He shoved one hard forearm under her, lifting her, and found a distended nipple with his mouth. He began sucking fiercely.

Lucy whimpered and strained. Her hands traveled over his body with frenzy. She stroked his hip, his waist. She rubbed his nipples, pinched them. His teeth grated hers in response. She gasped, her nails raking down his side. Shoz lifted his face from her breast and found her lips, brutally forcing them apart.

She gripped his penis, silky smooth, so very hot, wet. Her fingers played him. He gasped against her mouth, arching into her hand. Then he grabbed both of her wrists with one hand, forcing her arms over her head, quick as a wink. He held her immobile, a prisoner to his superior strength. She felt him touch her wet, slick recesses, and she shuddered convulsively.

"Like that, Lucy?"

"Yes."

He palmed her entirely. She throbbed heavily against his hand. Abruptly he kneed her thighs farther apart and thrust in.

It seemed like this was what Lucy had been waiting for, for so very long. He released her wrists so she could hold him, clutch him, sobbing into his neck. He moved fiercely, fast, pounding her, rocking her backward until her head knocked into the wall. She didn't care, didn't even notice. She was shattering into thousands of fiery pieces, and her cries echoed into the night.

"Lucy!" Heaving himself into her one last time, he began spasming heavily inside her. Lucy could feel every contraction.

They lay soaked and panting. Shoz slid off her, still holding her, one hand flopping across her belly. Lucy opened her eyes to look at him. She was smiling.

He smiled, too. "Like Sunday bronc-busting, huh?"

"I guess."

His smile faded, but his gaze was direct and searching. "I'm sorry. I meant to go slow. Things got out of hand."

"I didn't want it slow." She blushed at what she had said.

His grin reappeared. So did tiny crinkles at the corners of his eyes. He was so very handsome. "No, you didn't, did you?"

His gaze moved from her face to her breasts. He swept his hand over the bruised one, gently caressing her skin. "What happened?"

It wasn't so easy to answer. Lucy watched his palm brushing her nipple. It tightened into a hard, elongated nub. "I got into a fight with Carmen."

Shoz's hand stopped and he stared. "You and Carmen fought?"

Lucy thought she detected both amazement and concern in his tone. "Yes."

His expression grew grim. "And she did this?"

"It doesn't really hurt. It felt good to hit her."

"You hit her?"

Lucy nodded.

He suddenly smiled. "I hope it was a good one."

"It was—right across the face."

His eyes were wide. Then they narrowed. "Then she did this?"

"I didn't expect it."

"I'll bet you didn't." He cupped her breast and held it, almost protectively, possessively. "You ever fistfight before?"

"Never!"

"I didn't think so. Let me tell you something, Lucy, and don't forget it. This isn't Fifth Avenue. If you get in the gutter and fight, then you fight to win. And in the gutter there are no rules."

Lucy nodded, wide-eyed.

"If you ever come up against Carmen again, you fight to win. That means anything goes."

Their glances held. His gaze dropped to his hand as it moved lazily over her breast. "Does it hurt?" His tone was low.

"No," she whispered.

"I don't want to hurt you," he said, lowering his head. His kissed the contours of the bruise. Lucy's head fell back and she sighed.

"Am I hurting you?" His thumb toyed with her nipple while his mouth brushed her skin.

"N-no." Breathless.

His tongue traced the path his mouth had taken, only to detour around her nipple. "Feel better?"

"Yesss."

He drew her slowly into his mouth. "This time it will be slow and easy," he promised.

But it wasn't. The fires within both of them burned too brightly.

Lucy realized she had fallen asleep. She opened her eyes to find Shoz lying on his side, his head propped up on one hand, his other palm on the mattress, his fingertips just touching her arm. He was watching her.

Now, passion momentarily spent, Lucy felt awkward. She smiled slightly, uncertainly. He didn't smile back, but his gaze roamed her face intently.

For lack of a better topic, she said, "Did I sleep for long?"

"Maybe a half an hour."

Lucy rolled onto her side, facing him. His glance moved to her breasts and then right down to her toes before returning to her eyes. Lucy blushed, embarrassed at being stared at while she slept naked, and knowing she should be scandalized for her lack of modesty—and morals. But she wasn't. In fact, she was just as curious, and her glance wandered down his body, noting every detail with great interest.

She wondered what would happen now.

Would he just get up and go, back to his own bed, back to the one he shared with Carmen?

"What is it? Why are you frowning?"

Lucy looked at him.

"More regrets?" His tone changed, became mocking.

Instantly she shook her head. "No. No regrets."

His mouth was tight. He reached out to finger a curl. "Good."

"Shoz? Do you love her?"

He didn't have to ask who she was referring to, and he didn't hesitate, not for a second. "No."

"You must have loved her once."

"I never loved her. I'm not that kind of man."

Lucy wanted to ask him exactly what that meant, but was afraid of his answer. "But you love Roberto."

He smiled. "Yes. I love Roberto."

Lucy leaned back on the pillow. He made a face and cupped her chin. His mouth was very close. "When you start thinking too hard, I can feel it. Now what? Feel free."

She smiled, but it faded. "About what happened. In Paradise. At the ranch."

He made a sound and rolled onto his back, staring up at the beamed ceiling.

She sat up so she could see his face. "What did happen?"

"I didn't steal that damn horse."

"I want to believe you. Tell me what happened."

He shot upright, and the look he gave her was scathing. "*Now* you want to believe me? Why? Because I'm a good fuck?"

There was so much bitterness in his tone that Lucy hurt for him. She touched his arm; he drew away. "No!" she protested.

"Then why?"

"Because—because I know you better now. Because I see the kind of father you are, a wonderful father, and Roberto isn't even your natural son. Because I don't think you did it, but I need to hear about it from you."

He had flushed at her compliment about his fatherhood. He looked out the window. Outside, the night was like a black wall, thick and impenetrable.

"I hated the party and I wanted to have a smoke in peace and quiet," he said. "And I was waiting for you." He looked at her.

She colored a little.

"When I went into the barn, the old groom was already dead and the horse was already tacked. The groom was the inside man, Lucy, and at the last minute the thieves killed him. Probably out of greed—why split their prize three ways? And probably because he was too old to keep up with them. Or maybe they just didn't give a damn; who knows? That's what happened.''

''I'm so sorry,'' Lucy cried, genuinely anguished. ''I thought . . . I thought . . . I never thought it could have been that groom! And he was new, just some down-and-out drifter that Grandpa hired before you came. Oh God! What did I do!''

''Sure you didn't want to get back at me, just a little?'' His tone was biting.

She shook her head earnestly. ''No. Not even a little. I was so upset thinking it was you!''

He softened. ''Now I believe *you*.''

She wanted to ask him many more questions, especially about his conviction in New York. But she didn't dare. She sensed she had pressed far enough for tonight. Besides, his soft tone had affected her, and so did the lazy gleam coming into his eyes. And then she was undone. He pulled her into his embrace, his lips almost but not quite touching hers.

''Want to try and get it right one more time?''

Lucy nodded weakly. But they just couldn't seem to ''get it right''.

32

Shoz was never one to sleep late, and that day was no exception even though he hadn't slept more than a few hours the night before. He slipped into his own room, leaving Lucy soundly asleep with a small smile on her lips. Fortunately, Carmen wasn't within.

He felt a bit guilty and shoved it aside. What was done

was done, and he owed Carmen very little, if anything. Besides, he could tell that she hadn't bothered to return last night, and had slept somewhere else—probably with some-one else, as well. He grabbed a towel and headed outside for an early morning swim.

He liked being up at this hour when the rest of the valley slept. The sun would be a pale sand-colored ball if he could see it, which, because of the height of the valley's rim, he couldn't. This was the one time of day when the valley was actually cool and pleasant and the few creatures who in-habited it were visible. Across the creek an antelope grazed. A pair of jackrabbits leapt out of his path. Lizards scrambled for cover before the shadow of his bare feet. Other than the few animals, there was no one and nothing to disturb him, except his thoughts.

He didn't want to think about last night, but when he did, he was physically jolted from head to toe. He had a damn warm feeling inside, and it had been many years since sleeping with a woman had left him warm instead of cold. The sex had been as good as it could be, he suspected, between a man and woman, but what he kept remembering was other things, like that absurd compliment she'd paid him. Even now, buck-ass naked and submerging himself completely in the tepid water of the creek, he felt ridicu-lously pleased. He was a good father, wasn't he? He had a helluva lot of shortcomings, but that wasn't one of them.

He wished Roberto were his son.

He wished Lucy were the boy's mother.

Stunned, he came up sputtering, almost choking. He wasn't just obsessed—he was losing his mind!

Still, as he walked back to the house, there was no de-nying that he felt good, really good, almost like a schoolboy in love. More insanity, but the sky had never seemed bluer or the day brighter.

Carmen was waiting for him when he returned.

She was furious. "You were with her!"

Shoz rubbed his hair with the towel, then tossed it aside. "What of it?"

"What about me!"

He pulled on a soft, worn white cotton shirt. "I guess you had a good time last night, too."

She moved forward to slap him, but he caught her wrist. Annoyance, not anger, was evident in his expression. "Don't start."

Carmen yanked free. "I want her out of here."

Shoz sat down on the bed, leaning against the headboard, watching her. Carmen advanced. "I want her out of here! You said she's dangerous to us! Get rid of her!"

"I will," Shoz said slowly. "In a few weeks."

"In a few weeks! Get rid of her now!"

He didn't like explaining himself to her, and normally, he wouldn't. But because he had wronged her, he supposed, he did. "I have to go to Matamoros in a few days to sell the guns. When I get back, I'll free her."

"Take her with you! Free her there!"

"No." It was final and they both knew it.

Carmen paced angrily. She turned. "And tonight? Will you go to her tonight?"

"Will you go to Pedro?"

She blanched. "Shoz, that's crazy! Where—"

"Carmen, don't bother. Let's stop the games. I know what you do when I'm not here, and I always have."

She stared.

He stood and went to the bureau, picking up a razor strop.

"You could at least pretend that you care!"

He soaped his face. "Why? Nothing's changed between you and me, and you know it, Carmen."

She balled her hands into fists. "I'm not leaving."

"Did I ask you to?"

"I won't stay here with her!"

He dipped the blade into the basin of water and began scraping it over his skin. "I didn't ask you to do that, either."

"You're a bastard."

"I guess so."

"I'm going to stay with Pedro. When she's gone and you get lonely, maybe, I'll come back."

He laid down the strop to look at her in the mirror. "Roberto stays here."

She gave him a murderous look and stormed out.

Lucy awoke at noon.

She was scandalized. She bolted up, wondering why Carmen hadn't come banging on her door as usual to rouse her before seven. Then remembrance flooded her, and she fell back against the pillows.

She thought of Shoz and smiled dreamily. He was heaven. Last night had been heaven. His touch was sinfully exquisite, and remembering, she felt a powerful surge of desire. Which was amazing, considering he had made love to her again at dawn, sliding into her while she was half-asleep, stroking her lazily, whispering for her to wake up. She had, and they had finally gotten it "right".

But it wasn't just the lovemaking. It felt so good to have cleared the air about the horse theft, to have settled and shelved that particular source of tension. It felt good to have talked. She didn't think they had ever had a conversation before without anger and tension.

And he had been very upset about her fight with Carmen, and a little amazed, if she had read him right. Lucy sobered. She hoped she would never have to use his advice, but she would certainly never forget it.

Thinking about Carmen cast a shadow upon the day. Now what would happen? Shoz couldn't keep two women, could he? Much less in the same house. Her heart sank sickeningly. She knew in that precise moment that she was not a woman to share. She would have to fight to win. Carmen would have to go.

She got up and hurriedly dressed. Normally she would have been up early enough to get fresh water and bathe, but not today. She thought about Linda toiling alone in the kitchen and was struck with guilt. She rushed into the hall.

She saw no one until she got to the kitchen, where Linda was just pulling a roast hen from the oven to test it for doneness. "Linda, I'm sorry!" Lucy cried, striding forward. "Here, let me do that! Why don't you sit and cool off?"

"Did you sleep well, *niña*?" Linda asked, not letting her

take the pan from her as she placed it on the counter. She shook the drumstick and ambled back to the oven.

Lucy reddened. "I am sorry . . ."

Linda looked at her, and Lucy saw that she had been sincere, not suggestive. "Yes, I did."

"Good. Now, go and rest. It's too hot today. There's no work for you here."

"What?"

"El padrone has ordered it."

Lucy stared. Shoz had freed her from her kitchen duties. He hadn't just slept with her, he had been thoughtful enough to rid her of the hateful work here. Her first reaction was to be thoroughly pleased.

Then she watched Linda slicing potatoes, her face flushed, her dress stained and damp, and all her joy vanished. She came forward, taking the knife from Linda's hand. "I'm going to help anyway," she said firmly. "There is too much to do for one person."

Linda smiled. "Thank you, *niña*."

Some time later, when the meal was almost done, Lucy saw him outside, through the wide-open window. He was approaching the house with Roberto, strolling with that particular masculine swagger of his. Her hands stilled in the midst of their task of draining the boiled potatoes. She had to admire that semistrut. She had to admire him. He was clad in his tight Levis, with his shirt tucked in but open to his belt buckle, and she glimpsed enough form and flesh to recall just how virile he was in fact, as well as appearance.

He saw her as well and his steps slowed. His eyes brightened instantly and their gazes held. Lucy smiled shyly. He smiled, too, then his brow furrowed and he scowled. Her heart sank a little.

He disappeared from view as he went up the porch steps, and then the front door slammed. Lucy turned to see him hovering in the doorway.

"What are you doing?"

"I . . ." She found herself looking at his mouth, at his throat. His dark skin glistened where his shirt hung open, and the denim-encased bulge of his groin was overly suggestive. She lowered her gaze.

For just a moment a brief silence came between them. "Dammit, I said you don't have to work here. Linda! I told you Lucy won't be working in the kitchen anymore!"

Lucy interrupted before Linda could speak. "She told me, Shoz, but I decided to help her anyway. There's too much work here for one person, and I don't mind, truly."

He blinked at her.

She smiled hopefully, and saw the softening in his eyes. "Carmen can help."

"Carmen never helps," Lucy said.

"She's going to start."

Lucy thought about how she had taken Carmen's place in Shoz's bed. "I really don't mind. And I think it's better if Carmen and I keep our distance right now. I think it's better—" she looked at him boldly and flushed "—if she stays away from the house."

He understood her exactly, because she could see him fighting a small dry smile. "Carmen has decided to bunk with Pedro."

Lucy's eyes widened. So he did know about her infidelities!

"And I think you're right," he said.

A few moments later they sat down to eat, just the three of them, Roberto, Shoz, and Lucy. Lucy did not see Carmen at all during the next two days.

It was siesta time, and Lucy and Roberto were on their way for what had been, before Shoz's return, their daily swim. The past couple of days, Lucy and Shoz had taken the siesta together, but early this morning he had gone hunting. Lucy was humming and holding Roberto's hand. He skipped alongside her.

The tune died in her throat as she saw a familiar gypsy-clad figure rushing toward her from the houses behind the remuda. Lucy hadn't seen hide nor hair of Carmen since the night she had first slept with Shoz. She stiffened and stopped to wait for their imminent confrontation.

"What's wrong?" Roberto asked.

Lucy realized she was clenching his hand. She released it, rubbing his back. "Nothing, *niño*, nothing."

"So," Carmen huffed, without even a glance at her son, "the *bruja* thinks she is the new woman, eh?"

"Hello, Carmen."

"Do you really think *you* can possibly keep a man like *that*?" Carmen's gaze raked her contemptuously.

"Yes, I do," Lucy said. The reply was more automatic than anything else, because she had tried very hard not to think about the future at all.

"Ha! I have been his woman for five years, and I know him better than anyone. You he will tire of—soon."

"We will see."

"Did he tell you?"

Lucy dreaded asking. "Did he tell me what?"

Carmen's smile was a study in malicious triumph. "That he plans to get rid of you in a few weeks."

"What?" She couldn't contain her surprise and shock.

"*In a few weeks!* He told me the other day that he plans to free you in a few weeks. And then he will return to me— as always!"

Lucy's heart beat thickly and painfully. "Of course I must leave," she said with dignity. "I want to go home. I want very much to go home."

"Good! Because you will!" She turned to go, and paused. "Enjoy his bed while you can, *perra*."

Lucy watched her leave, shaken. Carmen was probably lying, but she was upset—just as Carmen had intended. Worse, the issue she wanted so much to avoid had been thrown right in her face—making it unavoidable. She did have to go home, sooner or later. Didn't she?

Of course she did.

But later would be better than sooner.

What was she thinking?

And was Carmen lying, or telling the truth?

Roberto tugged on her hand, breaking into her thoughts. "Don't let Mama make you sad."

"I'm not sad," she said, bending to hug him. "Not at all."

"Do you love Papa?"

Lucy jerked back. Although Roberto was a child of six he had undoubtedly understood every word. Did he know, too, that Shoz slept in Lucy's room now? He regarded her solemnly, his eyes big and black. "Roberto, do you mind your papa and me being good friends?"

"I'm glad Papa likes you!" he cried.

"Your mama's not very happy," Lucy said cautiously.

"That's because you're prettier and Papa likes you more."

At the moment, Lucy thought. "Roberto, do you miss your mama?"

He didn't hesitate. "I like it better when she stays down there." He looked past the remuda toward the adobe homes beyond it. Carmen was just entering one of the houses. His gaze turned to Lucy. "She can't yell at me when she's down there."

"Some people just have a temper, Roberto. She doesn't mean it." She stroked his hair.

His expression was far too old for a young boy, and his words far too wise. "Yes, she does. She doesn't like me. She doesn't like me because Papa loves me."

Lucy felt a tear slip down her cheek. "He loves you very much."

"Do you love my papa?"

She smiled, but another tear fell. "Yes, I do. Very much." She bent to embrace him. "And I love you, too."

"I wish you were my mama," he said, clinging.

Shoz came back later that day, and despite Carmen's disturbing words, Lucy was overjoyed to see him. Yet that night, together in her bed after frenzied lovemaking more appropriate for two lovers reunited after weeks instead of hours, he pulled her close and lifted her chin. "What is it?"

"Nothing."

"Something's upsetting you, and don't say it isn't."

She had learned he was sensitive that first night they had shared. Another facet of his character which, she thought, he would hide if he could. "Carmen and I had words."

"She's a bitch. Ignore her. She's succeeded in doing exactly what she wanted, which was to make you unhappy."

She turned more fully into his hard, sweat-slickened

body, nuzzling the crook between his neck and shoulder. "I'm not unhappy."

"What did she say?"

She leaned back on the pillows to look at him. "She said that in a few weeks you plan to free me."

He regarded her steadily. "I do."

She attempted a smile and failed. "I have to go home."

"Yes. You have to."

They looked at each other for a pregnant moment. Then they reached out to each other simultaneously. This time their lovemaking was more frantic than before—and tinged with desperation.

33

"Lucy?"

There was no answer. Shoz poked his head into her room, but she wasn't there. He wondered where she had gone off to, and if Roberto was with her, because he was also not in the house. It was siesta time, the heat particularly thick and intense, making everyone and everything more sluggish and sleepy than usual. He had thought to share the siesta with Lucy. It was too damn hot to do more than sleep, and he didn't need Lucy in order to do that. He would rather not admit the truth—that it was comforting to sleep with her beside him. It was something he could become very accustomed to.

The house was silent. He padded through on bare feet, seeking the coolness of the stone floors, his shirt hanging open but sticking to his torso. Linda was just finishing up in the kitchen, and when he asked, she told him that Lucy and Roberto had gone to the creek, probably for a swim.

"It's what they usually do during the siesta, Padrone," she added.

He had certainly noticed Roberto's friendship with Lucy. It disturbed him. The little boy was like a dry sponge, greedily soaking up the affection Lucy gave him. He so obviously needed a warm, caring mother. When he had first met Lucy Bragg, he would have never thought her mother material, far from it, but he had been wrong. One day she would be a fine mother with her own children—and that disturbed him as much as anything.

He suspected that she genuinely cared for Roberto. And although the boy needed her attention, it could only be temporary, and maybe when she left, more damage than good would have been done. He didn't want Roberto hurt.

He should tell her to stay away from the boy.

Grim, he made his way to the river. He heard their laughter and splashing before he saw them, and a pleasurable warmth spread rapidly through him. As he came closer, he watched their antics. Roberto would dive under the water, then emerge with all the fanfare of a baby whale, splashing Lucy. Submerged up to her neck, she waited for his attack, only to spray him back. Shoz softened right to his very bones.

It was bittersweet. She didn't belong here, not in Death Valley and not with them. With every day that passed, increasing their intimacy but bringing their separation that much closer, he knew it more. But she looked as if she belonged. She acted like the boy's mother, and she cooked and cleaned for him and shared his bed as if she were his wife. But she was neither of those things, not Roberto's mother, not his wife, she was just an illusion of those things, and very soon she would be gone and the illusion would be reduced to nothing more than a dusty memory.

If he dared admit it, her leaving would not just be difficult for Roberto, it would be difficult for him, too.

"Shoz!" Her cry was happy and she popped up, smiling. "Come join us!"

"Papa!" Roberto called enthusiastically.

Shoz's smile faded. "Get back in the water, Lucy, dammit!" he barked. Her chemise and blouse were translucent, her red petticoat molded to her thighs and crotch. "What if one of the men saw you?"

Lucy wasn't smiling anymore, and she had obediently sunk back down, up to her neck. "I'm always careful."

He was mad. He was mad because she was an intruder, worming her way into his family, where she didn't belong and would never belong. He was mad because she was his, at that moment, and he had never been so possessive before—if some other man even looked at her, he would kill him. He was maddest of all because in reality, she wasn't his at all.

"Shoz?" she asked, hurt.

"You should know better," he said gruffly, wishing he'd been kinder.

"I'm sorry."

"It's all right." He wanted to apologize, too. But he didn't know how, so he just swallowed it. He jammed his hands in his pockets. He wouldn't interrupt Roberto's fun just for his own sake. "I'm going to lie down," he said, although he was loath to leave them.

"Don't leave, Papa," Roberto cried.

"Come join us," Lucy urged. "The water's wonderful."

He wanted to, but was frankly embarrassed to horse around like some kid. The kid in him had died a long time ago; he wouldn't even know what to do if he got in that water with them. He turned to leave, not wanting to but resigned, when he was thoroughly drenched with water from head to foot.

He wheeled and stared incredulously, water dripping down his face and into his eyes, while Lucy and Roberto erupted into gales of laughter. He tried to scowl ferociously, but failed, making them laugh harder. "What the hell?"

"It wasn't me," Lucy said, wide-eyed and innocent and grinning.

"It wasn't me," Roberto echoed with the identical tone and expression.

"It must have been a helluva fish," Shoz said, making them both roar hilariously. It had been a long time since he had cracked a joke, and he found his mouth softening helplessly into a smile.

"Come on in," Lucy urged, her tone low and husky. His glance flew to hers, and she gave him a particularly inviting look. There was nothing subtle in her seduction. He wasn't immune, not at all; his blood boiled instantly, dangerously. Slyly, sensing her power, she stood and crooked a finger at him. "Come here."

Now was not the time to become aroused, but she was every man's dream, beautiful and sexy, her breasts straining the sheer blouse, nipples hard, her tone promising the fulfillment of untold fantasies. With a jolt he realized that if she chose to exercise it, she had immense power over him. He hoped she would never realize just how much.

"Please, Papa," Roberto screeched, jumping up and down.

"Please," Lucy whispered.

He looked at her, and she hit the water as hard as she could with her hand, causing it to spray him in the face—and his mouth had been open. He sputtered, shaking like a dog; she and Roberto laughed riotously. An instant later he dove shallowly in. She squealed and tried to leap out of the way, but he caught her around her knees and brought her under.

When they came up, she was wedged in his embrace, giggling. He was laughing, too, feeling absurdly pleased with himself. "With me, you can never win," he stated smugly.

She was in his arms, her body flush against his, knee to knee, hip to hip, and chest to chest. Her eyes danced. "Honey," she drawled, "I just did!"

He knew he would have to tell her that night.

After dinner, while Lucy helped Linda with the dishes, Shoz went to Roberto's room to oversee the boy's preparations for bed. Roberto was sitting on the bed, waiting for him, in a thin pair of cotton pajama bottoms. He smiled when his father entered.

"Already washed up?"

"Yes, Papa."

Shoz lifted his hands and inspected them, then took a soft earlobe between his fingers and rubbed it gently. "Ears?"

"Yes, Papa. I washed my face and hands and feet and ears and brushed my hair!"

"Teeth?"

He scowled.

"Brush your teeth," Shoz said with paternal sternness. Roberto reluctantly got up to obey. When the boy had come back, Shoz helped him climb into bed, covering him with the top sheet. Although it was still quite hot and uncomfortable out, Roberto liked to sleep with something covering him. He ran his hand through the boy's wet, neatly combed hair. "Sleep tight, now," he murmured.

Roberto nodded, his gaze moving past his father. Shoz turned to see Lucy hesitating in the doorway.

She smiled. "May I come in?"

"Of course," Shoz said.

Roberto sat up, beaming. "Will you tell me a story? Tell me about the time Colin took the canoe out into the ocean. Papa, he's only two years older than me and he lives on the ocean!"

"Really?" Shoz regarded Lucy questioningly. Her smile was soft. "Mother and Daddy always used to tell us bedtime stories when we were young. I thought Roberto would enjoy it, too."

Carmen never even said good night to her son, much less sent him to sleep with fairy tales. In the dark intimacy of the evening, he felt none of the anger that he had felt earlier, just the piercing of poignant heartache. How could he protect Roberto from the hurt he would feel when Lucy was gone? How could he protect Roberto when he was finding it more and more difficult to protect himself? Did she realize what she was doing to their lives?

"I don't want to intrude," Lucy added.

"You're not," he said quickly. But the irony wasn't lost on him, not at all—she had already intruded into their existence, and irrevocably she had already disrupted it. He gestured, and she came forward to sit on the bed, smoothing back Roberto's cowlick with one supple hand. While Roberto begged her for a story, Shoz's gut twisted into a knot. He should not let this go on. He absolutely must end it. He should have never brought her here, into the midst of their lives, and if he were smart, he would send her back to her family as soon as possible.

But he wasn't as strong as he had thought he was, because he knew he wouldn't free her a day sooner than he had to. He sat beside Lucy at Roberto's feet and listened to her tell an anecdote about one of her brothers, acutely uncomfortable. The situation mesmerized him, illusion nearly defying reality. This was how he had been raised, and it brought back powerful memories. This was what he had always thought he would have one day, until fate and Marianne Claxton had dealt him the first bitter blow. Tonight the illusion was reality, but he was sane enough to know it as a sham. This was not his family no matter how much it seemed so, and he would never have a family like this.

Shoz watched Lucy kiss Roberto good night. He bent and dusted the boy's cheek with his own mouth. He sighed and they left him with the small lamp on and the door ajar.

In Lucy's room, Shoz stood and stared out the window, seeing nothing but blackness, while Lucy undressed. He listened to the now familiar sounds of her clothes sliding down her body, of her footsteps as she moved about, of the splash of water as she bathed quickly and then rinsed out her things. Feelings he had thought were dead had merely lain dormant and were too intense to deny any longer. Like the hot gases of a volcano, he could feel the pressure building. Eruption was imminent. *How had his life come to this hellish existence?*

Before Lucy's advent into his life, he had accepted his fate unquestioningly, taking the blows with the instincts of a jungle cat, always landing on his feet. Survival in an inhospitable reality became the ultimate driving force, the overriding challenge—and distraction. The bitterness he could have entertained would have wasted valuable energy. Brooding was not in his nature. Until now. He realized her departure would affect him in no small way. Her presence had upset the careful rhythm and arrangement of his life. What had once been acceptable was now nearly unbearable.

"Shoz?" Her hand touched his back. "What is it?"

He turned, expressionless. "Tomorrow morning I'm leaving. I'll be back in a week or ten days."

Disappointment made her cry out.

He ignored her dismay, but it wasn't easy, and continued relentlessly. "After I return, I'll fulfill my promise and free you."

Her face turned white.

He moved away from her, shrugging off his shirt and tossing it onto the room's lone chair. She didn't protest. What had he expected? Maybe, foolishly, he had hoped she would tell him that she wanted to stay.

"I want to come with you," she said abruptly.

He turned, his mouth clamping into a hard line. "No."

"Where are you going?"

It didn't matter if she knew. "Matamoros."

"Take me with you!"

"I can't. I have business to take care of."

"What kind of business?"

"It's better if you don't know, Lucy," he said, and from her expression, he saw that she understood it was illegal.

Lucy tried not to be upset by that knowledge. All she knew was that she would not let him go again without her. If he would free her when he returned, then she must spend every moment they had left with him, she must. "Please take me with you!"

He walked away stiffly. If he took her with him to Matamoros, he would be ten kinds of an idiot not to free her there, as long as everything went well and remained under control. Matamoros was on the gulf. The Braggs were in Casitas. Once Lucy alerted them to her presence in Matamoros, it would take them a week to travel there. By the time they arrived in the small coastal town, he would be back at Death Valley, once again swallowed up by the voracious Sierras. It could not have been arranged better.

He did not want to take her to Matamoros. He wanted to delay the inevitable.

"Why do you want to come, Lucy?"

Her nostrils flared and her eyes were misty. She was naked and utterly lovely. She came to him and placed her palm on his own bare chest. "I want to be with you."

Her nudity hadn't undone him, and now, it wasn't her proximity. Her words were his undoing, and he capitulated completely, as completely as a man of his caliber could. "All right."

She cried out happily and embraced him fiercely. As he held her, he told himself that he was doing the right thing, the only thing. Lucy had to be freed, and the situation could not have been better in terms of his own safety. But he decided not to say anything, not yet. He didn't want to raise her hopes, just in case trouble arose as it had the last time, when he had intended to leave her in Casitas.

Because suddenly he had a bad feeling.

34

He had that same bad feeling riding into Matamoros, and there was no reason for it.

It was several days later. Everything was arranged. Tomorrow Shoz would meet his buyer, one Jorge Lopez, and they would conclude the transaction. Tonight Lucy and Shoz would stay at the Matamoros Hotel, while his men camped in a canyon just outside of town. On this side of the border, Shoz was not worried about American government agents. If the coast guard picked up Jorge with the stolen army guns, it wasn't his problem, and he would be long gone. He expected everything to run smoothly. Tomorrow Shoz would leave Lucy at the hotel and return to Death Valley a helluva lot richer. But he couldn't shake the bad feeling. He was tense with expectation—and with frustration.

Every second brought him and Lucy closer to their separation. He might not be ready to let her go, but he had no damn choice. She was blissfully unaware, but he didn't delude himself the tiniest bit. She might miss him, but she would be ecstatic to be back in the bosom of her family. And in another month she would be back in the Bragg mansion, dressed in diamonds and silk, fending off dozens of beaux—and not missing him at all.

"Look, the Gulf!"

Lucy's happiness and enthusiasm wrung the smallest smile from him. He studied her, not for the first time thinking how pretty she was. Especially when she was so happy and all smiles to prove it. The look she gave him was intimate and warm. He could feel her excitement. "Matamoros isn't much," he warned. Tonight he would tell her that tomorrow he was leaving without her.

"But it's not Death Valley," she returned, with no dimming of enthusiasm.

He couldn't have agreed with her more.

In the bright sunlight, Matamoros sat before them on the flat plain, sparkling like a diamond, with the blue, blue waters of the Gulf her setting. She was a good-sized town of white adobe homes and low-fronted stores, red-tiled roofs and timbered frames. The streets were wide, flat, and dusty. The small harbor, naturally protected by two fingers of marshy land, was spiked with masts and dotted with rocking vessels, mostly those owned by the local fishermen. There were one or two steamers in port, however. This close to the Gulf, there was a gentle, pleasant breeze.

They rode down the wide main thoroughfare, with Lucy exclaiming over everything as though she had never been to civilization before—as if Matamoros were something grand. "Look, a restaurant!" Her tone was wistful. "Oh, look! A mercantile and a milliner's! And look at the hotel! Is that where we're staying?"

"It's the only one in town," he said dryly.

The hotel was a two-storied, whitewashed building with three wide archways leading to an inner courtyard and garden. He didn't blame Lucy for being excited. It was amazing that she had adjusted to Death Valley the way she had, without even a single complaint. Of course she would miss the finer side of life terribly—the kind of life he could never give her.

They checked into the hotel quickly, with Lucy clinging to his arm as if to hide, and blushing at the stares of the clerk and two male guests lounging in the cool, spacious lobby. "Oh, it's lovely," Lucy cried when they entered their room.

He gave her a thorough glance. He hadn't thought about it before, but the way Lucy was dressed invited a particular kind of lewd stare—and once he left, she was going to be here for a week, alone. Downstairs, the clerk and the two male guests had beaten a hasty retreat when leveled with his murderous yet eerily flat gaze. He would make damn sure it wouldn't happen again, and after he was gone, she would just have to stay holed up in the hotel room for her own protection. He intended to arrange it.

"Why are you staring at me?"

"I have to go out for an hour or two."

"Without me?"

"It's business."

She was disappointed, but didn't complain. "All right."

Impulsively he leaned down and kissed her, something he'd never done before. She was surprised; so was he. To break the awkward moment, he told her that he would order some hot food and have it sent up.

When he had gone, Lucy went to the glass doors leading to their balcony and pulled them open. Sheer white drapes pushed by the breeze fluttered against her body. There was all the nomal activity of a small town in the street below, and Lucy found it vastly welcoming. Lady friends strolled with parasols and shopping bags, chatting animatedly. A few women walked with their children; a small boy kicked a ball down the opposite boardwalk. He hit a distinguished gentleman in a blue linen jacket and white trousers, who paused to reprimand him. A cotton-clad farmer wearing sandals, and a fisherman in knee-high rubber boots, came out of a saloon. Two dusty vaqueros entered it.

After a few minutes, Lucy saw Shoz leave the hotel and cross the street. At the sight of him, she smiled. She thought he was going to enter the bank facing the hotel, but instead he went into the post office adjacent to it. Lucy wondered what business he was conducting in this sleepy port town. She strongly suspected it was illegal and felt a pang of fear for his sake.

Gloom began to rise in her, fed by her fear for him, her

agitation over his possible criminal pursuits, and the knowledge that they would return to Death Valley and in a couple
of weeks he would free her. She shook it off. Today they
were here in this quaint hotel, and she intended to enjoy
being with the man she loved more and more every moment.
She didn't want to spoil the day by facing the dilemma that
was awaiting her in two weeks.

She inspected the room with rising spirits. It was large
and spacious and airy, dominated by the four-poster bed
with its white, fresh coverings. There were white eyelet
curtains on the windows and a pale beige Abusson rug on
the floor. There were two bergères in green and white striped
silk, a little worn but infinitely inviting. Between them was
a small mahogany table that could be used for dining. There
was a fine bureau of pale pine, and a gilt-edged mirror over
it. They had their own bathroom with running water, and
a large window over the tub let the sunlight pour in.

It felt so good to be in a town and out of that hellish
valley. If she didn't know that after this trip she would be
leaving Shoz, forever, she would be completely thrilled.

Lucy wandered to the mirror and frowned. Seeing herself
reminded her too uncomfortably of how the men downstairs
had looked at her. Her clothes might be fine for Death
Valley, where nobody would see her, but here she looked
like a trollop in Carmen's gypsy garments. She had wanted
to explore the town, but she just couldn't do it dressed like
this.

She sighed. She had also wanted to dine in that restaurant.
It had been so long, an eternity, since she had gone out for
an evening, much less been waited on instead of doing the
serving. But she couldn't go out like this. She would have
to ask Shoz to get her some clothes. Then it occurred to
her that if he was involved in something shady, maybe he
intended to lie low at the hotel. Lucy was terribly disappointed by the possibility.

She took a bath, luxuriating for a long time in the white
porcelain tub and the hot, soapy water. Once upon a time
she had taken baths for granted—and just about everything

else. Never again, she vowed, would she be so shallow and naive.

More than two hours had passed and Shoz had not returned. Lucy, wrapped in a thick white towel, picked at the dinner sent up by room service. She reluctantly realized that if he had ordered them a meal in the room, he didn't plan on going out at all and she certainly didn't have to worry about her clothes. Another thirty minutes ticked by, and Lucy grew worried. She staked out the balcony as twilight fell. Then she saw him crossing the street and she called out, filled with relief. Of course, he didn't hear her.

She was waiting at the door when he knocked, smiling with anticipation. She opened it and flew into his arms, missing his frown.

"What's this?" he asked, dropping a big white box on one of the bergères so he could hug her properly, with both hands.

"I was worried," she admitted, clinging.

His gaze actually became limpid, but his tone was gruff. "Yeah?"

"Is everything all right?"

"There's been a delay," he said, running his hands over the thick towel and her rump. "We'll have to stay here for the whole week."

Her eyes widened, and she shrieked and rocked him. He laughed. "I didn't think you'd find that too hard to take."

She looked at him, her hands around his neck. "Do you mean we get to stay here, in this hotel, for an entire week?"

"That's right."

She snuggled against him. "I don't mind."

His hands stroked her hair, which was loose. He released her. "Why don't you dress while I take a quick bath."

She blinked.

"Don't you want to dine at that restaurant we saw?"

Her face lit up, then her expression fell. "Shoz, I can't."

"Why not?"

"I can't go out in Carmen's clothes."

"Damn right you can't." He turned to the striped chair

and handed her the box. "Tomorrow we'll get you anything else you need."

Lucy barely heard. Laughing, her expression identical to a child's on Christmas morning, she sat on the bed and tore open the box. She exclaimed in delight when she pulled out a pale green silk tailor-made with a boned bodice and pleated back. It was an unerringly elegant day ensemble, with wide leg-o'-mutton sleeves and even wider lapels. A fresh cream shirtwaist with four rows of tiny ruffles went with it. Thoughtfully he had included all the proper underthings, even a corset, which she was certain she needed if she was to wear the tiny-waisted outfit. "I love it! Thank you!"

She jumped up to hug him happily.

Lloyd walked into the back room of Fernando's saloon, holding a telegram, his expression grim.

"What is it?" Rathe leapt to his feet. He was alone with his brother Nick, and they had been passing the time playing cards. Brett and Storm had disappeared as they did so often for some privacy; Derek and a few men had gone across the border for more supplies. Rathe refused to budge from Casitas, as it was as close as he could get to where his daughter had last been. And Nick would not leave his younger brother alone.

"News. Finally."

"What?" Rathe demanded. "Spill it, man!"

"Our informer was a bit late in relaying this information, but there's no real harm done, because there's been a delay. The deal is going to take place in one week, in Matamoros."

Rathe froze, stunned.

Nick frowned. "One week? That barely gives us enough time."

"Just barely," Lloyd said.

"Oh, it gives us enough time," Rathe said, his eyes chilling, his tone harsh. "I don't care how many horses I kill to get there, but I'll make it."

"Relax," Nick soothed. "We can just make it, but we don't have time to plan thoroughly. We'll have to leave today."

"To hell with plans! What kind of plans do we need? I only need my fucking gun."

Lloyd and Nick exchanged grim looks. "I'll round up everyone," Lloyd said, leaving.

Before Nick could speak, Rathe jumped on him. "Don't start with that crap that we have to bring him back to Texas alive! I don't care that he wasn't in cahoots with Red and Jake and that Mr. Lloyd Government Man says Lucy would have never been kidnapped if he hadn't been jailed! She was kidnapped, and if it was Nicole or Regina, you'd want to blow his head off, too!"

"I would. But he was wrongly incarcerated for the horse theft, and every man deserves a fair trial—not murder. And Lloyd does want him alive, Rathe, and he represents our government."

Rathe laughed. "As if I care."

"You'll feel differently when you see Lucy alive and unharmed."

Rathe's blue eyes were stricken. "And what if she's not? What then!"

"Then I'll help you kill him," Nick said flatly.

That night they dined on grilled oysters and drank French champagne. Shoz had also bought clothes for himself, shocking Lucy when he appeared dressed casually yet classically in a white linen suit with a double-breasted sack jacket. With his dark good looks, he seemed every inch the gentleman, and as if he belonged on a hundred-foot yacht. At her first glimpse of him, Lucy was speechless.

They dined out-of-doors on the patio, serenaded by the soft sighing of the wind in the trees and the groaning of the moored boats rocking in the harbor. The sky was full of stars. Shoz's gaze barely left her, and Lucy found herself with a rapt, intense audience. She regaled him with amusing stories, and was rewarded time and again with the flash of his white teeth or his husky laughter. When they left the restaurant, it was to walk arm in arm like honeymooners. They strolled barefoot on the beach and gazed at the moon-drenched water. That night after they made love slowly and tenderly, Lucy wept and Shoz held her, helpless to stop the flood of tears.

The next day he was better than his word. After riding out to inform his men of the delay, he took her shopping. She discovered another aspect of Shoz's character: he was unstintingly generous. He bought her another ready-made day ensemble, this one candy white with a scooped neck and elbow-length sleeves. And when she admired a stunning off-the-shoulder evening gown in draped purple chiffon, he bought that for her, too, despite her demi-protests.

They ate dinner in a little dive behind one of the saloons, Lucy in her green silk, Shoz in his white suit. The place had three adobe walls and half a sagging roof, with rickety wooden tables and a sandy floor. Behind the counter, the obese proprietor prepared the food. The other patrons were all locals: farmers, fishermen, and two clerks in their rolled-up shirt-sleeves. Shoz and Lucy were regarded with suspicion that quickly changed to the tolerance reserved exclusively for love-struck lovers. They feasted on fresh fish fried before their very eyes and crisp chips, and washed it all down with quarts of warm salted beer. Afterward they fell into the big four-poster bed in their room, too stuffed to do more than laugh and hold each other and sleep.

That night they ordered room service and ate stark-ass naked. What began innocently evolved into lechery. He couldn't resist tasting the too sweet red wine on her lips, instead of from his glass. When a drop fell on her nipple, tightening it, he licked it off. When he dribbled the liquid over her belly, she protested, but feebly. When the red wine trickled between her legs, she watched fascinated as he got down on his knees as if in worship and followed the trail with his tongue.

The week went too fast, a blur of her silks and his linens, of star-filled nights and sunstruck awakenings. One night they even stole into Brownsville, just across the border, for a change of venue. It was crazy and they knew it, but the thick right-off-the-hoof steaks were worth it, and when they snuck back, they were drunk and satisfied and laughing at their foolishness.

At the end of the week, Lucy saw the abrupt change in

Shoz. Where he had been carefree and open, he became dark and closed. She saw him start to pull away from her, and was helpless to stop him. No amount of teasing and no amount of kissing would bring back his quick grin and chase away whatever demons had possessed him. Once when he thought he was alone, she caught him with such a dark, bleak expression that she was frightened. Too frightened to ask what was wrong. It was the sixth day.

"Are you worried about tomorrow?" she finally asked, pretending to be more interested in adjusting the sleeves of her white dress than in his answer. They were preparing to go out for some lunch and she stood in front of the mirror.

He sat on the bed clad only in his jeans, very male and very dark, watching her from behind. He had already gone out that morning, and Lucy had glimpsed him entering the post office across the street. "Tomorrow will be fine," he said tightly. "Tomorrow I will conclude my business."

In the mirror she raised her gaze to look at him, both wanting and not wanting to know what his "business" was. She was certain that she was better off in ignorance.

"And tomorrow," he said, staring at her back and her reflection, "I'm going to return to Death Valley—and leave you here."

She whirled. "What!"

"I'm not a liar, Lucy," he said, standing. "I promised you your freedom, and tomorrow you'll have it."

She was white. She momentarily couldn't speak.

"Don't worry," he said. "I've arranged everything. You can stay here at the hotel; the room and your meals are paid for. There's a post office right across the street; you can wire your family. They should make it here in about a week. That will give me enough time to disappear," he added mockingly.

"You—you've planned this?"

"I'm not a liar," he said harshly.

Tears came to her eyes. She knew she did not want to leave him, not now, and it was the only thing she cared about. "Is it so easy for you," she asked brokenly, "to keep your promise?"

"No!" he exploded. "It's the hardest damn thing I've ever done!"

Hope soared within her. "Then break it!"

"What?" he gasped.

Her chin lifted, her heart thundered. "Break your promise."

"What in hell are you saying?"

"I'm saying . . ." She faltered. "I love you."

Shoz stared.

Lucy's mouth trembled.

He grabbed her arms, immobilizing her. "Then marry me," he said. "Marry me."

35

The Catholic priest in the old church mission just outside of Matamoros refused to marry them. When he asked Shoz if he was an observant Catholic, Shoz answered unblinkingly in the affirmative. The priest took his word, utter lie that it was, but when he asked Lucy, she grew quite red, and proceeded to give him an account of her family history, despite Shoz's sharp jab to her ribs. Her grandmother was observant, and her mother's parents had been equally devout and Irish to boot. The priest prodded her for more relevant information and Lucy grew redder. "Well, I will try, I promise, it's in my blood . . ."

The justice of the peace in Brownsville performed the rites with no hesitation; that is, once Shoz handed him a few greenbacks on the side. When they rode back into Matamoros, the sun was just setting, and they were legally wed.

Lucy was having a case of nerves. She had squelched every warning bell that had sounded, once again stubbornly doing what she wanted to without daring to think about the consequences. Now that it was done, now that she was his wife, she felt somewhat faint. And very nervous.

He hadn't said a word to her since they had left the justice of the peace in Brownsville. Dismounting at the livery behind the hotel, Lucy stole another glance at his rigid profile. He didn't look particularly happy; in fact, he looked grim and angry.

His gaze seared her. "Having regrets?"

His tone was mean and she was taken aback. "I'm just worried," she admitted, tears coming to her eyes. He was obviously the one with regrets.

He scowled as the livery boy took their horses away, hands jammed in his jeans. Lucy felt her mouth tremble and vowed she would not cry. With a sigh, he pulled her to him. The feel of his body was familiar and reassuring on the one hand, yet she felt utterly insecure on the other. Why had a barrier suddenly come between them?

She looked up at him out of blurry eyes.

She saw the moment he let his mask slip, she saw the softness enter his eyes, concern and worry cross his features. "Don't worry," he said hoarsely. "We'll figure it out." She closed her eyes in relief and he kissed her.

Lucy most definitely wanted to talk, but once back in their hotel room, he guided her to the bed. He forced her chin up so she would have to look into his eyes. "Do you really love me?"

She melted. "Yes."

It was the answer he apparently wanted, needed, because he kissed her hard, intensely, and then made love to her with the same passion. Any thoughts Lucy had of protesting were swept away. This was the Shoz she knew and loved, and when they were together like this, she had no doubts at all.

That night they stayed up until dawn making plans. They would not live at Death Valley. "It's no place for my wife," Shoz said seriously. "We'll head south, deeper into Mexico. With the money from this sale, I should be able to buy us some land. A few more deals and we'll be sitting pretty."

"What are you doing, Shoz?"

He refused to meet her apprehensive gaze. "It's better if you don't know, Lucy."

Her heart sank.

Once they were safely in the heart of Mexico, they would inform Lucy's family of the circumstances. Lucy's stomach twisted when she thought of her parents. She loved them dearly, and hated hurting them. She knew they would be devastated about her marriage to a man like Shoz. But if they only knew him . . . which was impossible. The one thing she wanted most in this world was to bring Shoz home to New York to meet her family and become a part of it, and this could never be. Although he hadn't stolen Derek's stud, he was doing something illegal now, and there was his criminal record and escape from New York prison to account for. She was afraid to ask him what crime he had committed in New York.

They decided to return first to Death Valley for Roberto. Shoz would not leave the little boy behind. He intended to adopt the boy, and was sure he could pay Carmen off to gain her assent. Lucy was less certain, but was filled with hope that maybe the boy would become their son. She urged Shoz to keep their marriage a secret, certain that Carmen would never let Roberto go if she knew the truth.

At dawn Lucy finally fell asleep, reassured and dreaming of a ranch in central Mexico and an idyllic family life. Shoz restlessly watched her. He was just starting to believe that they had really done it.

That he had really done it. Lucy was impulsive and used to doing what she wanted, but he knew much better. Was there any hope for them?

He couldn't give her any of the things she dreamed of, or the life she was bred to. Once her infatuation with him faded, would she become bitter and angry? He could not imagine her homesteading in Mexico, but then again, he had never thought she would adapt to Death Valley so well, either.

It didn't really matter. She was his wife now. He felt a powerful surge of nameless emotion at the thought. He had married her because he hadn't been ready to let her go, and once she was his wife, he'd never have to let her go. He'd never been possessive about any woman before. It was frightening.

At sunrise he shrugged on his blue shirt and jeans, giving up any hope of sleeping, and left the room quietly. He had donned a thin suede jacket to hide the gun he was packing low on his thigh. Sometime today Lopez would dock, and he intended to meet him. The gun was merely a precaution, because he did not expect any trouble.

As he walked down the wide stairs, the hairs began to rise on the nape of his neck. He had a terrible sense of warning. His steps slowed, for he trusted his instincts too much not to heed them. He did not enter the lobby. He flattened himself against the wall and peered around the corner. It was empty except for the clerk.

At this hour, the clerk finishing up the last of his midnight shift should be red-eyed and dozing at the desk. Not only was the clerk keenly alert—he was no damn hotel employee. Although Shoz had never seen him before, he could smell the law a mile away. And this man was an agent, no doubt about it.

Outwardly Shoz remained impassive, but adrenaline pumped through his body, and under his jacket he was beginning to sweat profusely.

Somehow, the law had been tipped off.

He silently hurried back upstairs, his mind racing. Feds or Braggs? It had to be the former, because the latter could not have possibly found his whereabouts here in Matamoros. Entering their room quietly, he locked the door. He went to the window, left open for the breeze, careful to stay near the wall to avoid being seen—or shot by some trigger-happy lawman.

The town was just coming awake. He could hear the gulls cawing and the fishermen calling to each other on the wharf. Across the street there was a small eatery, and the fragrant smells of sizzling bacon and strong coffee came wafting out. Someone in the alley between the post office and bank ducked out of sight.

It had been Lucy's father, Rathe Bragg.

He was sure of it.

His mind worked like lightning. If it was the Braggs and

not the Feds, they wanted Lucy. If they had a hired detective in place in the lobby, then they knew where Lucy was, for they would have ascertained this information from any of the hotel staff. He was certain they had only just arrived in town that morning, or in the blackness of the night, for he was too astute not to have noticed them if they had come any time earlier.

If the Braggs were here, they wanted Lucy first and him second. He could leave her here and make a run for it on his own. Or he could use her as a hostage, as a bargaining chip for his freedom. That had been the original plan, he thought wryly. Only now, he knew it was too late for that.

Because he wasn't going to leave her behind.

His mind was churning. How had the Braggs found him here in Matamoros? How had they shown up precisely on the last day of his stay here? Had he been betrayed? By Lopez? By one of his own men? He ruled them all out instantly. Then who? What if the Braggs were working with the Feds? The thought was chilling.

He went to the bureau. "Get up!"

Lucy awoke when he threw his extra pair of jeans at her, with a shirt following. "Put those on!"

"What?" She was wide-awake instantly and turning deathly white. "What's happening?"

"Get dressed now." He didn't look at her. "We're moving. Wear my clothes and hat and make sure all your hair is out of sight."

"Oh God," Lucy cried, leaping from the bed and stumbling into his jeans. "It's the law, isn't it? They've found you!"

Near the window, he saw her father again, in the alley, rifle in hand. The man was looking right up at him. Shoz could have sworn that their gazes met for a bare moment. But that was impossible. He turned and watched as Lucy fumbled with the buttons of his shirt. "Want to stay behind?"

She froze and stared at him, panting.

He cursed and finished buttoning up the shirt for her, jamming it into her pants roughly. She did not look like a boy. He gave her his jacket to hide her bosom and her figure. In his clothes, with her hair hastily pinned up under his hat, she now appeared sexless. Except for her small bare feet. But that couldn't be helped, because he had only one pair of boots and she had only her own shoes.

He grabbed her arm, causing her to cry out. If he wasn't so intent on escape, he would be brooding over the fact that she had failed to answer his succinct question—*Did she want to be left behind?* Why hadn't she just denied it?

He propelled her to the door and listened, unlocked it, cracked it. The hallway was silent and empty.

But he knew for a fact that Rathe Bragg was in the alley watching the hotel. One of their men was in the lobby, posing as a clerk. How many more men were in the rooms of this hotel, on this floor? How many others were downstairs? He had to get to the small livery out back where their horses were. The most direct route to the stable was via the room opposite theirs, which faced the back garden, which adjoined the hotel-affiliated stable. Was someone in that room? It would be infinitely easier to leave Lucy behind before he ventured forth to find out. But if he was taking her with him, he didn't dare; he didn't trust her. It was her family out there.

They stepped into the hall. Lucy whimpered in fear. Shoz held her tightly with one hand, drawing his knife with the other. They pressed against the wall by the door of the opposite room. "I'm going in; don't move."

She nodded, white and speechless, her pupils unnaturally dilated.

He released her, half expecting her to scream for help, but if she hadn't already screamed, then maybe she wouldn't. He tested the knob slightly—it was unlocked. Slowly he swung the door open, stepping back to Lucy and out of the way of any gun that might be pointed at the doorway from within. "Tell him not to shoot when I say so," he whispered.

She stared at him.

"Now," Shoz said.

"Don't shoot," Lucy cried.

Shoz stepped partly into the doorway, saw the man hesitating with his gun cocked, and threw his knife, before his opponent could even fire. He took him in the heart and the man fell with a gasp, the gun dropping to the floor. Shoz grabbed Lucy, wheeled her in, shut and locked the door, and propelled her to the glass doors on the far wall. Lucy was shaking. On the way to the balcony, he pulled the knife from the dead man's chest, wiped it front and back on the man's pants, and stuck it back in his belt. Except for Lucy's cry, they hadn't made a sound.

"I'm going to throw up," Lucy gasped.

"No you're not," Shoz said, pushing her against the wall. He stared outside while beside him, she wretched dryly.

Were there men out back? Shoz peered through the window carefully at the back gardens and didn't see anyone. It was too fortunate to be possible. He searched the area again, and was certain this time that no one was within it. They could use the balcony to drop to the ground. The livery, was only a short distance away, and once they were across the lawn, the trees would provide cover. There was only one other open stretch, the path between the hotel and livery, which was directly across from the alley where Rathe Bragg was hidden.

"Now what?" Lucy whispered.

"We're jumping," he said grimly, wrapping his arm around her waist and pushing them both out of glass doors before she could protest. Instantly they froze against the glass, directly under the overhanging edge of the roof. Shoz thought he had heard something—from the roof above.

Shoz listened. He heard nothing. He kept listening. Lucy was breathing harshly, distracting him, and in his hold, she shook. After more intent concentration, he was rewarded with the sound of a broken piece of tile skittering over the edge of the roof and falling to the ground below—from almost directly above them.

There was someone on the roof.

Lucy had heard it, too, and she was frozen in his embrace, her gaze cast up at the dark overhang above their heads.

Abruptly Shoz reached inside the doors to lock them from within, then pulled them closed. Now they were locked outside on the balcony—and just in case Lucy had second thoughts, she was temporarily contained. "Don't move," he whispered in her ear. He lifted her chin. "Are you going to scream?"

Her eyes went wide with surprise and outrage.

It was on the tip of his tongue to tell her that it was her family out there, stalking him, stalking them, to test her. He didn't.

Shoz went to the left edge of the balcony, climbed over the railing, then leapt for the adjacent terrace. Five feet were between the two and he made it easily. Staying away from the glass doors, just in case someone was inside, he climbed onto the railing, pressed against the building, clawing it for grip. He had to hunch down so he would fit beneath the overhang of the roof. He listened and heard the guard above him walking away. Which meant that his back was turned.

Quick as a cat, Shoz gripped the roof's edge and hurled himself up. Tiles broke and slid. He was on his hands and knees when the agent turned and saw him. Shoz reached for his knife; the agent lifted his rifle. Shoz threw his blade while the man cocked his gun. Shoz was faster. His target dropped.

On his hands and knees, keeping purposefully low, Shoz scrambled for the man, because he had not a doubt that he would need his knife again. The man was still alive. Shoz retrieved the knife, waiting for shouts to erupt from the street below. If someone had been watching their partner and seen him fall . . .

But no shouts came. The cards had turned. On this hand, so far, luck was riding him like a winner.

He re-joined Lucy on the balcony. Her eyes were frightened, questioning. He grabbed her arm. "Sorry," he said, hustling her to the edge of the balcony. "Bend your knees, drop, and roll."

She stiffened when she realized what he was doing, and when he lifted her over the railing, she cried out. "Shoz! No, please!"

His heart went tight—he didn't want her hurt. "Bend your knees and roll when you hit the ground, Lucy," he ordered, lowering her as far as he could. His arms felt like they were being ripped out of his sockets. He let her go.

She landed and went down and lay still. He was over the

railing and hanging from the balcony with the speed of a cat burglar. He landed hard, winced, and rolled, came up on all fours and scrambled to her. "Are you okay?" he asked huskily, lifting her to a sitting position.

"Yes," she gasped. Then her eyes darkened. "You bastard!"

He got up, dragging her with him.

"You could have warned me."

There was no time to argue. He had expected her to be madder than a hornet for heaving her over the second-story balcony. He grabbed her arm and they ran hard across the lawn to the safety of some trees at the edge of the hotel's property. To their right, if they peered past the trunks, they would see the main street, just a hundred feet away. A dirt alley that bisected the main street lay at their feet, and directly across it was the livery and their horses.

To their right was also Rathe Bragg, hidden between the bank and post office, just on the other side of the main street, with the rest of his family and all the Pinkertons they had hired undoubtedly staking out the hotel and the entire town. Shoz dared to look and saw no one and nothing on the broad thoroughfare, except for a passing dray. The timing could not be better; the dray would shield them from her father's—and any cohort's—view. "Let's go!"

Shoz and Lucy ran across the short distance of the road into the stable. A boy was forking hay. Shoz didn't wait; he was already grabbing one of their saddles from the tack room and barking at the boy to grab the other one. The boy obeyed with alacrity and no small amount of curiosity. Three minutes later, their horses were tacked and ready.

Shoz shoved money into the boy's hand as Lucy mounted. He also yanked the kid's beaten hat from his head and jammed it on. Shoz grabbed Lucy's reins. "You won't need these," he said, his gaze lancing her. Why couldn't he trust her? She was his wife. She loved him. But he was afraid she would see her father and change her mind.

She was affronted. "I can ride better if—"

"Forget it."

With that, he spurred his mount forward, and they came out of the barn at a fast walk. They were going to have to run for it sooner or later, but if they could get out of town disguised as they were, they might have a chance to escape. Shoz was tempted to cut across the back garden, but had no doubt that the livery was being watched—that they were being watched—and it would be damn suspicious. Instead, they would try to ride sedately out of town right under the Braggs' collective noses, hoping that they would not be identified.

They walked up the alley toward the main street. Shoz sat slouched low with the kid's hat hiding his face. Lucy looked like a gangly boy in his jacket and Stetson—or so he prayed. They stepped onto the main street, the bank and post office directly across from them—as was the alley where Rathe Bragg hid. Sweat drenched Shoz's body. He could feel their unseen eyes. Would her father recognize her? Recognize him? He waited for the searing pain of a bullet, but it did not come.

Nothing happened. The seconds slowly ticked by. They turned left. Their horses, sensing their riders' tension, moved with tight, coiled energy, fighting the hold and the pace Shoz kept. Lucy rode on Shoz's left, away from the north side of the street, where her father lay in wait. They rode knee to knee. Shoz muttered to her to keep her head down. She obeyed. Ahead of them lay open country, but beyond that were the mountains, which offered them their only hope.

If they could walk undetected out of town, they just might make it.

In the alley, Rathe squatted behind a barrel, squinting at the riders passing practically in front of him. He was impatient; he wanted them to get out of his line of vision, so he could watch the hotel where Shoz Cooper and Lucy had a room. Behind him, Nick said, "Why is that rider sweating like a pig at high noon when it's still so cool out?"

The two riders were past them now, and Rathe and Nick edged around the corner of the bank to watch the rumps of their horses. Nick was right, the rider was sweating like a pig. Something else struck a discordant note: their mounts were tense and collected as if ready to gallop at the drop of a hat. Rathe looked at the boy, frowning because some-

thing was familiar. A flash of pale skin drew his attention—
and he saw the bare heels of his feet.

Nobody went with bare feet.

Such tiny bare feet, even for an adolescent boy.

But not for a girl.

He jumped up, aiming his rifle very, very carefully.
"What are you doing!" Nick cried.

"It's them," Rathe said very calmly, and he fired.

Shoz heard the gun's retort at the same time that he felt
the bullet strike his neck. Lucy screamed. He was already
spurring his horse into a gallop as blood poured from the
wound. They raced out of town.

He rode bent for hell. He ignored the searing pain, the
sticky wetness of his shirt on his shoulder. He ignored Lucy,
who was shouting at him. If he was going to die, he would
die, but until that moment, he'd ride for freedom, giving it
all he was worth. They raised a cloud of dust as they galloped
past the last houses in Matamoros. Then they heard the
thunder rumbling behind them.

The mountains were hours away. But if they could outride
their enemy, they would make the foothills sooner, where
they might be able to get lost. The problem was, at this
pace, they would kill their mounts quickly.

"Oh my God," Lucy cried, looking over her shoulder.
"Shoz, we have to stop! God, you're bleeding . . ."

The pain in his neck had reduced itself to a stinging
numbness. He knew exactly how many men were following
him, because Fernando had told him how many men the
Braggs' had invaded Casitas with. But the noise the Braggs's
private army made was deafening, and he had to look back,
to see a small army in hot pursuit.

He had a bad feeling.

Like his luck had just run out.

After a few miles, their horses began to tire. Shoz was
feeling a bit dizzy from the loss of blood. Yet if they could
make it another couple of miles, there were gorges they
could enter and disappear into, at least slowing down their
enemy. They had to make it. He spurred his mount on.

Another mile passed. As their own mounts flagged, so
did those behind them. Lucy was screaming at him again,

screaming that they had to stop. Shoz twisted and saw that the gap between them and the Braggs had remained the same. There was hope after all.

"We'll never make it," Lucy cried. "There's blood all over your shirt. Please!"

"We'll make it," he gritted.

He spoke too soon. Weak and dizzy, he failed to ride his mount at that breakneck speed as he should. When his mount stumbled slightly, exhausted, Shoz lost his balance. He felt the courageous animal buckling as if time had slowed. Somehow he jumped free of the horse before it hit the dirt and crushed one of his legs. Still holding Lucy's reins, he was dragged a few yards before her horse came to a terrified, blowing halt.

He got to his feet and lunged for her mount, to leap up behind her and push on. But he was weak and not as fast as he should have been. Lucy had already slid off and was screaming and running to him.

"Get back on," he shouted hoarsely, through the thick, choking dust.

"We have to stop," Lucy screamed, pushing at him, preventing him from getting to her mount. He saw that she was crying. Of course she wanted to stop. She had to have seen her family. New pain seared him, and it wasn't completely physical.

She was crying incoherently about the blood. Shoz grabbed her and dragged her toward the quivering horse while she fought him every step of the way. The mount shied and backed away. Lucy suddenly dug in her heels and slapped him hard across the face.

He was stunned for a moment, stunned and dizzy, while the thundering of the Pinkerton army grew louder and louder, coming closer and closer. "You're going to die, you bastard," she was shouting, sobbing.

He let go of the reins, and the gelding jumped away. It was too late, the cavalry of riders was drumming down on them, but she wasn't right, he wasn't going to die, not if he could help it.

The hundred riders came to a halt, surrounding them. The dust cloud enveloped them. They could not see through it, and their world was reduced to one of sounds: the horses blowing and stomping, saddles creaking and groaning, bits jangling, Lucy's sobs. A hundred rifles were cocked almost simultaneously.

The dust settled.

He looked up to face the most formidable foe he had ever had, a hundred Pinkertons and the Braggs. Everyone sat motionless on their mounts looking down upon them, with a hundred rifles aimed at his heart. Shoz was determined not to collapse, but he was dizzy and he swayed, while Lucy sank to the ground, weeping at his feet. It was over.

It was finally, irrevocably, over.

PART THREE

HEAVEN AND HELL

HAVANA, CUBA

36

Near Havana, December 1897

The coal-burning freighter moved north out of Havana Bay before heading east toward the Straits of Florida. The sky was a delicate shade of azure blue, the waters of the Caribbean translucent and nearly turquoise. The freighter chugged gently through the bay, leaving a single cloud of black smoke in its wake. Behind the ship, Cuba grew smaller with every passing moment; her tropical palms waving above pearl-white beaches; green, jagged mountains rising above the thick, lush jungles; the scene peaceful, picturesque, idyllic. The vessel's sole passenger was unaffected, standing easily on the deck near the railing, for he only looked forward, never back.

Shoz stood with his legs apart and rode the ship's rhythmic lurching as if he'd been born to it. He'd been in the Caribbean long enough to be indifferent to the vista he was leaving behind him, but not long enough to be indifferent to the suffering he was also leaving behind. Shoz lifted his face to the hot sun and let the light drench him. The warm feel of it could not erase the images he would probably associate forever with Havana. Nothing could erase those images. The sickness and starvation, the death and dying. Emaciated children begging for food beside piles of corpses. Their mothers grabbing pitifully at his clothes, begging for something, anything, as he passed by. But Shoz had long ago given away his last dollar.

When he had agreed to take weapons to the rebels in Cuba, he had never expected to find such tragedy, nor had he anticipated becoming so involved. Yet no one could spend any length of time in Cuba and remain neutral, not when faced with this enormous conflict and with the poignant suffering. But even had he known, he would have come anyway. They hadn't given him any choice.

And just the reminder of those few days after he'd been captured outside of Matamoros brought another image to his mind, one that still came too easily and too frequently, one that even the horrors of a revolution could not erase, one with red hair and blue eyes. He still hated her. No matter that she had knuckled under to her family, and he could well imagine the pressure they had exerted upon her. If she had really loved him—if their marriage hadn't been some rich girl's whim—she would have never signed those divorce papers. He would never forgive her, and he would never forget.

He had arrived in Havana four months ago. As he'd agreed, he had transported the guns directly to Cuba. The rebels did not question his mercenary motives or his claim that the U.S. authorities were too close for comfort and he needed a temporary change of venue. As it was, they had been having trouble recently with the Spanish blockade, and welcomed placing the burden of running it on Shoz's shoulders.

General Valeriano Weyler y Nicolau had also just arrived from Spain, with the goal of crushing the uprising. The rebels wanted independence; Weyler was determined to reestablish Spain's stranglehold upon the island and was ruthlessly using all the means at his disposal. The rebels were nervous and wary, with good cause. They insisted he deliver the guns to one of their hideouts, and gave him four men to aid him. Shoz delivered the shipment to a working plantation a few miles from Havana, which was used as a base by the rebels. There they were stormed by the Spanish, and Shoz found himself in the midst of the fighting. The rebels succeeded in defending their position and escaping into the hills, Shoz with them. Running away with the rebels was a matter of survival.

Since Shoz's real purpose in coming to Cuba was to spy, once he was ensconced within the rebel army deep in the hills of Havana province, he stayed there. Soon he was an accepted leader. Most of the rebels were farmers, and the need for skilled leadership was crucial. The war consisted of continuous guerrilla engagements and sabotage, the one side against the other, striking as frequently and destructively as possible. Neither side offered any mercy to the other. Civilian casualties were careless and atrocious. Shoz tried to avoid all engagements that would hurt the innocent, and concentrated his band of rebels in attacks he deemed to be most damaging and effective: on the supply lines of the Spanish troops and on the corrupt government itself.

Shoz was hardened; he had endured the hell of the past months and seen the worst anyone could see. Yet his stomach turned over just from the memories. He was keenly aware that McKinley was negotiating with Spain for a cessation of hostilities, Cuban independence, and reparations. Shoz was certain that McKinley would never come to terms with Spain, for the situation in Cuba had escalated dangerously. There were now more than two hundred thousand Spanish troops in Cuba, and that kind of buildup meant that Spain's recent assurances to McKinley in the negotiations were all lies. Spain had said it would grant autonomy, but if she was building up such a massive army, she was intending a final and decisive assault on the rebels, one that would crush them into oblivion. Shoz had been called to Washington to report in person, and he had the numbers to back up his convictions.

The freighter chugged into the straits. Shoz stared ahead at the blue-green sea. In another couple of hours he would be able to make out the Florida Keys. Something inside him clenched up tight.

And he wasn't thinking of Washington, oh no. He was thinking of New York.

New York—just a short train ride from the capital.

He smiled, his expression hard and cynical. Coincidence was the great joker in life, a wild card; one never knew when it would be dealt. But he'd just gotten it.

Because it was the funniest coincidence that he should be summoned to Washington now, when he'd spent the past months in Cuba, only making one brief trip to Death Valley. It was a helluva coincidence that he would be just in time

to make another side trip—this one north. That he would
be just in time to celebrate Lucy Bragg's birthday—and her
second marriage.

Shoz and Lucy hadn't had a chance, not once they were
surrounded by the Braggs and their private army; a dozen
agents had instantly descended on him, cuffed him, and
thrown him on a horse. He had barely managed to retain
consciousness on the hard ride across the border, and the
gallop to Brownsville, the closest American town, had
seemed endless. Shoz knew it was only his anger and his
pride that kept him upright in the saddle. He didn't see
Lucy; she rode far behind him, protectively surrounded by
her family.

He was thrown in jail and tended by the town doctor.
Although he was weak and had lost a lot of blood, the
doctor assured him that the bullet had only creased his neck,
lucky man that he was. Shoz would have laughed at the
doctor's choice of words, except that he was in too much
pain.

But soon Shoz had other things to distract him, like the
tall, thin man with the cold blue eyes whose presence he
suddenly became aware of. The man was no regular Pinkerton. He had "government" written all over him, and Shoz
didn't like it. If things could possibly get worse, he sensed
they would.

"We're going to have a little chat," the man said, leaning
comfortably against the bars of Shoz's cell. "I think you'll
be very interested in what I have to say."

"I don't think I'm going anywhere."

The man smiled. "On the contrary, I think you are. My
name is Lloyd."

Shoz shifted to try and gain some comfort, which was
impossible because he'd refused painkillers and the ache in
his neck was getting worse. But before Lloyd could start,
the door to the jail flew open, and his wife ran in.

Shoz sat up, all physical distress forgotten.

She looked like hell. She was dusty and dirty, her hair
loose and snarled, her nose and eyes red from crying.

"Shoz!" She ran to the cell and grabbed the bars. "Are you all right?"

"I'm okay." He forgot Lloyd's presence; he heaved himself to his feet. "Lucy . . ."

Her expression wrenched at him. She waited for him to continue, pale and trembling. But he didn't know what to say. For some crazy reason, he wanted to reassure her that everything would be all right, that they would be all right, but he couldn't, not when their world was being ripped apart right in front of them. Not when he had just lost his freedom, which was the same as his life. Not when he knew there was no hope, not for him, not for them. Not anymore.

She reached out her hand through the bars. "Don't worry. Shoz, I—"

Lucy could not finish what she was saying, because the door behind her opened with a bang and her father strode in, looking enraged enough to murder. He was followed by his sister, Storm. "Lucy!"

Lucy didn't turn around. The look she gave Shoz was at once tear-filled and full of desperate, unspoken promises. Then Rathe grabbed her from behind and dragged her away from the cell. "I want you to stay away from him!"

"Let me go. I want to talk to him. You can't stop me. After all, I'm sure Aunt Storm told you, he's my hus—"

Rathe actually clapped his hand over her mouth, propelling her outside, Lucy's aunt protesting and rushing after them. The door slammed behind them; it was the last time Shoz saw Lucy.

His heart was thundering and he was gripping the bars of his cell for support. Sweat trickled from his temple. Lloyd spoke, drawing his attention. "Why *did* you marry her?"

Shoz didn't look at him and went weakly to the cot, sinking down on it. He had no intention of answering.

"She's a beautiful girl," Lloyd said. "Lust? Somehow, I don't think so. Let me warn you, Mr. Cooper, even though your wife cannot testify against you, we can put you away for the next hundred years, even without her testimony."

Shoz laughed weakly. That particular point of law had never occurred to him. "Don't bother trying to convince me," he said harshly. "I've already tasted American justice. I believe you."

"Good. That makes my job easier." Lloyd approached to take up the position Lucy had vacated. "I have a proposition for you, Shoz. One I think will interest you."

"The only thing that interests me is my freedom."

"Good. Then listen to this: You keep on smuggling guns to the Cubans, only you do it personally and successfully. And when you are thick with the thieves, so to speak, you begin to spy. You report everything to me—every detail of the war, every move the rebels make, every move the Spanish make."

"What's in it for me?"

"Your freedom, of course."

And suddenly there was hope.

Shoz was barely able to believe his good fortune. All he had to do was continue what he had been doing, with the little hitch of actually transporting the weapons to Cuba himself, making contact with the rebels, and involving himself more deeply in their affairs. In exchange for this, he would receive a presidential pardon for all of his crimes.

His record would be wiped clean. It would cease to exist.

There was a kink or two. There was no time limit on his services. He would spy for the United States government until there was no need to do so anymore. Without the intervention of a country like America, the Cuban war for independence could drag on indefinitely. Also, the criteria for the presidential pardon were vague—he must spy and do it well. Still, there was no choice. Shoz was being delivered from the very gates of hell. He was not going to go back to prison, something he had sworn to himself long ago that he would never do. And just as important, he had a chance to put his past behind him, and once this affair was finished, he could start over as a new man.

Would Lucy wait for him?

She was his wife—she would have to.

He was desperate now to see her again, because this time he could reassure her, this time he could promise her a future. Suddenly, where there had been only pain, there was excitement; where there had been blackness, there was light.

It was only a few hours after his "talk" with Lloyd that some of his peace was shattered. He had been dozing despite the steady pain of his neck. He heard the door to the jail slamming open, then he heard Rathe Bragg's furious voice. "Wake up!"

Shoz opened an eye.

"If you think you're going to get away with this, you're dreaming!"

Shoz sat up.

"I don't know how the hell you married my daughter, you son of a bitch, but you're going to pay for it, do you understand? You're going to spend the rest of your life paying for what you did!"

"I didn't force your daughter to marry me."

"You seduced her!"

Shoz laughed. He decided not to let Bragg in on the truth—she had, in fact, seduced him.

"You think this is funny? You won't think it's so funny when you're back on a chain gang."

Shoz went very still. "There won't be any chain gang."

"No?" Bragg grinned. It was taunting. "You think you can get away with kidnapping my daughter—and using her?"

Bragg didn't know about his deal with the government, and warning bells began to go off. Rathe Bragg was very powerful, and with his family behind him, more so. If they chose to oppose the government, then what? "I didn't use your daughter, Bragg."

"You bastard! When I think of you touching her, I could kill you!"

"Nobody's going to kill anyone," Lloyd said, entering with Derek. "I don't want you in here."

Rathe drew a roll of papers from his jacket. "Let him out, or let me in," he said. "I have something for him to sign."

"You shouldn't be in here, son," Derek said. He was grim. "Rathe, we have to talk."

"I have something for him to sign," Rathe repeated stubbornly. "And I sure as hell am not leaving until he does."

Shoz wanted to know just where the Braggs stood—where Derek Bragg, the family patriarch, stood. He sensed that Derek would hold the family together in the position he chose. He stared at him. "Has he told you? Has Lloyd told you about our deal?"

Derek winced. "Yes, he told me."

"What deal?" Rathe cried, looking from Shoz to his father. "What the fuck are you talking about?"

No one answered. Rathe looked at Lloyd. "This had better not be what it sounds like!"

"Rathe, Shoz is not going to be tried for kidnapping your daughter. He is going on a mission for the United States government."

Rathe stared for a split second. "You lousy double-crossing bastard!" Derek put a hand on his shoulder; he shook it off.

"Use your head and think," Lloyd said. "America has interests to protect in Cuba. Shoz is in with the rebels. Who better to spy for us and protect our interests? Protect your interests? Protect Maravilla—and you and your family's other investments? Who—"

"I don't believe this!"

Derek grabbed Rathe. "Unfortunately, son, this is out of our hands."

Rathe threw him off. "You're siding with him!"

"I'm not siding with him. We're not being given a choice here, Rathe, and I've given it some serious thought. Lucy is all right. We'll fix this marriage and take care of her so that no one will ever know *anything*. I will never permit the scandal that would come from a trial for Lucy's abduction, *never*. If the government wants to send him to Cuba, it doesn't change how we're going to take care of Lucy so that she isn't hurt any more than she is already."

Rathe was silent.

"Would you permit the scandal of a trial, Rathe? Would you? Dammit, son, use your head!"

Rathe cried out in frustration. He turned on Lloyd. "All along you knew about this, didn't you? You lied to me, used me and my family and our resources—to capture your ready-made spy!''

"That's right," Lloyd said easily. "I'm sorry."

In the cell, Shoz relaxed. The Braggs were not going to go up against the government and use their considerable power to thwart the deal of his lifetime. He was going to Cuba.

Rathe whirled. "You may think you're getting off, but you're not. You are going to pay for what you've done, and I'll make sure of it. I'll make sure they keep you in Cuba so long, you'll forget what America looks like. Cuba will be your prison, you son of a bitch—you wait and see."

"After doing real time in New York, Mr. Bragg, Cuba will be paradise."

Suddenly Rathe smirked. "Is that so? I was just there. Once upon a time it was paradise—now it's sheer hell!"

"Enough!" Derek said. "This isn't getting anybody anywhere. Do you have the papers?"

Rathe nodded, unrolling documents. "I don't care if I have to put a loaded gun to your head, but you're signing."

Lloyd unlocked the cell door, and Derek and Rathe entered. Shoz sat up straighter. Derek pulled a pen out of his vest. Rathe smiled coldly and held the papers down on the cot. "Sign on the X."

"What is this?" Shoz asked.

"You'd better sign," Derek warned.

"I've promised them you'd sign, Cooper," Lloyd said. "Or no deal."

"They're divorce papers," Rathe gritted. "*Sign*. Sign or I blow the whistle on this goddam deal."

Shoz froze. Even his heart had stilled. He said, "I'm not signing." He didn't think it through, he refused to think it through, refused to consider the consequences—prison. He knew himself well enough to know he meant what he said with every fiber of his being.

Rathe Bragg went crazy, lunging for him, with murder his obvious intention. He was dragged away by both Lloyd and Derek, the two men reassuring him that Shoz would come around. Shoz smiled, a hard sneer. But he was sweating.

Later Lloyd returned to convince him that his freedom was more important than his marriage, and that if he did not sign, he was going to prison for the rest of his life. Shoz knew he was right, he should sign—but he never lifted that pen. Derek Bragg also returned, grimly reiterating what Lloyd had stated, then adding even more arguments, but Shoz did not budge. He had made up his mind.

Very late that night, Lloyd entered the jail, carrying the papers. Shoz had been unable to sleep, his mind wrestling futilely with some means of escape from this impossible predicament. He hadn't found one, but now, at the sight of Lloyd, he sat up and began to sweat.

"I thought I made it clear," he said, never taking his eyes from Lloyd, "I'm not signing."

Lloyd unlocked the door to his cell as if he hadn't heard him. "I think you're going to change your mind, Cooper."

Shoz smiled. "Think again."

Lloyd unrolled the papers, holding them in front of him. "She doesn't want you, Cooper."

Shoz blinked, the typed words of the document coming into focus, a signature at the bottom of the page, near where he was supposed to sign, becoming distinct. Ugly, black comprehension started to set in.

"She didn't need any convincing; it was just a lark after all."

Lucy Bragg. Her dainty signature danced across the page, blurring. He whitened, shocked. Full understanding hit him, hard. *She had signed.*

She doesn't want you anymore. Lloyd's word's echoed, or was he repeating them? His heart began to pound, his blood surged. She had signed. *She had signed away her half of their marriage.*

Damn her. *Damn her!*

"I'll leave this with you," Lloyd said, throwing the documents on the cot with a pen. "No point in holding out now." He left.

Shoz didn't move. Not for a long time. But when he did, it was to sign his name with a flourish.

37

New York City, December 1897

Tomorrow she was going to be married. Lucy did not know whether to laugh or cry. She sat at her dressing table and stared grimly at her reflection. She did not look like a happy bride. She looked more like a widow.

Abruptly Lucy got up to pace around the room that had been hers since she was a child. It was very large, with one area dominated by the canopied bed, the other given over to a plush sofa and several armchairs. The room was decorated in shades of ivory and white. The four double windows on the far wall looked out on Central Park. Lucy pushed one open. It was a cold winter day, and the park, carpeted thickly with snow, sparkled in the sun. The chilling air seemed to invigorate her. At least, it eased some of the awful apathy that possessed her.

Today was her birthday, her twenty-first birthday. She should be happy, considering how lucky she was. Already over the hill, she was about to wed one of the finest catches in New York. She should be thanking her father. She should be grateful.

The problem was, she wasn't any of those things.

His image loomed, dark, mocking.

Aghast, Lucy tried to shove it away. He no longer invaded her thoughts so frequently; indeed, there were times when she did not think of him at all for an entire day—and then she would remember, and in the remembering, know she had not forgotten him at all.

And probably never would.

The hurt was long since gone. There was only anger in its stead.

Her parents had been right. He was not the man for her. He was a bum and a bastard. There was only one person he cared about, and that was his mercenary self. She was better off without him, and she knew it. *If he had cared at all for her, he would have never signed those papers.*

It had been a shock.

Lucy barely remembered the ride back to Brownsville. She had been in a state of hysteria, thinking Shoz was dying from the gunshot wound. There was so much blood. Once in town, she was hustled to a hotel room with her aunt Storm. Lucy had begged her aunt to let her find Shoz. Storm had grabbed her roughly. "What is going on, Lucy? What is it?"

Lucy didn't give a thought to the consequences of revealing the truth. "I don't want him to die!" she sobbed. "Please let me go to him!"

"I don't understand." But Storm was pale with comprehension.

"I love him! He's my husband!"

Storm held her and rocked her while she wept, assuring her that he would not die, and that she would bring word of his condition—but under no circumstances could Lucy see him. She left after Lucy promised to wait for her return. Lucy had done no such thing. The instant her aunt had disappeared, Lucy had fled to find Shoz.

Now she knew part of the truth. While she had been at the jail, her aunt had gone to her father with the news of their marriage. Setting off her father's determination to keep them apart and see them divorced. And as always, Rathe Bragg succeeded in whatever he decided to do.

Lucy had been weak with relief to find Shoz bandaged and awake, if pale, but so clearly alive and recovering. She had been so afraid he would die!

Her father's sudden furious entrance ruined her chance to speak with him and comfort him, which she so badly wanted to do. Rathe dragged her from the jail, across the street, and back to her hotel room.

"How dare you!" Lucy was furious. "I'm going back there, damn it; I have every right—"

"You have no rights!" her father shouted, raising his hand.

Lucy shrank against the wall. Never had she seen her father so enraged—and so close to violence. She did not move, understanding that he was fighting for control—and that the violence he so barely restrained was directed at her.

He recovered. There was no sound in the small room except for their harsh, uneven breathing. "Daddy?"

Rathe turned away, covering his face with his hands. "My God! I almost hit you!"

Lucy went to him and touched his broad back. "It's all right. I understand. You're afraid for me. You love me."

Rathe turned to her and embraced her hard. Lucy closed her eyes and clung. This was the father she knew and loved—her god since she had been a tiny girl, someone who could make anything right.

But this time, her illusions were rudely shattered. He didn't fix her world. He destroyed it.

Rathe insisted she never see Shoz again. He insisted they divorce. Lucy refused. She demanded to see Shoz; Rathe forbade it. Beneath their battle of wills existed intense, anguished emotions, and soon they were embroiled in a frightening screaming match. Neither her aunt Storm nor her grandfather could reconcile the two. And to make matters worse, everyone was on her father's side, everyone was trying to convince her that she must divorce Shoz and begin her life anew. Lucy stopped telling them that she loved him. Apparently no one was listening to her, apparently no one cared.

That evening her grandfather brought her the papers. Despite the trauma of the day, Lucy was exhausted and dozing. At her grandfather's knock, she sat up. He came in carrying cocoa, but she saw only the documents in his hand.

"Did I wake you?"

"No."

"Brought you some hot chocolate." He smiled.

Lucy couldn't smile back. She was still too close to tears.

She watched Derek sit by her feet and hand her the mug. "How is he?"

Derek grimaced. "He's sleeping. No fever, strong as ever."

Lucy could at least relax on that score. "Please help me, Grandpa. Please don't let him go to prison."

Derek could not lie. "He's not going to prison, Lucy."

Lucy gasped. "What has happened!" For one inane moment, she thought that Derek had somehow managed to save the man she loved.

"The government is sending him to Cuba, Lucy."

"Cuba!"

"We support the rebels—and Shoz has been supplying them with guns."

Lucy turned her face away. So that was what he had been doing, smuggling guns to revolutionaries. When she looked up, she was smiling. "So he's actually a hero?"

"Lucy," her grandfather said tightly, "he's no hero. He's an escaped felon and a gunrunner—and those guns were stolen army carbines. He is not the man for you under any circumstances."

Her spirits crashed. "You liked him in Paradise."

"I did—and I do. Man to man. But not for my granddaughter."

"It doesn't matter." Her eyes clouded. "It's too late. Everyone seems to be forgetting that I'm his wife, Grandpa, and nothing can change that. What will happen after Cuba?"

Derek hesitated. "It's not my place to say." He reached out to stroke her hair. "I'm afraid you're wrong, Lucy."

She stared.

"He's already signed divorce papers. It didn't take very long to convince him."

"I don't believe you." *But somehow she did.*

"It's your turn now," her grandfather said softly.

Lucy looked at the paper he was holding out through blurry eyes. But she saw his scrawled name. "You forced him." Inside herself, she was starting to die, just a little.

"No, honey. We didn't have to force him and we didn't have to pay him off, although Rathe would have done both."

Lucy was in shock. This couldn't be happening. She

didn't want to believe what she was seeing. And the worst part of it was that she could not deny that deep inside, she did believe it. Had he ever said he loved her? Miserably Lucy had to admit that all along, she hadn't really understood why he'd married her. Their marriage had been an impulsive act. She had never even tried to fool herself and think that he loved her. Apparently their marriage had meant little or nothing to him.

"I'm sorry, Lucy," Derek said, standing. "I'll leave the papers here. You sign them when you feel up to it. Tomorrow we'll go back to Paradise."

Lucy wished she were at Paradise right now. How she needed her mother.

"Honey," her grandfather said gently, "you're young, smart, and strong—not to mention beautiful. In no time at all, this will be behind you. You'll forget it. Time does that. There'll be another man for you, Lucy, trust me."

Lucy didn't answer. She couldn't.

"And you don't have to worry about scandal. We'll keep this hushed up—no one will know. No one will know anything. Trust me."

Her grandfather had been wrong about the scandal. They arrived back in New York City the first week in August, Lucy, her parents and brothers, and Joanna. The coincidence was bizarre. In Texas there had been no word of her abduction in the papers, but Texas was Derek Bragg's domain. And Paradise protected its own. The kidnapping was no secret there, although all the details were, yet as always in Paradise, Lucy was treated with friendliness and respect, as if the sore episode had never occurred.

The day after they returned to New York, the headlines were screaming with the news that had been so successfully contained in Texas. "Heiress Returns to Society After Abduction!" "Bragg Heiress Survives Kidnapping!" The sensational Hearst paper, the *New York Journal*, led the attack with the headline. "Bragg Heiress Spends Month with Kidnapper in Mexico!"

Lucy was still too numb over Shoz's rejection to care, but her parents were furious and upset. She was instantly hustled off to Newport for the last few weeks of the summer. Lucy could have been in Hong Kong for all that it mattered. She never left the Bragg estate—some days she never even left her room. She slept most of the time and had lost her appetite. Her parents fretted and tried to get her to go visit her friends and accept those callers who came. Lucy paid them no attention. She even turned away Leon Claxton without seeing him, despite his message that he would be leaving the States soon and he must speak with her. She just did not care.

And then one day toward the end of the summer, the fog lifted. The depression disappeared. And suddenly Lucy was angry.

Shoz wasn't suffering over her, she was sure of that. He was in Cuba somewhere, but knowing him, he was a survivor—and he had already forgotten her. So why should she mourn him? She was Lucy Bragg, he was a nobody. She was the best thing that could have happened to him, he was the worst that could have happened to her. She wouldn't deny that she had loved him, and maybe she still did, but she would return to the living with a vengeance. She would show anyone who cared to notice that she did not give a damn about the miserable bastard, not at all!

Before Lucy sailed forth to find her friends, she had to see Leon. Technically he was her beau, and she had been terribly rude to turn him away when he had called. She was even sorry now that she had not paid him more attention when he had visited her in Paradise. But there was no point in dwelling on that! She sent him a brief note, and the next day, he arrived to see her.

Lucy decided to receive him in the music room, which was bright and cheerful, especially in the sunny afternoons. She was nervous; Leon was the first person other than family whom she was seeing since her return from Texas. What would his reaction to the scandal be?

"I'm glad to see you, Leon," she said, entering the room, her smile hesitant.

He stood, looking dashing in white trousers and a navy linen jacket. His gaze swept her. "That wasn't the impression I got last week."

Lucy felt uncomfortable under his scrutiny. "I wasn't feeling well last week. Surely you can understand that."

"Oh, I think I can understand."

There was a bite in his tone. He wasn't at all the doting admirer he'd been last spring. Lucy sat beside him, concentrating on pouring them both lemonade. "Your message said you're leaving. Where are you going?"

Leon watched her every move. "My father and Roosevelt have encouraged me to go back into the Foreign Service. I've been posted to San Juan; I leave tomorrow."

"San Juan?"

"Puerto Rico," he said shortly.

This wasn't going at all well; he seemed grim, if not angry. "Are you upset?"

"Why would I be upset, Lucy? Because the woman I intended to marry was abducted by some hoodlum cowboy and kept prisoner for weeks on end?"

Shoz's name had been in the papers, so of course Leon knew, but she had not expected such a blatant attack. "It wasn't my fault. Believe me, if I could change what happened this summer, I would."

"Would you?" he asked sarcastically, his regard piercing. "Would you really?"

Lucy jumped to her feet. "What does that mean!"

"It means that maybe the abduction never happened." Leon was standing, too. "Maybe you ran off willingly with Cooper!"

Lucy gasped.

"I saw the two of you the night of your grandfather's party," Leon shouted. "In each other's arms, kissing! You were willing then, Lucy, weren't you?"

"You came here to accuse me, to attack me?"

He grabbed her. "You wanted him that night—I saw! Did you want him enough to run off with him? Or did he kidnap you? Did you sleep with him, Lucy? All those nights, just the two of you, alone, in the mountains . . . Did he rape you?"

"Let go!" Lucy wrenched free, furious and shaken. "He abducted me, I was his prisoner! I'm a victim—not a criminal to be accused in this disgusting manner!"

"When I first met you, I thought that at last I had found a woman who would be a perfect wife. My perfect wife. But I was wrong!"

Before Lucy could respond, he had taken her in his arms, pressing her completely against his hard body. "Did you like it, Lucy?" he demanded.

Lucy was stiff, stunned, and horrified at the feel of his arousal. "You had better leave, Leon, please."

For a moment he did not respond, his eyes glittering, his body throbbing against hers. Then he tore himself free, and without another word, he strode angrily from the room.

Lucy sank onto the couch. It took her some time to recover from all that had passed between them. She was no fool, and she understood that Leon's anger came from jealousy and bitter disappointment—he had probably loved her once, before all this had happened. She could even feel somewhat sorry for him—especially as he was correct in his worst suspicions. But there was no excuse for his behavior. He was a gentleman; he certainly knew better.

The next morning, Lucy called upon Joanna, whose parents also had a cottage in Newport. Joanna greeted Lucy with a smile, and the two friends hugged.

"So tell me about it," Joanna said, once they were seated comfortably in a small parlor with lemon cakes and tea.

"There's nothing to tell," Lucy said casually. She thought about Leon's horrible accusations.

"Oh, Lucy, you were with him for almost two months! You can tell *me*. I'm your best friend; I already know about the two of you anyway."

Lucy felt distinctly uneasy, remembering how Joanna had witnessed her and Shoz in an intimate embrace when they had been traveling to Paradise by automobile. "Joanna, I know you'll never say anything unseemly."

"Of course I wouldn't!"

Lucy's uneasiness increased, but she told herself that she was being silly. She managed to avoid Joanna's prying questions, but there was no mistaking her friend's avid interest. Before she left, Joanna invited her to a croquet party being held by her mother later that week. Lucy promised to attend. She was eager to reimmerse herself into society and get any unpleasantness associated with the scandal over with as soon as possible.

Lucy arrived at the croquet party on a perfect, sunny August day. She had dressed with particular care, and she wore a lacy white dress, one she considered fetchingly romantic, and, secretly, too innocent for her now. Knowing that her abduction was still the biggest scandal in town, Lucy was determined that she should appear as beautiful and carefree as ever—as if untouched by the events of the summer.

Joanna's parents treated her as they always had, as if she were a dear member of the family. While Lucy chatted with them casually, she peeped carefully around at the ensemble on the lawn, from beneath the large brim of her straw hat. She found that while she was trying to discreetly observe everyone, *they* were all trying to discreetly observe *her*. A little shaken, Lucy left Joanna's parents, heading for Joanna and a group of their girlfriends on the other side of the lawn. They were not just watching the croquet players—they were watching her.

She was stopped by one of the players, a young redheaded man she had known most of her life. "It's good to see you, Lucy; glad you're back," he said with a wide smile.

There was only politeness in his tone, but there was something in his smile and his gaze that she did not like, something she could recognize now only too well—lurid male interest in her person. "Thank you, Brian," she said, more coolly than she'd intended.

Before she could leave, he actually restrained her, gripping her gloved hand. "It's a beautiful day for croquet. Are you going to play?"

Lucy did not like the fact that he had not let go of her, and that he was crowding her. She curtly told him that she hadn't decided, and practically wrenched herself free. She hurried over to her girlfriends.

"Oh, Lucy, I'm so glad you're feeling better," cooed Janine Taylor-Smith, embracing her.

"We have been *dying* for you to get out; you must tell us all about it!" Elizabeth Sinclair cried. "Joanna said he's so dangerous—and so handsome."

Lucy froze. She managed to say stiffly, "Who?"

"Who?" Elizabeth and Janine broke into gales of laughter, Joanna giggling, too. "Why, that man—the one who kidnapped you—that Mr. Cooper."

Lucy shot Joanna a confused, perturbed look. She had asked her not to say anything. Joanna shrugged. "Well, he is handsome," she returned.

"Did he?" Janine asked slyly.

"Did he what?" Lucy could barely get the words out.

"You know," Janine whispered. "Did he touch you? Kiss you? Did he—"

"Excuse me," Lucy said abruptly, turning. She hurried away, hearing them explode into giggles again. Her heart was thundering. She should have expected this—she *had* expected it—but it was awful.

She slipped into the house to use the washroom to refresh herself and regain her composure. It was quiet and cool inside, but when Lucy approached the powder room, she heard female voices within, and she hesitated, not wanting to see anybody just yet. She froze in the hallway when she realized that the two ladies were discussing her.

"Only Lucy Bragg would have the gall to try and pretend that nothing's happened."

"Maybe nothing did happen." Lucy did not recognize either of the voices, which were muffled by the partially closed door.

"Nothing happen?! I heard she's ruined, I heard it practically firsthand!"

The door opened. Both ladies came out of the powder room and froze, stunned to see her standing there. Lucy managed to look them right in the eye. Somehow she held her head high and smiled, as if she hadn't heard every horrible word. "Why, hello, Mrs. Currey, hello, Mrs. Livingston. Isn't it the perfect day for croquet?"

Before they could find their tongues, Lucy slipped past them into the powder room and locked the door. There she took a few deep breaths to still her trembling. When she had become calmer, she had also become mad.

Who the hell was that Margaret Currey to throw stones at her! She had been having an affair with Rose Abbott's husband for the past year—and she was no widow! And as for her friends . . . Lucy shook with anger. It was clear now that they were enjoying her brief fall from grace. They could not know anything, and were hoping for the worst—because she was prettier and richer than they were, and her family was more powerful than theirs. In short, they were jealous! Lucy slammed the bathroom door behind her and strode down the hall. Let them hope for the worst! Let them laugh behind her back! Who were they, anyway? Janine was not only barely pretty, but engaged to a fat oaf just for his blue blood—since she had none of her own. Her father had been nothing but a butcher before he became the owner of one of the largest meat-packing companies in the East. And as for Elizabeth, she could trace her ancestors back to the *Mayflower*, but her family was practically impoverished, and everyone knew Elizabeth *had* to marry for money— and a lot of it.

As for Joanna . . . Lucy's steps slowed. Lucy knew Joanna was a follower, and if she was in a crowd, she would concur with everyone else. Lucy did not believe that she would really harbor the same feelings as her other supposed girlfriends would. Still, if she was really a friend, she should at least attempt to stick up for Lucy.

Lucy re-joined the party, determined to enjoy herself and ignore any gossip that might be flowing behind her back. Meanwhile she spent a good deal of her time fending off her new admirers. None of the young men there knew that Leon Claxton was no longer her beau as Lucy now assumed, yet they had all suddenly taken a roaring interest in her. She was surrounded by suitors the entire afternoon, vying for her attention—and any favors she might grant behind closed doors, she realized. She found she was quite adept at handling them—flirting with ease to a precise, instinctive point before making it clear that that was all it was, flirtation and nothing more—not ever. And all the while she enjoyed the open jealousy and resentment her "girlfriends" could not manage to conceal. By the time Lucy left, she felt that she had put Janine and Elizabeth and a few others in their proper places, but she was drained.

The summer could not end soon enough. Lucy went

everywhere, determined to bury the scandal and disprove
the gossip that she was "ruined," yet the scandal would
not die. And as difficult as it was, she did not want to go
back to Radcliffe, where the scandal would follow her and
in essence she would have to go through the same charade
over and over with her classmates. Her parents agreed that
she should take a leave of absence until things died down.

Lucy delayed her return to New York, even though everyone left Newport after the last weekend in August. The
peace and quiet was welcome, although the solitude gave
her too much time to think—and remember. Shoz Cooper
still invaded her thoughts frequently, and despite her anger
at him, she could not shake him from her mind. Then, at
the end of September, she received a note from her father
asking her to return to New York. She was curious as to
why her father was so impatient for her to return. It didn't
take her long to discover the reason. She had barely walked
through the front doors of their home on Fifth Avenue when
he descended upon her, beaming.

"Darling," he said, hugging her. "I'm so glad you're
back! I've arranged a marriage for you!"

Lucy froze, shocked.

"And I think you'll be very pleased."

38

Lucy wondered if she was doing the right thing marrying
Leon Claxton tomorrow. She wondered if, at the last minute,
she dared beg off. If she was honest with herself, she would
admit she wanted to beg off.

In the midst of dressing for the evening, clad only in her
underthings, Lucy sank onto a chaise. She didn't love Leon.
She didn't love anybody. Once, once she had loved Shoz,

but those feelings had long since died, and only the fierce anger remained.

And Leon didn't love her. Maybe he had once, last spring, before he had come to Paradise, and before she had been held prisoner by Shoz. It had been clear to Lucy from their last meeting in August that he was very angry with her, and when she had returned to New York, she had been shocked that her father had arranged this marriage.

Because Leon had so clearly shown his feelings for her, Lucy was sure he was only marrying her for her money and the Bragg connection, with all the power it would bring him. Lucy knew from the gossip that despite the scandal, Marianne and Roger Claxton had still favored her as his bride, and Marianne had made it quite clear on one occasion when their paths had crossed that she was responsible for convincing her son to marry "in these unfortunate circumstances". Marianne had been smiling, yet rude and condescending—Lucy was certain that she had gone out of her way to corner her and make her point that she would not be fooled by Lucy's pretenses, that she knew Lucy was ruined, and that this was Lucy's last and only chance at real social redemption.

That encounter had disturbed Lucy, as it had been intended to, and Lucy realized Marianne did not like her in the least. She supposed it was because she was coming to her son "ruined". Lucy imagined that Leon had been pushed quite hard by Marianne to accept her, and the proof was in the short, curt note of apology that finally arrived by telegraph a month after her betrothal.

At first Lucy had refused to marry Leon—because she didn't love him. She had closed her ears stubbornly to her father's arguments, finding herself thinking more and more about Shoz—and what they had briefly had. But it hadn't taken Lucy long to come to her senses. She was an intelligent woman, and in 1897 there weren't that many options open to any woman. She could stay with her family and grow old, a spinster sheltered first by her parents, then, when they were gone, by one of her brothers. She could become a shopgirl or schoolteacher. Or she could marry Leon, or someone else like him, and it would never be for love, because she would never love anyone else again. If she married Leon, she could start over immediately, putting the past behind her. She would live abroad as a diplomat's wife, have children—in short, make a real life for herself. The choice was obvious.

She would not call it off. She wanted back what she had once had, or at least a semblance of it. Lucy was determined to be happy. Leon had finally written to her, their last encounter apparently forgotten, and had assured her that they would not live in New York and would spend most of their time, at least in the immediate future, abroad. The idea almost made her happy.

Although Lucy had reasoned through this many times, especially as the wedding grew nearer, and always reached the same decision, the niggling panic remained. It was just nerves, she assured herself. Every bride was nervous. Every bride had doubts. She needed time with Leon as his wife. Time would bring mutual respect and friendship and, she hoped, caring. Unbidden, she remembered the hot love-making she had shared with Shoz. No, she didn't expect that. Although she knew Leon was still attracted to her, she would try not to think about sharing his bed.

There was a knock on her door. Lucy pulled on a dressing gown and opened it. She was surprised to see her father and mother there, already dressed for the evening. "Hello, Daddy, Mother."

"You're not dressed yet?" Her father stepped in. "I'm sorry we're interrupting."

"I'll hurry." She met her mother's warm yet worried gaze. "I'm fine," she reassured her. "I've just been day-dreaming."

Rathe handed her a flat velvet jeweler's box. "We wanted to give you your birthday present." He grinned. "So you can wear it."

"Oh, Daddy!" Lucy sat down to open the box. It was a breathtaking necklace of rubies and diamonds, fit for royalty. She had received many gifts of jewelery in her life, but never anything as stunning and valuable as this. "It's beautiful!"

"Very," Grace said, coming to help her try it on. "It's

too much for a girl of twenty-one, but—'' suddenly her eyes teared ''—you're getting married.'' She hugged her daughter. ''Oh, Lucy! I just can't believe it!''

''Neither can I.'' Lucy laughed nervously. She went to the mirror to admire the choker. She thanked and hugged them both.

''Lucy,'' her father said, ''there's one other thing.''

''Rathe, for God's sake, not now!'' Grace cried.

''Then when?'' he demanded. ''On her wedding day?''

''That would be better than right now!''

''What are you two arguing about?'' Lucy asked.

Rathe reached into his tuxedo and withdrew some folded papers. ''I think we've forgotten something, Lucy.''

Lucy was confused as he unfolded the three sheets carefully. She looked at her mother, who was angry. She looked back at her father, and suddenly she knew. Her heart slammed to a stop.

''You can't get married until you sign these,'' Rathe said quietly.

The divorce papers. Lucy had forgotten about them. Hadn't she? She turned away. She had refused to sign them in Brownsville after her rescue and Shoz's capture, until the issue was set aside and allowed to cool down. Yet during the past months she had always known deep in the back of her mind that she hadn't signed those papers, that she and Shoz were still husband and wife. God, was she ever a fool! He was a lousy bastard and she wanted him out of her life! It was over, it had been over for so very long, and if she dared to admit it, it had been over before it had even begun.

She turned. ''Okay, Daddy.'' She smiled too brightly while a tear ran down her cheek. ''It's about time, don't you think?''

Shoz arrived at east Sixty-second Street on foot, having chosen to walk. He leaned against the cold stone wall of Central Park and calmly lit a cigarette. Dragging deeply, he stared across Fifth Avenue at the Bragg mansion. His pose was relaxed, but he was not.

Only a few hours ago he had been in Washington in a grueling meeting with some of the top brass of the McKinley administration. Members of the State and Defense departments and the Pentagon had been present. They had grilled him for hours on the Cuban situation, and fortunately, Shoz had had all the answers. At the end, he was finally given his chance when the assistant secretary of the navy, Roosevelt, had asked him for his own opinion. Shoz had given it with no holds barred.

He told them that the promises of the Spanish government to grant autonomy were bunk, and he warned them that the situation was escalating and would soon be out of control. Even if the Spanish did grant the Cubans autonomy, it was too late—they would never settle for it now. Cuba was a powder keg about to explode.

Shoz wasn't tense from the long meeting he had endured. He was rigid with anticipation, and dammit, he did not like it. He was practically breathless because he was so close, because he was going to see *her*.

She still had a hold on him, a dangerous hold, and he'd thought it had been broken long ago.

It was already dark, but the street was well lit, and his shadow stretched out along the sidewalk under the iron streetlamps. The upper floors of the Bragg mansion were dark, the floors where the family obviously lived. Where Lucy lived. The ground floor, though, was well lit. Shoz waited for an hour. When his watch told him it was ten, he knew he had missed them and he cursed. She had obviously gone out for the evening with her family.

A bribe got him the information he wanted. She had been escorted by Leon Claxton to the Claxton residence for the rehearsal dinner. The whole family was in attendance, except for her youngest brothers, as was the Who's Who of New York.

Don't be a fool, he told himself.

But he went anyway.

39

Ten minutes later, he arrived at the Claxton mansion, which he was already intimate with. He didn't hesitate. The front entrance was brightly lit, and Fifth Avenue was lined with the private carriages and automobiles of the guests, their coachmen and drivers chatting beneath the streetlamps, bundled up in their heavy winter coats. Shoz was dressed in a fine black suit for the meeting he had attended in the capital. His hair had been cut the day before, and was carefully parted in the center. Smiling, he entered as any guest would, and he was greeted with a polite "Good evening" by the majordomo.

His blood was pulsing thickly in his veins. From the marble-floored foyer, he could hear the raucous conversation and the laughter of the party drifting to him from the salon. Laced into the humming of animated voices was the tinkle of fine crystal and the strains of a piano. Shoz strode down the hall. He paused on the threshold of the salon, his gaze sweeping the hundred or so guests.

There were several salons in the house. This one was the largest, except for the ballroom, and was filled to overflowing. Shoz scanned the glittering crowd, the women in brightly colored gowns and jewels, their shoulders bare, hair swept up, the men in formal evening attire. He did not see Lucy.

But he saw her parents. They were not the only people there whom he recognized. He stared at Leon, who was tall, blond, handsome, and so very at ease in his elegant surroundings. He saw Marianne's husband, Roger, and realized that the man he was talking to with the silver mane of hair was Derek Bragg. Next to Derek was one of his

sons, the earl, and his blond wife, the actress. Shoz cursed
when he realized that the whole Bragg clan, or most of it,
was in town for Lucy's wedding. He did not need to be
discovered by them just now.

Two guests dispersed on the far side of the room and
revealed the hostess, Marianne, petite and stunning in silver
chiffon. Had she been in the center of the crowd, he would
have never seen her, but standing there against the back
wall, she was momentarily in view. Just for an instant he
could see her perfectly. She must have felt his gaze, because
she glanced his way. Her gaze widened visibly.

Shoz sighed and turned away, going not toward the foyer
but down the hall instead. His stride slowed when he saw
a familiar form, a woman, approaching in the dimly lit
corridor, closing her reticule. It was Lucy's friend, Joanna,
and looking up, she gasped.

Shoz nodded curtly and continued past her. He let himself
into the library. He went straight to the Queen Anne desk
and poured himself a tumbler of the finest scotch whiskey,
which was Roger's preferred drink, as he had found out so
many years ago.

Of course, an instant later the door opened, admitting
Marianne. She closed it, leaning her back against it, staring
at him.

He lifted his glass. "Beautiful as always, Marianne. To
the best hostess in New York."

"You would have the nerve to come here!" But her tone
was calm and wary, unlike her words, and she didn't move
from the door—nor did she take her gaze from him.

Shoz let his hip find the side of the desk and he sipped
his scotch. Marianne said, "What are you doing here? What
do you want?"

Even across the distance of the library, Shoz could feel
her physical reaction to him. He could smell it. She was
still a bitch in heat, and he found it amusing. But what she
had done last summer hadn't been amusing, not at all.
"Maybe I want to settle old scores."

"What does that mean?"

He was the predator now. He knew her too well for her
to pull the wool over his eyes; she sounded as if she had

no idea what he was referring to. Of course, she could not know of the first score he had in mind—that was private, unfinished business with his dear ex-wife—but certainly she hadn't forgotten the night of Derek Bragg's eightieth birthday. Yet her next words showed him that she had—or else she was a very clever actress.

"I told you a year ago, no, just after you escaped prison, that I was sorry. I am sorry! I didn't think you would go to jail!"

"You plant your diamond ring in my pocket and call the police and tell me you didn't think I would go to jail? Come now, Marianne, we both know the truth; you were a jealous, vindictive bitch, and nothing gave you more satisfaction than to set me up and put me away."

"All right! I was jealous, but if you hadn't gone back to her after I found you together the first time, that would have been the end of it! Truthfully, now I am sorry it went so far! I'm sorry you went to prison for a crime you didn't commit! But you liked the danger, you bastard, you liked screwing my maid under my nose!"

"Frankly," Shoz said, carelessly but truthfully, "I can't remember *any* details."

"You shit."

"And you know that score isn't the one I have in mind." She was genuinely confused. "What do you mean?"

"I mean you tried to kill me, and I haven't forgotten it."

"What are you talking about!"

He slipped off the desk, and walked toward her. "I'm talking about a hot, humid night in Paradise, Texas, remember? Why did you shoot me, Marianne? Because I wouldn't ball you?"

He was close enough now for her to slap him, but he caught her wrist and wrenched it, hurting her. "I didn't! It wasn't me! I swear it! I don't know who shot you that night!"

Shoz believed her. She was a lying bitch, but he recognized the truth when he saw it, and he saw it in her eyes. He released her. She rubbed her wrist, but never took her gaze from his.

"If it wasn't you, then who?"

"I have no idea." She lifted her chin. "Is that why you came? To—punish me?"

He heard the tremor. He saw the glitter in her eyes. There had been women in the past months, women whose names he didn't know and didn't care to know, women whose faces and bodies he didn't remember, and tonight his lust was thick in his blood, and he could easily satisfy it and her. He knew she was thinking of that other time, six, no, seven years ago, when he'd broken out of prison and so crudely taken her in her boudoir. "No," he said, smiling. "I didn't come here to punish you, Marianne."

Her nostrils flared. He started to turn away. She touched him. "But it was I who told the sheriff about you, Shoz, all about you."

He froze. He turned slowly. Dark rage burned in his eyes. "I should have known."

Her smile was fragile. Her breasts rose and fell shallowly. She still held his arm. He could see her nipples straining erectly against the chiffon of her gown. He felt nothing for her, nothing except disgust. He jerked his arm free and gave her his back. He owed her, but it seemed like a pittance compared to what he owed Lucy Bragg.

He heard her breathing behind him. "You bastard," she finally said, and she left, slamming the door behind her.

He exhaled and started for his scotch. The doors to the balcony behind the desk were ajar, he saw for the first time. A draft of frigid air was coming in. He began to lift his scotch when, to his amazement, the doors swung open, pushed from outside. Standing on the terrace in her ruby-red gown was Lucy Bragg.

Lucy's dress was off-the-shoulder and sleeveless, and she was shivering. Although she had wrapped her arms around herself for warmth, she didn't move to come in. She could only stare. It was like seeing a ghost.

He stared back, the snifter still in his hand, every bit as stunned as she. He recovered first. He lifted the whiskey. "Another toast. To the bride. To the bride and her new life."

Lucy thought she might faint. He drank, draining the

entire contents of the glass, and she watched the long line of his tanned throat and his Adam's apple as he swallowed. God! Just the sight of him was enough to bring back every memory she had, from hot, hard ones to soft, silky ones—and then came remembrance of his betrayal. Of how casually and carelessly he had tossed aside their marriage—and her. Lucy suddenly stepped inside, no longer cold, her blood surging.

He hadn't moved. "Spying?"

"Don't flatter yourself. You have more nerve than anyone I know to come here, tonight!"

"Are you asking me to leave?" he asked mockingly.

"Asking?" She still hadn't stepped away from the doors, afraid of what she might do if she began to move. "I'm telling you. Get out, *now.*"

"What's wrong, princess?" he said softly, stepping toward her. "You're shaking. Somehow I don't think it's from the cold."

"Don't come near me!"

He paused by the butler's bar, laughing. "Now *you* flatter *yourself.*"

It hurt. How she hated him. And he, damn him, was so cool, so calm, so clearly unaffected by their encounter. She watched him refill his glass with scotch. "If you're not leaving, then I am," she said, striding forward.

She never got past him. Quick as a wink he grabbed her arm, whipping her about so she was facing him, so close their breaths mingled. "Not yet."

Her heart actually skipped a beat from the contact with him. Lucy tried to pull away, but his grin, and the glitter in his eyes, made her go still. She would not play this game, his way, whatever it might be. She would not amuse him. "Why are you here, Shoz? Why?"

His smile was a sneer. "I'm here to congratulate the bride, of course. To celebrate—with my darling ex-wife."

The sarcasm and hatred in his voice fueled Lucy's own anger—he had no reason to hate her, and she had every reason to hate him. "Your darling ex-wife has no intention of celebrating with the bastard she was stupid enough to marry."

"You didn't mind being my wife a few months ago."

Lucy lifted her chin, again attempting to pull her wrist free from his powerful grip, but failing. Her heart was beating hard and unsteadily. His gaze held hers for an endless moment, and in that span of time a million hot, heady, explicit memories of their lovemaking flooded her mind. Seeing the growing heat in his gaze, she was sure he was recalling the same thing she was. "I was young, innocent, and very, very foolish."

His gaze darkened. For once, he did not have a response, and Lucy felt the barest sense of triumph. It died rapidly, though, beneath the heat of his regard. The fires banked there were hard and hot and angry, and she saw them darkening with every second that ticked by. Lucy realized he was just as angry as she was.

The cruel smile covered his face again. His gaze dropped lasciviously, intently. And that was enough—Lucy felt her breasts grow tight and hot, felt her nipples hardening.

"Who do you think you're fooling, Lucy?" Shoz said harshly. "You still want me—I can feel it."

He was right, but she would not ever admit it, not to him, and not, now, to herself. "Tomorrow I am marrying Leon Claxton. You are the one fooling yourself, Shoz."

He laughed, finally releasing her. "You and Leon. A pair of real blue bloods. I wish you well. But don't you think you might find him a bit dull after your first husband?"

She rubbed her wrist, wanting to strike him and wondering if she dared. "I hate my first husband. He ruined my life. Leon is a gentleman—a rich gentleman. He can give me everything I want. All you could give me is a hellhole in Mexico!"

His smile disappeared. He lifted his glass, cold and angry. "To the diplomat's wife. To her happiness."

Lucy backed up. His anger was strong enough for her to feel, and she knew she had gone too far, she should leave now—but she didn't. "You mock him—and me—because you can never be anything but what you are!"

"A lousy ex-con?"

Lucy regretted instantly throwing his own dirt back at him. Then she looked up sharply, recalling the conversation she had overheard between him and Marianne. "Marianne sent you to prison? She accused you of something you didn't do?"

"So you were spying."

They hadn't known she was out there on the terrace, so it was the truth, the wrenching truth. The implications were too mind-boggling for her to grasp completely right now, but it dawned on her that Shoz had chosen a certain path in his adult life because he'd been unjustly accused of a crime by a malicious and powerful woman. She was stunned, and worse, she realized she was appalled at how he had paid for something he had not done.

"So you still have a touch of compassion in your heart for me."

Lucy recovered, fast. "You're dreaming." She turned abruptly, unreasonable panic filling her.

He pounced on her, his fingers digging into the bare skin of her shoulder. "Admit it." It was a demand; his breath brushed her ear.

"I won't admit any such thing," she cried, trying to yank free. She didn't want to be so close to him, she was afraid to be so close to him. "If you won't leave, then let me go!"

"I can't let you go," he said harshly, reeling her into his arms.

Contact with the full length of his body made her freeze, while the glitter of his eyes and his touch and hardness sent tingles racing down her spine. Lust and rage, rage and lust. She saw it in his eyes, felt it in her own veins. In that moment, she was no different from him, they were one and the same.

The corners of his mouth curled. "And it's not just compassion you feel for me," he said softly, a lover's whisper. His one arm was a clamp around her back. His other hand stroked her bare shoulder, her neck. "Admit it. I won't let you go until you tell me you still want me—that you're still crazy with wanting me."

"No," Lucy moaned. "I won't, not ever!" She twisted in his arms again, but it only served his purposes in rubbing her belly against his massively swollen groin. She stilled, panting, knowing she was going to give in very shortly if she did not manage to free herself. She had to concentrate on her anger, but now she felt only lust.

"Leon will never excite you like this," he said harshly, his hand closing over her buttock and lifting her closer.

Lucy screamed in fury and struck him blindly with both fists, on his chest. Instantly he caught her wrists and jammed them down between their bodies, increasing the pressure of his body on hers so that her hands were pinned between them. She opened her mouth to scream again, but never managed to get any words out. He kissed her. With his hand he forced her to keep her mouth open, raping her with his tongue, showing her how he wanted to rape her with his manhood.

Lucy would have bitten off his tongue if he hadn't kept her jaw pried open; but then the fury faded, and all that was left was the heat and the pent-up desire that had never left her in all the time they had been apart. She touched his rampaging tongue with her own, and her hands, pressed against his belly, curled into the pleats of his shirt.

He backed her up against the wall. His kisses were voracious, his hands now roaming freely over her back and buttocks, and it dawned on Lucy that he had no intention of stopping, that in just a few moments he would be pushing up her skirts and penetrating her, right there, against the wall, in the library—at her rehearsal dinner.

Everything was happening too fast. Somehow she had to stop this, stop him. Stop herself. She felt him press his palm against her womanhood. He was more than preoccupied, he was maddened by his own lust, and Lucy wrenched away from him, slipping on the floor in her heels and falling to her knees. She scrambled away and lunged to her feet and put the couch between them.

For a scant instant, shock was etched on his features, shock that she had left him so close to the consummation of their passion. And then his expression was wiped clean. She needed time to recover, but apparently he did not. He straightened his bow tie, staring her right in the eye. "Who's fooling whom?" he asked shortly. "Who's the little liar?"

Lucy closed her eyes briefly, panting and trembling, feeling very, very shaken. "I still hate you. Go away."

His smile was twisted, and when he spoke, it was with absolute conviction "The feeling is mutual, *princess*."

Her eyes flew open. "Why do you hate me?"

"Did you think I might love you?"

So much hurt and pain rose so rapidly from somewhere so deep in her soul that Lucy was immobilized by it. He came toward her. His hands, large and hard, found her shoulders. "But that doesn't change anything, does it? Lust has nothing to do with love, or with hate—as we both know firsthand."

They stared at each other for an endless moment. Around them, the noise of the party swelled and rose, but the fact did not penetrate as the library door was opened and closed. I have to get away from him, Lucy thought. I have to think. This can't have happened, it can't!

"How dare you!" Marianne cried.

Lucy gasped when she realized Marianne had entered the room again and was standing furiously beside them. Shoz barely acknowledged her. His gaze was filled with loathing. She knew it was not for Marianne—but for herself.

"If you don't leave," Marianne hissed, "I'm going to call the Braggs in here. Now, get out!"

Shoz gave Lucy another glance. "Tell the *lucky* groom I send my best," he mocked, and then he was striding out, slamming the door fiercely behind him.

Lucy looked at Marianne, her future mother-in-law, a blush staining her cheeks, terribly relieved that Marianne hadn't walked in just a moment sooner. "It wasn't what you thought," she said, then went silent at the fury she saw contorting the woman's face.

She reminded herself that this was Shoz's former mistress and Leon's mother. That this was a woman ruthless enough to accuse a man of a crime he had not committed and send him to prison for it. In essence, this woman was some kind of monster. Warily, Lucy straightened. She was, however, not prepared for Marianne's assault.

"You little whore!"

"You can't talk to me that way!"

"Oh yes I can," Marianne said. "After all, we both know *you* know Shoz intimately."

Lucy flushed, but only with fresh anger. "You're forgetting something, Marianne. We *both* know Shoz intimately, wouldn't you say?"

Marianne was momentarily taken aback. Lucy felt a moment of wicked satisfaction until the other woman recovered. "I advise you to watch yourself before casting stones. I also suggest you stay away from him if you want to marry my son. Because my son will not tolerate infidelity from his bride—or his wife."

"I have advice for you," Lucy said, ignoring Marianne's gasp. "I'm marrying your son—not you. My life is just that—mine."

"You are a fool, Lucy!" Marianne was furious. "Don't throw your life away. Leon will take you where you want to go—Shoz can do nothing for you outside of the bedroom. Do you understand?"

"Oh, I understand," Lucy said, thinking of Marianne being an adulteress, and then maliciously sending Shoz to jail. She was filled with fury, and it was all directed at the woman who would become her mother-in-law on the morrow. "I understand more than you know, Marianne."

And with that, she turned on her heel and left her hostess standing there alone.

40

Going to the Claxtons' had been stupid, and now Shoz was in a deadly, black humor. Clad only in trousers and a pair of black suspenders, Shoz dragged on a cigarette, staring out the hotel window at the city's night lights.

He knew he should be anywhere but here, alone in this

dreary room, alone with his bleak thoughts. Dammit! His fist hit the windowsill. Hard. The pain was welcome. He shook his hand, wondering if he'd cracked a bone.

She still felt like she belonged to him. She still felt like his. Even though it had been a very long time since they'd been together, even though she had betrayed him by divorcing him, even though she was about to marry another man—*even though she had never really loved him*—she still felt like his. He couldn't stand knowing that tomorrow afternoon she would wed Leon, a man who was everything he was not—as Lucy had been so quick to point out.

Not for the first time, he dared to admit his deepest, most secret feelings—he was sorry he had divorced her so precipitously that day in Brownsville.

Of course, she had divorced him *first*. There was no point in brooding. It was over, it had been over for a very long time; soon she would belong to Leon Claxton. Her feelings had been very clear: she despised him. She was marrying now for money and position—everything he did not have. He smiled grimly. But he had one thing she wanted, and she could deny it until she took her last breath—she wanted him.

He paced and chain-smoked. Too late, he knew he should have never seen her again at Marianne's. He would have relished her uncontrollable physical attraction to him, except that it went both ways. She lit him up like a volcano. Around her, he was barely containable. One moment he wanted to murder her, the next rape her, hurt her, and in the next, love her.

She was probably home by now. Home, and alone in her big bedroom, maybe asleep. The need he'd felt when he'd first seen her at Marianne's, and the anger, crashed over him again. Suddenly he knew he would never be able to sleep, not tonight, and he dressed quickly and strode from the room.

Outside, it was frigidly cold and starting to snow. Bareheaded, Shoz walked and walked, his hands deep in his suit jacket pockets, not caring that he hadn't worn an overcoat. The cold air felt good. The brisk pace felt better. This was what he needed, to get out and escape himself and his thoughts, even if it meant physically outdistancing them.

His footsteps slowed. He saw with dismay that he had walked all the way to Central Park. Had it been his intention all along? He cursed aloud, knowing he should turn back, knowing he wouldn't. He began walking uptown, at first slowly, then faster, the snow falling harder now. He crossed Sixtieth Street, then Sixty-first. His breath made puffy clouds in the frigid air, and his ears felt numb. On the corner of Sixty-second Street he finally stopped, panting. Dammit! He was such a fool!

He stood and stared at the Bragg mansion through the curtain of falling snow, all the upper floor lights extinguished, the downstairs windows shining with warmth. He wanted to leave.

But he couldn't.

Instead, he leaned against the lamppost and stared.

Then, impulsively, he started across the street.

After the rehearsal dinner, Lucy did not even try to sleep. Once alone in her bedroom, she didn't know whether to scream with relief or shout with frustration. Finally she was alone, she could think! The evening had turned out to be an interminable bore, Leon was an interminable bore, and Shoz was here, here in New York, and tomorrow was her wedding day. God, she couldn't go through with it!

She paced the room, barefoot, in her nightgown. A fire crackled in the hearth. How could she cry off at the last minute? How could she dare? And what about Shoz?

She was shaking. She took a few deep breaths to calm herself. She had two issues to sort out, and they weren't related. One thing was very clear—she could not marry Leon tomorrow.

She had been a fool to think she could. She was not a woman who could marry without love. Absurdly, that had been made clear by the flood tide of memories that seeing Shoz tonight had caused. She would send Leon a note early tomorrow morning. There was no explanation that was acceptable; her behavior—jilting him at the altar—wasn't acceptable, but there was no choice. Leon would be furious, his family would be furious—even her family would be angry. But her parents would come around, eventually.

It would be a big scandal, and on the heels of the last one, intolerable. Lucy sat down hard on the bed. She would not stay in New York, oh no. It would be years—if ever—before she could hold her head up in this town if she stood Leon up at the altar. She could go to Dragmore, or Paradise, or even to California with her aunt Storm and Uncle Brett. She had options, but staying here would not be one of them.

Despite the terrible thing she was doing, she felt a vast sense of relief. Far better to remain a spinster and her own master than to marry a man she barely knew and did not love. Somehow she would adjust to this new status, and all that it entailed; she would still have her family, and their love—she would manage without Society. Lucy thought about Shoz. In truth, she hadn't been able to get him out of her mind, not for a second, since she had seen him in the library at the Claxtons'. Her reaction to him infuriated her; worse, it frightened her. Clearly he could seduce her if she did not find the strength to resist him. But why had he come to New York, especially now? It was obvious that he harbored no fondness for her, just the same maddening lust that she felt for him. He had known she was about to wed. Had he come to cause trouble? If so, he had succeeded!

She would probably never marry now, not after doing this. Lucy sighed and walked to her closet. Hanging there among her vast wardrobe was her bridal nightgown. She touched it. It was the sheerest silk, with a daringly low lace bodice, slit high on one leg, right to her hip. Now she would never wear it. Impulsively she pulled her cotton nightgown over her head and let it fall to the floor. Then she slipped on the bridal gown and went to the mirror. She was beautiful, more than beautiful, mostly naked and very sexy, the gown so sheer, it revealed everything, the bodice so low, the tops of her nipples were visible. Suddenly, fantastically, she wished it were Shoz she was marrying tomorrow, that this gown was for him, that he was her bridegroom and they would have a storybook ending—the way it should be.

She walked away from the mirror. Would she ever stop being a fool? Shoz had only wanted one thing from her, while she had loved him. She had to pound that fact into her head. And what about the other facts she had learned tonight? He had gone to prison for a crime he hadn't committed, setting his life on a terrible course, one he hadn't deserved. He wasn't a real criminal, not at all. He was the victim of a ruthless woman's jealousy.

It made so much sense. It was the greatest relief. Lucy cursed Shoz for not declaring his innocence from the start, for not even bothering to explain the truth. Yet she also knew that although Shoz might have begun his path of lawlessness as a victim, he had taken to it readily. And there was no denying another fact: he was a hard, dangerous man, not the silky-soft gentleman lover of a schoolgirl's dreams. He was the biggest contradiction she knew.

Why was he in New York? And why did he hate her so? She hadn't done anything to him, but he had done everything to her.

She should try to sleep. It was almost two in the morning, and tomorrow she had to send Leon the note. Lucy hesitated, about to remove the bridal nightgown, then decided to sleep in it. After all, it was unlikely that she would ever be a bride after tomorrow. She turned off the lights except for those by her bedside, poked the crackling fire, then decided to leave it ablaze for the extra warmth it provided. She climbed into bed and knew she would never sleep, not tonight. There was a novel on her bedside table, a gift from Nicole. Lucy was about to reach for it when something caught her eye, and she stared at the balcony doors facing her bed. For a second she had thought the knob on the door had moved. And then it did move, it turned, and Lucy sat bolt upright with a cry. The door opened.

And standing there was Shoz.

They stared at each other.

Lucy was stunned. Reality seemed suspended. This wasn't possible. *What was he doing here?*

He was covered with snow, which was already beginning to melt. He smiled. It was a mocking smile, a dangerous smile. The look he was giving her was also dangerous. It swept her from head to toe. It was more than intimate, it suggested he was about to sample what he once had had. Lucy knew what he could see, knew she was no better than naked. She did not move. She remembered instantly how he had smelled, how he had tasted, and how he had felt when she had been in his arms just a few hours ago.

His smile widened. "Felicitations, princess," he said softly.

Lucy sat up straighter. "You shouldn't be here!"

He grinned, closing the door with his boot without turning away from her. His long fingers went to his tie, unknotting it. "Probably not."

Her heart was pounding hard enough that had she not been so experienced, she would have thought herself about to faint. But it was the anger and the desire. She slipped her feet to the floor, but did not leave the bed. "Shoz, you're crazy. My brothers are right down the hall. If they catch you, they'll kill you."

He pulled the tie free of his shirt and let it slip through his fingers and to the floor. "Then why don't you scream?" He smiled again; the effect was devastating.

Why didn't she? Lucy opened her mouth to shout for help, but said instead, "You son of a bitch. I hate you, but I don't want to see you back in prison, and you know it."

"You're right." He grinned. "I do know it."

She gripped the bedclothes. "What are you doing?"

He removed his jacket, and it also fell to the floor. "You know what I'm doing."

Lucy inhaled hard. "Stop. *Stop right now!*" He was casually removing a cuff link. "Or to hell with my being such a nice person, you don't deserve it, not from me, I will scream this house down!"

He removed the other cuff link. "We're definitely going to finish what we started at the Claxtons'—and you know it as well as I do."

She practically shredded the sheets in her hands at his blunt reference to the sexual act that was going to take place soon. "No! Get out! Get out of here now!"

"If you really wanted me to leave, you'd have screamed the moment I walked in instead of sitting there in that bed in a very open invitation."

Lucy's breasts heaved. He was right, damn him, but she was going to resist, he was not going to win.

His expression turned ugly. "Do you love him?"

She was breathing too fast and shallowly. She couldn't get any response out.

"Do you?" he related harshly.

"No!"

"You have a helluva way of showing it!" He hurled the cuff links with all the force he had, which was quite considerable, at the wall behind her. Lucy ducked. She ducked, heard them hit and fall to the floor. She was already leaping off the bed, running for the bathroom.

He had been waiting. The instant she moved, he moved. He leapt onto and off the bed and caught her on the other side before she took three steps, dragged her backward as she braked furiously, then lifted her and heaved her back onto the mattress. She bounced but came up scrambling for the other side. He grabbed her ankle and yanked. She sprawled facedown and was pulled back into the center of the bed. It dipped from his weight as he straddled her. She felt the strength of his thighs on her sides, the heat of his groin on her spine. He flipped her over abruptly so she was on her back staring up at him.

He was panting, too. Lucy didn't hesitate. She reached out to claw his face. He caught her hand and wrenched her wrists up over her head. With his other arm he lifted her up, forcing her to arch toward him uncomfortably. His knee parted her thighs, jamming into her. His mouth came down on hers, hard and bruising. Lucy tried to twist away, tried to buck him off. She writhed wildly, but caught between his thighs and body, with her wrists imprisoned in his powerful grip, it was hopeless. But she would not capitulate, and continued to struggle.

Mindless of her efforts to heave him off, he continued to terrorize her, kissing her hurtfully, forcing her mouth open, raping its interior with his tongue. His hold on her wrists was excruciating. His knee was hurting her, too. His arm beneath her back was contorting her spine, crushing her to his chest. She wondered if he would break her in two, and it increased her determination not to give in.

He finally pulled his mouth from hers. "Little hypocrite. Stop playing the virgin, Lucy."

Her eyes blazed. When he lowered his head to kiss her again, she quickly bit his jaw.

He cried out, yanking back, touching the wound. Lucy instantly struck him with her one free hand, balled into a fist. Furious, he caught her palm. "You little bitch!"

"I won't give in," she gritted. "You're going to have to rape me!"

His smile was frightening. "Do you think I won't?" For emphasis, he ground his thick, hard shaft into her.

Lucy stiffened, closing her eyes, panting hard. She heard him opening his zipper. Her pulse, already racing, roared. She was afraid he would touch her and discover the truth, that her resistance was only an act of extreme willpower, that her body was on fire for his.

And he did touch her. Abruptly he hauled her delicate nightgown up and delved between her thighs. Lucy tried to jerk free one last time, while he went still. Then she heard him laugh softly, in utter male satisfaction. "Liar," he said, stroking her. "Such a little liar."

Lucy couldn't stand it, and he had found her out anyway. She moaned as his mouth touched hers and opened to accept him more fully. She touched her tongue to his. He froze. She stroked him delicately, deliberately, then began seeking out every crevice and cranny she could find, with rising frenzy. Licking, sucking, lapping. He released her wrists and wrapped her in his arms. Their tongues warred fiercely, mated hotly. His throbbing groin settled against hers, bare flesh to bare flesh. With his palm he found her breast and possessed it roughly.

Lucy's nails tore down his back. Shoz lifted himself to pull out his shirt; Lucy yanked it apart, spilling the buttons over her body and the bed. Her hands found his bare chest, his ribs, his nipples. Pinching him, she moaned frantically into his mouth.

He touched her. He touched her and made a sound full of raw lust. He stroked her, parted her, then was apologizing even as he rammed into her.

It was a wild mating that was over almost as soon as it began. He pounded into her; she rose to meet him. They strained and bucked. Lucy cried out first, loudly, without shame, the keening call urging Shoz to faster, harder rampaging in an effort to catch up. He clapped his hand over her mouth to silence her as he convulsed deep inside her.

Lucy began to think almost immediately. Desperation brought instant coherence. He did not move off her; she did not let her arms slip from their embrace of him. Yet she was careful not to tighten her hold, although she wanted to. Oh dear God, she thought, I still love him.

She lay beneath him in utter confusion and total panic, gripping him fiercely. What would he do now? What should she say? God, there was so much to say, but he had rejected her once, divorcing her; what if he rejected her again? A terrible understanding—a terrible fear—was materializing, that there was so much to say but that even if she dared, he would not care, even if she tried, it would be impossible to breach the past. Her terrible fear grew that this was only a moment in their lives, a single and passing moment, maybe a final moment. She dared not think further; if she did, she would burst into tears. His face was buried in her neck, and she wanted desperately to kiss his temple, caress him. She did not have the courage.

Suddenly he rolled off of her.

Lucy did not move. He lay still for a moment, then got up and began tucking his shirt into his pants.

Lucy closed her eyes. No, this couldn't be happening. *This couldn't have happened.* Not this way. She heard him closing his fly. She sat up and found him buttoning his pants, watching her.

She had to say something. He couldn't leave. He couldn't leave her again. But he was doing just that—leaving her—again.

She attempted a too bright smile. "Well, that's one thing we do well together." She was afraid to be serious; levity was much easier. She hugged a pillow.

"But not without fighting," he said quietly.

Lucy stared.

He turned abruptly and reached for his jacket. Lucy fought an onslaught of fierce emotions that were going to leave her crying like a baby if she wasn't careful. "Shoz?"

He didn't look at her, but she knew he was listening.

She had to know. "How long will you be in New York?"

He shrugged on his jacket and stood before her. "I'm leaving for Cuba tomorrow."

"Tomorrow?"

He looked at her. "Disappointed?"

His words were uncharacteristically flat, instead of sarcastic and snide. Lucy couldn't answer. She wanted, desperately, to tell him that she was disappointed, but she had too much pride. He would only be amused. His response would be cutting, his only interest more sex. She lunged to her feet and ran into the bathroom. She fell onto her knees by the bathtub, gripping its white porcelain rim.

She strained to hear. She heard the floor creaking as he moved. She began to rock with the impending tears. She was choking with them. Her back was to the door, but she heard him come to stand in the entrance, felt him looking at her.

Don't go, she begged silently. Don't leave me! Not like this!

She dared to look at him. For a heart-stopping moment, she thought she saw compassion in his eyes; she thought he was going to come to her and hold her. But instead, his jaw tightening, he turned and left.

When Lucy heard the terrace doors shutting, she sagged against the tub. He was leaving tomorrow, but he was breaking her heart tonight. The tears finally came, unstoppable.

41

That next morning Lucy was ushered into one of the drawing rooms while Leon was summoned. She was rigid with nerves. She had realized on her way over to the Claxtons' that she could not just drop off a note, she had to tell

Leon in person that the wedding was off. She jumped when Leon strode into the room, smiling.

"Don't you know that it's bad luck for the groom to see the bride before the wedding?" he admonished in good humor.

Lucy wet her lips. "Leon . . . that's just it. I'm sorry, but I can't marry you."

"Is this a bad joke?"

"No."

He was stark white, stunned.

"I'm so sorry, Leon."

"Just explain to me why."

"I don't love you."

"What does that have to do with anything?" he shouted.

"I'm afraid it has everything to do with a marriage, Leon. I'll see myself out. Good-bye."

She left before he could respond, knowing she was a coward in wanting to avoid any further confrontation with him. She felt miserable for treating him so badly, but while she was driven home in one of the Bragg coaches, the guilt began to fade as another confrontation loomed before her. Fortunately, she ran into her mother in the foyer as she entered. Grace was putting on her cloak, no doubt about to leave, having much to do before the wedding that evening. "Mother, can we speak?"

"Lucy! It's eight-thirty. Where have you been first thing in the morning?"

Lucy handed her cape to a valet, waiting for him to depart before she spoke. "I went to see Leon, Mother."

"Why?"

"Because I've called off the wedding."

"You've called it off!"

"I don't love Leon. I can't marry him."

"Lucy, do you know what you've done? I thought you realized that this was for the best!"

"I just can't go through with it, Mother. I've seen how happy you and Daddy are too many times. If I can't have that kind of marriage, then I don't want to marry at all."

"Oh, dear." Grace quickly came to her to wrap her in an embrace. "Are you sure, Lucy?"

"Positive."

Grace stroked her hair. "I'll take care of everything. Why don't you go upstairs for a while."

"And Father?"

"I'll take care of him, too."

Lucy hugged her. "You are so wonderful to understand."

"I just hope you can try to understand your father," Grace replied softly. "He only wants the best for you."

"I know."

Her father was, of course, shocked and angry, so angry that he refused to speak with Lucy. The tension between them was awful, and had never been worse. When Rathe happened upon her in the house, he set his jaw and would not even look at her. He did not soften for several days, but when he did, he came to her room and gruffly told her that he only wanted her to be happy, and while he was sure she was making a mistake, it broke his heart for them to remain estranged. Lucy took the cue and embraced him. "I'll be all right, Daddy; you don't have to worry about me, you'll see."

He hugged her hard before releasing her. "I wish I could believe that."

Now that they were once again on good terms, Lucy was free to concentrate on finding Shoz. She hired a private detective, for Cuba was a big island and she was determined to know exactly where he had gone. She could not let things end this way between them. He thought her the lowest sort of tramp, about to marry Leon and sleeping with him on the night before her wedding. Why, right now he even thought she was married to Leon! Lucy was determined that he should know the truth, or part of it—that she had never loved Leon, that she had been pressured to marry him, and that she had, finally, begged off. The real problem was that she was afraid he might not even care.

While Lucy waited for news from her detective, she stayed close to home and studiously avoided all callers and hence all of the scandal she knew was swirling about the city. One week later, on New Year's Day, her detective provided her with the information she sought. Shoz had left New York on a freighter bound for the Caribbean. One of

the ship's stops was Havana, its only port of call in Cuba.
Did she dare?

Before she even asked herself the question, Lucy knew
she was going to go to Cuba in search of him. She was a
fool, for in her heart she knew she would follow him to the
end of the world—and not just to set the record straight.
She still loved him and was sorry she had finally signed
those damn divorce papers. She wanted, desperately, to be
with him. He still desired her, he had made that so very
clear, and that gave her some amount of power over him.
Would it be so bad to be his mistress? Maybe, one day,
they could overcome the past and recapture what they'd
once had. And if she was chasing a dream, so be it. There
was nothing for her here, nothing at all.

She booked passage on a passenger ship bound for Miami
on the sixth of the month. From there, the ticket agent
assured her, she would easily find a cruise ship headed for
Havana. It was quite a popular tourist spot, despite the
rebellion.

Lucy told her parents she was going to Dragmore, and
they did not question it. She made arrangements for two
passengers to travel to England, fortunately finding a ship
leaving the same day she was departing for Cuba. At the
last moment she would easily evade her chaperone, who
would sail without her. Lucy planned to leave her a note,
so that the poor woman would not think she had fallen
overboard.

In the few days she had left before departing, she packed
all she would need for an extended stay and began reading
everything she could find on Cuba. That was easily done;
it was the hottest political topic of the day, and the newspapers were full of accounts of the suffering of the rebels,
the massacres of the Spanish troops, and the epidemics
infesting General Weyler's *reconcetrado* camps. Lucy began to have a few doubts. It sounded as if she was going
into a veritable civil war. But her love was stronger than
reason, and on January sixth, a bleak, snowy day, she departed New York.

Lucy was seasick during the entire voyage. She spent just
one night on land in Miami, barely enough time to regain

her equilibrium. Fortunately, it was only another sixteen hours to Cuba, and when she arrived at Havana Harbor, she was relieved. She was still quite green and she wanted to set foot on land as soon as possible. She intended to reside in Havana at her father's villa, certain that it would be easier to find Shoz if she stayed in the capital than at Maravilla. Lucy stood at the railing as the large vessel was eased into the bottleneck harbor by a smaller tugboat. It was January thirteenth.

The day was warm and balmy. The skies were very blue, the waters of the Caribbean opaque and turquoise. Lucy gazed at the Castillo del Morro on her left as the ship passed by, a rather decrepit old castle that was now a defense fortification, a newly whitewashed lighthouse rising from its midst. Ahead of her, to the right, lay Havana, a charming city where colonial-style buildings abounded in bright sunlight, palm trees sighing in the breeze along the wide avenues. Lush green hills framed the city, a perfect backdrop. Lucy smiled, a sense of excitement pervading her.

She had succeeded in escaping New York; she was about to begin an adventure, perhaps even a new life. For the first time in almost six months, life seemed ripe with promise. She lifted her face to the warm sun and smiled.

The harbor was a bustling port, one of the most important for the tiny island. Most of the vessels anchored there were being loaded with sugar destined for the States. Smaller local fishing vessels bobbed beside them. And a Spanish man-of-war was at dock, a deadly reminder that this was a country in the grip of war.

The villa was in the center of town, on the Avenue Muralla, not far from the Iglesia de San Francisco, a magnificent old church dating back to the sixteenth century. Lucy hired a horse-drawn buggy to take her there, and even so, it could not accommodate all of her luggage. The driver promised to return later for the rest of her belongings. He clucked the mare forward across the cobbled street.

Lucy had not been to Cuba in years, and then only twice, yet the city did not seem to have changed. Although the hills around them were lush and green, the most fertile sugar-growing land was on the eastern side of the island.

Lucy knew all this from her visits to Cuba as a child. Maravilla was about twenty-five miles from Havana, bordered by softer slopes in the west and lush jungles in the east.

They passed through a teeming marketplace. Buyers and sellers shouted at each other in an endless cacophony; the crowd swirled around them. Vendors hawked their wares from stalls or big woven baskets at their feet. The stench of freshly caught fish assailed her, and Lucy glimpsed one vendor standing amidst his catch, a ton of long, silver-scaled marlin dumped at his feet. They left the market behind and turned in to a narrow, winding street.

Ahead of them a faint sound rose, like a muted roar.

It came again, a swelling echo.

"Sir, what is that noise?" Lucy asked the driver.

"I don't know, señorita."

They both listened and the sound became more distinct— it was the roar of a crowd. Indecipherable chanting followed. Lucy realized with curiosity and excitement that they were heading in the direction of the crowd; now she could hear applause and whistles.

They turned a sharp corner and abruptly entered a town square.

Lucy gasped. The small square was jammed with thousands of people. Even the green in the center was packed with bodies. The carriage moved forward a few paces and stopped. The street was so congested with people that all forms of vehicular traffic were impossible. The driver cursed and shouted and they inched forward before halting again.

"What is it? What's happening?"

"A protest, señorita," the driver cried with excitement. "A protest against autonomy. Cuba will never accept autonomy from Spain. José Marti is here!"

Lucy knew who José Marti was from the reading she had done. He had practically started the revolution singlehandedly, and the American press treated him like a hero. She looked where the driver was pointing. A man on a second-story terrace on the building beside them was speaking through a megaphone. It had to be Marti. He spoke with forceful charisma, firing up the crowd, stating that no Cuban would ever accept autonomy from the Spanish—it was freedom or death. When he had finished, the crowd roared in approval.

"He must be crazy to come to town and show himself like this!" Lucy cried, caught up in the excitement that Marti was generating.

"Sí, señorita, the Spanish have been trying to capture him for years."

Lucy stared at Marti in awe, wishing she could see him better. The carriage hadn't budged. They were in a sea of bodies, and it was clear that they would be stuck here for a very long time. "Am I going to have to walk?" Lucy asked, as Marti started to talk again. "Unless he finishes quickly, we'll be here all day."

"It's not far to Muralla Avenue," the driver said. "I can give you directions and follow with your bags when I can."

What harm could there be in walking? As interesting as Marti was, Lucy wanted to get to the villa and settle in— and find Shoz. She quickly made arrangements with the driver, then slipped out of the carriage. Lucy, who had been feeling fine from the moment she had set foot on solid land again, felt her breath catch and her stomach clench. There were so many people! She did not like the feeling of being trapped in this crowd at all. Panic was rising, although she told herself not to be silly. Already the crowd had jostled her away from the buggy, providing an impenetrable wall of human flesh, making it impossible for her to return to it, even had she wanted to. She needed air, desperately.

Lucy forced her way through the crowd, panic giving her unusual strength. She was near the park and she managed to push past four or five women to reach it. Lucy clung to the stone wall surrounding the park, panting, but it wasn't good enough. Lifting her skirts, careless of who should see, she climbed up so that she was standing on it. Her heart began to settle and she took great gulps of air. A few other people were standing on the wall, too, and Lucy began to look at them with interest. Many were young boys and teenagers. She began to enjoy her vantage point. The crowd around her on the ground was mixed, men, women, and children. Many wore worn cotton, the sign of the Cuban farmer and farm worker. Above them all, José Martí was crying out another fervent message that the government's promises were empty lies. They had promised reforms, but had the *reconcetado* policy ceased? Was the press free? Prisoners released? Autonomy was another empty promise, and even if it wasn't empty, they would never accept it, not ever!

Everyone in the crowd roared, the gustiest sound yet. Lucy gazed up at the terrace at Martí. She was on the side of the park closest to the balcony where he stood, and from her position, she could see him quite clearly now. He wore an ill-fitting suit, and had Indian features, his face high-cheekboned but flat and wide. He raised his fist in the air as he shouted.

The crowd echoed him. *"CUBA LIBRE! CUBA LIBRE! CUBA LIBRE!"*

The chant swelled and grew and reverberated around her. Lucy found herself caught up in the excitement, in the tremendous energy. She stared at the speaker, whose face was triumphant. The door behind him moved and another man stepped out onto the terrace and spoke urgently into Martí's ear.

Lucy froze. Her heart slammed to a stop. The other man was tall and dark and wearing faded Levis. It couldn't be. It could not be Shoz.

She would know him anywhere, even from this distance, even when his face was so close to the other man's that she couldn't see it. It was Shoz, she wasn't dreaming; he was here, in the middle of this protest!

He moved away from Martí, and Lucy saw his rough, dark features. She was trembling. Why was he here? What was he doing with the Cuban rebel leader?

She realized his gaze was sweeping the horizon, not the crowd, as if watching for someone or something. She couldn't take her eyes from him. Maybe he felt her stare, because suddenly he looked down—right at her.

Their gazes met and locked, and there was no mistaking his recognition and shock.

The crowd was still chanting, *"CUBA LIBRE, CUBA LIBRE!"* as they stared at each other. Lucy was vaguely aware that she was hearing glass breaking somewhere close by. Cries of approval sounded. The sound of more glass shattering caught her attention and Lucy turned to look behind her, but it was impossible to see anything other than the surging, angry ocean of people. The tone of the crowd had changed. Lucy heard hysteria, felt the frenzied intent. She also heard wood groaning and splitting, and then before her very eyes, she saw the carriage—her carriage—being overturned by a mob of shrieking youths.

Lucy froze, immobilized with fear. She saw a window in the building in front of her break as a huge rock hit it, thrown by someone in the crowd. More rocks began flying, some dangerously close, as one by one the windows in the same building began shattering. And all the while the roar of *"CUBA LIBRE, CUBA LIBRE"* echoed.

And then someone shoved her and she fell off the wall.

The crowd was packed so tightly that it kept her upright. Lucy looked up—but Shoz and Marti were gone. Disappointment claimed her for a second, then gave way to real panic. The crowd was jostling her, shoving her this way and that. Now the sounds of destruction and frenzy were everywhere around them—wood breaking, glass crashing, people screaming in exultation and in terror, the chanting of *"Cuba Libre,"* the sound of sirens, the frightened whinny of a horse. Someone pushed her so hard, she thought she would fall and be trampled to death. She screamed.

She was shoved again, this time hard from behind, and Lucy went down on her knees. Someone stepped on her hand and she screamed as dizziness assailed her. She must not faint, she must get up, or she would be trampled by the crowd! Terror gave her superhuman power, and Lucy clawed her way to her feet, her nails digging into the strangers around her, pushing back at them as they pushed at her.

Panting, on her feet, locked between people whom she could not see, Lucy did not try and fight the crowd. It was moving her forward, and she went with it, tears of panic streaking her cheeks. She could not breathe. The feeling of claustrophobia was stronger. The crowd surged ahead unevenly, and Lucy lost her balance again. She grabbed someone's shoulder, while something wet blowing warm air shoved her from behind. She heard a snort and realized it was a horse. Lucy screamed in terror as the horse's muzzle pushed her again, causing her to stumble into someone. She had to move aside or be run over. But she couldn't move, she was hemmed in by hard-packed bodies. A hand anchored itself in her hair.

Lucy tried to run from the horse, into the people blocking her way. The hand yanked her back. The horse's body pushed her forward.

"Lucy!"

Lucy half twisted, her hands going up to claw at the stranger who wouldn't release her hair. Beside her, the horse danced in place, his hooves brushing against her feet. With a snarl, Lucy grabbed the man's wrist as he wrenched at her scalp so painfully, she thought he would pull a great hunk of her hair from her head. Like an animal, she tried to bite him.

"Lucy!" Shoz shouted.

She recognized him and started to go limp. He rode the huge black forward, and Lucy felt the horse's hoof clip her ankle, its shoulder brush her. Shoz grabbed her by her armpits and hauled her up in front of him. Lucy clung to him. "Hold on!" he shouted.

She had no intention of ever letting go. The crowd swarmed all around them, but Shoz was very skilled and determined; he weaved his mount through as if threading a needle, barely avoiding trampling those he forced aside, using a crop ruthlessly, slashing at those in his path and moving them out of the horse's way. Lucy clung, shaking. The stallion danced and snorted, people shrieked in hysteria. Lucy heard the roar of a fire, smelled the smoke. Someone screamed in terror. There was an explosion, and out of the corner of her eye, she saw a building crumble.

And then they were free.

42

Not until they had ridden to the outskirts of Havana did they stop. Shoz pulled up the steaming stallion. Lucy abruptly slid from his lap, took two steps, and sank onto the ground. Shoz leaped down after her. "Are you all right?"

She was no longer trembling, but her breathing was shallow and fast. A series of explosions sounded, causing them both to jerk and look back the way they had come. They were on a hillside, and most of the city sprawled below them in a jumble of orange-tiled roofs. Lucy saw a thick cloud of smoke hanging over the center of Havana, marking where they had been. She thought about being caught up in that horrible riot and she shuddered. Then she turned her gaze to Shoz.

He was scowling and grim, and his eyes were sparking with anger. He was sweating, his blue cotton shirt half-open and clinging to his hard torso. His legs were braced apart hard, straining taut the fabric of his faded Levis, as he loomed over her. "Dammit, what the hell are you doing here!"

Lucy forgot about her near brush with death. Shoz was here—she had found him—but he didn't seem pleased to see her. To the contrary, he seemed furious. Slowly she got to her feet.

"I asked you a question."

She lifted her chin. "What a pleasant greeting."

"If you're looking for manners, than you're looking in the wrong place."

"Believe me, I know *firsthand* that you are thoroughly lacking in that department."

He smiled. "Mad, are we?"

"I wasn't mad until you made me mad."

Now he seemed pleased. What was she doing? She hadn't tracked him to Cuba to argue. "Shoz, please, I don't want to fight with you."

He ignored her. "What are you doing here, Lucy?"

"I had to leave New York."

His gaze narrowed.

"I didn't marry Leon."

He stared. Suddenly he grinned—and then he laughed. "You stood him up at the altar?" He hooted.

"It wasn't funny."

He was really laughing now. "Oh, that's funny, princess, that's really funny!"

Lucy clenched her fists. "Are you being obnoxious on purpose?"

"You still didn't answer my question. *What the hell are you doing in Cuba?*"

"I told you—I couldn't stay in New York, not with another scandal!"

Shoz grabbed her chin. His gaze pinned hers. "But Cuba? You have rich family all the hell over the world, and you run to Cuba?"

Lucy pursed her mouth shut. He was being a miserable bastard and suddenly she was all pride—she would never tell him that he was the reason she had come to Cuba!

He smiled, releasing her. "Wait a minute. This isn't just a coincidence, is it? You knew I was here, didn't you? You came because of me!"

"You arrogant son of a bitch!" Lucy cried. She slapped him across the face with all the strength she had, tears of anger in her eyes. She had followed him to Cuba, but she would never admit it, because he just didn't care. He had never cared. He was making fun of her.

He drew back. "Ow! What the hell was that for?"

"That was for just about everything." She wasn't aware that she was still posed to hit him.

He grabbed her wrist as she swung again, pulling her up close. "That's the thanks I get for saving your delectable ass?"

"You get no thanks from me for anything!"

"You're mad because I came to your room that night, aren't you? You're mad because you damn well enjoyed it."

"I'm mad because you're a selfish, self-serving bastard."

"It took two, baby." He yanked on her. "Or is it because I'm not falling all over you now? Is that it?"

"What did I ever see in you?"

That shut him up. They looked at each other, Shoz grim, Lucy red-faced with anger. Finally Shoz said, softly, "I could never figure that out."

And in that instant, Lucy's heart went out to him. He wasn't a bastard, it was all show. "Shoz . . ."

"I want you out of here. Don't you have any common sense? This country's in the middle of a bloody civil war! This country is no place for a woman, any woman, much less one like you!"

"What does that mean!"

"It means that you belong in your fancy New York mansion with your liveried servants, Lucy. Not here. Not now."

"You don't give me any credit."

"Sure I do." He grinned, and eyed her.

She stepped back, her breasts heaving. She watched him warily. She watched him leer, knowing it was on purpose, knowing he wanted to alienate her again. But then his interest genuinely changed, damn his soul to the depths of hell. Lucy recognized the bright light in his eyes too well. His gaze made a more thorough sweep of her person.

A frisson swept her, and Lucy was too experienced not to realize, with dismay, that his interest only fueled hers. She wanted him. Needed him. She had always wanted him.

She took another step away from him. "Contrary to what you believe, I came here for the anonymity Havana could provide me. To be alone, and—recover."

"I don't care why you came. This is no place for you to be, Lucy. You had better get on the next ship bound for home, and I mean it."

"I am not leaving," she gritted. "And it is *not* your affair!"

"Maybe I'm making it my affair."

A thrill swept her. "That's your business."

He was furious. Lucy had to contain herself not to show her own emotions, which were far from fury.

He turned away first, rigidly. "Where are you staying?"

"Daddy has a villa on Avenue Muralla."

"I'll take you there."

Lucy looked back at Havana. Already the smoke was drifting away, leaving a blue sky in its wake. The city was picturesque and still. It was hard to believe that such violence had just occurred within its deceptively serene confines. "All right, thank you."

He extended his hand. Now that the riot, and their argument, were far behind them, Lucy hesitated. She had never been more conscious of his rawly male appeal than at that precise moment.

As if comprehending her completely, he smiled. "Maybe it's not so bad—that you're here for a while."

Lucy didn't respond, waiting, even wary.

"We never have had enough time, just the two of us, have we, princess?"

She looked at him. "No, we haven't."

He stared. Lucy smiled and held out her hand. Instead of helping her mount, he gripped her hand, hard. "What are you up to, Lucy?"

"I told you," she said. "I came here to escape the scandal in New York. That's all."

"You're lying."

He had turned away; Lucy approached and laid her palm on his damp back. The texture of him was so familiar, hard and smooth, warm and wet. He jumped as if she'd stung him.

"I'm not," she said earnestly. "My reputation was in tatters after being your hostage in Death Valley. Somehow it was leaked to all the newspapers. We had to maintain that I was, er, unhurt." Her voice cracked. "I couldn't handle another scandal, I just couldn't."

"It'd be an even bigger scandal if they knew we'd been married." His tone and expression were mocking, indifferent; his gaze was not. It held hers, searched hers.

"I'm not ashamed of our marriage. I never was."

"Like hell."

"Believe what you want." The anger came back so easily. "You will anyway, won't you?" Now it was her turn to be bitter.

"That's right."

They had reached a standoff. Somewhat reluctantly Lucy allowed Shoz to help her mount; he climbed astride behind her. He urged the black into a slow trot, and for a while they rode in silence, each immersed in his or her own thoughts, but overwhelmingly aware of the other.

It wasn't comfortable. It had been so long since they had made love properly, and Lucy felt the enormity of her desire engulfing her like a tidal wave, and she was filled with yearning and anguish. She knew he felt it, too. His forearm braced her firmly across her abdomen, her back was glued to his chest, she sat in his lap. His body, against hers, felt as hard as steel and as tight and tense as a newly coiled spring.

"How are you involved with José Marti?"

He stiffened. "Don't ask."

The implications of his involvement began to seize her. "Shoz, if you're caught with him . . . !"

He laughed. "Suddenly concerned for my well-being?"

"Of course I am."

He was silent. Then his grip tightened, and his arm lifted, pressing into her breasts. His mouth, when he spoke, touched the side of her cheek. "You don't care about me. You never cared about me. You only care about what I can do for you in bed."

Lucy could barely breathe, his breath sending a delicious frisson through her. "Th-that's not true."

"Should I prove it?"

"Shoz, stop."

"Why?" His mouth moved over her cheek. His hand closed over her breast. "Face it," he said, his breath warm on her ear. "You start coming in your lacy French drawers when I barely touch you."

For one second, Lucy could not breathe, could not move. Then she wanted to kill him.

"Deny it all you want to," he said, releasing his hold and urging the horse on. "But that won't make it go away."

"Why did I ever like you?"

"For the same reason you still like me." He leered.

"I want to walk." She moved to slide off the stallion, but he held her firmly in place.

"Forget it."

She seethed silently. Nothing was going the way she had dreamed, nothing. "Why are you so mean?" she flung, before she could stop herself.

"You always did bring out my worst side."

There was such rueful sincerity in his tone that Lucy twisted around to look at him. Incredibly she saw his cheeks darkening with a blush. He looked away, avoiding eye contact. She thought, he is such a complex man. Unfortunately, she chose that moment to remember his sensitivity and love for Roberto in a series of sharp, focused images. She felt her own anger draining, and rising in its stead was an answering warmth. "How is Roberto?"

"He's fine."

"You still see him?" She faltered, thinking of Carmen.

"When I can."

She didn't want to know. "He's in Death Valley?"

He studied her. "Yes."

Lucy hid her gaze. Jealousy surged through her with such force, it made her feel momentarily faint. She didn't have a doubt that if Shoz periodically went to Death Valley, Carmen was there, still his mistress. God, she hated her—she hated him!

They did not speak anymore. Lucy still wanted to know what Shoz was doing here in Cuba, among the rebels, but Shoz refused to be drawn into a conversation. He was the only person she knew who could upset her so quickly, with just a word, or an innuendo. She felt drained from their encounter, the riot, her voyage. They began passing the homes of the well-to-do who resided in Havana's finer districts.

"We're almost there," Shoz told her, turning onto Avenue Muralla. He asked for the villa's street number, and Lucy told him. "Lucy, listen carefully."

His tone was very serious, and Lucy was all ears.

"It's very dangerous here in Havana, and in all of Cuba.

The situation is out of control. I want you to leave. And until you do, I want you to be very careful.''

"I'm not going to leave, Shoz," she said firmly. "But I will be careful."

He grimaced. "I want you to follow the rules. You don't go out unescorted. You stay to the areas of the city that are trouble-free, like this neighborhood. And Lucy, before doing anything, think it through first."

It was as if he cared about her safety, as if he really cared. "You sound like my mother," she joked. But she was agitated, and so very hopeful!

"This isn't a joking matter!"

"I'm sorry."

"One more thing. There's a secretary in the consulate, Janice. If ever you have a problem, or an emergency, just tell her that you need to reach me, or give her a message. Don't hesitate. Okay?"

"Is Janice also your mistress?"

"Oh, for crissakes!"

Lucy wished she'd held her tongue. "I'm sure there won't be any problems."

"Let's hope not," he returned. "We're here. *But think about leaving!*"

Lucy suddenly wanted to delay their parting, but Shoz slid her to the ground. The stallion shifted restlessly. Shoz's mouth was taut and tight. She wanted to invite him in, but before she could, he abruptly wheeled the big animal around. Lucy watched his back as he trotted away from her, wanting to call him back—or go with him. She stared after him until he was no longer visible.

The villa was white stucco with half an acre of tropical gardens and a small swimming pool. It was cool and spacious within, with a distinctly Caribbean flavor to its furnishings. Lucy had always loved the house.

She was greeted at the front door by the housekeeper, a big Negress named Venida. She seemed displeased with Lucy's presence, although not surprised, for her bags had already arrived with the driver she had left during the riot. However, all her luggage was still in the foyer, Venida seeming reluctant to exert herself to make Lucy comfortable.

"Please have my things brought up to the pink room, Venida. I'll stay there."

"But that's where your papa stays when he comes," Venida argued, scowling.

Lucy found herself explaining to the servant. "Daddy is not coming to Cuba, and I'm going to stay for some time. The pink room, please, Venida."

Before supper, which Venida waddled off to prepare with some grumbling under her breath, Lucy explored the villa, refamiliarizing herself with it. She unpacked a few things, then spent an hour soaking in the huge sunken tub in the master bath, sipping a brandy and relaxing. Her life seemed to have changed suddenly and dramatically.

Shoz was here. He had rescued her heroically, and for the first time since he had done so, Lucy could remember, and luxuriate in the memory. In all the memories. And he cared enough about her to warn her to be careful. Maybe it wasn't very much, but it was a start.

She was no longer shaken by the riots. Alone in the massive tub, pampering herself, it seemed hard to believe that outside the villa there existed a world of subterfuge and insurrection, of violence and revolution. She might have felt the tiniest shiver of excitement.

Her life was certainly no longer dull and dreary.

The next day Lucy set out to see those parts of Havana that were not proscribed. Venida made it clear where she should and should not go, and had the gall to instruct the coachman. Lucy supposed she was only trying to be helpful, but she did not like being told where she could and could not go.

One of her first stops was the American consulate.

Lucy wanted to meet the secretary Shoz had referred to, Janice. She was a short, plump woman in her forties, and Lucy was ashamed of having jumped to the wrong conclusion. She had picked an importune time to visit, for the consulate was a beehive of activity due to the riots of the day before. The wires between Washington and Havana seemed to be in constant use. "I'm sorry," Janice apologized, looking harried. A cacophony of typewriters, telegraphs, telephones, and voices made it hard to hear her. "But we're almost in a state of emergency; this is exactly the kind of trigger that might cause McKinley to declare war on Spain!"

Lucy shuddered at the thought. As the revolution dragged on, the American press had begun speculating on the possibility of American intervention to gain Cuban independence. When she had been in New York, the idea had seemed remote, but now, amidst the chaos of the consulate, it seemed very real, and frightening. "Janice, I'll come back another time."

She left, but not before overhearing Janice telling a cohort, excitedly, that the State Department had put the USS *Maine*, stationed at Key West, Florida, on alert. She hurried outside, into the sunny brightness of the Havana morning. Here, amidst the tall, stately buildings of the government district, it seemed peaceful and serene—as if the riots of yesterday and the revolution did not even exist.

Lucy wondered at the connection between Janice and Shoz. Janice was working for the United States government; Shoz was obviously deeply involved with the rebels. Was she a spy? A spy for the rebels? Why else would she be passing messages to Shoz? *Or was he a spy?* Exhilaration suddenly gripped Lucy, stopping her in her tracks. When they were in Brownsville, her grandfather had said that the government was sending Shoz to Cuba, to supply the rebels with guns. And if he was working with Janice, than he must be some sort of spy for the United States. Lucy didn't know whether to be terrified for Shoz, or proud of him.

On her fourth night in Havana, the Spanish governor-general held a small dinner party in honor of the new American consul, who had just arrived. Janice had secured Lucy an invitation. The American community in Havana was small and cohesive, and as a Bragg, she was a welcome addition and had already met most of the wives of the consulate staff. The evening affair was held at the governor-general's palace. Lucy was introduced to the ranking officials of the Spanish government, the rest of the foreign community, and their wives. She found the occasion to be little different from any New York ball. The men flirted openly with her; their wives were eager for a newcomer to relieve the tedium of their exile. And as she had just arrived from the States, everyone was eager to know the "real" mood in America. Would Washington really go to war for the sake of a few Cuban rebels?

Soon the group she was with began to discuss excitedly the latest exploits of one of the rebels, someone they called El Americano. As usual, he had attacked and harassed the Spanish troops right under the noses of the government, this time at Castillo del Morro, where a bomb had gone off, destroying part of the fortification and causing great chaos— and even more embarrassment. The Americans in the group appeared to admire him.

"Is he really an American?" Lucy asked, pale. She couldn't help thinking of Shoz.

"Oh, I don't think so," one of the consulate secretaries said. "He's called that because he speaks Yankee English, when most Cubans speak English with a British accent. They say he's dark as sin; he's probably part Indian and part Negro—and all Cubano." She laughed.

Lucy did not have time to dwell on her suspicions. For she saw Leon.

It was a great shock. He was standing across the room, staring at her coldly. She could not believe this coincidence; she went white. He turned away, but Lucy, recovering, excused herself and crossed the room.

"What are you doing here!"

"I should ask you," he said coldly. He eyed her bare shoulders with a combination of interest and distaste, and Lucy felt naked in her yellow sheath.

"I decided to leave New York," Lucy said.

"I'm the new American consul."

She gasped, stunned. "But I thought you were posted in Puerto Rico!"

"I was. This is a new assignment," Leon said, and rudely he turned and walked away, leaving her standing there alone.

"A very foolish man," someone said behind her.

Lucy whirled, embarrassed that someone had seen Leon cut her off.

"We haven't had a chance to speak, and I regret it greatly," General Valeriano Weyler said.

They had briefly been introduced, but had not talked. Lucy managed to smile, still shaken by Leon's presence in Havana. The general was tall and handsome, with tawny hair and olive skin and pale blue eyes—yet he was not attractive. He had an intensity that disturbed her. He was the general already infamous in the States for his policy of herding up the local population and confining them to limited areas, ostensibly to create fire-free zones where the rebels would not have any local support. According to sensational press reports, Weyler's camps were overcrowded and inadequately supplied, causing much pain and hardship and even death.

"Hello, General," Lucy said evenly.

He took her hand and kissed it. Lucy did not like the feel of his mouth on her skin. "You are a true beauty, my dear, a ravishing one. I see you have already met your new consul."

Was he merely making conversation, or was he prying? "Thank you," Lucy said. "Leon and I are old friends; our families are quite close."

"Indeed? A small world. Then you must be quite fond of Señor Claxton."

"He is my friend; once, he was a beau." Lucy didn't particularly care for the turn of conversation, or for admitting more than she wanted to.

"Ahh, yes, I see. The poor fellow looked somewhat surly."

"I'm sure you only imagined that."

"I like loyalty in a woman."

"I imagine you like loyalty in all those who serve you, General."

"Ahh," he said with a smile. "I knew you were as clever as you are beautiful. Have you had the time to visit Maravilla yet?"

"No, but soon I shall go." She was eager to see the plantation again. Weyler did not miss her mood.

"You cannot, of course, travel there yourself, because of the rebels. Perhaps I can be of service. Tomorrow I have a meeting with some of my local commanders not far from Maravilla. I will be happy to escort you there.''

Lucy's mind raced frantically. Her instincts warned her not to go anywhere with the general; on the other hand, what safer escort could she have? Even though she had only been in Havana a few days, she knew he was right, she could not go alone with her coachman to Maravilla. ''I don't know.''

''I will stop by your villa at eight tomorrow. You have the entire evening to decide.''

Lucy opened her mouth to protest, but he bowed and left. She was relieved, for their short conversation had somehow made her uneasy. She decided that no matter how much she wanted to see Maravilla again, she would not go with Weyler.

Lucy left the party just before midnight, being one of the first to depart. Her coachman was waiting; his face brightened at the sight of her. It was only a short drive back to her villa, and the night air was warm, still, and balmy. She realized, as Venida let her in, that she was tired, but pleasantly so; it had been an enjoyable evening. She smiled and hummed a little tune as she let herself into the luxurious pink room.

''Just where the hell have you been all night?''

''Shoz!'' Lucy cried.

43

''Where the hell have you been?''

Lucy recovered from the shock of finding him standing there in the middle of her bedroom. ''What are you doing here?!''

''Or rather,'' he gritted, his gaze sweeping her strapless

yellow sheath, "who the hell were you with?"

Lucy thought she heard a noise, and suddenly realized how compromised she was, with Shoz in her bedroom. She turned and shut the door quickly. "What does that mean?"

"It means who the hell are you sleeping with now!" Shoz shouted, and he flung his arm out, slamming his fist into the mirror above the mahogany bureau.

Lucy gasped as the mirror shattered, falling over the bureau and to the floor. Shoz stood motionless, holding his arm aloft, while blood from his hand began spotting the beautiful Aubusson rug. Lucy moved.

"What have you done!" she cried, rushing to him and taking his wrist.

"Dammit," he cursed. "Only you do this to me."

Lucy had already fled into the bathroom and returned with a fluffy pink towel, which she wrapped quickly around his hand. "For your information," she said stiffly, recalling his horrendous accusation, "I was at a party."

"With who?"

Before Lucy could answer, there was a sharp rapping on her door. "Miz Lucy, is that you? You all right?" It was Venida.

"No!" Lucy cried. "Don't—"

But Venida opened the door and saw the mirror. "Lawdy!" Then she saw Shoz.

For a moment the tableau was frozen. Shoz and Lucy standing together, his hand wrapped in the pink towel, Lucy holding his arm, Venida staring. Disapproval formed swiftly on her black face. "Well," she humphed. "I can see you got company and no need for me!" She turned and marched out with as much indignation as a two-hundred-and-fifty-pound woman could manage. She left the door open.

"Oh, God!" Lucy cried, running to the door and closing it. She leaned against it, breathless. "Of all the people, that nosy Venida! She won't say anything, will she?"

"Servants love to gossip," Shoz stated flatly.

Lucy moaned.

Shoz looked at the mirror and grimaced. "Stupid, real stupid. I'll replace it."

"Forget the mirror," Lucy snapped, frazzled now. She

grabbed his elbow and propelled him into the hallway. "I'm sure there's antiseptic in the kitchen, and at least there's soap."

Venida was in the kitchen smoking a cigarette when they came in. The kitchen was spotless, but when she saw them, she put it down, turned, and began banging pots and pans around. Lucy gave Shoz a warning look that said, "Shut up and sit," and approached her. Shoz sat at the kitchen table, saying nothing, but his mouth quirked. Venida slammed a lid on a pot.

"Do we have antiseptic?"

"In the pantry." She began to wipe down the scrupulously clean counter, with long, hard strokes.

Lucy soon found everything she needed, filled a bowl with water, and joined Shoz at the table. She began cleaning his hand. None of the cuts were deep, but she had to remove many splinters of glass.

"Whose party?"

She didn't look up. "I was at the governor-general's."

"Ah, yes. And how did you wrangle that invitation?"

Venida paused in her scrubbing of the countertop.

"Janice."

Shoz raised a brow.

Lucy looked up. "Just in case there's trouble, I thought I had better make her acquaintance."

Shoz's stern expression softened. "That was smart."

Lucy bit back a smile at his compliment, if it was such, and began dabbing antiseptic on his cuts. Venida made a noise.

Lucy looked at her. "I think the kitchen is clean enough, Venida; why don't you call it a night?"

"As you surely are about to do," she sniffed, and waddled out.

Lucy clenched her fists; Shoz laughed.

"She's not funny," Lucy hissed. "She's a big busybody—what was she doing upstairs anyway when you hit the mirror? Spying on me? She was certainly eavesdropping here in the kitchen!"

Shoz chuckled again, the sound warm, rich. "She's probably harmless. I think I like her."

"You would!" Lucy flared, yanking his hand forward and slapping more antiseptic on.

"Ow!"

"You would like anything that makes my life more difficult."

He said, "So how's the new American consul?"

Lucy froze. "You know? You know it's Leon?"

He nodded.

"Why didn't you warn me!"

"I didn't know you needed warning."

Lucy wrapped his hand in gauze and taped it. "That wasn't fair, what you said earlier." She had lowered her voice.

"What should I have thought?" He knew exactly to what she was referring. "It's one in the morning, and you come in singing, dressed to kill a man."

"You shouldn't have thought that," Lucy said, gathering up all the items she had used. She put them away, disposing of the soiled linens. She paused before Shoz, gripping the back of her chair. He stared at her.

The crisis past, Lucy was gripped with a very familiar longing. She could feel the increased beat of her heart, the tension in her spine. "Why did you come?"

"You know why I came."

She could barely breathe. "Then," she said huskily, "why don't we adjourn upstairs?"

He kicked back his chair, standing. Lucy lowered her gaze, afraid she would reveal too much of the intense desire—and emotion—she was feeling. He followed her upstairs wordlessly. Lucy paused in the bedroom, and heard Shoz close and lock the door behind them. She did not move, filled with excitement, yet filled with anguish, too.

This was what she wanted, why she had come to Cuba, to be with him, even if it was only in his bed. And this was why he had come, to sleep with her—and not for anything more. It was so bittersweet.

"Lucy," he whispered from behind, closing his large hands on her bare shoulders.

Lucy heard herself sigh as he pulled her pliant body against his. She arched into him.

"You are the most beautiful woman I know." His mouth touched her neck.

A wonderful thrill raced across her, yet it was as much, or more, in response to his words than to his touch. He had never given her such an extravagant compliment before. Tears flooded her eyes.

And then his hands slid across her bare collarbone, across the flat upper planes of her chest, and then down into her bodice. He gripped her breasts, his teeth finding the skin of her neck. Lucy reached behind her to grasp the fabric of his jeans, anchoring him more firmly against her. His phallus was already engorged, pulsing deeply in the cleft of her buttocks.

"I am going to die," she gasped.

"I'll help you," he said.

Something banged, a door, awakening Lucy. She was incredibly tired, as if she hadn't slept at all, and she rolled over, reaching for a pillow to cover her eyes as sunlight suddenly poured into the bedroom. As if someone had opened the blinds. Then she remembered—Shoz. She smiled, a warm, wonderful happiness assailing her.

"Jist ain't right, good folks ought to know better; now, if'n it was po' trash, why, then I'd understand, but good folks? Lawdy!"

Lucy gasped, realizing that Venida was in the bedroom, her eyes flying open. One look showed her that she was alone; Shoz had already left. Thank God!

"Such carryings-ons I neveh did see! 'Bout time you opened them eyes!"

Lucy sat up. "What time is it?"

Venida set a tray of hot chocolate down by the bed. "Seven."

"Seven!"

"You tol' me last night, when you first came in, to wake you at seven 'cause mebbe some general was goin' to come by. Or have you forgot?" Her hands fisted on her hips.

Lucy had told Venida to wake her just in case she changed her mind and decided to go to Maravilla. "Thank you, Venida," she said, her tone dismissive.

Venida walked to the door. "If'n your daddy knew the goin' ons in his house—in his bed—if he knew what his daughter was up to, he'd jist about die!" With that, she left.

Lucy's annoyance fled. She grinned like a cat, stretching luxuriously. Last night had been wonderful. Better than ever, oh yes. And she was in love, madly, hopelessly in love, again. Maybe she was a fool, but it was worth it!

Of course, nothing had been settled between them, and Shoz had not said when he would return. In truth, they had barely done any talking. He had taken her time and again like a starved man, and Lucy knew, finally, that his need for her was almost as great as hers for him. She had no doubt that he would come back to her.

Of course, she wanted more than just this, his visiting her in the dark of the night. But this was a beginning. She would make sure that his occasional visits became frequent, routine. She would become his mistress—his only one. And then, maybe, they could find something more.

But first, now, she had to decide if she was going to allow General Weyler to escort her to Maravilla or not.

Lightning struck her. What if she could help Shoz, show him she was more than a woman to warm his bed? Earn his appreciation, his gratitude? Lucy leapt from the bed, excited. What better way than to become friendly with the man in command of all the Spanish troops—the greatest enemy the rebels had? What if she could learn something of value to the rebels—to Shoz!

Miraculously Lucy was dressed and downstairs promptly at eight, appearing as fresh as if she had slept more than eight hours and not a mere two. She was a bit taken aback to see that her escort consisted of fifty heavily armed, mounted cavalry. She was also surprised to find herself sitting in a supply wagon next to the driver, while Weyler rode ahead with several other officers after greeting her at the front door.

It was a three-hour ride to Maravilla, and Lucy was upset to realize that she had no chance to eavesdrop on the general in order to help Shoz. She had obviously misjudged his interest in her at the party. She had no desire to converse with the driver of the buckboard, but the scenery was lush and gorgeous, and she had her memories of last night to keep her company.

Maravilla was five thousand acres of verdant, sugar-yielding hills fringed with tropical jungles and stretches of shell-white beach. Weyler dropped her off at the plantation house's front door, promising to return for her at four. Lucy thanked him, and waved until he had driven away.

Maravilla! Lucy turned exultantly. The big, white-shingled manor reminded her of the southern plantation homes she'd seen in Natchez. She turned slowly, pleased to find the house whitewashed and fresh-looking, the lawns carefully manicured, a profusion of pink and orange tropical blooms creeping along the drive and against the walls of the house. A long, gray-floored veranda ran the length of the front, furnished with white wicker chairs and sofas in green and pink striped upholstery. Huge potted ferns marked the four corners of the porch. Lucy noticed that the emerald-green shutters were closed on all the windows.

Lucy frowned. The place was very still and quiet, as if deserted, yet the manager lived here—or at least, he was supposed to. Lucy hurried up the porch steps to knock on the heavy door. There was no answer.

Lucy tried the door and found it locked. Her heart sank; she had a terrible feeling that the place had been abandoned. But that did not make sense. Lucy walked around to the back.

As it turned out, the house wasn't deserted, merely locked as a precaution against unruly, looting soldiers and rebels. The housekeeper let her in, introducing herself as Bamie. She explained that Harris, the manager, was out in the fields, supervising the day's work.

Lucy was pleased to see that everything was in order at Maravilla, as if the war had not touched the sugar plantation at all. Bamie informed her that in fact they had lost five hundred acres last year to a fire, which had broken out after a skirmish between the rebels and the Spanish troops. Other than that, the plantation had escaped the revolution un-scathed and in nearly full productive capacity. Lucy assured Bamie she would not be spending the night, but urged her to prepare a guest suite should she be able to come for a weekend. After a light lunch of crisply fried fish and delicious greens, Lucy decided to take a mount out to ride across the land, heeding Bamie's warning not to go too far.

Promptly at four, Weyler returned for her, and Lucy was ready. Again she rode in the buckboard while he rode ahead with his officers. They stopped to water the horses an hour after leaving the plantation. As he had done when they had paused to rest that morning, Weyler rode up to her. "I hope the wagon isn't too uncomfortable."

She gave him her best smile. "Not at all. I'm very appreciative of the escort. But I think I will stretch my legs."

He shouted a command to the soldier driving the wagon, who helped Lucy down while Weyler rode off to re-join his officers.

Lucy was certain they would not stop again before reaching Havana. This would be her last and only chance to spy, and she knew it. Her adrenaline was racing wildly. Afraid her excitement and fear showed, Lucy strolled along the creek, in the direction of the general. Weyler had dismounted and was in what appeared to be a deep conversation with a lieutenant. Lucy tried not to appear interested, ostentatiously viewing the scenery, yet she ambled closer until she could hear almost every word. She was surprised that there appeared to be a shortage of necessities for the Spanish troops, particularly meat, boots, and ammunition. New supplies were expected next week. This did not strike Lucy as important, but the fate of a rebel leader did. Apparently he had been interrogated to the general's satisfaction, because he was slated for a public execution the following day at noon. Lucy kept her facial expression impassive, but her heart was thumping madly. She turned to gaze up at a hawk soaring overhead, determined to tell Shoz about the execution. But did she even have time? She would have to instruct Janice to make sure Shoz got her message that very evening.

Feeling slightly faint, Lucy returned to the buckboard, unaware that Weyler had turned to watch her.

44

Lucy straightaway went to the consulate to ask Janice to have Shoz contact her. Although she stressed that it was urgent, Shoz had still not appeared at the villa by midnight, and Lucy had nearly paced a hole in the rug of her bedroom. Thinking he would enter her room as he had done the night before, from her terrace by way of the gardens below, Lucy stepped through the open balcony doors to wait outside.

The night was pitch-black, starless, and still, but it was also thickly sweet and fragrant. Lucy leaned on the polished mahogany railing, trying to pierce through the darkness blanketing the gardens and swimming pool below. Suddenly he swung over the rail and landed beside her as silently and unexpectedly as a jungle cat.

He did not give her a chance to speak, but grabbed her roughly. "What were you doing with General Weyler today?"

Lucy blinked in surprise, for only Venida and the rest of her household staff, and of course, Bamie, knew she had been escorted by the general to Maravilla. "How did you know I was with Weyler?"

He was furious. "That is none of your business. What in hell were you doing with him?"

"He escorted me to Maravilla, that's all."

"Maravilla!" It was an explosion, and he grabbed her. "I thought I told you—begged you—to be careful!"

"I was being careful," she protested angrily, trying to free herself from his grasp. "How better to travel there than with a military escort?"

"You shouldn't have gone at all! Didn't I make it clear? Cuba isn't safe, not for you, Lucy, not for anyone. What if Weyler's troops had been attacked? Dammit! And that's the one man I want you to stay away from. Do you understand me?''

He was hurting her, and she finally wrenched free. "I have a few questions of my own, dammit! You obviously have spies everywhere. Is Janice one of them? Is she the spy—or are you?''

"Don't worry about her, Lucy, or about me. You had better worry about yourself! Dammit! I can't spend my time worrying about you!''

Her heart skipped a beat. She touched him. "Do you? Worry about me?''

He refused to answer. "What is so urgent?''

Her hopes were winging, no matter how hard she tried to rein them in. Her fingers settled around his wrist. She could not let this go, not now, in the balmy intimacy of the Caribbean night. "Shoz? Do you worry about me?''

For a moment he did not move. She could hear him breathing, then he yanked his hand free. "What is so urgent?''

She straightened, certain that she had attained a small victory. Now she would attain another one. She told him about the rebel slated for public execution tomorrow at noon.

"How in hell did you find that out?''

"From General Weyler.''

He grabbed her again, this time shaking her. "What in hell did you do to make Weyler confide in you?''

"Let me go! You're hurting me!''

He ignored her. "He seduce you, Lucy? Is that it?''

She gasped. Outrage filled her. "Why don't you ask one of your spies! Apparently someone left a few details out!''

"You have ten seconds to answer me. One.''

He meant it. Lucy answered. "When we stopped on the way back to Havana, I happened to overhear him talking with his officers.''

"God!''

"What was so wrong with that?''

"You happened to overhear him?'' He was incredulous. "I pray you're not playing spy! Stay away from him. Or you might be very sorry.''

She bit her lip. "You could at least thank me for the information."

"Thank you for spying on Weyler? Forget it! I want you to mind your own business, Lucy, dammit!"

He still held her. He was so angry, so upset. Lucy knew then, with all her soul, that he was afraid for her. She swayed against him. "You still care about me."

He stiffened. Then he rudely ground his pelvis against hers. "That's what I care about, doll."

It hurt. Lucy refused to believe him, and she twisted free. Clouds broke, spilling moonlight on them both. His eyes blazed. "Sometimes I hate you," she said bitterly.

"Yeah, out of bed."

"Why did I bother to even tell you about that poor Cuban!"

"I can't figure that one out, either."

"Are you going to do something about it?"

"That, lady, is none of your concern!"

"I've only been in Cuba five days, and already I'm sick of everyone telling me that everything isn't my business!"

"Maybe you should try taking some advice—before you get hurt."

"There's something else I want to tell you."

"I'm all ears."

"They're expecting supplies for the troops within a few days."

"Where?"

"I don't know."

"Anything else?"

"No." Lucy folded her arms around herself, wondering what to do now. Shoz hadn't moved since she had stopped speaking. He was staring at her, and in the light spilling from her bedroom, she could just make out his shadowy features. She wished she could see his eyes more clearly. She didn't want him to go.

"Got an itch?" The words were rude, but his tone was not. It was a whisper, soft and gratingly sensual.

Lucy just looked at him.

His fingers touched her chin, raising it. His slight touch thrilled her the way no other man's ever had. If he wanted to, in moments, he could have her on her knees, begging for his attention. Lucy did not delude herself.

"Promise me," he said huskily, and Lucy rocked toward him, "Promise me you'll stay away from Weyler, promise me you won't go anywhere unescorted. Promise me you'll stay where you're supposed to stay, and do what you're supposed to do. Promise me, Lucy."

His tone was mesmerizing and sexy, despite his message. She was stunned when he pulled away from her and moved to the railing, about to leave.

"You—you're not staying?"

"I can't, not tonight."

She wanted to ask him why; she didn't dare. Anguish flooded her. She watched him straddle the rail, and when he was poised on top of it, she said, "You care about me, but you won't admit it. Well, I'm braver than you, because I'm not afraid to say it. I still care about you, Shoz; God help me, I do!"

She turned and ran into her bedroom, flinging the French doors closed behind her, and then she was clinging to their frame.

Daylight brought sanity, making her midnight confession seem foolish and melodramatic. She had only given him power over her, which he would not hesitate to use. Today she was determined not to dwell on Shoz, although she wondered if he would attempt to rescue the rebel prisoner. She had tremendous faith in him, she realized, for she did not doubt that he would succeed against the odds if he tried.

The world Lucy had so far moved in was carefully circumscribed by diplomatic dinners and the ladies' lavish luncheons, by the finest shopping in the city, and by her own elegant villa. Lucy decided that a tour of Havana was in order. There must be much more to the city than those fine shops of imported goods where all the diplomats and titled Spanish shopped. However, her driver did not want to take her around the city. Lucy had to threaten to go alone with a hired cab before he succumbed, albeit reluctantly.

And then she ordered him to take her to Havana Hill.

"You don't want to go there, señorita," he begged, clearly distressed.

"Yes, I do."

She knew that Havana Hill was one of the *reconcetrado* camps. Her driver's blunt refusal fueled her determination to go. She threatened to dismiss him, and they finally set off.

They soon left the stately, charming Havana Lucy was accustomed to behind. She grew somber as they entered Havana's slum neighborhoods. The buildings were low, squat, and crumbling adobe; tiles were missing from the roofs. Doorways were often open or doorless. Shops were empty, windows broken or boarded up. Lucy glimpsed an abundance of stray cats. Ragged clothes hung from some lines outside some of the tenement windows—so apparently someone lived there. But she did not see a soul, as if everyone were in hiding, and it was eerily quiet. Lucy felt distinctly uneasy.

Havana Hill was not deserted. To the contrary. The buggy stopped in front of a high wire fence. The fence stretched through the slums as far as Lucy could see—restricting everything and everyone on its inside from leaving its confines. Spanish soldiers patrolled its exterior and its gate.

"Oh my God," Lucy said. Not really aware of what she was doing, she stepped from the carriage, staring.

Within Havana Hill, people were everywhere. Old men and women and children sat on the street, on stoops, on upside-down garbage cans. Aimless and vacant-eyed. Poor people, skinny people, people half-clad in rags. Sick people, emaciated people. People who limped and hobbled, people with festering sores, people lying with fever. There were no young men, no teenage boys. The youngest children ran naked, thin and sticklike, their swollen, starved bellies testimony to their desperate plight.

Lucy realized she was clinging to the fence, trying not to faint. Two children ran up to her, no more than five or six, the boy clad only in a ragged shirt, the girl naked. They held out their palms. They begged.

Lucy reached into her purse, and through the fence, she gave them everything she had.

"Señora!"

Vaguely she was aware of a soldier questioning her. He sounded far away, but he was standing at her elbow. He demanded she state her business. It was the last thing she was aware of; she fainted.

"General Weyler." Lucy managed a warm smile. She had never known she could be such an actress, but too much was at stake.

"Señorita, I am honored." He ushered her into his cool, spacious office at military headquarters. The contrast with Havana Hill was gruesome, nauseating.

It was several hours later. Lucy had revived from her faint to find herself in the offices of the local camp commander. After she had explained who she was, she had been allowed to go. She had come directly here, to Weyler.

Shoz's words flashed through her mind: *Promise me you'll stay away from Weyler.*

"I need your help, General," Lucy said briskly.

"I am eager to give it."

"Good!" She went on to explain her intentions—she wanted to organize a relief effort for Havana Hill and any other concentration areas in Cuba. She would bring in food and medicine and organize volunteers to clean up the camps. Unsmiling, she waited for his reply.

"I'm afraid that is not possible."

"Why not?"

"It is the policy of the government not to allow any relief to the prisoners."

"That's inhumane."

"We are at war."

"Surely you can bend the rules."

"I'm afraid not." He stood. "Can I offer you some refreshment? Coffee? Tea?"

Lucy stood. "General, we must do something about those poor starving—dying—people!"

"Once the rebels cease hostilities, I assure you, they will be freed. That is the government policy."

Lucy debated arguing with him, and decided against it. "May I have permission to go into the camps?"

"Why?"

"To bring what comfort I can."

"I'm afraid not."

"I see." She smiled tightly. "Good day, General."

He grabbed her arm. Lucy froze. "Perhaps we can come to an *arrangement*."

Lucy looked at him, trembling with disbelief and anger. Surely she was misunderstanding him. "What kind of arrangement?"

"Perhaps an intimate dinner? Or lunch?"

"And after our meal?"

"You can convince me to accede to your request."

"On your sofa?" she said sarcastically.

"You should not be offended. You should be flattered. I find you incredibly desirable, my dear."

"I don't think so, General!" She turned and stormed to the door, her heart thundering.

"If you change your mind," General Weyler said, "please let me know."

Lucy slammed the door shut behind her. Outside, she sank against the wall, trembling. Why did she feel that she was getting deeper and deeper into something she could not control? With no way out?

That night Lucy did not sleep. Images from Havana Hill haunted her. Weyler was the most inhumane man she had ever met. She wished Shoz were here; she needed so very much to share with him what she had seen.

She soon realized she could not live with herself if she did not do something, anything, to help those poor inmates at Havana Hill. It seemed to be some vast moral obligation which she just could not escape. But what could she, Lucy Bragg, do? The inmates needed so much.

She had been sitting in bed; now she tossed the sheet aside and threw her feet on the floor. The solution was so obvious! The one thing she had was money, and a lot of it. She would buy all the relief supplies she could, and she could do it right here in Havana.

Her mind raced. The goods would have to be smuggled into Havana Hill. Shoz could do it; she knew he could. She would talk him into it when the time came, even if it meant using all the powers she had as a woman over him. And in the meanwhile, she would have to do a little research to find out what the inmates really needed.

She smiled, filled with a tremulous kind of anticipation, afraid, yet exhilarated. Deeper and deeper. Lucy knew she could stop this right now, before becoming irrevocably involved in breaking the law. Before becoming a part of a revolution.

But she could not.

45

He wondered what she wanted now.

He wondered if she was jerking him around on purpose.

Shoz hadn't seen Lucy in three weeks, not since their midnight encounter on the terrace of her home. From her balcony he'd gone directly to his men to make plans, and they had successfully rescued the rebel slated for execution that following day. In doing so, he had once again infuriated the authorities and General Weyler; he had been the subject of a massive manhunt in these past weeks, and he had been hiding deep in the jungles near Santiago. Despite the ensuing time, he hadn't been able to forget that encounter with Lucy—or her words.

"I'm braver than you," she had said, her face ivory in the moonlight, her eyes shimmering. "I'm not afraid to say it; I still care for you, Shoz!"

The words tore at him. They weren't real. He refused to believe she could have possibly meant what she said. He reminded himself savagely that she had eagerly divorced him, hadn't even come to say good-bye before she left with her all-powerful family—and somehow, as mad as he had

been, he had been waiting for that moment endlessly. But
she hadn't cared then, so why the hell would she care now?

In truth, he had been glad the circumstance of war had
forced him to stay away from Havana. His instinct for self-
preservation was strong. Now, in hindsight, he knew he
had loved her when she had been his wife. He was damned
determined not to make that same mistake—and he was
close to making it again.

Surprisingly, the anger over her betrayals, not just in
Matamoros, but with Leon as well, had begun to fade away.
Taking its place was raw frustration—and anxiety. In the
first week she had been in Cuba, Lucy had done every damn
thing she shouldn't, going out of her way, it seemed, to
court danger, turning the hairs on his temples gray. The
past few weeks had been unnaturally quiet, and he would
have been relieved if he didn't know her so well.

Not hearing from her, or about her, fed his anxiety. She
was up to something, meddling where she oughtn't; he could
feel it.

He had enough problems in his life without adding Lucy
to the list. Yet Fate seemed to be laughing at him, taunting
him with the woman he had once loved, just a little, testing
his patience and his resolve. But Shoz knew that as long as
Lucy was here, despite the past, he could not turn his back
on her. If he questioned his motivation too deeply, he would
have answers he did not care for, frightening answers.

Today Janice had sent him another message from Lucy—
and he had been alternately excited and dismayed. She said
that she urgently needed to see him. He knew how fanciful
she could be, yet he rode like hell back to Havana when
his man brought word from Janice. She would get him killed
yet, he thought grimly, yet he only saw one patrol and
evaded it easily.

Four days had certainly passed since she had given her
message to Janice when he arrived at the villa. It was very
early, the sun was bright, the birds chirping enthusiastically.
Most of her neighbors would still be asleep, and Shoz chose
to ring at the front door—it looked better than if someone
should happen to see him scaling her balcony wall. His
insides were tied in knots—and it had nothing to do with

the "urgency" she had communicated to Janice.

Venida answered, and the instant she saw him, she scowled. "Wondered when you'd show up."

"Good morning, Venida. May I come in?"

"Do I have a choice?"

Shoz laughed, the sound rich. "I'm not that bad."

She turned her back on him, waddling in. "You's probably the worst."

Shoz walked in behind her. "You needn't show me up. I know my way."

She snorted in disapproval and glared; Shoz bounded up the stairs. He knocked once and opened her door, his pulse racing, tension filling every fiber of his being.

She wasn't asleep. She sat on a plush chaise clad in an exquisite peach chiffon dressing gown, the fabric spilling over her curves like liquid silk. Shoz momentarily froze, his heart picking up a heavy beat, his groin tightening, reminding him that he hadn't been with a woman in a long three weeks. She became motionless, holding a porcelain cup near her lips.

His smile was mocking to hide his agitation. "You summon, and I obey."

She set the cup in its saucer, pursing her mouth, yet her gaze swept him, and it fed his hunger. Her laugh was shaky. "I wish."

She was at it again, and it infuriated him. "Really?" He stepped into the room, closing the door. "Stop playing games, Lucy; I don't like it."

She swung her incredible legs to the floor. "I'm not playing games. I stopped playing games with you a long time ago—when I realized I couldn't win."

He felt like smashing something. She was at it again, saying what he didn't want to hear, because if her words were sincere, he'd carry her off with him and never let her go, to hell with the past. "I think someone has emerged here as the winner, sweetheart, and it isn't me." His gaze raked her rudely, reflexively. The front of her robe had opened. She wore something silky and clinging beneath it in the same peach color. He wanted to rip it off.

"Why can't we both be winners? Why is this even a

competition? Why are you so angry first thing in the morning? Is it something I did, or said?''

He laughed, a hard sound. "As if you don't know.''

"I don't know. Surely you're not still referring to the past?''

He prowled forward. "The past? I never forget, I never forgive, but no, that's not what's on my mind.'' He paused in front of her. She sat up very straight, eyes clear and luminous and riveted to his. He watched her pulse leaping in her throat. Her nipples were hard, jutting through the thin fabric of her nightclothes. She was as aroused as he. "You know what's on my mind.''

"We have business to discuss,'' she said weakly.

"Later.'' His hand had its own volition; he touched her cheek. Her eyes flew closed and she leaned into his palm. Shoz thought he might explode, then and there. His hand drifted down her neck, her shoulder, and across her breast. He felt her heart slamming against her breastbone like a hardball in play.

Whatever was so urgent could wait. Abruptly he lifted her in his arms and fell on top of her on the bed. Their mouths had already fused wildly, and then he felt her nails on his back, under his shirt. She was as crazed with wanting it as he was. He forced a strong forearm under her back, lifting her breasts to his mouth, sucking one distended nipple feverishly. Her hands were on his groin, stroking his straining penis through the denim, kneading it. Shoz gasped, coming up for air. She freed him. He shoved her wispy bedclothes up to her hips, lifting her again, and then he took her in his mouth, as much as he could, his tongue delving into every slick fold he could find. A violent orgasm wracked her.

He spread her thighs wide and thrust into her. "Come again.''

She moaned in response as he drove himself into her. Liquid pooled beneath them. Shoz abruptly withdrew and flipped her onto her belly, jamming a pillow beneath her. He grasped her buttocks and entered her again. Lucy gasped, gripping the bottom of the headboard. Shoz watched his huge member plunging repeatedly into her slick, pink softness. When Lucy keened his name, he convulsed deep within her.

Afterward, they lay side by side, panting. Heady emotions were washing over him, but he would not succumb to the need to take her in his arms and just hold her. He sat up and looked at her; she was gazing up at him.

With his eyes he worshiped her body, her beauty, his glance roaming over her long legs, her full breasts. Once she would have blushed at such an open inspection, but now she only sat up, modestly smoothing her gown back into place. She had changed, he thought, the innocence was gone—he had changed her.

"That's one thing that hasn't changed," he said ruefully.

"Yes." Lucy gave him what might have been a smile, then left the bed to go to the bathroom. While she was gone, he fixed his own clothes and helped himself to some coffee from the silver pot on the tray by the chaise. Lucy returned, still clad in her peignoir.

"Where have you been? It's been three weeks."

"Have you been counting?"

"Yes, I have."

"In hiding."

Her eyes widened. "What happened?"

"I'm riding with the rebels, remember? This is a war, Lucy."

"The day after I told you about that rebel, the one slated for execution, he was rescued. It was you, wasn't it?"

"Don't ask me questions, Lucy. I'm not going to answer them."

Suddenly she smiled, and it was like a Caribbean sunburst after a tropical storm. "I knew you would rescue that prisoner!"

He said nothing.

"Weyler was furious." Seeing him jerk, she added quickly, "According to the gossip."

"You have stayed away from him?"

She sipped her coffee; he couldn't see her eyes. "Yes." She looked up. "Shoz, are you El Americano?"

He choked on his coffee. "What the hell!"

"It is you!"

He rose and stood before her furiously. "I don't want you to meddle in this damn war, Lucy! Jesus! You're putting yourself in danger—and you just might get me killed!"

She paled. She set her cup in its saucer shakily. "I'm sorry. Don't worry, really, I've never said a word, and I won't!"

"I didn't say I was him," Shoz ground out, low, unwilling to even say the nickname aloud.

"You don't trust me."

He saw the hurt in her eyes and paced away, feeling guilty because, in a way, she was right. God, she could turn him upside down. "It's not that I don't trust you," he said slowly. "I don't think you'd betray me on purpose, but I think it could happen by mistake."

"I'm smarter than that." She stood. "But you've never given me credit for anything, have you? Except for sex."

He winced. He thought about Death Valley, how she had changed there, been strong in the face of adversity, been like a mother to Roberto. "That's not true."

She turned her back on him and strode to her closet, then beckoned him to follow. Shoz saw that one corner in the back, hidden by her clothes, was piled high with crates. He counted six and figured there were at least a dozen.

He was puzzled. Lucy opened one on the top and withdrew a bundle, handing it to him.

His skin prickled. He unwrapped the package, growing grim. In it was a small first aid kit, containing iodine, vaccinations, gauze, chloroform, and other items. She handed him another bundle, in that was canned and dried foodstuffs. He looked at her.

"I have a ton of medical and food supplies in these trunks. But I have no way of getting them into Havana Hill. Will you help me?"

Shoz was furious. "Do you realize what you've done!"

"Of course."

"Do you realize that if you are discovered defying edicts of the Spanish government—"

She cut him off. "I'm aware of all of the consequences. I thought it out very carefully—and I did what I had to do.

I could not live with myself if I didn't try to bring relief to those poor, suffering souls!''

It took Shoz some time to grow as calm as she. He was in a state of disbelief. Was this the frivolous rich girl he had abducted last summer? He realized he was staring at her. God, she had changed more than he had thought. But then, he had changed too, hadn't he? "I don't want you doing this again."

She turned away, fingering some of the clothing hanging in the closet.

"It's too dangerous."

She whirled. "Shoz—if you help me, we can do it together. We can—"

"No!"

She stopped, drew herself up, exhaled. "All right. What about all of this?"

"I'll get it into the Hill."

Her eyes lit up; she smiled. "I knew you would!"

"I'll bring some men tonight."

"I'll tell Venida." Seeing his frown, she added quickly, "She already knows what I've been doing. I managed to get the first crates into the house when she was at the market, but, well, you know how she snoops. She discovered the boxes and I had to confide in her. But you can trust her, Shoz."

"You don't have to mention I'm coming tonight; she'll be asleep."

Lucy bit her lip. "I do have to tell her. So she can let you in." She briefly hesitated. "I won't be home tonight."

"Oh, really? Who's your latest conquest, Lucy?"

"It's not like that, not at all," she sparked. "Why do you always think the worst?"

He ignored her protest. "Where are you going?"

"Not that it's your business, but Captain Sigsbee is taking me to supper. He happens to be a friend of my Uncle Brett's."

Shoz scowled. Sigsbee was the captain of the USS *Maine*, which had docked at Havana two weeks ago, a response to the riots of the thirteenth and a potent reminder of the growing tension between Spain and the United States. "Sigsbee's old enough to be your father."

"Think what you want! You will anyway!"

"I've got to go," he said abruptly, "and get some men together."

She grabbed his arm, halting him. "You wouldn't do it, would you, unless you were sure you could smuggle those goods without getting caught?"

He was grim. "Do you want me to tell you it won't be dangerous?"

She studied him. "How dangerous? Shoz, I don't want you taking foolish risks."

"Why, Lucy? Why does it matter to you?"

"I wasn't lying the other night when I said I still care about you."

She was playing him again, smooth as could be, and she'd land him like some damn undersized catch if he wasn't careful. "Yeah, like you cared about Leon, right?"

"No," she said, so softly he wasn't sure she'd said anything at all.

She turned away to pour him more coffee. "I never cared about Leon."

"You sure had a lot of people fooled."

"Daddy arranged the marriage. I agreed because the scandal had ruined my life, and I wanted my place in Society back. But then I just couldn't go through with it."

He had ruined her life. Guilt struck him, hard. He had taken away her innocence, taken away her reputation, her standing among her peers. Did she really still care about him? Had she ever cared about him? *She divorced you so easily!* his mind cried. "If this is a game, I don't like it, not one bit."

She slammed her cup down. "I can talk myself blue with you, can't I? But it won't get me anywhere. Well, I have pride, too!"

He stood aggressively before her. "If you care about me, then why in hell did you divorce me?"

She stared. "Why did I divorce you?" She got to her feet, fighting-ready. "I beg your pardon—but I'm the one who should be asking that question!"

He didn't understand what she was saying and was only interested in an explanation that was long overdue. "Answer me, dammit! We had a good thing going, we were only married a few days, but the minute we got to Brownsville, you signed. If you really cared about me, you would have never given in to your daddy."

She gasped. "I never signed any papers in Brownsville! I refused to sign! I didn't sign them until the night of the rehearsal dinner—the day before I was supposed to marry Leon!"

His fists were clenched by his sides, and they shook. "Lucy," he said, his tone so soft, it was positively frightening, "Lloyd brought me the papers that first night I was in jail—and your signature was on them."

She went stark white. "I didn't sign them until the night before I was supposed to marry Leon! I didn't want to divorce you—I refused. I loved you! They brought *me* papers with *your* signature on them that night! And when I saw that you had signed . . ." She faltered, tears coming fast and hard. "When they brought me the papers, Shoz, there was only one signature on them, and it was yours."

Now he stared, comprehension beginning to dawn.

Lucy said, wretchedly, "You broke my heart—but I still wouldn't sign them."

So much struck him at once. But one fact stood out, one incredible fact—she hadn't signed those papers in Brownsville, she had held out until the last possible moment. He was so overwhelmed, he had to turn away. Almost to himself, he said, "Someone forged your signature to get me to sign."

Lucy was terribly shocked. "It wasn't Daddy, it wasn't Grandpa! They would never do something like that!"

Shoz had regained control, and he turned back to her. His eyes blazed. "No, they wouldn't. But I know who would." Their glances held. "Mr. Government Man. Lloyd."

"Oh, God." Lucy brushed at another onslaught of tears. "I still don't understand. Lloyd brought you papers with my signature, which was a forgery. And you signed them?" At his nod, she said, "But the papers I saw in Brownsville—

the same ones I signed in New York—only had one signature on them, yours.''

Shoz paced to the window, momentarily perplexed, then insight struck him. ''Lloyd wouldn't give a damn whether we were divorced or not, but he had to placate your family. Because I refused to sign at first, he couldn't just forge my name and whisk me away to Cuba. I could always get in touch with you and reveal the truth. Somehow he had to get me to sign—make me believe I'd signed—and he did that by forging your signature.''

Lucy was gaping at him.

''Once he'd done that, the rest was easy.'' Shoz shrugged. ''I signed, I thought it was legitimate, I wasn't going to cause more trouble. All he had to do was get me out of town so I'd never find out the truth. Meanwhile he could have a good forgery made of my name on a fresh set of papers, and no one would ever suspect. And it worked.''

''Shoz—you refused to sign?''

He was trapped. Too much was changing too quickly, and he wasn't ready to admit to her that he had been so in love with her that he hadn't intended to sign, facing prison instead. She hadn't betrayed him as he had thought, and he needed to get used to that idea. He could even imagine now how she would plan to wed Leon out of anger at his apparent rejection, the way he had bedded other women in the same kind of vengeance and rage. Reluctantly, roughly, he said, ''I'm a stubborn man and we had a good thing going. I wasn't ready for it to end.''

Lucy gripped the arm of the love seat beside her, staring at him. He knew she was trying to penetrate into the very depths of his heart and soul. Uncomfortably, he turned away, but then she cried out.

''Shoz, are you saying that the papers I signed in New York don't have your signature on them—that the signature is a forgery?!''

''There's no way in hell those papers have my signature on them, Lucy.''

Her hand found her chest, and she smiled, her eyes positively glowing. ''Don't you know what this means?''

He faced her warily.

"Shoz—you never signed the papers I signed—the divorce can't be valid. I'm still your wife!"

He stiffened. "Wait a minute."

"I'm still your wife," she repeated, stubbornly.

"That divorce is registered and official. In the eyes of the world, we're divorced."

"But it's not valid. Any court—"

"Hold on! If you think I'm going to take the government to court for forgery, you're out of your mind!"

She reeled as if he'd struck her.

He was angry at her reaction, and even angrier at himself for being so callous toward her feelings—and then regretting what he'd done. The situation was out of control and he didn't like it, not one damn bit. "I'd never win. And I have a presidential pardon at stake."

"I don't understand."

"I'm not at liberty to tell you details, Lucy."

She gasped. "Grandpa told me the government had sent you to Cuba. You are working for them, aren't you? You're a United States spy! And when this is over, you're going to get a pardon?"

He turned away. "Lucy, you have a big imagination."

"Damn you! You still don't trust me!"

He wheeled and gripped her shoulders. "Just leave everything alone! The past is the past, and the present is here and now. Don't push."

She set her mouth firmly. "I am your wife," she said, "and no matter what you say, you know it."

46

It was time to reveal himself. If the American consul had been anyone other than Leon, Shoz would have done so immediately upon his arrival in Havana. But because it was Leon, he had preferred keeping his work in Cuba secret. Now, however, he must at last come forth to communicate what he had learned. Too many lives were at stake.

He cursed the rebels, even as he admired them for their shrewdness. Just this morning the decision had been taken to plant an explosive on the *Maine* and blow her—and all aboard—up. Tonight. The goal was not to create an international furor, which it would, but to push the Americans over the brink and into war against Spain. For the Spanish government would be the first to be blamed.

It was brilliant, tactically speaking. Shoz had been hoping for American intervention to end the bloody impasse and free Cuba as much as the most fervent patriot. But he was an American; he could not sit on such knowledge and watch several hundred innocent Americans die. Nor could he do more than express a few reservations to his compatriots; he had worked too hard to become one of them, and if he had been a Cuban, he would have applauded the plan too.

He was at the consulate before anyone else, wishing there had been a way to give the information to Janice without damaging her position, but there wasn't. He paced outside the five-story brick building restlessly, watched by two stony marine guards. Leon's carriage drew up and he alighted. When he saw Shoz he froze, eyes widening in instant recognition.

They had never been properly introduced. But they had seen each other often enough at Paradise, when Leon had been the welcome guest, courting Lucy, and he the hired hand, watching their every move. He had a flashing remembrance of carrying Leon's bags up to his room the day he had arrived, and finding him there kissing Lucy.

"I don't believe this," Leon said.

"I'm sure you don't, *Consul*. We have business to discuss."

Leon moved past him. "I find that equally hard to believe."

"Frankly, I don't care what you believe," Shoz said, following him without an invitation. The two guards blocked his way. Shoz resigned himself to their rapid body search, and did not protest when they removed his revolver and knife.

Leon had watched. "Come to kill me?"

Shoz grinned. "Spooked, aren't we?" His expression changed. "Who would be stupid enough to travel in Cuba without weapons?"

Leon was grim, angry even. "This had better be good." With a word to the guards, he turned and spun on down the walk. Shoz followed, waiting while Leon unlocked the padlocked door. Inside the reception foyer, it was cool and dark.

Leon strode into his office, Shoz behind him. No one else was there yet, and Shoz was almost impressed with Leon's work ethic. Almost, but not quite. Leon went behind his desk, shrugging off his jacket. "What the hell are you doing in Cuba?"

"Business."

"I'll bet. I find this coincidence overwhelming as well."

"What coincidence?"

"You're being here, Lucy being here!"

"My being here has nothing to do with Lucy."

Leon gripped his desk. "Too bad you survived that gunshot in Paradise, too damn bad."

Shoz stared. "It was you?"

Leon smiled.

"You son of a bitch. I bet it was you."

"Really?" Leon was cool; the tables had turned.

Shoz forced a grim smile. He was almost certain that

Leon was enough of a coward and a bastard to have shot him in the back—because of Lucy.

"Why are you here?" Leon demanded.

"The Cubans are planning to plant a bomb on the *Maine*."

"What!?"

"I suggest you warn Sigsbee, and I suggest you do it today."

"How do you know such a thing? Why would they tell you?" Leon's eyes widened. "What kind of ploy is this?"

"I do business with the rebels, and before you think to turn me over to the Spanish, think again—think about your country's position in this mess."

Leon was stuck. The United States warned its citizens to stay out of Cuban affairs, but secretly condoned anyone supporting the rebels, especially those smuggling weapons and food to them—which was obviously the business Shoz referred to. But in this case, Leon thought, he would carefully consider betraying Shoz to the Spanish. "I want evidence. Otherwise I am not going to stir up a diplomatic hornet's nest. If this is a false alarm—and I really find it impossible to believe the Cubans would dare incur the wrath of America—I will have egg on my face."

"You fool," Shoz said. "I have no evidence. I'm telling you the truth. The *Maine* and all aboard her are in imminent danger. Do something about it."

They stared at each other. Leon said, coldly, "What do you possibly have to gain by all this?"

Just as cool, Shoz responded, "Nothing. I gain nothing."

"You never struck me as a patriot, Cooper. I think you want to stir up trouble, create an incident—with me at its center! And I think Lucy's the reason!"

"The reason for what?" Lucy said from the doorway.

Both men whirled. Lucy turned to Leon. "What are you two shouting about?"

Leon came out from behind his desk. Stalking her. "You don't seem surprised to see him, Lucy."

Lucy went red, too late realizing her mistake, and she backed up. "Of course I'm surprised! I . . ."

"Little liar," Leon said softly. "Now I think I understand. Everything."

Shoz grabbed Leon's arm. "Lucy and I ran into each other last week at a party. Don't jump to any conclusions," he warned.

Leon was red with rage. "Now I understand why Lucy is in Cuba. Because of you! Did you come together? How long has—"

"No!" Lucy protested. "Leon, you're wrong!"

Leon faced Shoz, his body taut as a wire, his face filled with loathing. "You never did abduct her, did you? The two of you ran off together! Rathe Bragg couldn't allow that, of course, so he chased you down, then invented that kidnapping story! You think I don't know about the two of you in Paradise? I saw you kissing her at the barn the night of the birthday party!"

"So it *was* you," Shoz said softly.

"Yes," Leon snarled. "Get out! Both of you, get out now!"

Lucy was pale and shaken. Shoz guided her across the street and into a café. She did not protest. He led her to one of the small tables in the back.

She sat hard. "What were you thinking of to go and see Leon!"

"I should ask you the same question."

She was angry. "I was passing by and I just stopped to say hello to Janice."

"Oh, really? Best friends now, are we?"

"Yes, we are friends." She leaned forward. "I couldn't help but hear the two of you! Why did you go see Leon, Shoz?"

"I had information to give to him, Lucy, important information." He watched her anger fade, watched the bright, avid interest leap into her eyes.

"What information? How important?"

"That is none of your business."

She clenched her fist with a small cry, then glanced nervously around. "We shouldn't be here. Rather, you shouldn't be here. And don't be patronizing—I'm tired of it.''

He sighed. "I'm not being patronizing, I just want you to keep out of this war.''

She grimaced.

A waiter came and he ordered them espresso. When he had left, Lucy leaned forward. "How did it go last night?''

"Maybe I should ask you.''

"Don't start. What happened last night?''

"I'm here, aren't I? It went fine.''

She exhaled in relief.

Their gazes held. Everything that had passed between them yesterday came back to him, hard. He had spent too much time since he had last seen her thinking about what he had learned and all that she had said. Soon he was going to believe that she still cared for him, soon his own feelings were going to demand attention and identification. Things were happening too fast, too damn fast. Why was he so afraid of her—of himself? What in hell did she see in him, anyway?

"What are you thinking?" she asked softly, touching his hand. "Have you thought about what we discovered yesterday—about the divorce?''

He rose to his feet. "If you're waiting for some sort of declaration, you're going to wait a long time.''

She smiled up at him confidently. "I'll wait. You see, Shoz, you're only fooling yourself now, you're not fooling me. I know you care about me, and sooner or later, you're going to know it too.''

Still smiling, she stood, and he watched her walk away.

Lucy was in the midst of dressing for supper aboard the *Maine* with Captain Sigsbee and his executive officers. She sat at her dressing table, applying a fine coat of powder to her face. It was hard to concentrate; she was torn between powerful, conflicting emotions. On the one hand, she was thrilled with the turn of events—thrilled that she was still Shoz's wife. She had not a doubt about that, and now she could freely admit to herself how much she loved him, how she had never stopped loving him. Most important, now that she knew he was her husband, she was going to work on him until the discord and strife of the past was finally forgotten, until he accepted his own feelings and accepted her again as his wife.

On the other hand, she was desperately worried about Shoz now that Leon knew he was in Cuba. She was positive that Shoz was the daring rebel leader, El Americano. Gossip ran rampant in the small American community, and she had heard that it was El Americano who had rescued the rebel destined for execution. It was no coincidence, she was sure, that she had warned Shoz about the man's fate and that a rescue had ensued.

She worried that Leon would make the same connection that she had—that Shoz was El Americano. Oh, why had Shoz gone to the consulate! Did he court danger on purpose? And she had overheard more of their conversation than she'd let on. If Leon had shot Shoz in Paradise, would he do something awful again? If he ever informed the Spanish authorities that Shoz was a spy, or worse, that he was El Americano . . . Lucy shuddered to think of what might happen should Shoz be caught.

And what if Leon should spread rumors about her and Shoz—rumors that were almost entirely the truth? What if Leon wrote to Marianne that she was here? Lucy was already anxious about Captain Sigsbee's relationship with her uncle Brett. If they happened to correspond, he would undoubtedly mention her presence in Cuba, yet it was more likely that Leon would do so first. Either way, her father would become informed, and Lucy had not a doubt that Rathe would personally come running to Cuba to bring his runaway daughter home.

There was a knock and Venida bustled in. "You's got yoreself a caller, Miz Lucy."

Lucy rose, hoping it was Shoz. Maybe she had finally made some headway with him. Picking up her elbow-length black gloves and reticule, Lucy hurried downstairs.

Halfway down the stairs, she froze. Leon stood in the hall below, clad in a white dinner jacket, hands in his pockets. The hairs on the nape of her neck prickled with warning.

"He's the one, isn't he?"

Slowly Lucy continued down the stairs. "This is a surprise, Leon." Her heart was tumbling; she knew he was referring to Shoz.

"Is he?"

She tried to steer the conversation in another direction. "What are you doing here, Leon? I don't mean to be impolite, but I'm on my way out."

"I know." He grinned, the expression ugly. Leon seemed to be somewhat drunk. "Dinner aboard the *Maine*, right? Well, I've been invited too. Shall we ride together?"

It was the height of rudeness to refuse, but Lucy did. "I don't think so, Leon."

He grabbed her arm. "Why not? Afraid? Or expecting your lover?"

"That's enough," Lucy cried, trying to wrench away. He let her go. "I'm going to have to ask you to leave!"

"You are going to be sorry," he yelled, and then he marched away. The front door slammed behind him.

Lucy trembled. She was certain she had just made a serious mistake. She should have diffused the situation; instead she had made it worse.

Shoz knew he should stay away; he couldn't.

Their encounter earlier that day troubled him. He was torn, wanting to believe her, and fighting with himself. It was becoming an act of major willpower not to trust her, not to believe her. He had to battle himself, because he was afraid he was seriously falling for her, and he just couldn't see how their relationship could survive the misunderstandings of the past and their terribly different backgrounds.

He was careful to avoid being seen as he entered the small estate. A quick glance told him no one appeared to be home. It was just after nine. Who had she gone out with tonight? The thought infuriated him—she had no trouble amusing herself when he wasn't around. Jealousy washed over him. It was the height of irony; he was never faithful to any woman, and his lovers were always jealous of him, but since he had slept with Lucy in New York, there had been no one else. This time, she was the one with the scores of suitors; he was the one filled with doubt and jealousy. Maybe he should accept her stand that she was his wife. He would put an end to this kind of socializing, fast.

He banged on the front door loudly, no longer caring who heard or who saw him. An endless five minutes passed before Venida answered, frowning. "You's gonna wake the dead! Ain't you got no manners?"

"Where is your mistress?"

"She's out," Venida said bluntly. "An' if you think you's gonna wait, she ain't comin' back till way late!"

"Where is she?"

The words were said so ominously, Venida blinked. "Why, she's gone to sup with Captain Sigsbee—aboard the *Maine*."

"Benito, what time is it, do you think?"

Lucy was standing on the side of the road, just a mile or so from the harbor. She was watching her coachman repair one of the carriage's wheels, which a terrible rut had wrenched from its axle. Benito paused to look at her. "I don't know, señorita. Maybe nine-thirty, maybe ten o'clock."

Lucy bit her lip. She was terribly late; she was supposed to have been met at the wharf by a crewman and dinghy at nine, to be rowed out to the *Maine*. Walking had been out of the question. She wore a low-cut green gown which revealed far more than it covered. Diamond-set emeralds sparkled at her throat, from her ears, and on her left wrist. The neighborhood they were in was a crumbling slum. To walk would have invited assault and robbery by thieves.

She sighed with resignation. "How much longer, Benito?"

"I think I've almost fixed it, señorita."

Lucy was relieved. It was distinctly uncomfortable to be stranded for so long in this run-down section of Havana. Maybe she could still find someone to take her out to the *Maine*.

A boom sounded.

It came from the direction of the docks, and both Lucy and Benito jumped. "What was that?" Lucy asked.

The words had barely left her mouth when a rapid series

of explosions roared, one after the other, and the entire night above the sea burst into bright white light. Lucy jerked back, against the coach. She stared, wide-eyed. Another series of explosions ripped open the sky.

"*Por Dios!*" Benito cried.

Shoz rode across Havana in a mad, reckless gallop. He spurred his lathered black on, not allowing him to falter. He almost ran down those pedestrians and vehicles in his way. When the horse went down, half a mile from the docks, Shoz leaped from his back, landed on his feet, went to his knees, and bounced back up again. And he ran.

He ran until he thought his lungs would burst. He ran with Lucy's image etched irrevocably in his mind. He ran cursing Leon, the fucking fool. He ran until his heart seemed about to falter and give out, the way his stallion's had.

He was a block from the harbor when she came into sight, sleek and white and full-masted, basking in the moonlight. There was a tourist liner a few hundred yards away from the battleship, and the melancholy sound of a bugler playing taps on its deck drifted across the water. The air was hot, still, the harbor dead and silent except for the haunting strains of the bugle.

And then a boom sounded. The *Maine* jackknifed. Another series of explosions ripped open the keel, thrusting it up to the bridge. Instantly the ship was engulfed in flames.

Although half a block away, Shoz felt the ground under his feet lurch, sending him sprawling onto his hands and knees. He screamed in protest. The battleship was a raging inferno, and sailors were dropping from its sides into the water like ticks from a flame, some of them ablaze. Shoz clawed the dirt, praying he would see Lucy leaping into the sea, unhurt, but he saw no such thing. He jumped to his feet and hurled himself the rest of the way to the docks.

And then it became a time for action; there was no time to think. Men were screaming, on fire, trying to escape the burning ship. Others were hurt, and in their attempt to swim to shore, drowning. Another explosion sent blazing masts hurling to the decks and into the sea. Shoz saw a man going under the orange-black gleaming surface of the water. He dove in after him.

The water was warm, and brilliantly aglow from the fire-ridden battleship. Shoz came up for air, saw the man he'd gone after bobbing on the surface before sinking again. Holding his breath, he thrust himself down, down, unerringly pushing through the water in the direction of the sailor. Shoz was rewarded when he felt the man's thrashing limbs. He hauled them both to the surface, his lungs straining for air, threatening to explode. Treading, holding the unconscious man, he began gulping oxygen in. Then he towed the man ashore.

The relief effort took hours. Shoz threw himself into it with the firemen, police, and soldiers who had come to the ship's rescue. Every time he dragged a victim ashore, some already dead, or so badly crushed and burned, they had little chance of surviving, he glanced around, icy fear gripping him anew, searching for Lucy among the survivors. But there was no sign of her.

After towing some dozen or so wounded from the burning sea, Shoz collapsed on the ground not far from one of the treatment centers that had been set up by the medics. He had no strength left. His body was exhausted and numb, except for a pain in his heart that was so fierce, he was afraid to recognize it. But it wouldn't go away. It grew stronger. His mind was becoming coherent, savagely so, screaming at him.

She's dead!

She was on that ship, she's dead!

He realized he was gripping the dirt and trying to deny it when he knew there was no possibility she had survived. He was crying like a child. Crying his heart out, crying his guts out. He couldn't stop. There was fury in his tears, and he raised his fist at the sky and cursed the God he did not believe in. Then he cursed himself, blaming himself, blaming himself for not warning the *Maine,* for not warning her, blaming himself, God, why did he have to realize now how much he loved her, and yes, dammit, needed her? How could he go on like this?

In the chaos of the night, he was left alone. There were

a few solicitous inquiries by those thinking he was one of the explosions's victims until they realized he was lost in his own grief. Shoz wasn't sure how long he lay in the dirt sobbing. He wiped his eyes with a bare, salty forearm; apparently he had shed his shirt and boots some time ago. He inhaled, exhaled. He looked at the dirt, at the moon, anywhere but at the now-glowing skeleton of the battleship. Finally he looked at the ship again. Tears quickly blurred his vision.

He lunged to his feet. Slowly he began walking away from Havana Harbor. Behind him, in her death throes, the USS *Maine* began to sink. Shoz did not look back.

47

"Shoz!" Lucy called.

He was trudging away from the docks. His shoulders were slumped and he seemed so very tired, even defeated. Her heart went out to him. She was very proud of what he had done. She had arrived at the harbor to discover the *Maine* ablaze, shortly after hearing the explosions. Sometime later Lucy had glimpsed Shoz dragging a poor unconscious sailor from the sea. Lucy hadn't been able to go to him, however; she had been swallowed up by the relief effort, administering first aid to victim after victim until she barely knew what she was doing. Now, holding up the hem of her torn, dirty gown, her feet bare (having long since broken one high heel and removed her shoes), her jewels incongruously glinting fire around her face, she stumbled after Shoz.

"Shoz! Shoz! Wait!"

He stopped, trancelike, then slowly turned his head.

Lucy hurried to him, needing to be with him immensely

in that moment. Needing his comfort after all the horror she had witnessed, and wanting to offer him the same. "Are you all right?"

At first he did not react, staring as if she were an apparition risen from the dead, then he swept her into his embrace.

Lucy was stunned by his onslaught. He held her hard and fiercely against his frame. His face was buried against her neck. His hands stroked down her back, shaking with some unnamed, barely restrained emotion. Her lips felt the bare skin of his chest; he tasted like the sea. She clung back, relishing the moment, wanting it to never end.

"Are you all right?" she asked again, when he let a few inches slip between them.

He still held her. His voice was hoarse. "God, Lucy, I thought . . ."

She stared at him. "You thought what?"

In answer, he cupped her face and kissed her, his hands warm and strong and callused. Lucy allowed herself to succumb to the pleasure of the kiss, just for a minute. He embraced her again.

He put his arm around her and they walked a few paces back toward the harbor. "I thought you were on that ship," he said gruffly.

"You didn't see me with the other volunteers? I saw you rescuing some of the sailors."

"No, I didn't see you."

They sat down on a pile of heavy beams, Shoz clad only in his jeans, Lucy in her ripped and torn evening gown. He still had his arm around her, and she leaned against him wearily. She scouted for Leon, but she did not see him among the chaos of fire wagons and ambulances, firemen and medics, volunteers and victims. Lucy's stomach churned. "I was almost aboard her tonight."

"I know."

"Shoz, Leon was on board."

"I know."

"You know!"

"I saw him after he was rescued. He was badly burned. He died, Lucy."

Lucy gasped. Only a few hours ago, Leon had been

alive—and so angry at her. Had he still been in love with her? What did it even matter? He had done a terrible thing in shooting Shoz in Paradise, but she couldn't hate him, and certainly he didn't deserve this fate. "I can't believe it. No one deserves to die like that."

Shoz said, low, "I warned him. Today I warned him about this, but the fool thought I was out to embarrass him and create an incident. He didn't treat my warnings with the professionalism he should have because of his personal feelings for me."

"You knew!"

"If he had put the *Maine* on alert, this entire night might have never happened."

"And Leon might still be alive," Lucy murmured, dazed by the magnitude of what Leon had failed to do—and why.

Lucy stared at the bow and the naked burnt masts of the *Maine*, all that was left above the waterline. Shoz asked her why she hadn't been on board, his hand on her shoulder, kneading her flesh soothingly, helping to ease the horror of the night. She told him about how they'd lost a wheel, which was why she had never made it aboard the battleship.

They fell into an exhausted silence, neither one making any move to leave, leaning on each other. Wagons rolled past them, taking load after load of victims to the hospitals. Relief workers hurried to and fro. A pair of soldiers rode by.

They watched the activity around them with detached interest. Lucy was very aware of the bond between them; it seemed stronger than ever, and different. For the first time they seemed to be more than lovers, they seemed to be partners, friends.

Shoz finally stood. "I'll find us some transportation and take you home."

Lucy nodded, unable to refrain from smiling in both gratitude and pleasure. Not just because she was exhausted, but because their relationship had suddenly, drastically, changed for the better.

Lucy awoke early despite the toll of the night before. Bright tropical sunlight was streaming through the open balcony doors. She hadn't slept well at all, despite her utter exhaustion, for her dreams had been filled with the bloody deaths she had witnessed the previous night. She had even dreamed of Leon, badly burned but alive and accusing her of leaving him for Shoz.

Upon awakening, her first coherent thought was that the *Maine* had been blown up, so many had died, Leon had died. And Shoz had been here with her last night.

He had taken her home as he had promised. Lucy could not remember the ride, but she did remember him soothing a shocked Venida that she was indeed all right before helping her upstairs. Lucy could recall little else, so apparently she had slept for a while.

She opened her eyes to find him on the chaise, clad only in his jeans, sipping pungent coffee. She froze at the sight of him; he set the cup down. It was the first time he had stayed the entire night with her, and they hadn't even slept together. A jumbled kind of soaring elation swept her, and she sat up, her hopeful gaze gaining his attention.

"Good morning," Shoz said. His expression was impossible to read.

She managed a smile. She realized that she was utterly nude beneath the sheets; he had obviously undressed her last night. Into her happiness came a hot, heady desire. "You stayed."

"I wanted to make sure you're all right."

She sat up straighter, holding the sheet against her chest. "Last night was hell."

"Yeah," he said roughly.

Lucy started wondering how she might get Shoz to approach—and climb into bed with her. She wanted him; after last night, she *needed* him.

Silence filled the room, stretching taut between them. The birds outside broke it with their cheerful morning songs. Shoz stood. Her gaze was drawn to his hard, muscular body, the bare chest and lean torso, the tight Levis. God, how she needed him; he could chase away all the awful memories that had haunted her sleep, even if only for a while.

"I should go," he said, and he walked toward her.

She gripped the sheet. "I don't want you to go."

"I know." He sat by her hip, taking her hands in his. "I don't want to go."

"Then don't."

He pulled her forward; the sheet fell to her waist. His eyes, drifting from her mouth to her breasts, grew distinctly smoky. "Do you know what you're saying?"

"Yes."

"No, I don't think you do." He held her tightly, their bodies not quite touching. "This time," he warned, "it's you and me—no Leons, no Sigsbees, just you and me."

Her heart leapt in excitement and joy. "I understand."

"This time, there won't be any turning back."

She made a sound, swaying closer.

"You belong to me, Lucy, and I don't share what's mine."

"Yes." It was a whispered breath.

His face tightened, as if he fought to control his own emotions. Abruptly he got up and locked the door. He came to her with long, hard strides, his hands already working the zipper of his jeans, the fabric of his groin already becoming taut. He yanked them down his legs. Lucy's breath got stuck somewhere in her chest. His gaze met hers, hot, intense. He pulled the sheet from her body. "This time there won't be anything—or anyone—between us."

"Oh God," Lucy said, before he slid her beneath him.

He took her like it was the last time—or the first. Lucy's response was just as fevered and impatient, just as frenzied and exultant. Hot and hard, their mouths fused, hands rough and soft everywhere. Shoz had never been one for words in bed; this time he told her, his voice low and husky, how beautiful she was, how much he wanted her, and how afraid he had been that he had lost her. It was like a dream. When he slid deeply into her, Lucy wept in ecstasy. After, holding him, she wept again. She thought that his face, pressed against hers, was moist as well.

They fought afterward.

After their glorious lovemaking, he told her that she had to leave Cuba and return home. "Cuba's no place for a woman alone," he had said softly, his hand caressing the curve of her hip. "There's a freighter outbound this afternoon; I'll try to get you on it."

"No."

His eyes darkened. "Why not?"

"I've told you from the beginning that I won't leave."

"You know as well as I do what the tragedy last night means! Cuba was never safe—and now it's going to be worse. You can't stay here alone."

"I'm not alone."

"What the hell does that mean?"

"It means that I have you."

He laughed derisively. "I can't baby-sit you! I shouldn't even be in Havana these days! Things are going to break loose, Lucy, and I won't be around to save your neck when it needs saving."

"I'm not leaving Havana, Shoz."

He lunged from the bed to dress. Lucy watched him, tight-lipped and so terribly sad after the closeness she had thought they had found. He paused at the door. "Be ready to leave this afternoon, Lucy."

"I won't," she cried, frightened by the implacable expression on his face. His only answer was one long, dark look. Tears welling, she hurled a book at the door as it slammed behind him, and it just happened to be a Bible. "Go to hell," she cried.

She wasn't going to leave Cuba, not with him here, not with war apparently just around the corner. Never. But would it always be this way between them? Lucy wondered miserably. One moment extreme passion, the next extreme anger? Had the closeness she had thought they had shared been merely an illusion? Was she being a fool?

Lucy chose to treat the day as if Shoz had not stated that she should be ready to depart the country that afternoon. She went to the consulate, determined to assess the state of affairs for herself. It was in a state of chaos, as she had expected, but she boldly elbowed her way to Janice, anyway. "You shouldn't be here," the secretary said, looking harassed.

"I was there last night; I have to know what's happening."

"So far," Janice said grimly, "two hundred and fifty-seven men have died. Lucy, you should get out of Cuba. Look at this."

She pointed to a bold headline on top of the many papers on her desk. It was a wire from the States, and the first line read: PUBLIC BLAMES SPAIN CLAMORS FOR WAR.

"It's only a matter of time," Janice said.

Lucy left, dismayed. American intervention would help the desperate rebels attain their independence, and Lucy had already been swept up in their cause. Before today, before Shoz's threat, Lucy had hoped for her country's intervention. But she had never considered what a war between Spain and the United States might really mean. And suddenly she was afraid.

As she returned to the villa, the image of hostile troops entrenched on Havana's streets, facing each other, smoke obscuring the scene, guns and artillery firing, soldiers dying, civilians running, buildings crumbling, Havana aflame, etched itself in her mind.

Was she wrong to insist on remaining in Cuba now? But she just couldn't leave Shoz, not if there was going to be a war!

Once she had returned, she hurried into the kitchen to find Venida, who suddenly loomed as a source of stability and comfort. Venida was unpacking a dozen boxes.

"What are you doing?" Lucy asked.

"I's been all over Havana this mornin'," Venida said. "One thin's for sure, when the fightin' starts, we ain't gonna starve."

Lucy's heart skipped a beat; Venida had been stocking up on canned and dried foodstuffs. "So you think there will be a war."

"I's afraid, Miz Lucy, I's afraid."

When Shoz didn't come that afternoon, Lucy began to breathe easier, thinking he had changed his mind, that he would not send her away from Cuba. That night Lucy thought about nothing other than war, afraid of all that might happen, afraid not just for herself, but for Shoz, imagining the fighting, the bloodshed, him fleeing deep into the jungle to escape Spanish troops. It was almost midnight when he stepped into her room, and Lucy was so glad he had come.

"What's going to happen?"

"War. It's only a matter of time. My guess is American troops will arrive in a month or two."

"That long?"

"Congress will debate, and they have to be mobilized, supplied, coordinated, transported—that long." His look was grim.

"What is it? What's wrong?"

"I couldn't get you on that freighter, but I've arranged alternate transportation. Get dressed."

"Now!"

"You're going back to the States—tonight."

She drew herself up. "No."

"You're going, Lucy."

"Only if you come with me."

"I can't come."

"Of course you can come!" she cried, her heart thundering, her palms wet. "Shoz, I can't leave without you!"

His expression tightened. "I won't let you stay."

Lucy was so desperately afraid. Staring back at him with real panic, she knew that this time she was going to lose, this time he would do as he willed. "Why can't I stay? Why won't you leave? You've done enough for the United States! My family can help if you're worried about the government and your pardon!"

"My work isn't done, it's only beginning." He smiled ruefully. "I can't leave these people, Lucy. They need me."

She blinked. "This has nothing to do with the presidential pardon, does it? This is no longer just a job for you, is it?"

"It hasn't been just a job for a very long time, and no, this doesn't have anything to do with the damn pardon for my crimes." His gaze met hers.

Her heart swelled with pride against a backdrop of choking terror. "You believe in *Cuba Libre*."

"I believe in *Cuba Libre*," he said.

An hour later, Lucy said good-bye to Venida in the dimly lit foyer of the villa. The big woman was sniffling noisily, and her dark eyes glistened with tears. She rocked Lucy in her arms. "You listen to Mistah Shoz an' you do everythin' he says," she ordered, bossy to the end.

"I'll try," Lucy said, crying. "Thank you for being such a good friend, Venida. I don't know what I would have done without you."

"You's would have got yorese'f in loads mo' trouble, that's what," she said, wiping her eyes with her apron.

"Come with me," Lucy cried impulsively, grabbing her hands.

"I wish I could, Miz Lucy, but I got me two grown boys, and they's got good wives and little childs heah. I can't leave my family now."

Lucy hugged her again, weeping anew. It was Shoz who finally separated them, murmuring that they had to go. "I'll be back, I promise," Lucy said.

Venida managed to smile, waving farewell.

Once outside and mounted, Lucy was silent, sick with their impending separation. She had stopped pleading with Shoz when he had explained quietly to her why she must go. He was a survivor, and he intended to survive this war. He intended to ensure his own safety, and that of his men. What he did not need was her presence in a war-ravaged land, constantly distracting him. She would be an extra, real burden, she would preoccupy him; because of her, he might find that stray bullet. And they both knew that with the passage of the merest amount of time, no matter how dangerous the risk, he would ride the length and breadth of Cuba just for a glimpse of her.

Lucy knew Shoz, and she knew that if she managed to defy him and remain in Cuba, she would be his Achilles' heel. Silent, numb, she had resigned herself to departing. But it was happening so fast. And God, she had a feeling she just couldn't shake, the worst feeling—that it was going to be a very long time before she ever saw him again.

Their horses' hooves had been wrapped in burlap so they wouldn't make any noise as they left the city. It was a blessedly dark, starless night. Because of the destruction of the *Maine* the night before, Spanish patrols were everywhere. A network of alleys crisscrossed the city, and Lucy and Shoz stayed exclusively within their confines until they were out of Havana. They followed a narrow dirt track north and then turned toward the coast. A short time later, they had crested the last dunes and rode down to a sandy stretch of beach below them. In the near-black night, the breakers frothed starkly white against the purple sea and pale beach. Lucy could see a yacht bobbing at anchor, waiting for her. Her heart was shattering into tiny little pieces.

They came to a stop. The man who would take her to Key West sauntered forward with a greeting. Shoz slipped from his horse and came to her. Lucy slid down into his arms. She clung to him. She told herself she would not cry.

"It's not forever," he said gently.

"Oh God," she gasped, and she wept.

"Lucy . . ." He faltered, embracing her hard. The man turned away, gazing out at the sea. Lucy tore her face from his chest to stare up at him. "I love you."

"I do, too," he said gruffly.

"Get word to me," she demanded, gripping him tightly.

"If you don't hear from me, it's because I couldn't get through—don't think the worst."

She cried again.

"Listen to me: I'll be all right." He forced her chin up. "Don't you believe me?"

She nodded, she did, but she was so afraid, and she didn't. War made even the immortal mortal.

He kissed her. Shoz finally pulled free and took her arm, walking her down to the water until it lapped their feet.

The man held the small rubber dinghy that would take him and Lucy to the yacht. A lonely star blinked. Lucy grabbed Shoz's hand, held it like a lifeline. Gently he pried her loose, kissed her nose, and lifted her into the dinghy. He tossed in her one small bag. She watched him standing in the knee-deep water. The dinghy moved as the man pushed it into the surf, then he leaped in. He began rowing; Shoz was already ten feet from her, then fifteen. She could not, would not, take her eyes off him.

"Wait for me," he said.

She lifted her hand, watching him as the dinghy took her farther and farther away, watching him as he grew smaller and smaller, watching him until he became a speck on the shore, watching him until she couldn't see him anymore.

PART FOUR

THE FIRES OF PARADISE

PARADISE, TEXAS

48

September 1898

Seven long months had passed since Lucy had returned to New York from Cuba. Congress had declared war on April 19, and the president had called for 125,000 volunteers to augment the small regular army. Three regiments were to be composed of frontiersmen with special qualifications as horsemen and marksmen. One of those regiments was commanded by Colonel Leonard Wood, and second in command was Theodore Roosevelt.

The regiment was quickly nicknamed Roosevelt's Rough Riders, and in June they engaged in their first victory in Cuba in the bloody Battle of Guasimas. A spectacular and even more bloody victory followed on July 1, when the Rough Riders led a courageous assault on the San Juan Hills, taking them and sending the Spanish fleeing. The hills commanded Santiago—thus began the siege of Santiago. Delicate negotiations ensued, and on July 17 the Santiago garrison surrendered and Spain had fallen.

The fighting had been over for two months now, but Lucy had not heard from Shoz since early June—before the Battle of Guasimas. The letter she had received had been too brief. He had written a bit about the impending war and everyone's expectations, but not much else. But he had written that he missed her, one single line that meant more to her than anything else could have, except the words "I love you". She had supposed that they, too, would come in time.

Now she did not know what to think. Lucy was tired of waiting for word that did not come. Where was he? Why hadn't she heard from him? Every day she expected him to

suddenly appear on her doorstep, and every night she went
to bed sick with disappointment and growing dread. What
if he had been hurt? What if he had been killed?

Whenever that kind of horrible thought arose, she
quenched it instantly. Shoz wasn't dead. If he were, she
would know it, she would feel it, she was certain. No, he
wasn't dead, but maybe he was hurt, or in trouble. Then
again, the arduous peace negotiations had not yet been con-
cluded, and American troops still remained in Cuba. Maybe
he had remained behind as well, for some nefarious purposes.

Lucy cabled the American consul in Havana several
times. Leon's replacement had not seen or heard from Shoz
since early August. Lucy turned to her father for help.

Her parents knew nearly everything. When she had arrived in New York on the first of March, they had just found
out from Marianne Claxton that Lucy was in Cuba, and that
Shoz was there, too. Leon had obviously written to his
mother before he had died, as Lucy had feared he would.

But now Lucy had no more secrets to keep. She bluntly
reaffirmed her love for Shoz, then went on to tell them how
his signature on her divorce papers was a forgery—and that
they were still man and wife. "And I am going to be his
wife in every sense of the word when he returns from
Cuba," she ended.

Rathe was furious, so furious he disappeared for several
days. When he returned, Lucy discovered that he had gone
to Washington to confront Lloyd, determined to get to the
truth. Because Rathe could not seem to discuss anything
involving Shoz with her at all, Lucy found out from Grace
that Lloyd had indeed forged Shoz's original signature onto
a fresh set of divorce papers, using the artist from the
Brownsville Chronicle. As Shoz had guessed, Lloyd had
never thought it possible that his deception would be uncovered.

While Rathe was gone, Grace had become her confidante.
Although Lucy loved her mother dearly, she had never been
quite as close to her as to her father, for her mother was so
fervently involved in her various political and social causes.
Now they became very close. Her mother listened to the

incredible tale of all her daughter's adventures. "I am so proud of the woman you have become," she said when Lucy had finished. Lucy didn't think she would ever forget those words.

After his return from Washington, Rathe never brought up the topic of Shoz again, yet Lucy knew he was by no means reconciled to her marriage to him. She was also certain that her mother was encouraging him to bend, and she could only hope that one day he would forget the past, and think of the future instead.

But now she needed his help, and boldly she turned to him. "I want to find Shoz Cooper, Daddy," she told Rathe.

They were in his oak-paneled study, and Rathe's pleasant expression faded. "This is no young girl's infatuation, is it, Lucy?" he asked quietly. He'd had a long seven months to adjust to the fact that his daughter was still married to the man who had abducted her.

"No, Daddy, it's not. The young girl you keep trying to hold on to grew up a long time ago."

Heavily he sat down. "Your mother keeps telling me to give the man a chance, that he was an innocent victim of Marianne's spite and that now he's a bloody hero."

She leaned forward on his desk eagerly. "I wish you would."

His response was to open the drawer of his desk. He handed her a slip of paper containing Lloyd's name, a telephone number, and an address in Washington, D.C. Tears in her eyes, Lucy hugged him.

Grace wished her well, and Lucy left for Washington immediately upon making an appointment to see Lloyd. Her excitement at having found him turned to anger over how he had duped Shoz into signing away his half of their marriage. She reminded herself that that was the past, and locating Shoz was her utmost goal; there was no point in bringing up his treachery at all.

Lloyd told her that Shoz had left Cuba in July, finally released from his duties there—and he did not know where he had gone.

Lucy was momentarily crushed. If he had left in July, why hadn't he come to her? She sat in his office fighting not to show her torn emotions, while Lloyd rose to his feet, impatient and obviously wanting her to go.

But Lucy didn't move. Shoz hadn't come for her, and she didn't know why. She couldn't accept that. He had told her to wait for him, and even if he hadn't, she would have. Why hadn't he come?

Lucy organized her thoughts. She knew what she wanted—she wanted him. He was all right, unhurt, he was not in Cuba. She would find him. Oh, she would find him. If he thought he could leave her behind, he was wrong. She would hunt his miserable hide down.

"Miss Bragg," Lloyd prodded. "I'm afraid I have another appointment."

Lucy looked up, eyes wide as an idea struck her. "Do you know now where his old hideout in Mexico is? Death Valley?" Shoz had gone to Roberto—she knew it!

"Yes," Lloyd said slowly. "It was always understood that we could reach him there if he wasn't in Cuba, and besides, a part of our deal was to send supplies there on a monthly basis to provide for the woman and child."

Lucy froze, her excitement replaced by a sickening fear. All the time he had been in Cuba, he had provided for Carmen and her son through U.S. auspices. She told herself that of course he had to make sure they were cared for when he was gone, but the sick feeling remained. "I'd like the exact directions," she said. "You see, I'm going to Death Valley."

He shrugged and told her how a man named Foster in San Antonio had packed the supplies into Death Valley every month, and he told her how to contact him. Lucy finally rose to her feet, but she did not thank him.

"It's not Miss Bragg," she said coolly, "or have you forgotten your little deception in Brownsville? *It's Mrs. Cooper.*"

His eyes widened for a fraction of a second, but Lucy was already sailing out the door.

Death Valley.

The feeling of déjà vu was strong for Lucy as, two weeks later, she and the guide named Foster made the final, treacherous descent into the hellhole where once she had been Shoz's prisoner. As her mount picked his way down the steep, rocky trail, Lucy was a bundle of taut nerves. She could already feel the valley closing in on her, like some mythical monster, could feel its desire to swallow her up— and never let her out again. But that was just fantasy, she reminded herself, gazing up at those pale, soaring yellow walls. They spanned the trail overhead, blocking out the sky. Lucy wondered if one day those walls wouldn't decide to just come crashing down on whoever dared to enter here.

There was no winter in Death Valley. It was hot, so hot, airless, arid. They left the descent and reached the flat basin. Blazing yellow sand stretched away from her, low scrubs fought viciously for a hold on life. And all around her were those familiar, overpowering walls, blocking out the sky, the sun, all sense of reality.

The valley struck her as a living thing that was, at the same time, dead. She stared at Foster's back. He, too, seemed affected by the valley—usually he was quite garrulous, and he had entertained her frequently with amusing anecdotes of his well-worn life. But this past hour he had been uncharacteristically silent. He must feel the valley's eerie spirit too.

The valley suddenly opened, and the sky appeared above them. Lucy breathed again. She was sweating heavily, and she blotted her face with a handkerchief. Was Shoz here? Would they finally be reunited?

Déjà vu. They rode past a scene that was identical to the one she had witnessed the first time she had entered the valley as Shoz's prisoner. Women paused in their tasks by the flat, sluggish creek, staring. Children who had been racing in games of tag turned to gaze at them. Even the toddlers making sand pies in the earth stopped, regarding them.

The outline of the adobe structures ahead grew clearer. Lucy's heart was pounding fiercely now. On the one hand there was such joy—on the other, if he had been living here with Carmen, she would kill him.

They rode up to the front of the house. Déjà vu. With a screech, Carmen came flying out of the house and down

the porch steps in a blur of rainbow colors, just as she had
a year and a half ago.

And Lucy knew he wasn't here.

Carmen halted; Lucy stopped her mount. Carmen's eyes
went wide; Lucy stared back. The two women regarded
each other. Lucy's heart was thundering. Carmen, her enemy, once her rival—still her rival? The woman was as
stunning as ever; she would turn any man's head. "Is Shoz
here?"

Carmen's fists found her hips. "His *puta* returns. No."

"I'm afraid you're mistaken, Carmen. I'm not his
whore—you're his whore. I'm his wife."

Carmen reeled back, shocked. "Liar! Liar!"

"Was he here?"

"Yes!"

Her heart clenched. "Is he coming back?"

Carmen's chin lifted. "Yes."

"Then I'll wait," Lucy said, slipping off her mount. He
hadn't come for her, she thought in terrible distress, and he
had been here, he was returning here.

"You will not." Carmen strode to her, took her shoulder,
and spun her roughly around.

Anger ignited. Lucy knocked the other woman's hand
away, hard. *"Don't touch me."*

Carmen's smile was a nasty baring of her teeth. "You
can leave now."

"I'm not leaving. Where is Roberto? In his room?" She
didn't wait for an answer, she pushed past Carmen, but
every instinct she had was attuned to the other woman's
response.

It came. Carmen shrieked in hatred and grabbed Lucy's
elbow, wrenching her back. Lucy doubled up her arm and
socked Carmen with all her might, a powerful blow to her
nose. With a cry of pain, Carmen fell into the dust on her
backside, holding her bleeding nose.

Panting, Lucy stood over her. "If you touch me again,
I will really hurt you." The words were hard and flat.

"Now, wait a minute," Foster cried. "You gals—"

"Stay out of this, Mr. Foster," Lucy warned. Carmen

still sat sprawled in the dust, her palm covering her nose. "Do you understand me, Carmen?"

The look of hatred Carmen sent her was intense.

Lucy turned and walked into the house, feeling no sense of triumph, sober at having done what she'd had to do. Déjà vu. Everything was so familiar, the cool white walls, the stone floors, Carmen's things scattered around the living room. "Roberto?" she called softly. The house was so quiet, so lifeless, like some sleeping, brooding giant. "Roberto?" She pushed open the door to his room. She gasped.

The room was empty, abandoned, a sterile shell of what it had been. Roberto was obviously gone and not coming back. Suddenly Lucy lunged into Shoz's room across the hall. All of his heavy law books were gone—not a volume remained on the shelves. She threw open the armoire and pushed through the clothes within. All Carmen's—not a single item of man's clothing. She ran back outside.

Carmen sat on the steps of the porch, holding a wet rag to her nose. Foster stood over her. "He's not coming back!" Lucy cried, powerful joy surging through her. "He's taken Roberto and he's not coming back!"

Carmen stood. "He'll come back," she spat. "He always comes back to me."

Lucy suddenly felt sorry for her. "There's no reason for you to stay now, Carmen; we both know he's not coming back. You can leave with us tomorrow morning."

Carmen raised her chin proudly. "I'm not leaving. And he will come back."

They left Death Valley at daybreak: Lucy and Foster. As they rode away, Lucy turned to look back at Carmen's colorful figure standing in front of the house, glaring after them. Tremendous pity welled up within her for the other woman, her onetime rival for the man she loved. Carmen refused to leave the valley. But she was not alone. The outlaws still lived here, and there was the lost village with its inhabitants. Last night Carmen had danced passionately in front of a bonfire for the applauding men, their gypsy queen. Queen of the valley and all within.

Did Carmen really believe that Shoz would come back?

Lucy hoped not. Yet an image would not leave her, a terrible, poignant image of an old, gray woman running from the house every time a visitor came to the valley—expecting a man who never came.

49

September 1898

Shoz disembarked at the railhead in Paradise.

Strong memories had assailed him from the moment he had first arrived in Galveston, a few weeks ago, and had continued as he had gone on to Death Valley to get Roberto, just as they continued now. Lucy's presence seemed to linger everywhere, embracing him fiercely.

When he had left Cuba toward the end of July, he had almost gone directly to New York for Lucy. He missed her terribly, he could barely stand it. But she had his letter; she knew he was safe and on his way. Roberto was just a small lonely child who missed his father, who could not completely understand why there had been this year-long separation, and from Cuba, Mexico was on the way to New York. But most important, after picking up Roberto, he had to pay a crucial call in Paradise—it was time to set the record straight with the family patriarch, Derek Bragg.

Lucy was his wife, she belonged to him. He couldn't live without her, didn't even want to—he loved her. Living in hell, facing the dark jaws of death, made a man face his deepest, darkest emotions, his deepest, darkest fears.

He wasn't going to question why she loved him anymore. It was time to accept it, time to embrace the future—their future.

Now he wanted the acceptance of her family, if not their

approval. He sensed that his best chance was with Derek, and that eventually, once he gained the old man's acceptance, her father and mother would come around.

From Paradise it was a short ride to the D&M, with Roberto wide-eyed, taking in all the sights with awe, as he had done since they had left Death Valley. He also squirmed with excitement, for Shoz had told him that the D&M was Lucy's grandparents' home.

Miranda greeted them at the door, drying her hands on her apron. She blinked in surprise at Shoz, then took in Roberto standing beside him. "Mr. Cooper. This is a surprise!"

He smiled, showing one rare dimple. "You used to call me Shoz, ma'am," he said, hastily removing his hat. He gave Roberto a look; the boy imitated his father. "This is my son, Roberto."

Miranda smiled. "Well, then, Shoz, won't you come in? Hello, Roberto. I'll bet you would love some chocolate cookies still warm from the oven!"

Roerto nodded solemnly.

Miranda shooed them in. Her lucid gaze held Shoz immobile for a moment, and he had the fleeting feeling that she knew why he was here, and was not at all surprised. "You wish to see my husband?"

Shoz nodded. He waited impatiently while she went to fetch him, his mouth suddenly dry, as nervous as an adolescent at his first barn dance. What if he couldn't convince the old man that he was good enough for Lucy? Hearing Bragg's footfalls, Shoz looked up. The older man stared. "Hello, Shoz."

"Mr. Bragg."

A silence fell. Miranda took Roberto into the kitchen. Derek finally gestured and they walked into his office. Neither man sat. "I've come to discuss your grandaughter."

"Why with me?"

"You're the head of this family, and I want to make amends. I know if I gain your approval, the rest will come, eventually."

"You're asking for a lot."

"I'm asking for my due. To be judged fairly. I've got

my pardon now, and you damn well know I earned it. I'm
a free man—and I love Lucy.''

"I see." Derek sat down, but Shoz remained standing.
"I know you earned your pardon, Shoz, because I've kept
in touch with certain people in Washington—just as I've
kept in touch with my son and granddaughter.''

Now it was Shoz's turn to be puzzled. "And?"

"And I learned a lot about you. Six months ago I also
received a ten-page letter from Lucy. I would say that now
I know just about everything worth knowing about you,
Shoz.''

"And?" he demanded again. "Do you know that our
divorce is phony? That Lucy is still my wife?"

"I know about the divorce and Lloyd."

"So am I going to get your blessing or not?"

"You deserve a whole lot more than just my blessing,"
Derek said softly.

Lucy's spirits were low by the time she arrived at the
D&M. She had already cabled the Pinkerton agency from
San Antonio and instructed them to contact her in Paradise.
She would not waste any time in hiring detectives to find
Shoz. Where the hell could he be if he had left Death Valley
with Roberto?

Lucy was tired and desperately craving a bath when the
buggy she had hired in Paradise finally drove her up the
long, winding drive toward the big white ranch house. Despite her frustration and worries, it was soothing and peaceful to be back in Paradise, it was like a long-awaited
homecoming. Lucy turned to watch the Thoroughbred yearlings in the whitewashed paddock gallop alongside her
buggy, stretching out their young limbs, testing themselves,
running for the sheer joy of it, and she smiled. She turned
to look up at the house on the hill. Purple and white petunias
spilled across the veranda in gay profusion. Lucy smiled
again.

"Lucy!"

Lucy froze. Suddenly her pulse roared in her ears. What
she had heard could not possibly be real.

Lucy turned as Roberto flew across the lawn to her. She

opened her arms wide. He halted abruptly, beaming but hanging back shyly.

Shoz is here, she managed to think. "What's this?" she cried. "No hug?"

He grinned and raced into her embrace. When she let him go, she wiped tears from her eyes. "Is your father here?"

"He's inside," Roberto said.

"Come on, then." Lucy took his hand. Her mind could barely grasp what was happening; elation pumped in her veins. *Shoz is here.* Here!

Lucy raced through the foyer, heard his voice, and without pausing, skidded into the parlor. Shoz saw her at that exact moment. He was sitting on the sofa; he froze. Then his eyes sparked and he jumped to his feet with a glad cry she could not mistake. "Lucy!"

Before she could move, he was on her and hauling her into his embrace. He kissed her. Lucy melted, clinging, tears of joy streaming down her face.

He kissed her endlessly, and it became hot and hard, his tongue thrusting deeply into her mouth, his body pressing against hers hungrily. They had forgotten they were not alone, they had forgotten Roberto and her grandparents. Miranda was shooing Derek and Roberto out of the room; neither Shoz nor Lucy noticed. All Lucy could comprehend was that they were together again, finally, and God, she had missed him, missed him so much. When they finally came apart, panting and shaking, she was crying. "Where have you been!"

"I told you to wait for me in New York!"

They stared at each other, barely able to comprehend one another.

"Come on," Lucy said, clutching Shoz's hand. Although they were miraculously alone, the parlor was not private enough. Barely swallowing her happy laughter, she pulled Shoz behind her and they ran out of the house.

They ran outside and down the porch steps and to the old white swing her grandfather had built for Miranda back in 1841. Lucy's laughter finally escaped, bubbling merrily, uncontainable, and Shoz laughed, too, the sound warm and rich.

"I went to Death Valley, looking for you." She held his hands—or he held hers.

"Didn't you get my letter?"

"What letter?" she cried. She was in his arms again. He was kissing her again. He was tall and powerful and male and she clung, never wanting to let go. His hands slid down her, shaking in passion; his body trembled. But so did Lucy's. He began kissing away the tears that still fell.

Shoz suddenly broke free to put his arm around her, and they stumbled down the hill. He kissed her ear. Lucy tried to kiss his mouth, which was impossible as they slipped and tripped down the slope. "I missed you so much," he growled, his hand tightening on her waist.

"I love you so much," she said, as he led her into the first barn they came to.

His response was indistinct and he pushed her up the ladder. They fell into the hay of the loft, grabbing wildly at each other's clothes. He fumbled with the buttons of her shirtwaist, she yanked his shirt from his trousers and ripped it open, eagerly touching the bare, hot, hard flesh of his abdomen.

"Hell," he said, and tore her blouse open as well. They both laughed.

Their laughter died. Shoz pushed aside her undergarments to bare her breasts and bury his face between them. Lucy went completely still. He came up for air, then touched her, caressed her, gently, softly, then faster and faster. Lucy arched beneath him and pulled his mouth to hers. Teeth grinded, hips pumped. Shoz shoved up her skirts. She wrenched his fly open. He thrust his huge rock hardness deep inside her.

Afterward they talked. There was so much to catch up on. Shoz found out that Lucy had never gotten his second letter, and Lucy found out why he had not come for her first, and of course, it made so much sense.

They talked about the war. After San Juan, the government had wanted Shoz to stay in Cuba to continue spying among the rebels, but he had insisted on leaving. The war had been bloody, the casualities terribly high. He had escaped unscathed, fortunately, and he admitted rawly that a day hadn't passed that he hadn't thought of her.

Lucy wanted to know about Carmen. Shoz had paid her well, and in return he had adopted Roberto—actually, the paperwork had been filed just before he'd left for Cuba a year ago. As far as Carmen went, and Shoz had smiled with amusement, he hadn't touched her since he and Lucy became lovers in Death Valley. Lucy was terribly pleased.

She had dreamed of the day he would ask her to marry him again, and rectify the divorce, but she could not restrain herself. Sitting up, magnificently naked, while he lay casually on his back, head on his hands, she blurted, "I want to get married."

He looked at her. His mouth quirked. "We're already married, or have you forgotten?"

Her eyes widened. "Now you realize! I want us to get married again, properly. Officially we are divorced—only you and I and my parents and grandparents know the truth. So we *have* to get married."

"Lucy." He sat up, serious. "Why are you so determined to be my wife?"

She became very still, as serious as he was, sensing the tremendous importance of the question. "Because I love you."

"Why?"

"Because you're the finest man I know." She smiled, her eyes blurring a little, wanting to chase away his dark demons once and for all. "I realized I loved you in Death Valley, when I saw what a wonderful, warm, loving father you are. But I fell in love with you in Paradise. You tried to be dark and dangerous—and you are—but you're also the bravest, strongest man I know. My mother thinks you're a hero—and so do I."

"All right."

"All right?" Her heart leapt. "You accept?"

"I do."

Lucy gave a cry of joy and beamed. She was ecstatic, even if he was the one who was supposed to do the proposing and even if they were already married—sort of. And to her surprise, Shoz was smiling, too, and the smile reached clear into his soul.

Lucy dragged Shoz into the house with her and found her grandparents with Roberto in the kitchen with glasses of milk and apple pie. "We're getting married again and you're the first to know!" Lucy cried to her grandparents.

A wide smile suffused Derek's face, and Miranda beamed. Derek came to them and wrapped Lucy in a hug. "About damn time," he said softly.

For once, Miranda did not chastise his language, and she, too, embraced her granddaughter. "I knew it!" she cried. "I knew it from the start! I'm so happy for you, darling!"

Derek smacked Shoz's shoulder. Their gazes met and held for one intimate moment. Miranda reached up to clasp his face and pull him down to kiss his cheek. He blushed.

"When's the date?"

"Tomorrow," Shoz said.

"June," Lucy said.

They looked at each other in gentle dismay. "I want to get married tomorrow," he said firmly.

"We can't get married tomorrow." Lucy was serene.

"Why the hell not?"

"Because I want a big wedding—and that takes preparation and time."

He stared at her.

"Darling," Miranda said, "a big wedding would not be seemly; after all, this is either your second wedding or a renewal of your vows, depending upon how one chooses to view matters. And there was the scandal. No, it should be small and intimate, just family and a few good friends, but we can make it stunning. And you have to wait for her parents," she added to Shoz.

He smirked, the victory seemingly his. Lucy smiled back, much too sweetly. "Oh no," she said. "I want a *big* wedding. In June. I always wanted to get married in June, in Paradise, right here, outside on the lawn."

Shoz growled.

Worriedly Miranda said, "Just how big a wedding did you have in mind, my dear?"

"I want at least a thousand guests," Lucy said with relish. "I want *all* of Daddy's and Grandpa's friends and *half* of New York Society and *most* of Texas. And the *entire* family, of course." She smiled wickedly. "I want this to be the wedding of the *century*—after all, it's not every day a girl gets married for the *second* time—to the man of her dreams."

"Oh dear," Miranda said.

Shoz couldn't sleep.

He wondered if his happiness was as evident as Lucy's. She was walking around as if floating on air—and he felt the same way. Now, outside in the black of midnight, he strolled down to one of the paddocks to stare at the moon, think, and wait.

Lucy and Miranda had done nothing but talk and plan the wedding of the century since this afternoon, and an hour ago he had left them ensconced in the library, still planning. Although he was very impatient to have her in his arms again, and he had been waiting for hours for her to go up to bed so he could sneak from the guest room to her bedroom, he had watched her animatedly conversing with her grandmother all evening with endless patience and fond tolerance. The power of his feelings for her no longer frightened him; he just had to get used to them. But the power he had to make her so happy was another thing, and watching her while trying not to be so obviously cow-eyed, he swore he would devote the rest of his life to her happiness, and gladly. That she loved him so much left him awed and breathless, but he knew she could never love him as much as he loved her. It just couldn't be possible.

A cloud crossed the face of the moon, a chilly breeze nipped his ears, and he shoved his hands deeper into the pockets of his heavy wool jacket. One of the yearlings snorted nervously and took off, tail high, white socks flashing in the darkness. The other colts bolted after him, and Shoz wondered what was making them jumpy, but he didn't hear anything.

Like the clouds, his thoughts drifted to the future. Only Lucy would have the bravado to have a huge wedding after the scandal. She wanted an extravaganza, and now he had decided she deserved it. He could wait—as long as they were never apart again.

They hadn't discussed it, but he wanted children, lots of them, soon. First, though, he wanted to take Lucy to Bakersfield to visit his parents, Jack and Candice Savage—he wanted to show her off. His homecoming was long overdue, and the thought of it warmed him immensely. They would go before June, of course.

And just as it was time to go home, it was time to shed the alias he had acquired so many years ago. It was time to bury Shoz Cooper and truly leave the past behind. He was Shoz Savage, Shozkay Savage if his full name be known, the son of Jack and Candice, two people he respected and loved more than anyone, other than Lucy. He would be married in the name he had been born with, and from this day forward, he would be Shoz Savage and only Shoz Savage.

He grinned in the blackness around him. For the first time in too many years to count, he felt free. Happy and free.

One of the yearlings screamed in fright. At that precise moment, Shoz sniffed the acrid odor in the air. His heart clenched, he turned. Shocked, he stared up the hill at the big white ranchhouse. The ground floor was red and ablaze.

Shoz ran.

50

Lucy had fallen asleep on the sofa in the library. After her grandmother left her to retire, she found she was too keyed up with excitement over the wedding to even consider going upstairs to sleep. She indulged in a brandy. Soon her emotions settled, and she realized she was exhausted and drained. It was as much emotional as physical, not just from the wedding plans but from finally finding Shoz and achieving her greatest dreams. Lucy fell into a heavy, deep slumber. She thought she heard her grandmother calling her, but she was so tired, she did not want to wake up. When she finally did, terribly groggily, she thought it was a dream. Yet it had been so real, and Miranda's voice had been so full of fear.

She smelled the smoke.

And a blazing light at the window made her turn her head.

Lucy gasped when she saw the huge old oak tree outside the French doors ablaze—the flames licking at the windows. In the next instant she saw fire creeping merrily along the floor where it joined with the wall under the doors.

Panting and beginning to choke on the smoke that was filling the library, Lucy turned, her spine pressed into the sofa. She gasped at the sight that now greeted her—half of the far wall was aflame—and with it, the massive mahogany doors, cutting off her means of escape.

Lucy screamed.

Cries of ''Fire! Fire!'' split the air as hands from the bunkhouses realized that the ranchhouse was on fire. Pumping his legs, Shoz ran harder than he'd ever run before, up the hill, fighting its slope, while the flames licked at the porch and the sides of the house, creeping up the walls, dancing higher and higher. He had almost reached the porch when Derek came crashing out the front door, the old man carrying Roberto through the flaming porch and hurling them forward and onto the damp grass. The boy was wrapped in a blanket, and miraculously, Derek's pajamas were only singed.

Shoz reached them. He grabbed his son. ''Are you all right?''

''Yes, Papa.'' Roberto was wide-eyed.

''Where's Miranda?'' Derek shouted, levering himself to his feet.

''I don't know.''

"I sent her to get Lucy—they should have been out before me!"

Shoz grabbed the old man to prevent him from launching himself mindlessly back into what was fast becoming an inferno. It was then that Miranda came running from the house, her white robe trailing red flames.

Derek dove on top of her, using his body to smother the flames. Shoz saw flames kindling on his pants leg, and he whipped off his heavy jacket to beat them out. Moments later the couple lay unhurt, panting and coughing in the grass. Shoz hauled Derek off his wife, grabbing her. "Where's Lucy? *Where's Lucy?*"

"I don't know! She's not in her room—I thought she was with you!"

Shoz grabbed his jacket and flung it over his head and pounded up the steps and into the flames.

"The library!" Miranda screamed after him. "I left her in the library!"

Fire licked his boots, his feet and legs became hot. He ran through the crackling flames and into the foyer. Fire licked the walls and danced along the lowest steps of the stairs. Shoz felt his knee burning and beat out a flame with his bare palms.

Screaming her name, he ran down the hall.

Fire raced behind him, straining at his heels.

"Lucy!" He watched the hall wall begin to glow, turning from white to living red. He reached the library door in time to see it erupt into flames. He heard her scream.

Without pausing, he hurled himself into the door and went crashing into the room.

He broke through the doors and burst through the flames so quickly, he was only singed. The curtains were ablaze, leaping gold and red in the windows, and the rugs were just igniting. Flames raced along the baseboards of the wall and began to claw their way up them. Smoke hung heavy in the room. Lucy stood in the middle of the room, with nowhere to go. She saw him and catapulted into his arms.

A quick glance outside told him there was no escape through a window or the French doors. Protecting her with his body and his jacket, he ran hard through the doorway. Flames singed his knees and buttocks.

As he ran down the hall, his toes seemed to be burning. He seemed to be trodding on fire. He swung Lucy into his arms. He had never run faster; flames reached out from the walls for the denim of his thighs. And then they were in the foyer and he rushed out the burning front doorway and across the burning porch.

He wasn't aware of falling. But he was on the ground with Lucy when they doused him with water, again and again. For just a moment he lay gasping, the relief of the water quickly gone, his knees and thighs and toes and a spot on his cheek burning. Lucy. He levered himself up and clutched her face.

"Lucy!"

She coughed. She coughed and wretched and clung to him, and Shoz went limp beside her.

Derek was squatting next to them while dozens of men were fighting the blaze with hoses and by hand with buckets of water. "You okay?" Derek asked anxiously. "Shoz, Lucy, you okay?"

Shoz stared at Lucy as she gulped air. "Yes," she said hoarsely, coughing again. "Shoz?"

"I'm here." He flopped onto his back, groping for her hand. She clung, but so did he.

Shoz didn't protest as the old man's hands probed him for injuries. "You're one lucky man," Derek said. "Your boots are burned—and your socks—and I guess your toes will have a few blisters. An ember got your cheek, and there are a few burns on your knees. You're okay."

"Grandma?" Lucy asked, sitting up groggily.

"She's fine. She took Roberto down to the mess house."

Shoz sat up, too. The three of them were faced with the house. It was an inferno—there would be no saving it. Flames engulfed it, blazed into the heavens. He looked at Derek and saw the old man staring, his face taut with controlled emotion, his face ghostly white. Lucy took his hand, sharing one look with Shoz. "Oh, Grandpa."

He didn't say anything. He couldn't speak.

Shoz watched the house burning and thought about how

this one strong man had brought his young wife here in 1840 and built this house and everything around it with his own two hands, with his own sweat and blood and tears. He had braved and fought this land to provide a legacy for his wife and children. In doing so, he had more than conquered what he'd set out to tame; he had created an empire and a dynasty. Vast respect filled Shoz, and with it, a terrible sadness.

By daybreak the fire finally died. Only piles of charred timbers and the blackened stone fireplaces and chimneys remained. No one had slept through the long night; now everyone was dispersing to begin the day's chores. Lucy stood with Shoz, his arm around her waist, staring at the burned wreck of the house.

"Do you really think it started in the kitchen?" Lucy asked.

"It sure looks that way." One of the maids had sobbingly admitted to having a boyfriend visiting her while she had been cleaning up, the last one to leave—and he had been smoking. "It wouldn't take much for the house to catch, not after that dry summer."

"Grandpa and Grandma are taking this terribly."

"They're both strong. They have each other. They have the ranch, Paradise. They'll make it."

"Grandpa looked so old last night," Lucy said brokenly. A few hours ago he had been pale and gaunt, looking every one of his eighty years, looking tired and defeated. Miranda had actually been walking stooped. "And Grandma, when she finally started crying . . ."

"We'll stay and give them our support until they've recovered from the shock."

"Thank you," Lucy said, kissing him.

They found her grandparents walking around the ruins, hand in hand. Lucy and Shoz approached hesitantly, but were determined to help them through the crisis. "I think we all deserve Cook's flapjacks this morning." Lucy attempted to be cheerful.

Derek turned. "Not a goddamn thing to save except the fireplaces." It was announced matter-of-factly, causing

Shoz and Lucy to exchange startled glances.

"I think we should have brick fireplaces," Miranda said firmly.

"All right." Derek turned to them. "We're going to rebuild immediately."

Lucy exchanged a delighted glance with Shoz. "Rebuild!"

Derek looked at her. "Why so surprised? I've got a ranch to run. Can't do it from the hotel in town."

"I . . ." Lucy grinned at Shoz.

"Before we rebuild so immediately, I want to hire an architect," Miranda stated.

"An architect!" Derek groaned. "What do you have in mind, woman?"

"Well, at my age, I'm entitled to a little luxury."

"We had luxury."

"I want a marble bathroom and a swimming pool."

"I can agree to that."

"And stone floors this time."

"All right. You got an architect in mind?"

"I've heard there's a top man in Austin." Miranda smiled at Derek, who grinned back.

Shoz looked at Lucy and saw the plea in her eyes. He slipped his arm around her waist and pulled her close. "We want to stay here and help you rebuild."

"Can you handle a hammer?"

"Yes, sir."

"You're on. Right after breakfast, get a crew up here to start hauling the debris out. Lucy, you can take your grandmother to Austin to hire that architect. But don't come back without any plans!"

Lucy took her grandmother's hand. "We can go to Austin first thing tomorrow."

"What's wrong with today?" Miranda asked.

Lucy looked at Shoz with a bubble of laughter. He was smiling, too.

"If we're having a June wedding, we'd better start right now!" Derek pointed out.

Lucy took Shoz's hand. "I think I'll be gone for a few days, darling."

"That's all right," he chuckled. "I'm going to be too tired from all this work we've got to do to be a very attentive fiancé."

"Maybe we should make a real spacious guest wing," Derek said thoughtfully, staring at Lucy and Shoz. "With a nursery—or two."

"Or a guest villa!" Miranda cried excitedly. "We could clear the woodland out back—the views would be charming!"

As her grandparents continued to make new plans, with growing excitement, Lucy took Shoz's hand and led him away. "You don't mind staying and helping them rebuild?"

A breeze lifted a tendril of her hair and pushed it into her eyes. Shoz moved it away. "I want to stay and help them, Lucy. Besides, they'll be pressed for time, because of our June wedding."

She melted against him. "Do you really mind?"

"Waiting until June? No. Not when it makes you so happy."

She touched his face, careful not to touch the gauze covering the burn on one cheekbone. "You make me happy, Shoz. If we married tomorrow, I'd be just as happy."

"You mean we can change the date?"

She heard the teasing note and laughed while his arms went around her. His mouth tenderly brushed her nose. "From tragedy to triumph," he murmured. "We're not the only happy ones."

Lucy followed his regard and watched her grandparents; Derek was pointing, Miranda was nodding enthusiastically.

"Look at them," he said softly. "Married over fifty years, partners over fifty years, lovers for more than half a century. A few hours ago they were shocked, almost defeated. Now they're fighting back—together—and enjoying every moment of the new challenge."

She leaned back to look up at his handsome face, marveling anew at his sensitivity—and at how lucky she was.

"One day," he said huskily, his gray eyes fierce with emotion, "we will be like that."

Tears burned Lucy's eyes, momentarily blurring her vision. "Did I tell you today how much I love you?"

He stiffened. "No. Lucy . . ." He stroked the high bones of her face. "You could have died today. God! But you know, you do know . . ."

"You risked your life for me," Lucy replied gravely. "When you're ready to say the words, I'll listen, but I don't need them, Shoz. I do know."

He cupped her elbows, pulling her against him. "I'm ready to say those damn words," he whispered. "I love you, Lucy."

She smiled and, just a little, she cried.

EPILOGUE

Paradise, Texas
June 1899

Lucy Bragg and Shoz Savage were married on June the tenth, eighteen hundred and ninety-nine. The ceremony took place out-of-doors on the hill by an old white swing. The bride, although it was her second marriage, wore white: a couture Worth gown from Paris, scandalously straight, with an endless tulle train that made her appear to be walking in clouds. During the ceremony, she wept. The groom, in a dashing black tuxedo, was tense, solemn, and nervous. During the vows, the groom lifted the bride's veil to wipe away her tears with his handkerchief. After the ceremony, many guests commented on how touching it had been.

Over a thousand guests attended. The entire family, of course: the Braggs of New York, the d'Archands of San Francisco, Lord and Lady Shelton of Dragmore, and all their children and grandchildren. The bride's father, the millionaire-industrialist Rathe Bragg, gave away the bride with a wide smile. Although it was not quite traditional, after the ceremony he made the first toast, almost directly to the groom, an apology for past doubts and a welcome to the family. The groom blushed and the bride wept again.

The groom's seven-year-old son, Roberto, had acted as his best man during the ceremony, trying to be somber but unable to repress his terrific excitement. The bride's mother, one of the well-known leaders of the Progressive Reform movement, Grace Bragg, was her daughter's matron of honor. She also made an untraditional toast during the reception, referring to her new son-in-law as a real hero. Later, she spent most of the evening on the dance floor in uninhibited and uncharacteristic abandon.

The groom's parents were just as pleased and just as emotional. His father, the California rancher Jack Savage, could not stop smiling; neither could his wife, Candice.

The three Savage brothers attended with their wives, and so did the groom's sister, Christina, now the Princess Zemstov, with her husband, the Prince of Lubrovic.

There were many illustrious guests, including Senator Claxton, although his wife was mysteriously absent, President McKinley and his wife, and the now famous ex-Rough Rider, Theodore Roosevelt. Dancing began almost immediately after the ceremony, outdoors on a wood-planked floor covered with sawdust to the tune of a rowdy Spanish band. It continued until the wee hours of the morning, when the last of the guests finally departed to their lodgings.

The wedding was written up in all of the nations's leading journals despite efforts to keep it out of print. They called it the Wedding of the Century.

The bride, it was said, was a leading Society heiress who had been kidnapped by the groom just a few years ago. The groom, it was said, was a lawyer who had been erroneously imprisoned for a theft he did not commit. He had abducted the bride in a jailbreak, fleeing with his captive into the heart of Mexico. There they had fallen in love, only to be wrenched apart when her father tracked them down.

The scandal had ruined her, while he had mysteriously disappeared. It was hinted that more than just an abduction had occurred; some said they had even been married and divorced secretly at the time. And then just when she was about to marry the diplomat Leon Claxton, she, too, disappeared.

To this day, there is a legend that holds that she followed him to Cuba, where he was a great rebel leader called El Americano by friend and foe alike, and together they lived and loved and fought for *Cuba Libre* until it came to pass.

It was a story America immediately loved. It was the Love Story of the Century. The Triumph of True Love. No one was unaffected by it, and many wept over it. They became America's Darlings.

This, then, was their story, but here the story does not end. For the day following the glorious celebration, the family patriarch, Derek Bragg, gave the bride and groom his wedding present, the D&M and his majority shares of Bragg Enterprises. The groom was speechless, the bride was not.

And so the Saga continues.

Don't Miss
Brenda Joyce's Next Historical Romance,
SCANDALOUS LOVE,
Coming Soon From Avon Books

The Bragg saga does indeed continue! In *Scandalous Love* you will meet Lucy Bragg's cousin, Nicole Shelton, the daughter of the Earl of Dragmore. Like Lucy, Nicole is intelligent and headstrong. Unlike Lucy, she doesn't have a single proper Victorian bone in her body. Scandal has stalked Nicole relentlessly. It appears to be stalking her again when she meets the virile, unattainable Duke of Clayborough, a man who is forbidden to her. Yet their affair is destined to do more than shock society, for Nicole's destiny is to become his duchess, proving that, sometimes, dreams do come true. . . .

America Loves Lindsey!

The Timeless Romances
of #1 Bestselling Author

Johanna Lindsey

PRISONER OF MY DESIRE
75627-7/$5.99 US/$6.99 Can

Spirited Rowena Belleme *must* produce an heir, and the magnificent
Warrick deChaville is the perfect choice to sire her child—though it
means imprisoning the handsome knight.

*Be Sure to Read These Other
Timeless Lindsey Romances*